# Les Misérables

## Volume V: Jean Valjean

# Les Misérables

## Volume V: Jean Valjean

# Victor Hugo

MINT EDITIONS

*Les Misérables* was first published in 1862.

This edition published by Mint Editions 2020.

ISBN 9781513279800 | E-ISBN 9781513284828

Published by Mint Editions®

 MINT
EDITIONS
minteditionbooks.com

Publishing Director: Jennifer Newens
Design & Production: Rachel Lopez Metzger
Project Manager: Micaela Clark
Translated by: Isabel F. Hapgood
Typesetting: Westchester Publishing Services

# Contents

BOOK THIRD. MUD BUT THE SOUL

BOOK FOURTH. JAVERT DERAILED

BOOK FIRST

THE WAR BETWEEN FOUR WALLS

# I

## The Charybdis of the Faubourg Saint Antoine and the Scylla of the Faubourg Du Temple

The two most memorable barricades which the observer of social maladies can name do not belong to the period in which the action of this work is laid. These two barricades, both of them symbols, under two different aspects, of a redoubtable situation, sprang from the earth at the time of the fatal insurrection of June, 1848, the greatest war of the streets that history has ever beheld.

It sometimes happens that, even contrary to principles, even contrary to liberty, equality, and fraternity, even contrary to the universal vote, even contrary to the government, by all for all, from the depths of its anguish, of its discouragements and its destitutions, of its fevers, of its distresses, of its miasmas, of its ignorances, of its darkness, that great and despairing body, the rabble, protests against, and that the populace wages battle against, the people.

Beggars attack the common right; the ochlocracy rises against demos.

These are melancholy days; for there is always a certain amount of night even in this madness, there is suicide in this duel, and those words which are intended to be insults—beggars, canaille, ochlocracy, populace—exhibit, alas! rather the fault of those who reign than the fault of those who suffer; rather the fault of the privileged than the fault of the disinherited.

For our own part, we never pronounce those words without pain and without respect, for when philosophy fathoms the facts to which they correspond, it often finds many a grandeur beside these miseries. Athens was an ochlocracy; the beggars were the making of Holland; the populace saved Rome more than once; and the rabble followed Jesus Christ.

There is no thinker who has not at times contemplated the magnificences of the lower classes.

It was of this rabble that Saint Jerome was thinking, no doubt, and of all these poor people and all these vagabonds and all these miserable people whence sprang the apostles and the martyrs, when he uttered this mysterious saying: *"Fex urbis, lex orbis,"*—the dregs of the city, the law of the earth.

The exasperations of this crowd which suffers and bleeds, its violences contrary to all sense, directed against the principles which are its life, its masterful deeds against the right, are its popular *coups d'état* and should be repressed. The man of probity sacrifices himself, and out of his very love for this crowd, he combats it. But how excusable he feels it even while holding out against it! How he venerates it even while resisting it! This is one of those rare moments when, while doing that which it is one's duty to do, one feels something which disconcerts one, and which would dissuade one from proceeding further; one persists, it is necessary, but conscience, though satisfied, is sad, and the accomplishment of duty is complicated with a pain at the heart.

June, 1848, let us hasten to say, was an exceptional fact, and almost impossible of classification, in the philosophy of history. All the words which we have just uttered, must be discarded, when it becomes a question of this extraordinary revolt, in which one feels the holy anxiety of toil claiming its rights. It was necessary to combat it, and this was a duty, for it attacked the republic. But what was June, 1848, at bottom? A revolt of the people against itself.

Where the subject is not lost sight of, there is no digression; may we, then, be permitted to arrest the reader's attention for a moment on the two absolutely unique barricades of which we have just spoken and which characterized this insurrection.

One blocked the entrance to the Faubourg Saint Antoine; the other defended the approach to the Faubourg du Temple; those before whom these two fearful masterpieces of civil war reared themselves beneath the brilliant blue sky of June, will never forget them.

The Saint-Antoine barricade was tremendous; it was three stories high, and seven hundred feet wide. It barred the vast opening of the faubourg, that is to say, three streets, from angle to angle; ravined, jagged, cut up, divided, crenelated, with an immense rent, buttressed with piles that were bastions in themselves throwing out capes here and there, powerfully backed up by two great promontories of houses of the faubourg, it reared itself like a cyclopean dike at the end of the formidable place which had seen the 14th of July. Nineteen barricades were ranged, one behind the other, in the depths of the streets behind this principal barricade. At the very sight of it, one felt the agonizing suffering in the immense faubourg, which had reached that point of extremity when a distress may become a catastrophe. Of what was that barricade made? Of the ruins of three six-story houses demolished expressly, said some. Of the prodigy of all wraths, said others. It wore the lamentable aspect of all constructions of hatred, ruin. It might be asked: Who built this? It might also be said: Who destroyed this? It was the improvisation of the ebullition. Hold! take this door! this grating! this penthouse! this chimney-piece! this broken brazier! this cracked pot! Give all! cast away all! Push this roll, dig, dismantle, overturn, ruin everything! It was the collaboration of the pavement, the block of stone, the beam, the bar of iron, the rag, the scrap, the broken pane, the unseated chair, the cabbage-stalk, the tatter, the rag, and the malediction. It was grand and it was petty. It was the abyss parodied on the public place by hubbub. The mass beside the atom; the strip of ruined wall and the broken bowl,—threatening fraternization of every sort of rubbish. Sisyphus had thrown his rock there and Job his potsherd. Terrible, in short. It was the acropolis of the barefooted. Overturned carts broke the uniformity of the slope; an immense dray was spread out there crossways, its axle pointing heavenward, and seemed a scar on that tumultuous façade; an omnibus hoisted gayly, by main force, to the very summit of the heap, as though the architects of this bit of savagery had wished to add a touch of the street urchin humor to their terror, presented its horseless, unharnessed pole to no one knows what horses of the air. This gigantic heap, the alluvium of the revolt, figured to the mind an Ossa on Pelion of all revolutions; '93 on '89, the 9th of Thermidor on the 10th of August, the 18th of Brumaire on the 11th of January, Vendemiaire on Prairial, 1848 on 1830. The situation deserved the trouble and this barricade was worthy to figure on the very spot whence the Bastille had disappeared. If the ocean made dikes, it is thus that it would build. The fury of the flood was stamped upon this shapeless mass. What flood? The crowd. One thought one beheld hubbub petrified. One thought one heard humming above this barricade as though there had been over their hive, enormous, dark bees of violent progress. Was it a thicket? Was it a bacchanalia? Was it a fortress? Vertigo seemed to have constructed it with blows of its wings. There was something of the cesspool in that redoubt and something Olympian in that confusion. One there beheld in a pell-mell full of despair, the rafters of roofs, bits of garret windows with their figured paper, window sashes with their glass planted there in the ruins awaiting the cannon, wrecks of chimneys, cupboards, tables, benches, howling topsyturveydom, and those thousand poverty-stricken things, the very refuse of the mendicant, which contain at the same time fury and nothingness. One would have said that it was the tatters of a people, rags of wood, of iron, of bronze, of stone, and that the Faubourg Saint Antoine had thrust it there at its door, with a colossal flourish of the broom making of its misery its barricade. Blocks resembling headsman's blocks, dislocated chains, pieces of woodwork with brackets having the form of gibbets, horizontal wheels projecting from the rubbish, amalgamated with this edifice of anarchy the sombre figure of the old tortures endured by the people. The barricade Saint Antoine converted everything into a weapon; everything that civil war could throw at the head of society proceeded thence; it was not combat, it was a paroxysm; the carbines which defended this redoubt, among which there were some blunderbusses, sent bits of earthenware bones, coat-buttons, even the casters from night-stands, dangerous projectiles on account of the brass. This barricade was furious; it hurled to the clouds an inexpressible clamor; at certain moments, when provoking the army, it was covered with throngs and tempest; a tumultuous crowd of flaming heads crowned it; a swarm filled it; it had a thorny crest of guns, of sabres, of cudgels, of axes, of pikes and of bayonets; a vast red flag flapped in the wind; shouts of command, songs of attack, the roll of drums, the sobs of women and bursts of gloomy laughter from the starving were to be heard there. It was huge and living, and, like the back of an electric beast, there proceeded from it little flashes of lightning. The spirit of revolution covered with its cloud this summit where rumbled that voice of the people which resembles the voice of God; a strange majesty was emitted by this titanic basket of rubbish. It was a heap of filth and it was Sinai.

As we have said previously, it attacked in the name of the revolution—what? The revolution. It—that barricade, chance, hazard, disorder, terror, misunderstanding, the unknown—had facing it the Constituent Assembly, the sovereignty of the people, universal suffrage, the nation, the republic; and it was the Carmagnole bidding defiance to the Marseillaise.

Immense but heroic defiance, for the old faubourg is a hero.

The faubourg and its redoubt lent each other assistance. The faubourg shouldered the redoubt, the redoubt took its stand under cover of the faubourg. The vast barricade spread out like a cliff against which the strategy of the African generals dashed itself. Its caverns, its excrescences, its warts, its gibbosities, grimaced, so to speak, and grinned beneath the smoke. The mitraille vanished in shapelessness; the bombs plunged into it; bullets only succeeded in making holes in it; what was the use of cannonading chaos? and the regiments, accustomed to the fiercest visions of war, gazed with uneasy eyes on that species of redoubt, a wild beast in its boar-like bristling and a mountain by its enormous size.

A quarter of a league away, from the corner of the Rue du Temple which debouches on the boulevard near the Château-d'Eau, if one thrust one's head bodily beyond the point formed by the front of the Dallemagne shop, one perceived in the distance, beyond the canal, in the street which mounts the slopes of Belleville at the culminating point of the rise, a strange wall reaching to the second story of the house fronts, a sort of hyphen between the houses on the right and the houses on the left, as though the street had folded back on itself its loftiest wall in order to close itself abruptly. This wall was built of paving-stones. It was straight, correct, cold, perpendicular, levelled with the square, laid out by rule and line. Cement was lacking, of course, but, as in the case of certain Roman walls, without interfering with its rigid architecture. The entablature was mathematically parallel with the base. From distance to distance, one could distinguish on the gray surface, almost invisible loopholes which resembled black threads. These loopholes were separated from each other by equal spaces. The street was deserted as far as the eye could reach. All windows and doors were closed. In the background rose this barrier, which made a blind thoroughfare of the street, a motionless and tranquil wall; no one was visible, nothing was audible; not a cry, not a sound, not a breath. A sepulchre.

The dazzling sun of June inundated this terrible thing with light.

It was the barricade of the Faubourg of the Temple.

As soon as one arrived on the spot, and caught sight of it, it was impossible, even for the boldest, not to become thoughtful before this mysterious apparition. It was adjusted, jointed, imbricated, rectilinear, symmetrical and funereal. Science and gloom met there. One felt that the chief of this barricade was a geometrician or a spectre. One looked at it and spoke low.

From time to time, if some soldier, an officer or representative of the people, chanced to traverse the deserted highway, a faint, sharp whistle was heard, and the passer-by fell dead or wounded, or, if he escaped the bullet, sometimes a biscaïen was seen to ensconce itself in some closed shutter, in the interstice between two blocks of stone, or in the plaster of a wall. For the men in the barricade had made themselves two small cannons out of two cast-iron lengths of gas-pipe, plugged up at one end with tow and fire-clay. There was no waste of useless powder. Nearly every shot told. There were corpses here and there, and pools of blood on the pavement. I remember a white butterfly which went and came in the street. Summer does not abdicate.

In the neighborhood, the spaces beneath the portes-cochères were encumbered with wounded.

One felt oneself aimed at by some person whom one did not see, and one understood that guns were levelled at the whole length of the street.

Massed behind the sort of sloping ridge which the vaulted canal forms at the entrance to the Faubourg du Temple, the soldiers of the attacking column, gravely and thoughtfully, watched this dismal redoubt, this immobility, this passivity, whence sprang death. Some crawled flat on their faces as far as the crest of the curve of the bridge, taking care that their shakos did not project beyond it.

The valiant Colonel Monteynard admired this barricade with a shudder.—"How that is built!" he said to a Representative. "Not one paving-stone projects beyond its neighbor. It is made of porcelain."— At that moment, a bullet broke the cross on his breast, and he fell.

"The cowards!" people said. "Let them show themselves. Let us see them! They dare not! They are hiding!"

The barricade of the Faubourg du Temple, defended by eighty men, attacked by ten thousand, held out for three days. On the fourth, they did as at Zaatcha, as at Constantine, they pierced the houses, they came over the roofs, the barricade was taken. Not one of the eighty cowards thought of flight, all were killed there with the exception of the leader, Barthélemy, of whom we shall speak presently.

The Saint-Antoine barricade was the tumult of thunders; the barricade of the Temple was silence. The difference between these two redoubts was the difference between the formidable and the sinister. One seemed a maw; the other a mask.

Admitting that the gigantic and gloomy insurrection of June was composed of a wrath and of an enigma, one divined in the first barricade the dragon, and behind the second the sphinx.

These two fortresses had been erected by two men named, the one, Cournet, the other, Barthélemy. Cournet made the Saint-Antoine barricade; Barthélemy the barricade of the Temple. Each was the image of the man who had built it.

Cournet was a man of lofty stature; he had broad shoulders, a red face, a crushing fist, a bold heart, a loyal soul, a sincere and terrible eye. Intrepid, energetic, irascible, stormy; the most cordial of men, the most formidable of combatants. War, strife, conflict, were the very air he breathed and put him in a good humor. He had been an officer in the navy, and, from his gestures and his voice, one divined that he sprang from the ocean, and that he came from the tempest; he carried the hurricane on into battle. With the exception of the genius, there was in Cournet something of Danton, as, with the exception of the divinity, there was in Danton something of Hercules.

Barthélemy, thin, feeble, pale, taciturn, was a sort of tragic street urchin, who, having had his ears boxed by a policeman, lay in wait for him, and killed him, and at seventeen was sent to the galleys. He came out and made this barricade.

Later on, fatal circumstance, in London, proscribed by all, Barthélemy slew Cournet. It was a funereal duel. Some time afterwards, caught in the gearing of one of those mysterious adventures in which passion plays a part, a catastrophe in which French justice sees extenuating circumstances, and in which English justice sees only death, Barthélemy was hanged. The sombre social construction is so made that, thanks to material destitution, thanks to moral obscurity, that unhappy being who possessed an intelligence, certainly firm, possibly great, began in France with the galleys, and ended in England with the gallows. Barthélemy, on occasion, flew but one flag, the black flag.

# What is to Be Done in the Abyss if One Does Not Converse

Sixteen years count in the subterranean education of insurrection, and June, 1848, knew a great deal more about it than June, 1832. So the barricade of the Rue de la Chanvrerie was only an outline, and an embryo compared to the two colossal barricades which we have just sketched; but it was formidable for that epoch.

The insurgents under the eye of Enjolras, for Marius no longer looked after anything, had made good use of the night. The barricade had been not only repaired, but augmented. They had raised it two feet. Bars of iron planted in the pavement resembled lances in rest. All sorts of rubbish brought and added from all directions complicated the external confusion. The redoubt had been cleverly made over, into a wall on the inside and a thicket on the outside.

The staircase of paving-stones which permitted one to mount it like the wall of a citadel had been reconstructed.

The barricade had been put in order, the tap-room disencumbered, the kitchen appropriated for the ambulance, the dressing of the wounded completed, the powder scattered on the ground and on the tables had been gathered up, bullets run, cartridges manufactured, lint scraped, the fallen weapons re-distributed, the interior of the redoubt cleaned, the rubbish swept up, corpses removed.

They laid the dead in a heap in the Mondétour lane, of which they were still the masters. The pavement was red for a long time at that spot. Among the dead there were four National Guardsmen of the suburbs. Enjolras had their uniforms laid aside.

Enjolras had advised two hours of sleep. Advice from Enjolras was a command. Still, only three or four took advantage of it.

Feuilly employed these two hours in engraving this inscription on the wall which faced the tavern:—

LONG LIVE THE PEOPLES!

These four words, hollowed out in the rough stone with a nail, could be still read on the wall in 1848.

The three women had profited by the respite of the night to vanish definitely; which allowed the insurgents to breathe more freely.

They had found means of taking refuge in some neighboring house.

The greater part of the wounded were able, and wished, to fight still. On a litter of mattresses and trusses of straw in the kitchen, which had been converted into an ambulance, there were five men gravely wounded, two of whom were municipal guardsmen. The municipal guardsmen were attended to first.

In the tap-room there remained only Mabeuf under his black cloth and Javert bound to his post.

"This is the hall of the dead," said Enjolras.

In the interior of this hall, barely lighted by a candle at one end, the mortuary table being behind the post like a horizontal bar, a sort of vast, vague cross resulted from Javert erect and Mabeuf lying prone.

The pole of the omnibus, although snapped off by the fusillade, was still sufficiently upright to admit of their fastening the flag to it.

Enjolras, who possessed that quality of a leader, of always doing what he said, attached to this staff the bullet-ridden and bloody coat of the old man's.

No repast had been possible. There was neither bread nor meat. The fifty men in the barricade had speedily exhausted the scanty provisions of the wine-shop during the sixteen hours which they had passed there. At a given moment, every barricade inevitably becomes the raft of *la Méduse*. They were obliged to resign themselves to hunger. They had then reached the first hours of that Spartan day of the 6th of June when, in the barricade Saint-Merry, Jeanne, surrounded by the insurgents who demanded bread, replied to all combatants crying: "Something to eat!" with: "Why? It is three o'clock; at four we shall be dead."

As they could no longer eat, Enjolras forbade them to drink. He interdicted wine, and portioned out the brandy.

They had found in the cellar fifteen full bottles hermetically sealed. Enjolras and Combeferre examined them. Combeferre when he came up again said:—"It's the old stock of Father Hucheloup, who began business as a grocer."—"It must be real wine," observed Bossuet. "It's lucky that Grantaire is asleep. If he were on foot, there would be a good deal of difficulty in saving those bottles."—Enjolras, in spite of all murmurs, placed his veto on the fifteen bottles, and, in order that no one might touch them, he had them placed under the table on which Father Mabeuf was lying.

About two o'clock in the morning, they reckoned up their strength. There were still thirty-seven of them.

The day began to dawn. The torch, which had been replaced in its cavity in the pavement, had just been extinguished. The interior of the barricade, that species of tiny courtyard appropriated from the street, was bathed in shadows, and resembled, athwart the vague, twilight horror, the deck of a disabled ship. The combatants, as they went and came, moved about there like black forms. Above that terrible nesting-place of gloom the stories of the mute houses were lividly outlined; at the very top, the chimneys stood palely out. The sky was of that charming, undecided hue, which may be white and may be blue. Birds flew about in it with cries of joy. The lofty house which formed the back of the barricade, being turned to the East, had upon its roof a rosy reflection. The morning breeze ruffled the gray hair on the head of the dead man at the third-story window.

"I am delighted that the torch has been extinguished," said Courfeyrac to Feuilly. "That torch flickering in the wind annoyed me. It had the appearance of being afraid. The light of torches resembles the wisdom of cowards; it gives a bad light because it trembles."

Dawn awakens minds as it does the birds; all began to talk.

Joly, perceiving a cat prowling on a gutter, extracted philosophy from it.

"What is the cat?" he exclaimed. "It is a corrective. The good God, having made the mouse, said: 'Hullo! I have committed a blunder.' And so he made the cat. The cat is the erratum of the mouse. The mouse, plus the cat, is the proof of creation revised and corrected."

Combeferre, surrounded by students and artisans, was speaking of the dead, of Jean Prouvaire, of Bahorel, of Mabeuf, and even of Cabuc, and of Enjolras' sad severity. He said:—

"Harmodius and Aristogiton, Brutus, Chereas, Stephanus, Cromwell, Charlotte Corday, Sand, have all had their moment of agony when it was too late. Our hearts quiver so, and human life is such a mystery that, even in the case of a civic murder, even in a murder for liberation, if there be such a thing, the remorse for having struck a man surpasses the joy of having served the human race."

And, such are the windings of the exchange of speech, that, a moment later, by a transition brought about through Jean Prouvaire's verses, Combeferre was comparing the translators of the Georgics, Raux with Cournand, Cournand with Delille, pointing out the passages translated by Malfilâtre, particularly the prodigies of Cæsar's death; and at that word, Cæsar, the conversation reverted to Brutus.

"Cæsar," said Combeferre, "fell justly. Cicero was severe towards Cæsar, and he was right. That severity is not diatribe. When Zoïlus insults Homer, when Mævius insults Virgil, when Visé insults Molière, when Pope insults Shakspeare, when Frederic insults Voltaire, it is an old law of envy and hatred which is being carried out; genius attracts insult, great men are always more or less barked at. But Zoïlus and Cicero are two different persons. Cicero is an arbiter in thought, just as Brutus is an arbiter by the sword. For my own part, I blame that last justice, the blade; but, antiquity admitted it. Cæsar, the violator of the Rubicon, conferring, as though they came from him, the dignities which emanated from the people, not rising at the entrance of the senate, committed the acts of a king and almost of a tyrant, *regia ac pene tyrannica.* He was a great man; so much the worse, or so much the better; the lesson is but the more exalted. His twenty-three wounds touch me less than the spitting in the face of Jesus Christ. Cæsar is stabbed by the senators; Christ is cuffed by lackeys. One feels the God through the greater outrage."

Bossuet, who towered above the interlocutors from the summit of a heap of paving-stones, exclaimed, rifle in hand:—

"Oh Cydathenæum, Oh Myrrhinus, Oh Probalinthus, Oh graces of the Æantides! Oh! Who will grant me to pronounce the verses of Homer like a Greek of Laurium or of Edapteon?"

# III

## Light and Shadow

Enjolras had been to make a reconnaissance. He had made his way out through Mondétour lane, gliding along close to the houses.

The insurgents, we will remark, were full of hope. The manner in which they had repulsed the attack of the preceding night had caused them to almost disdain in advance the attack at dawn. They waited for it with a smile. They had no more doubt as to their success than as to their cause. Moreover, succor was, evidently, on the way to them. They reckoned on it. With that facility of triumphant prophecy which is one of the sources of strength in the French combatant, they divided the day which was at hand into three distinct phases. At six o'clock in the morning a regiment "which had been labored with," would turn; at noon, the insurrection of all Paris; at sunset, revolution.

They heard the alarm bell of Saint-Merry, which had not been silent for an instant since the night before; a proof that the other barricade, the great one, Jeanne's, still held out.

All these hopes were exchanged between the different groups in a sort of gay and formidable whisper which resembled the warlike hum of a hive of bees.

Enjolras reappeared. He returned from his sombre eagle flight into outer darkness. He listened for a moment to all this joy with folded arms, and one hand on his mouth. Then, fresh and rosy in the growing whiteness of the dawn, he said:

"The whole army of Paris is to strike. A third of the army is bearing down upon the barricades in which you now are. There is the National Guard in addition. I have picked out the shakos of the fifth of the line, and the standard-bearers of the sixth legion. In one hour you will be attacked. As for the populace, it was seething yesterday, to-day it is not stirring. There is nothing to expect; nothing to hope for. Neither from a faubourg nor from a regiment. You are abandoned."

These words fell upon the buzzing of the groups, and produced on them the effect caused on a swarm of bees by the first drops of a storm. A moment of indescribable silence ensued, in which death might have been heard flitting by.

This moment was brief.

A voice from the obscurest depths of the groups shouted to Enjolras: "So be it. Let us raise the barricade to a height of twenty feet, and let us all remain in it. Citizens, let us offer the protests of corpses. Let us show that, if the people abandon the republicans, the republicans do not abandon the people."

These words freed the thought of all from the painful cloud of individual anxieties. It was hailed with an enthusiastic acclamation.

No one ever has known the name of the man who spoke thus; he was some unknown blouse-wearer, a stranger, a man forgotten, a passing hero, that great anonymous, always mingled in human crises and in social geneses who, at a given moment, utters in a supreme fashion the decisive word, and who vanishes into the shadows after having represented for a minute, in a lightning flash, the people and God.

This inexorable resolution so thoroughly impregnated the air of the 6th of June, 1832, that, almost at the very same hour, on the barricade Saint-Merry, the insurgents were raising that clamor which has become a matter of history and which has been consigned to the documents in the case:—"What matters it whether they come to our assistance or not? Let us get ourselves killed here, to the very last man."

As the reader sees, the two barricades, though materially isolated, were in communication with each other.

# IV

## Minus Five, Plus One

After the man who decreed the "protest of corpses" had spoken, and had given this formula of their common soul, there issued from all mouths a strangely satisfied and terrible cry, funereal in sense and triumphant in tone:

"Long live death! Let us all remain here!"

"Why all?" said Enjolras.

"All! All!"

Enjolras resumed:

"The position is good; the barricade is fine. Thirty men are enough. Why sacrifice forty?"

They replied:

"Because not one will go away."

"Citizens," cried Enjolras, and there was an almost irritated vibration in his voice, "this republic is not rich enough in men to indulge in useless expenditure of them. Vain-glory is waste. If the duty of some is to depart, that duty should be fulfilled like any other."

Enjolras, the man-principle, had over his co-religionists that sort of omnipotent power which emanates from the absolute. Still, great as was this omnipotence, a murmur arose. A leader to the very finger-tips, Enjolras, seeing that they murmured, insisted. He resumed haughtily:

"Let those who are afraid of not numbering more than thirty say so."

The murmurs redoubled.

"Besides," observed a voice in one group, "it is easy enough to talk about leaving. The barricade is hemmed in."

"Not on the side of the Halles," said Enjolras. "The Rue Mondétour is free, and through the Rue des Prêcheurs one can reach the Marché des Innocents."

"And there," went on another voice, "you would be captured. You would fall in with some grand guard of the line or the suburbs; they will spy a man passing in blouse and cap. 'Whence come you?' 'Don't you belong to the barricade?' And they will look at your hands. You smell of powder. Shot."

Enjolras, without making any reply, touched Combeferre's shoulder, and the two entered the tap-room.

They emerged thence a moment later. Enjolras held in his outstretched hands the four uniforms which he had laid aside. Combeferre followed, carrying the shoulder-belts and the shakos.

"With this uniform," said Enjolras, "you can mingle with the ranks and escape; here is enough for four." And he flung on the ground, deprived of its pavement, the four uniforms.

No wavering took place in his stoical audience. Combeferre took the word.

"Come," said he, "you must have a little pity. Do you know what the question is here? It is a question of women. See here. Are there women or are there not? Are there children or are there not? Are there mothers, yes or no, who rock cradles with their foot and who have a lot of little ones around them? Let that man of you who has never beheld a nurse's breast raise his hand. Ah! you want to get yourselves killed, so do I—I, who am speaking to you; but I do not want to feel the phantoms of women wreathing their arms around me. Die, if you will, but don't make others die. Suicides like that which is on the brink of accomplishment here are sublime; but suicide is narrow, and does not admit of extension; and as soon as it touches your neighbors, suicide is murder. Think of the little blond heads; think of the white locks. Listen, Enjolras has just told me that he saw at the corner of the Rue du Cygne a lighted casement, a candle in a poor window, on the fifth floor, and on the pane the quivering shadow of the head of an old woman, who had the air of having spent the night in watching. Perhaps she is the mother of some one of you. Well, let that man go, and make haste, to say to his mother: 'Here I am, mother!' Let him feel at ease, the task here will be performed all the same. When one supports one's relatives by one's toil, one has not the right to sacrifice one's self. That is deserting one's family. And those who have daughters! what are you thinking of? You get yourselves killed, you are dead, that is well. And tomorrow? Young girls without bread—that is a terrible thing. Man begs, woman sells. Ah! those charming and gracious beings, so gracious and so sweet, who have bonnets of flowers, who fill the house with purity, who sing and prattle, who are like a living perfume, who prove the existence of angels in heaven by the purity of virgins on earth, that Jeanne, that Lise, that Mimi, those adorable and honest creatures who are your blessings and your pride, ah! good God, they will suffer hunger! What do you want me to say to you? There is a market for human flesh; and it is not with your shadowy hands, shuddering around them, that you will prevent them from entering it! Think of the street, think of the pavement covered with passers-by, think of the shops past which women go and come with necks all bare, and through the mire. These women, too, were pure once. Think of your sisters, those of you who have them. Misery, prostitution, the police, Saint-Lazare—that is what those beautiful, delicate girls, those fragile marvels of modesty, gentleness and loveliness, fresher than lilacs in the month of May, will come to. Ah! you have got yourselves killed! You are no longer on hand! That is well; you have wished to release the people from Royalty, and you deliver over your daughters to the police. Friends, have a care, have mercy. Women, unhappy women, we are not in the habit of bestowing much thought on them. We trust to the women not having received a man's education, we prevent their reading, we prevent their thinking, we prevent their occupying themselves with politics; will you prevent them from going to the dead-house this evening, and recognizing your bodies? Let us see, those who have families must be tractable, and shake hands with us and take themselves off, and leave us here alone to attend to this affair. I know well that courage is required to leave, that it is hard; but the harder it is, the more meritorious. You say: 'I have a gun, I am at the barricade; so much the worse, I shall remain there.' So much the worse is easily said. My friends, there is a morrow; you will not be here to-morrow, but your families will; and what sufferings! See, here is a pretty, healthy child, with cheeks like an apple, who babbles, prattles, chatters, who laughs, who smells sweet beneath your kiss,—and do you know what becomes of him when he is abandoned? I have seen one, a very small creature, no taller than that. His father was dead. Poor people had taken him in out of charity, but they had bread only for themselves. The child was always hungry. It was winter. He did not cry. You could see him approach the stove, in which there was never any fire, and whose pipe, you know, was of mastic and yellow clay. His breathing was hoarse, his face livid, his limbs flaccid, his belly prominent. He said nothing. If you spoke to him, he did not answer. He is dead. He was taken to the Necker Hospital, where I saw him. I was house-surgeon in that hospital. Now, if there are any fathers among you, fathers whose happiness it is to stroll on Sundays holding their child's tiny hand in their robust hand, let each one of those fathers imagine that this child is his own. That poor brat, I remember, and I seem to see him now, when he lay nude on the dissecting table, how his ribs stood out on his skin like the graves beneath the grass in a cemetery. A sort of mud was found in his stomach. There were ashes in his teeth.

Come, let us examine ourselves conscientiously and take counsel with our heart. Statistics show that the mortality among abandoned children is fifty-five per cent. I repeat, it is a question of women, it concerns mothers, it concerns young girls, it concerns little children. Who is talking to you of yourselves? We know well what you are; we know well that you are all brave, parbleu! we know well that you all have in your souls the joy and the glory of giving your life for the great cause; we know well that you feel yourselves elected to die usefully and magnificently, and that each one of you clings to his share in the triumph. Very well. But you are not alone in this world. There are other beings of whom you must think. You must not be egoists."

All dropped their heads with a gloomy air.

Strange contradictions of the human heart at its most sublime moments. Combeferre, who spoke thus, was not an orphan. He recalled the mothers of other men, and forgot his own. He was about to get himself killed. He was "an egoist."

Marius, fasting, fevered, having emerged in succession from all hope, and having been stranded in grief, the most sombre of shipwrecks, and saturated with violent emotions and conscious that the end was near, had plunged deeper and deeper into that visionary stupor which always precedes the fatal hour voluntarily accepted.

A physiologist might have studied in him the growing symptoms of that febrile absorption known to, and classified by, science, and which is to suffering what voluptuousness is to pleasure. Despair, also, has its ecstasy. Marius had reached this point. He looked on at everything as from without; as we have said, things which passed before him seemed far away; he made out the whole, but did not perceive the details. He beheld men going and coming as through a flame. He heard voices speaking as at the bottom of an abyss.

But this moved him. There was in this scene a point which pierced and roused even him. He had but one idea now, to die; and he did not wish to be turned aside from it, but he reflected, in his gloomy somnambulism, that while destroying himself, he was not prohibited from saving some one else.

He raised his voice.

"Enjolras and Combeferre are right," said he; "no unnecessary sacrifice. I join them, and you must make haste. Combeferre has said convincing things to you. There are some among you who have families, mothers, sisters, wives, children. Let such leave the ranks."

No one stirred.

"Married men and the supporters of families, step out of the ranks!" repeated Marius.

His authority was great. Enjolras was certainly the head of the barricade, but Marius was its savior.

"I order it," cried Enjolras.

"I entreat you," said Marius.

Then, touched by Combeferre's words, shaken by Enjolras' order, touched by Marius' entreaty, these heroic men began to denounce each other.—"It is true," said one young man to a full grown man, "you are the father of a family. Go."—"It is your duty rather," retorted the man, "you have two sisters whom you maintain."—And an unprecedented controversy broke forth. Each struggled to determine which should not allow himself to be placed at the door of the tomb.

"Make haste," said Courfeyrac, "in another quarter of an hour it will be too late."

"Citizens," pursued Enjolras, "this is the Republic, and universal suffrage reigns. Do you yourselves designate those who are to go."

They obeyed. After the expiration of a few minutes, five were unanimously selected and stepped out of the ranks.

"There are five of them!" exclaimed Marius.

There were only four uniforms.

"Well," began the five, "one must stay behind."

And then a struggle arose as to who should remain, and who should find reasons for the others not remaining. The generous quarrel began afresh.

"You have a wife who loves you."—"You have your aged mother."—"You have neither father nor mother, and what is to become of your three little brothers?"—"You are the father of five children."—"You have a right to live, you are only seventeen, it is too early for you to die."

These great revolutionary barricades were assembling points for heroism. The improbable was simple there. These men did not astonish each other.

"Be quick," repeated Courfeyrac.

Men shouted to Marius from the groups:

"Do you designate who is to remain."

"Yes," said the five, "choose. We will obey you."

Marius did not believe that he was capable of another emotion. Still, at this idea, that of choosing a man for death, his blood rushed back to

VICTOR HUGO

his heart. He would have turned pale, had it been possible for him to become any paler.

He advanced towards the five, who smiled upon him, and each, with his eyes full of that grand flame which one beholds in the depths of history hovering over Thermopylæ, cried to him:

"Me! me! me!"

And Marius stupidly counted them; there were still five of them! Then his glance dropped to the four uniforms.

At that moment, a fifth uniform fell, as if from heaven, upon the other four.

The fifth man was saved.

Marius raised his eyes and recognized M. Fauchelevent.

Jean Valjean had just entered the barricade.

He had arrived by way of Mondétour lane, whither by dint of inquiries made, or by instinct, or chance. Thanks to his dress of a National Guardsman, he had made his way without difficulty.

The sentinel stationed by the insurgents in the Rue Mondétour had no occasion to give the alarm for a single National Guardsman, and he had allowed the latter to entangle himself in the street, saying to himself: "Probably it is a reinforcement, in any case it is a prisoner." The moment was too grave to admit of the sentinel abandoning his duty and his post of observation.

At the moment when Jean Valjean entered the redoubt, no one had noticed him, all eyes being fixed on the five chosen men and the four uniforms. Jean Valjean also had seen and heard, and he had silently removed his coat and flung it on the pile with the rest.

The emotion aroused was indescribable.

"Who is this man?" demanded Bossuet.

"He is a man who saves others," replied Combeferre.

Marius added in a grave voice:

"I know him."

This guarantee satisfied every one.

Enjolras turned to Jean Valjean.

"Welcome, citizen."

And he added:

"You know that we are about to die."

Jean Valjean, without replying, helped the insurgent whom he was saving to don his uniform.

# V

## The Horizon Which One Beholds from the Summit of a Barricade

The situation of all in that fatal hour and that pitiless place, had as result and culminating point Enjolras' supreme melancholy.

Enjolras bore within him the plenitude of the revolution; he was incomplete, however, so far as the absolute can be so; he had too much of Saint-Just about him, and not enough of Anacharsis Cloots; still, his mind, in the society of the Friends of the A B C, had ended by undergoing a certain polarization from Combeferre's ideas; for some time past, he had been gradually emerging from the narrow form of dogma, and had allowed himself to incline to the broadening influence of progress, and he had come to accept, as a definitive and magnificent evolution, the transformation of the great French Republic, into the immense human republic. As far as the immediate means were concerned, a violent situation being given, he wished to be violent; on that point, he never varied; and he remained of that epic and redoubtable school which is summed up in the words: "Eighty-three." Enjolras was standing erect on the staircase of paving-stones, one elbow resting on the stock of his gun. He was engaged in thought; he quivered, as at the passage of prophetic breaths; places where death is have these effects of tripods. A sort of stifled fire darted from his eyes, which were filled with an inward look. All at once he threw back his head, his blond locks fell back like those of an angel on the sombre quadriga made of stars, they were like the mane of a startled lion in the flaming of an halo, and Enjolras cried:

"Citizens, do you picture the future to yourselves? The streets of cities inundated with light, green branches on the thresholds, nations sisters, men just, old men blessing children, the past loving the present, thinkers entirely at liberty, believers on terms of full equality, for religion heaven, God the direct priest, human conscience become an altar, no more hatreds, the fraternity of the workshop and the school, for sole penalty and recompense fame, work for all, right for all, peace over all, no more bloodshed, no more wars, happy mothers! To conquer matter is the first step; to realize the ideal is the second. Reflect on what progress has already accomplished. Formerly, the first human races beheld with terror the hydra pass before their eyes, breathing on the waters, the dragon which vomited flame, the griffin who was the monster of the air, and who flew with the wings of an eagle and the talons of a tiger; fearful beasts which were above man. Man, nevertheless, spread his snares, consecrated by intelligence, and finally conquered these monsters. We have vanquished the hydra, and it is called the locomotive; we are on the point of vanquishing the griffin, we already grasp it, and it is called the balloon. On the day when this Promethean task shall be accomplished, and when man shall have definitely harnessed to his will the triple Chimæra of antiquity, the hydra, the dragon and the griffin, he will be the master of water, fire, and of air, and he will be for the rest of animated creation that which the ancient gods formerly were to him. Courage, and onward! Citizens, whither are we going? To science made government, to the force of things become the sole public force, to the natural law, having in itself its sanction and its penalty and promulgating itself by evidence, to a dawn of truth corresponding to a dawn of day. We are advancing to the union of peoples; we are advancing to the unity of man. No more fictions; no more parasites. The real governed by the true, that is the goal. Civilization will hold its assizes at the summit of Europe, and, later on, at the centre of continents, in a grand parliament of the intelligence. Something similar has already been seen. The amphictyons had two sittings a year, one at Delphos the seat of the gods, the other at Thermopylæ, the place of heroes. Europe will have her amphictyons; the globe will have its amphictyons. France bears this sublime future in her breast. This is the gestation of the nineteenth century. That which Greece sketched out is worthy of being finished by France. Listen to me, you, Feuilly, valiant artisan, man of the people. I revere you. Yes, you clearly behold the future, yes, you are right. You had neither father nor mother, Feuilly; you adopted humanity for your mother and right for your father. You are about to die, that is to say to triumph, here. Citizens, whatever happens to-day, through our defeat as well as through our victory, it is a revolution that we are about to create. As conflagrations light up a whole city, so revolutions illuminate the whole human race. And what is the revolution that we shall cause? I have just told you, the Revolution of the True. From a political point of view, there is but a single principle; the sovereignty of man over himself. This sovereignty of myself over myself is called Liberty. Where two or three of these sovereignties are combined, the state begins. But in that association there is no abdication. Each sovereignty concedes a certain quantity of itself, for the purpose of forming the common right. This quantity is the same for all of us. This identity of concession which each makes to all, is called Equality. Common right is nothing else than the protection of all beaming on the right of each. This protection of all over each is called Fraternity. The point of intersection of all these assembled sovereignties is called society. This intersection being a junction, this point is a knot. Hence what is called the social bond. Some say social contract; which is the same thing, the word contract being etymologically formed with the idea of a bond. Let us come to an understanding about equality; for, if liberty is the summit, equality is the base. Equality, citizens, is not wholly a surface vegetation, a society of great blades of grass and tiny oaks; a proximity of jealousies which render each other null and void; legally speaking, it is all aptitudes possessed of the same opportunity; politically, it is all votes possessed of the same weight; religiously, it is all consciences possessed of the same right. Equality has an organ: gratuitous and obligatory instruction. The right to the alphabet, that is where the beginning must be made. The primary school imposed on all, the secondary school offered to all, that is the law. From an identical school, an identical society will spring. Yes, instruction! light! light! everything comes from light, and to it everything returns. Citizens, the nineteenth century is great, but the twentieth century will be happy. Then, there will be nothing more like the history of old, we shall no longer, as to-day, have to fear a conquest, an invasion, a usurpation, a rivalry of nations, arms in hand, an interruption of civilization depending on a marriage of kings, on a birth in hereditary tyrannies, a partition of peoples by a congress, a dismemberment because of the failure of a dynasty, a combat of two religions meeting face to face, like two bucks in the dark, on the bridge of the infinite; we shall no longer have to fear famine, farming out, prostitution arising from distress, misery from the failure of work and the scaffold and the sword, and battles and the ruffianism of chance in the forest of events. One might almost say: There will be no more events. We shall be happy. The human race will accomplish its law, as the terrestrial globe accomplishes its law; harmony will be re-established between the soul and the star; the soul will gravitate around the truth, as the planet around the light. Friends, the present hour in which I am addressing you, is a gloomy hour; but these are terrible purchases of the future. A revolution is a toll. Oh! the human race will be delivered, raised up, consoled! We affirm it on this barrier. Whence should proceed that cry of love, if not from the heights of sacrifice? Oh my brothers, this is the point of junction, of those who think and of those who suffer; this barricade is not made of paving-stones, nor of joists, nor of bits of iron; it is made of two heaps, a heap of ideas, and a heap of woes. Here misery meets the ideal. The day embraces the night, and says to it: 'I am about to die, and thou shalt be born again with me.' From the embrace of all desolations faith leaps forth. Sufferings bring hither their agony and ideas their immortality. This agony and this immortality are about to join and constitute our death. Brothers, he who dies here dies in the radiance of the future, and we are entering a tomb all flooded with the dawn."

Enjolras paused rather than became silent; his lips continued to move silently, as though he were talking to himself, which caused them all to gaze attentively at him, in the endeavor to hear more. There was no applause; but they whispered together for a long time. Speech being a breath, the rustling of intelligences resembles the rustling of leaves.

# VI

## Marius Haggard, Javert Laconic

Let us narrate what was passing in Marius' thoughts.

Let the reader recall the state of his soul. We have just recalled it, everything was a vision to him now. His judgment was disturbed. Marius, let us insist on this point, was under the shadow of the great, dark wings which are spread over those in the death agony. He felt that he had entered the tomb, it seemed to him that he was already on the other side of the wall, and he no longer beheld the faces of the living except with the eyes of one dead.

How did M. Fauchelevent come there? Why was he there? What had he come there to do? Marius did not address all these questions to himself. Besides, since our despair has this peculiarity, that it envelops others as well as ourselves, it seemed logical to him that all the world should come thither to die.

Only, he thought of Cosette with a pang at his heart.

However, M. Fauchelevent did not speak to him, did not look at him, and had not even the air of hearing him, when Marius raised his voice to say: "I know him."

As far as Marius was concerned, this attitude of M. Fauchelevent was comforting, and, if such a word can be used for such impressions, we should say that it pleased him. He had always felt the absolute impossibility of addressing that enigmatical man, who was, in his eyes, both equivocal and imposing. Moreover, it had been a long time since he had seen him; and this still further augmented the impossibility for Marius' timid and reserved nature.

The five chosen men left the barricade by way of Mondétour lane; they bore a perfect resemblance to members of the National Guard. One of them wept as he took his leave. Before setting out, they embraced those who remained.

When the five men sent back to life had taken their departure, Enjolras thought of the man who had been condemned to death.

He entered the tap-room. Javert, still bound to the post, was engaged in meditation.

"Do you want anything?" Enjolras asked him.

Javert replied: "When are you going to kill me?"

"Wait. We need all our cartridges just at present."

"Then give me a drink," said Javert.

Enjolras himself offered him a glass of water, and, as Javert was pinioned, he helped him to drink.

"Is that all?" inquired Enjolras.

"I am uncomfortable against this post," replied Javert. "You are not tender to have left me to pass the night here. Bind me as you please, but you surely might lay me out on a table like that other man."

And with a motion of the head, he indicated the body of M. Mabeuf.

There was, as the reader will remember, a long, broad table at the end of the room, on which they had been running bullets and making cartridges. All the cartridges having been made, and all the powder used, this table was free.

At Enjolras' command, four insurgents unbound Javert from the post. While they were loosing him, a fifth held a bayonet against his breast.

Leaving his arms tied behind his back, they placed about his feet a slender but stout whip-cord, as is done to men on the point of mounting the scaffold, which allowed him to take steps about fifteen inches in length, and made him walk to the table at the end of the room, where they laid him down, closely bound about the middle of the body.

By way of further security, and by means of a rope fastened to his neck, they added to the system of ligatures which rendered every attempt at escape impossible, that sort of bond which is called in prisons a martingale, which, starting at the neck, forks on the stomach, and meets the hands, after passing between the legs.

While they were binding Javert, a man standing on the threshold was surveying him with singular attention. The shadow cast by this man made Javert turn his head. He raised his eyes, and recognized Jean Valjean. He did not even start, but dropped his lids proudly and confined himself to the remark: "It is perfectly simple."

# VII

## The Situation Becomes Aggravated

The daylight was increasing rapidly. Not a window was opened, not a door stood ajar; it was the dawn but not the awaking. The end of the Rue de la Chanvrerie, opposite the barricade, had been evacuated by the troops, as we have stated, it seemed to be free, and presented itself to passers-by with a sinister tranquillity. The Rue Saint-Denis was as dumb as the avenue of Sphinxes at Thebes. Not a living being in the crossroads, which gleamed white in the light of the sun. Nothing is so mournful as this light in deserted streets. Nothing was to be seen, but there was something to be heard. A mysterious movement was going on at a certain distance. It was evident that the critical moment was approaching. As on the previous evening, the sentinels had come in; but this time all had come.

The barricade was stronger than on the occasion of the first attack. Since the departure of the five, they had increased its height still further.

On the advice of the sentinel who had examined the region of the Halles, Enjolras, for fear of a surprise in the rear, came to a serious decision. He had the small gut of the Mondétour lane, which had been left open up to that time, barricaded. For this purpose, they tore up the pavement for the length of several houses more. In this manner, the barricade, walled on three streets, in front on the Rue de la Chanvrerie, to the left on the Rues du Cygne and de la Petite Truanderie, to the right on the Rue Mondétour, was really almost impregnable; it is true that they were fatally hemmed in there. It had three fronts, but no exit.—"A fortress but a rat hole too," said Courfeyrac with a laugh.

Enjolras had about thirty paving-stones "torn up in excess," said Bossuet, piled up near the door of the wine-shop.

The silence was now so profound in the quarter whence the attack must needs come, that Enjolras had each man resume his post of battle.

An allowance of brandy was doled out to each.

Nothing is more curious than a barricade preparing for an assault. Each man selects his place as though at the theatre. They jostle, and elbow and crowd each other. There are some who make stalls of paving-stones. Here is a corner of the wall which is in the way, it is removed;

here is a redan which may afford protection, they take shelter behind it. Left-handed men are precious; they take the places that are inconvenient to the rest. Many arrange to fight in a sitting posture. They wish to be at ease to kill, and to die comfortably. In the sad war of June, 1848, an insurgent who was a formidable marksman, and who was firing from the top of a terrace upon a roof, had a reclining-chair brought there for his use; a charge of grape-shot found him out there.

As soon as the leader has given the order to clear the decks for action, all disorderly movements cease; there is no more pulling from one another; there are no more coteries; no more asides, there is no more holding aloof; everything in their spirits converges in, and changes into, a waiting for the assailants. A barricade before the arrival of danger is chaos; in danger, it is discipline itself. Peril produces order.

As soon as Enjolras had seized his double-barrelled rifle, and had placed himself in a sort of embrasure which he had reserved for himself, all the rest held their peace. A series of faint, sharp noises resounded confusedly along the wall of paving-stones. It was the men cocking their guns.

Moreover, their attitudes were prouder, more confident than ever; the excess of sacrifice strengthens; they no longer cherished any hope, but they had despair, despair,—the last weapon, which sometimes gives victory; Virgil has said so. Supreme resources spring from extreme resolutions. To embark in death is sometimes the means of escaping a shipwreck; and the lid of the coffin becomes a plank of safety.

As on the preceding evening, the attention of all was directed, we might almost say leaned upon, the end of the street, now lighted up and visible.

They had not long to wait. A stir began distinctly in the Saint-Leu quarter, but it did not resemble the movement of the first attack. A clashing of chains, the uneasy jolting of a mass, the click of brass skipping along the pavement, a sort of solemn uproar, announced that some sinister construction of iron was approaching. There arose a tremor in the bosoms of these peaceful old streets, pierced and built for the fertile circulation of interests and ideas, and which are not made for the horrible rumble of the wheels of war.

The fixity of eye in all the combatants upon the extremity of the street became ferocious.

A cannon made its appearance.

Artillery-men were pushing the piece; it was in firing trim; the fore-carriage had been detached; two upheld the gun-carriage, four were at the wheels; others followed with the caisson. They could see the smoke of the burning lint-stock.

"Fire!" shouted Enjolras.

The whole barricade fired, the report was terrible; an avalanche of smoke covered and effaced both cannon and men; after a few seconds, the cloud dispersed, and the cannon and men reappeared; the gun-crew had just finished rolling it slowly, correctly, without haste, into position facing the barricade. Not one of them had been struck. Then the captain of the piece, bearing down upon the breech in order to raise the muzzle, began to point the cannon with the gravity of an astronomer levelling a telescope.

"Bravo for the cannoneers!" cried Bossuet.

And the whole barricade clapped their hands.

A moment later, squarely planted in the very middle of the street, astride of the gutter, the piece was ready for action. A formidable pair of jaws yawned on the barricade.

"Come, merrily now!" ejaculated Courfeyrac. "That's the brutal part of it. After the fillip on the nose, the blow from the fist. The army is reaching out its big paw to us. The barricade is going to be severely shaken up. The fusillade tries, the cannon takes."

"It is a piece of eight, new model, brass," added Combeferre. "Those pieces are liable to burst as soon as the proportion of ten parts of tin to one hundred of brass is exceeded. The excess of tin renders them too tender. Then it comes to pass that they have caves and chambers when looked at from the vent hole. In order to obviate this danger, and to render it possible to force the charge, it may become necessary to return to the process of the fourteenth century, hooping, and to encircle the piece on the outside with a series of unwelded steel bands, from the breech to the trunnions. In the meantime, they remedy this defect as best they may; they manage to discover where the holes are located in the vent of a cannon, by means of a searcher. But there is a better method, with Gribeauval's movable star."

"In the sixteenth century," remarked Bossuet, "they used to rifle cannon."

"Yes," replied Combeferre, "that augments the projectile force, but diminishes the accuracy of the firing. In firing at short range, the trajectory is not as rigid as could be desired, the parabola is exaggerated, the line of the projectile is no longer sufficiently rectilinear to allow of its striking intervening objects, which is, nevertheless, a necessity of battle, the importance of which increases with the proximity of the enemy and the precipitation of the discharge. This defect of the tension of the curve of the projectile in the rifled cannon of the sixteenth century arose from the smallness of the charge; small charges for that sort of engine are imposed by the ballistic necessities, such, for instance, as the preservation of the gun-carriage. In short, that despot, the cannon, cannot do all that it desires; force is a great weakness. A cannon-ball only travels six hundred leagues an hour; light travels seventy thousand leagues a second. Such is the superiority of Jesus Christ over Napoleon."

"Reload your guns," said Enjolras.

How was the casing of the barricade going to behave under the cannon-balls? Would they effect a breach? That was the question. While the insurgents were reloading their guns, the artillery-men were loading the cannon.

The anxiety in the redoubt was profound.

The shot sped the report burst forth.

"Present!" shouted a joyous voice.

And Gavroche flung himself into the barricade just as the ball dashed against it.

He came from the direction of the Rue du Cygne, and he had nimbly climbed over the auxiliary barricade which fronted on the labyrinth of the Rue de la Petite Truanderie.

Gavroche produced a greater sensation in the barricade than the cannon-ball.

The ball buried itself in the mass of rubbish. At the most there was an omnibus wheel broken, and the old Anceau cart was demolished. On seeing this, the barricade burst into a laugh.

"Go on!" shouted Bossuet to the artillerists.

# VIII

## The Artillery-Men Compel People to Take Them Seriously

They flocked round Gavroche. But he had no time to tell anything. Marius drew him aside with a shudder.

"What are you doing here?"

"Hullo!" said the child, "what are you doing here yourself?"

And he stared at Marius intently with his epic effrontery. His eyes grew larger with the proud light within them.

It was with an accent of severity that Marius continued:

"Who told you to come back? Did you deliver my letter at the address?"

Gavroche was not without some compunctions in the matter of that letter. In his haste to return to the barricade, he had got rid of it rather than delivered it. He was forced to acknowledge to himself that he had confided it rather lightly to that stranger whose face he had not been able to make out. It is true that the man was bareheaded, but that was not sufficient. In short, he had been administering to himself little inward remonstrances and he feared Marius' reproaches. In order to extricate himself from the predicament, he took the simplest course; he lied abominably.

"Citizen, I delivered the letter to the porter. The lady was asleep. She will have the letter when she wakes up."

Marius had had two objects in sending that letter: to bid farewell to Cosette and to save Gavroche. He was obliged to content himself with the half of his desire.

The despatch of his letter and the presence of M. Fauchelevent in the barricade, was a coincidence which occurred to him. He pointed out M. Fauchelevent to Gavroche.

"Do you know that man?"

"No," said Gavroche.

Gavroche had, in fact, as we have just mentioned, seen Jean Valjean only at night.

The troubled and unhealthy conjectures which had outlined themselves in Marius' mind were dissipated. Did he know M. Fauchelevent's opinions? Perhaps M. Fauchelevent was a republican. Hence his very natural presence in this combat.

In the meanwhile, Gavroche was shouting, at the other end of the barricade: "My gun!"

Courfeyrac had it returned to him.

Gavroche warned "his comrades" as he called them, that the barricade was blocked. He had had great difficulty in reaching it. A battalion of the line whose arms were piled in the Rue de la Petite Truanderie was on the watch on the side of the Rue du Cygne; on the opposite side, the municipal guard occupied the Rue des Prêcheurs. The bulk of the army was facing them in front.

This information given, Gavroche added:

"I authorize you to hit 'em a tremendous whack."

Meanwhile, Enjolras was straining his ears and watching at his embrasure.

The assailants, dissatisfied, no doubt, with their shot, had not repeated it.

A company of infantry of the line had come up and occupied the end of the street behind the piece of ordnance. The soldiers were tearing up the pavement and constructing with the stones a small, low wall, a sort of side-work not more than eighteen inches high, and facing the barricade. In the angle at the left of this epaulement, there was visible the head of the column of a battalion from the suburbs massed in the Rue Saint-Denis.

Enjolras, on the watch, thought he distinguished the peculiar sound which is produced when the shells of grape-shot are drawn from the caissons, and he saw the commander of the piece change the elevation and incline the mouth of the cannon slightly to the left. Then the cannoneers began to load the piece. The chief seized the lint-stock himself and lowered it to the vent.

"Down with your heads, hug the wall!" shouted Enjolras, "and all on your knees along the barricade!"

The insurgents who were straggling in front of the wine-shop, and who had quitted their posts of combat on Gavroche's arrival, rushed pell-mell towards the barricade; but before Enjolras' order could be executed, the discharge took place with the terrifying rattle of a round of grape-shot. This is what it was, in fact.

The charge had been aimed at the cut in the redoubt, and had there rebounded from the wall; and this terrible rebound had produced two dead and three wounded.

If this were continued, the barricade was no longer tenable. The grape-shot made its way in.

A murmur of consternation arose.

"Let us prevent the second discharge," said Enjolras.

And, lowering his rifle, he took aim at the captain of the gun, who, at that moment, was bearing down on the breach of his gun and rectifying and definitely fixing its pointing.

The captain of the piece was a handsome sergeant of artillery, very young, blond, with a very gentle face, and the intelligent air peculiar to that predestined and redoubtable weapon which, by dint of perfecting itself in horror, must end in killing war.

Combeferre, who was standing beside Enjolras, scrutinized this young man.

"What a pity!" said Combeferre. "What hideous things these butcheries are! Come, when there are no more kings, there will be no more war. Enjolras, you are taking aim at that sergeant, you are not looking at him. Fancy, he is a charming young man; he is intrepid; it is evident that he is thoughtful; those young artillery-men are very well educated; he has a father, a mother, a family; he is probably in love; he is not more than five and twenty at the most; he might be your brother."

"He is," said Enjolras.

"Yes," replied Combeferre, "he is mine too. Well, let us not kill him."

"Let me alone. It must be done."

And a tear trickled slowly down Enjolras' marble cheek.

At the same moment, he pressed the trigger of his rifle. The flame leaped forth. The artillery-man turned round twice, his arms extended in front of him, his head uplifted, as though for breath, then he fell with his side on the gun, and lay there motionless. They could see his back, from the centre of which there flowed directly a stream of blood. The ball had traversed his breast from side to side. He was dead.

He had to be carried away and replaced by another. Several minutes were thus gained, in fact.

# IX

## Employment of the Old Talents of a Poacher and that Infallible Marksmanship Which Influenced the Condemnation of 1796

Opinions were exchanged in the barricade. The firing from the gun was about to begin again. Against that grape-shot, they could not hold out a quarter of an hour longer. It was absolutely necessary to deaden the blows.

Enjolras issued this command:

"We must place a mattress there."

"We have none," said Combeferre, "the wounded are lying on them."

Jean Valjean, who was seated apart on a stone post, at the corner of the tavern, with his gun between his knees, had, up to that moment, taken no part in anything that was going on. He did not appear to hear the combatants saying around him: "Here is a gun that is doing nothing."

At the order issued by Enjolras, he rose.

It will be remembered that, on the arrival of the rabble in the Rue de la Chanvrerie, an old woman, foreseeing the bullets, had placed her mattress in front of her window. This window, an attic window, was on the roof of a six-story house situated a little beyond the barricade. The mattress, placed cross-wise, supported at the bottom on two poles for drying linen, was upheld at the top by two ropes, which, at that distance, looked like two threads, and which were attached to two nails planted in the window frames. These ropes were distinctly visible, like hairs, against the sky.

"Can some one lend me a double-barrelled rifle?" said Jean Valjean.

Enjolras, who had just re-loaded his, handed it to him.

Jean Valjean took aim at the attic window and fired.

One of the mattress ropes was cut.

The mattress now hung by one thread only.

Jean Valjean fired the second charge. The second rope lashed the panes of the attic window. The mattress slipped between the two poles and fell into the street.

The barricade applauded.

All voices cried:

"Here is a mattress!"

"Yes," said Combeferre, "but who will go and fetch it?"

The mattress had, in fact, fallen outside the barricade, between besiegers and besieged. Now, the death of the sergeant of artillery having exasperated the troop, the soldiers had, for several minutes, been lying flat on their stomachs behind the line of paving-stones which they had erected, and, in order to supply the forced silence of the piece, which was quiet while its service was in course of reorganization, they had opened fire on the barricade. The insurgents did not reply to this musketry, in order to spare their ammunition. The fusillade broke against the barricade; but the street, which it filled, was terrible.

Jean Valjean stepped out of the cut, entered the street, traversed the storm of bullets, walked up to the mattress, hoisted it upon his back, and returned to the barricade.

He placed the mattress in the cut with his own hands. He fixed it there against the wall in such a manner that the artillery-men should not see it.

That done, they awaited the next discharge of grape-shot.

It was not long in coming.

The cannon vomited forth its package of buckshot with a roar. But there was no rebound. The effect which they had foreseen had been attained. The barricade was saved.

"Citizen," said Enjolras to Jean Valjean, "the Republic thanks you."

Bossuet admired and laughed. He exclaimed:

"It is immoral that a mattress should have so much power. Triumph of that which yields over that which strikes with lightning. But never mind, glory to the mattress which annuls a cannon!"

# X

## Dawn

At that moment, Cosette awoke.

Her chamber was narrow, neat, unobtrusive, with a long sash-window, facing the East on the back court-yard of the house.

Cosette knew nothing of what was going on in Paris. She had not been there on the preceding evening, and she had already retired to her chamber when Toussaint had said:

"It appears that there is a row."

Cosette had slept only a few hours, but soundly. She had had sweet dreams, which possibly arose from the fact that her little bed was very white. Some one, who was Marius, had appeared to her in the light. She awoke with the sun in her eyes, which, at first, produced on her the effect of being a continuation of her dream. Her first thought on emerging from this dream was a smiling one. Cosette felt herself thoroughly reassured. Like Jean Valjean, she had, a few hours previously, passed through that reaction of the soul which absolutely will not hear of unhappiness. She began to cherish hope, with all her might, without knowing why. Then she felt a pang at her heart. It was three days since she had seen Marius. But she said to herself that he must have received her letter, that he knew where she was, and that he was so clever that he would find means of reaching her.—And that certainly to-day, and perhaps that very morning.—It was broad daylight, but the rays of light were very horizontal; she thought that it was very early, but that she must rise, nevertheless, in order to receive Marius.

She felt that she could not live without Marius, and that, consequently, that was sufficient and that Marius would come. No objection was valid. All this was certain. It was monstrous enough already to have suffered for three days. Marius absent three days, this was horrible on the part of the good God. Now, this cruel teasing from on high had been gone through with. Marius was about to arrive, and he would bring good news. Youth is made thus; it quickly dries its eyes; it finds sorrow useless and does not accept it. Youth is the smile of the future in the presence of an unknown quantity, which is itself. It is natural to it to be happy. It seems as though its respiration were made of hope.

Moreover, Cosette could not remember what Marius had said to her on the subject of this absence which was to last only one day, and what explanation of it he had given her. Every one has noticed with what nimbleness a coin which one has dropped on the ground rolls away and hides, and with what art it renders itself undiscoverable. There are thoughts which play us the same trick; they nestle away in a corner of our brain; that is the end of them; they are lost; it is impossible to lay the memory on them. Cosette was somewhat vexed at the useless little effort made by her memory. She told herself, that it was very naughty and very wicked of her, to have forgotten the words uttered by Marius.

She sprang out of bed and accomplished the two ablutions of soul and body, her prayers and her toilet.

One may, in a case of exigency, introduce the reader into a nuptial chamber, not into a virginal chamber. Verse would hardly venture it, prose must not.

It is the interior of a flower that is not yet unfolded, it is whiteness in the dark, it is the private cell of a closed lily, which must not be gazed upon by man so long as the sun has not gazed upon it. Woman in the bud is sacred. That innocent bud which opens, that adorable half-nudity which is afraid of itself, that white foot which takes refuge in a slipper, that throat which veils itself before a mirror as though a mirror were an eye, that chemise which makes haste to rise up and conceal the shoulder for a creaking bit of furniture or a passing vehicle, those cords tied, those clasps fastened, those laces drawn, those tremors, those shivers of cold and modesty, that exquisite affright in every movement, that almost winged uneasiness where there is no cause for alarm, the successive phases of dressing, as charming as the clouds of dawn,—it is not fitting that all this should be narrated, and it is too much to have even called attention to it.

The eye of man must be more religious in the presence of the rising of a young girl than in the presence of the rising of a star. The possibility of hurting should inspire an augmentation of respect. The down on the peach, the bloom on the plum, the radiated crystal of the snow, the wing of the butterfly powdered with feathers, are coarse compared to that chastity which does not even know that it is chaste. The young girl is only the flash of a dream, and is not yet a statue. Her bed-chamber is hidden in the sombre part of the ideal. The indiscreet touch of a glance brutalizes this vague penumbra. Here, contemplation is profanation.

We shall, therefore, show nothing of that sweet little flutter of Cosette's rising.

An oriental tale relates how the rose was made white by God, but that Adam looked upon her when she was unfolding, and she was ashamed and turned crimson. We are of the number who fall speechless in the presence of young girls and flowers, since we think them worthy of veneration.

Cosette dressed herself very hastily, combed and dressed her hair, which was a very simple matter in those days, when women did not swell out their curls and bands with cushions and puffs, and did not put crinoline in their locks. Then she opened the window and cast her eyes around her in every direction, hoping to descry some bit of the street, an angle of the house, an edge of pavement, so that she might be able to watch for Marius there. But no view of the outside was to be had. The back court was surrounded by tolerably high walls, and the outlook was only on several gardens. Cosette pronounced these gardens hideous: for the first time in her life, she found flowers ugly. The smallest scrap of the gutter of the street would have met her wishes better. She decided to gaze at the sky, as though she thought that Marius might come from that quarter.

All at once, she burst into tears. Not that this was fickleness of soul; but hopes cut in twain by dejection—that was her case. She had a confused consciousness of something horrible. Thoughts were rife in the air, in fact. She told herself that she was not sure of anything, that to withdraw herself from sight was to be lost; and the idea that Marius could return to her from heaven appeared to her no longer charming but mournful.

Then, as is the nature of these clouds, calm returned to her, and hope and a sort of unconscious smile, which yet indicated trust in God.

Every one in the house was still asleep. A country-like silence reigned. Not a shutter had been opened. The porter's lodge was closed. Toussaint had not risen, and Cosette, naturally, thought that her father was asleep. She must have suffered much, and she must have still been suffering greatly, for she said to herself, that her father had been unkind; but she counted on Marius. The eclipse of such a light was decidedly impossible. Now and then, she heard sharp shocks in the distance, and she said: "It is odd that people should be opening and shutting their carriage gates so early." They were the reports of the cannon battering the barricade.

A few feet below Cosette's window, in the ancient and perfectly black cornice of the wall, there was a martin's nest; the curve of this nest formed a little projection beyond the cornice, so that from above it was possible to look into this little paradise. The mother was there, spreading her wings like a fan over her brood; the father fluttered about, flew away, then came back, bearing in his beak food and kisses. The dawning day gilded this happy thing, the great law, "Multiply," lay there smiling and august, and that sweet mystery unfolded in the glory of the morning. Cosette, with her hair in the sunlight, her soul absorbed in chimæras, illuminated by love within and by the dawn without, bent over mechanically, and almost without daring to avow to herself that she was thinking at the same time of Marius, began to gaze at these birds, at this family, at that male and female, that mother and her little ones, with the profound trouble which a nest produces on a virgin.

# XI

## The Shot Which Misses Nothing and Kills No One

The assailants' fire continued. Musketry and grape-shot alternated, but without committing great ravages, to tell the truth. The top alone of the Corinthe façade suffered; the window on the first floor, and the attic window in the roof, riddled with buckshot and biscaïens, were slowly losing their shape. The combatants who had been posted there had been obliged to withdraw. However, this is according to the tactics of barricades; to fire for a long while, in order to exhaust the insurgents' ammunition, if they commit the mistake of replying. When it is perceived, from the slackening of their fire, that they have no more powder and ball, the assault is made. Enjolras had not fallen into this trap; the barricade did not reply.

At every discharge by platoons, Gavroche puffed out his cheek with his tongue, a sign of supreme disdain.

"Good for you," said he, "rip up the cloth. We want some lint."

Courfeyrac called the grape-shot to order for the little effect which it produced, and said to the cannon:

"You are growing diffuse, my good fellow."

One gets puzzled in battle, as at a ball. It is probable that this silence on the part of the redoubt began to render the besiegers uneasy, and to make them fear some unexpected incident, and that they felt the necessity of getting a clear view behind that heap of paving-stones, and of knowing what was going on behind that impassable wall which received blows without retorting. The insurgents suddenly perceived a helmet glittering in the sun on a neighboring roof. A fireman had placed his back against a tall chimney, and seemed to be acting as sentinel. His glance fell directly down into the barricade.

"There's an embarrassing watcher," said Enjolras.

Jean Valjean had returned Enjolras' rifle, but he had his own gun.

Without saying a word, he took aim at the fireman, and, a second later, the helmet, smashed by a bullet, rattled noisily into the street. The terrified soldier made haste to disappear. A second observer took his place. This one was an officer. Jean Valjean, who had re-loaded his gun, took aim at the newcomer and sent the officer's casque to join the soldier's. The officer did not persist, and retired speedily. This time the warning was understood. No one made his appearance thereafter on that roof; and the idea of spying on the barricade was abandoned.

"Why did you not kill the man?" Bossuet asked Jean Valjean.

Jean Valjean made no reply.

# XII

## Disorder a Partisan of Order

B ossuet muttered in Combeferre's ear:
"He did not answer my question."

"He is a man who does good by gun-shots," said Combeferre.

Those who have preserved some memory of this already distant epoch know that the National Guard from the suburbs was valiant against insurrections. It was particularly zealous and intrepid in the days of June, 1832. A certain good dram-shop keeper of Pantin des Vertus or la Cunette, whose "establishment" had been closed by the riots, became leonine at the sight of his deserted dance-hall, and got himself killed to preserve the order represented by a tea-garden. In that bourgeois and heroic time, in the presence of ideas which had their knights, interests had their paladins. The prosiness of the originators detracted nothing from the bravery of the movement. The diminution of a pile of crowns made bankers sing the Marseillaise. They shed their blood lyrically for the counting-house; and they defended the shop, that immense diminutive of the fatherland, with Lacedæmonian enthusiasm.

At bottom, we will observe, there was nothing in all this that was not extremely serious. It was social elements entering into strife, while awaiting the day when they should enter into equilibrium.

Another sign of the times was the anarchy mingled with governmentalism (the barbarous name of the correct party). People were for order in combination with lack of discipline.

The drum suddenly beat capricious calls, at the command of such or such a Colonel of the National Guard; such and such a captain went into action through inspiration; such and such National Guardsmen fought, "for an idea," and on their own account. At critical moments, on "days" they took counsel less of their leaders than of their instincts. There existed in the army of order, veritable guerilleros, some of the sword, like Fannicot, others of the pen, like Henri Fonfrède.

Civilization, unfortunately, represented at this epoch rather by an aggregation of interests than by a group of principles, was or thought itself, in peril; it set up the cry of alarm; each, constituting himself a centre, defended it, succored it, and protected it with his own head; and the first comer took it upon himself to save society.

Zeal sometimes proceeded to extermination. A platoon of the National Guard would constitute itself on its own authority a private council of war, and judge and execute a captured insurgent in five minutes. It was an improvisation of this sort that had slain Jean Prouvaire. Fierce Lynch law, with which no one party had any right to reproach the rest, for it has been applied by the Republic in America, as well as by the monarchy in Europe. This Lynch law was complicated with mistakes. On one day of rioting, a young poet, named Paul Aimé Garnier, was pursued in the Place Royale, with a bayonet at his loins, and only escaped by taking refuge under the porte-cochère of No. 6. They shouted:—"There's another of those Saint-Simonians!" and they wanted to kill him. Now, he had under his arm a volume of the memoirs of the Duc de Saint-Simon. A National Guard had read the words *Saint-Simon* on the book, and had shouted: "Death!"

On the 6th of June, 1832, a company of the National Guards from the suburbs, commanded by the Captain Fannicot, above mentioned, had itself decimated in the Rue de la Chanvrerie out of caprice and its own good pleasure. This fact, singular though it may seem, was proved at the judicial investigation opened in consequence of the insurrection of 1832. Captain Fannicot, a bold and impatient bourgeois, a sort of condottiere of the order of those whom we have just characterized, a fanatical and intractable governmentalist, could not resist the temptation to fire prematurely, and the ambition of capturing the barricade alone and unaided, that is to say, with his company. Exasperated by the successive apparition of the red flag and the old coat which he took for the black flag, he loudly blamed the generals and chiefs of the corps, who were holding council and did not think that the moment for the decisive assault had arrived, and who were allowing "the insurrection to fry in its own fat," to use the celebrated expression of one of them. For his part, he thought the barricade ripe, and as that which is ripe ought to fall, he made the attempt.

He commanded men as resolute as himself, "raging fellows," as a witness said. His company, the same which had shot Jean Prouvaire the poet, was the first of the battalion posted at the angle of the street. At the moment when they were least expecting it, the captain launched his men against the barricade. This movement, executed with more good will than strategy, cost the Fannicot company dear. Before it had traversed two thirds of the street it was received by a general discharge from the barricade. Four, the most audacious, who were running on in front, were mown down point-blank at the very foot of the redoubt, and this courageous throng of National Guards, very brave men but lacking in military tenacity, were forced to fall back, after some hesitation, leaving fifteen corpses on the pavement. This momentary hesitation gave the insurgents time to re-load their weapons, and a second and very destructive discharge struck the company before it could regain the corner of the street, its shelter. A moment more, and it was caught between two fires, and it received the volley from the battery piece which, not having received the order, had not discontinued its firing.

The intrepid and imprudent Fannicot was one of the dead from this grape-shot. He was killed by the cannon, that is to say, by order.

This attack, which was more furious than serious, irritated Enjolras.—"The fools!" said he. "They are getting their own men killed and they are using up our ammunition for nothing."

Enjolras spoke like the real general of insurrection which he was. Insurrection and repression do not fight with equal weapons. Insurrection, which is speedily exhausted, has only a certain number of shots to fire and a certain number of combatants to expend. An empty cartridge-box, a man killed, cannot be replaced. As repression has the army, it does not count its men, and, as it has Vincennes, it does not count its shots. Repression has as many regiments as the barricade has men, and as many arsenals as the barricade has cartridge-boxes. Thus they are struggles of one against a hundred, which always end in crushing the barricade; unless the revolution, uprising suddenly, flings into the balance its flaming archangel's sword. This does happen sometimes. Then everything rises, the pavements begin to seethe, popular redoubts abound. Paris quivers supremely, the *quid divinum* is given forth, a 10th of August is in the air, a 29th of July is in the air, a wonderful light appears, the yawning maw of force draws back, and the army, that lion, sees before it, erect and tranquil, that prophet, France.

# XIII

## Passing Gleams

In the chaos of sentiments and passions which defend a barricade, there is a little of everything; there is bravery, there is youth, honor, enthusiasm, the ideal, conviction, the rage of the gambler, and, above all, intermittences of hope.

One of these intermittences, one of these vague quivers of hope suddenly traversed the barricade of the Rue de la Chanvrerie at the moment when it was least expected.

"Listen," suddenly cried Enjolras, who was still on the watch, "it seems to me that Paris is waking up."

It is certain that, on the morning of the 6th of June, the insurrection broke out afresh for an hour or two, to a certain extent. The obstinacy of the alarm peal of Saint-Merry reanimated some fancies. Barricades were begun in the Rue du Poirier and the Rue des Gravilliers. In front of the Porte Saint-Martin, a young man, armed with a rifle, attacked alone a squadron of cavalry. In plain sight, on the open boulevard, he placed one knee on the ground, shouldered his weapon, fired, killed the commander of the squadron, and turned away, saying: "There's another who will do us no more harm."

He was put to the sword. In the Rue Saint-Denis, a woman fired on the National Guard from behind a lowered blind. The slats of the blind could be seen to tremble at every shot. A child fourteen years of age was arrested in the Rue de la Cossonerie, with his pockets full of cartridges. Many posts were attacked. At the entrance to the Rue Bertin-Poirée, a very lively and utterly unexpected fusillade welcomed a regiment of cuirassiers, at whose head marched Marshal General Cavaignac de Barague. In the Rue Planche-Mibray, they threw old pieces of pottery and household utensils down on the soldiers from the roofs; a bad sign; and when this matter was reported to Marshal Soult, Napoleon's old lieutenant grew thoughtful, as he recalled Suchet's saying at Saragossa: "We are lost when the old women empty their pots de chambre on our heads."

These general symptoms which presented themselves at the moment when it was thought that the uprising had been rendered local, this fever of wrath, these sparks which flew hither and thither above those deep masses of combustibles which are called the faubourgs of Paris,— all this, taken together, disturbed the military chiefs. They made haste to stamp out these beginnings of conflagration.

They delayed the attack on the barricades Maubuée, de la Chanvrerie and Saint-Merry until these sparks had been extinguished, in order that they might have to deal with the barricades only and be able to finish them at one blow. Columns were thrown into the streets where there was fermentation, sweeping the large, sounding the small, right and left, now slowly and cautiously, now at full charge. The troops broke in the doors of houses whence shots had been fired; at the same time, manœuvres by the cavalry dispersed the groups on the boulevards. This repression was not effected without some commotion, and without that tumultuous uproar peculiar to collisions between the army and the people. This was what Enjolras had caught in the intervals of the cannonade and the musketry. Moreover, he had seen wounded men passing the end of the street in litters, and he said to Courfeyrac:— "Those wounded do not come from us."

Their hope did not last long; the gleam was quickly eclipsed. In less than half an hour, what was in the air vanished, it was a flash of lightning unaccompanied by thunder, and the insurgents felt that sort of leaden cope, which the indifference of the people casts over obstinate and deserted men, fall over them once more.

The general movement, which seemed to have assumed a vague outline, had miscarried; and the attention of the minister of war and the strategy of the generals could now be concentrated on the three or four barricades which still remained standing.

The sun was mounting above the horizon.

An insurgent hailed Enjolras.

"We are hungry here. Are we really going to die like this, without anything to eat?"

Enjolras, who was still leaning on his elbows at his embrasure, made an affirmative sign with his head, but without taking his eyes from the end of the street.

# XIV

## Wherein Will Appear the Name of Enjolras' Mistress

Courfeyrac, seated on a paving-stone beside Enjolras, continued to insult the cannon, and each time that that gloomy cloud of projectiles which is called grape-shot passed overhead with its terrible sound he assailed it with a burst of irony.

"You are wearing out your lungs, poor, brutal, old fellow, you pain me, you are wasting your row. That's not thunder, it's a cough."

And the bystanders laughed.

Courfeyrac and Bossuet, whose brave good humor increased with the peril, like Madame Scarron, replaced nourishment with pleasantry, and, as wine was lacking, they poured out gayety to all.

"I admire Enjolras," said Bossuet. "His impassive temerity astounds me. He lives alone, which renders him a little sad, perhaps; Enjolras complains of his greatness, which binds him to widowhood. The rest of us have mistresses, more or less, who make us crazy, that is to say, brave. When a man is as much in love as a tiger, the least that he can do is to fight like a lion. That is one way of taking our revenge for the capers that mesdames our grisettes play on us. Roland gets himself killed for Angélique; all our heroism comes from our women. A man without a woman is a pistol without a trigger; it is the woman that sets the man off. Well, Enjolras has no woman. He is not in love, and yet he manages to be intrepid. It is a thing unheard of that a man should be as cold as ice and as bold as fire."

Enjolras did not appear to be listening, but had any one been near him, that person would have heard him mutter in a low voice: "Patria."

Bossuet was still laughing when Courfeyrac exclaimed:

"News!"

And assuming the tone of an usher making an announcement, he added:

"My name is Eight-Pounder."

In fact, a new personage had entered on the scene. This was a second piece of ordnance.

The artillery-men rapidly performed their manœuvres in force and placed this second piece in line with the first.

This outlined the catastrophe.

A few minutes later, the two pieces, rapidly served, were firing point-blank at the redoubt; the platoon firing of the line and of the soldiers from the suburbs sustained the artillery.

Another cannonade was audible at some distance. At the same time that the two guns were furiously attacking the redoubt from the Rue de la Chanvrerie, two other cannons, trained one from the Rue Saint-Denis, the other from the Rue Aubry-le-Boucher, were riddling the Saint-Merry barricade. The four cannons echoed each other mournfully.

The barking of these sombre dogs of war replied to each other.

One of the two pieces which was now battering the barricade on the Rue de la Chanvrerie was firing grape-shot, the other balls.

The piece which was firing balls was pointed a little high, and the aim was calculated so that the ball struck the extreme edge of the upper crest of the barricade, and crumbled the stone down upon the insurgents, mingled with bursts of grape-shot.

The object of this mode of firing was to drive the insurgents from the summit of the redoubt, and to compel them to gather close in the interior, that is to say, this announced the assault.

The combatants once driven from the crest of the barricade by balls, and from the windows of the cabaret by grape-shot, the attacking columns could venture into the street without being picked off, perhaps, even, without being seen, could briskly and suddenly scale the redoubt, as on the preceding evening, and, who knows? take it by surprise.

"It is absolutely necessary that the inconvenience of those guns should be diminished," said Enjolras, and he shouted: "Fire on the artillery-men!"

All were ready. The barricade, which had long been silent, poured forth a desperate fire; seven or eight discharges followed, with a sort of rage and joy; the street was filled with blinding smoke, and, at the end of a few minutes, athwart this mist all streaked with flame, two thirds of the gunners could be distinguished lying beneath the wheels of the cannons. Those who were left standing continued to serve the pieces with severe tranquillity, but the fire had slackened.

"Things are going well now," said Bossuet to Enjolras. "Success."

Enjolras shook his head and replied:

"Another quarter of an hour of this success, and there will not be any cartridges left in the barricade."

It appears that Gavroche overheard this remark.

# XV

## GAVROCHE OUTSIDE

Courfeyrac suddenly caught sight of some one at the base of the barricade, outside in the street, amid the bullets.

Gavroche had taken a bottle basket from the wine-shop, had made his way out through the cut, and was quietly engaged in emptying the full cartridge-boxes of the National Guardsmen who had been killed on the slope of the redoubt, into his basket.

"What are you doing there?" asked Courfeyrac.

Gavroche raised his face:—

"I'm filling my basket, citizen."

"Don't you see the grape-shot?"

Gavroche replied:

"Well, it is raining. What then?"

Courfeyrac shouted:—"Come in!"

"Instanter," said Gavroche.

And with a single bound he plunged into the street.

It will be remembered that Fannicot's company had left behind it a trail of bodies. Twenty corpses lay scattered here and there on the pavement, through the whole length of the street. Twenty cartouches for Gavroche meant a provision of cartridges for the barricade.

The smoke in the street was like a fog. Whoever has beheld a cloud which has fallen into a mountain gorge between two peaked escarpments can imagine this smoke rendered denser and thicker by two gloomy rows of lofty houses. It rose gradually and was incessantly renewed; hence a twilight which made even the broad daylight turn pale. The combatants could hardly see each other from one end of the street to the other, short as it was.

This obscurity, which had probably been desired and calculated on by the commanders who were to direct the assault on the barricade, was useful to Gavroche.

Beneath the folds of this veil of smoke, and thanks to his small size, he could advance tolerably far into the street without being seen. He rifled the first seven or eight cartridge-boxes without much danger.

He crawled flat on his belly, galloped on all fours, took his basket in his teeth, twisted, glided, undulated, wound from one dead body to another, and emptied the cartridge-box or cartouche as a monkey opens a nut.

They did not dare to shout to him to return from the barricade, which was quite near, for fear of attracting attention to him.

On one body, that of a corporal, he found a powder-flask.

"For thirst," said he, putting it in his pocket.

By dint of advancing, he reached a point where the fog of the fusillade became transparent. So that the sharpshooters of the line ranged on the outlook behind their paving-stone dike and the sharpshooters of the banlieue massed at the corner of the street suddenly pointed out to each other something moving through the smoke.

At the moment when Gavroche was relieving a sergeant, who was lying near a stone door-post, of his cartridges, a bullet struck the body.

"Fichtre!" ejaculated Gavroche. "They are killing my dead men for me."

A second bullet struck a spark from the pavement beside him.—A third overturned his basket.

Gavroche looked and saw that this came from the men of the banlieue.

He sprang to his feet, stood erect, with his hair flying in the wind, his hands on his hips, his eyes fixed on the National Guardsmen who were firing, and sang:

> "On est laid à Nanterre,
> C'est la faute à Voltaire;
> Et bête à Palaiseau,
> C'est la faute à Rousseau."

> "Men are ugly at Nanterre,
> 'Tis the fault of Voltaire;
> And dull at Palaiseau,
> 'Tis the fault of Rousseau."

Then he picked up his basket, replaced the cartridges which had fallen from it, without missing a single one, and, advancing towards the fusillade, set about plundering another cartridge-box. There a fourth bullet missed him, again. Gavroche sang:

> "Je ne suis pas notaire,
> C'est la faute à Voltaire;
> Je suis un petit oiseau,
> C'est la faute à Rousseau."

> "I am not a notary,
> 'Tis the fault of Voltaire;
> I'm a little bird,
> 'Tis the fault of Rousseau."

A fifth bullet only succeeded in drawing from him a third couplet.

> *"Joie est mon caractère,*
> *C'est la faute à Voltaire;*
> *Misère est mon trousseau,*
> *C'est la faute à Rousseau."*

> *"Joy is my character,*
> *'Tis the fault of Voltaire;*
> *Misery is my trousseau,*
> *'Tis the fault of Rousseau."*

Thus it went on for some time.

It was a charming and terrible sight. Gavroche, though shot at, was teasing the fusillade. He had the air of being greatly diverted. It was the sparrow pecking at the sportsmen. To each discharge he retorted with a couplet. They aimed at him constantly, and always missed him. The National Guardsmen and the soldiers laughed as they took aim at him. He lay down, sprang to his feet, hid in the corner of a doorway, then made a bound, disappeared, reappeared, scampered away, returned, replied to the grape-shot with his thumb at his nose, and, all the while, went on pillaging the cartouches, emptying the cartridge-boxes, and filling his basket. The insurgents, panting with anxiety, followed him with their eyes. The barricade trembled; he sang. He was not a child, he was not a man; he was a strange gamin-fairy. He might have been called the invulnerable dwarf of the fray. The bullets flew after him, he was more nimble than they. He played a fearful game of hide and seek with death; every time that the flat-nosed face of the spectre approached, the urchin administered to it a fillip.

One bullet, however, better aimed or more treacherous than the rest, finally struck the will-o'-the-wisp of a child. Gavroche was seen to stagger, then he sank to the earth. The whole barricade gave vent to a cry; but there was something of Antæus in that pygmy; for the gamin to touch the pavement is the same as for the giant to touch the earth; Gavroche had fallen only to rise again; he remained in a sitting posture, a long thread of blood streaked his face, he raised both arms in the air, glanced in the direction whence the shot had come, and began to sing:

> *"Je suis tombé par terre,*
> *C'est la faute à Voltaire;*
> *Le nez dans le ruisseau,*
> *C'est la faute à. . . "*

> *"I have fallen to the earth,*
> *'Tis the fault of Voltaire;*
> *With my nose in the gutter,*
> *'Tis the fault of. . ."*

He did not finish. A second bullet from the same marksman stopped him short. This time he fell face downward on the pavement, and moved no more. This grand little soul had taken its flight.

# XVI

## How from a Brother One Becomes a Father

At that same moment, in the garden of the Luxembourg,—for the gaze of the drama must be everywhere present,—two children were holding each other by the hand. One might have been seven years old, the other five. The rain having soaked them, they were walking along the paths on the sunny side; the elder was leading the younger; they were pale and ragged; they had the air of wild birds. The smaller of them said: "I am very hungry."

The elder, who was already somewhat of a protector, was leading his brother with his left hand and in his right he carried a small stick.

They were alone in the garden. The garden was deserted, the gates had been closed by order of the police, on account of the insurrection. The troops who had been bivouacking there had departed for the exigencies of combat.

How did those children come there? Perhaps they had escaped from some guard-house which stood ajar; perhaps there was in the vicinity, at the Barrière d'Enfer; or on the Esplanade de l'Observatoire, or in the neighboring carrefour, dominated by the pediment on which could be read: *Invenerunt parvulum pannis involutum*, some mountebank's booth from which they had fled; perhaps they had, on the preceding evening, escaped the eye of the inspectors of the garden at the hour of closing, and had passed the night in some one of those sentry-boxes where people read the papers? The fact is, they were stray lambs and they seemed free. To be astray and to seem free is to be lost. These poor little creatures were, in fact, lost.

These two children were the same over whom Gavroche had been put to some trouble, as the reader will recollect. Children of the Thénardiers, leased out to Magnon, attributed to M. Gillenormand, and now leaves fallen from all these rootless branches, and swept over the ground by the wind. Their clothing, which had been clean in Magnon's day, and which had served her as a prospectus with M. Gillenormand, had been converted into rags.

Henceforth these beings belonged to the statistics as "Abandoned children," whom the police take note of, collect, mislay and find again on the pavements of Paris.

It required the disturbance of a day like that to account for these miserable little creatures being in that garden. If the superintendents had caught sight of them, they would have driven such rags forth. Poor little things do not enter public gardens; still, people should reflect that, as children, they have a right to flowers.

These children were there, thanks to the locked gates. They were there contrary to the regulations. They had slipped into the garden and there they remained. Closed gates do not dismiss the inspectors, oversight is supposed to continue, but it grows slack and reposes; and the inspectors, moved by the public anxiety and more occupied with the outside than the inside, no longer glanced into the garden, and had not seen the two delinquents.

It had rained the night before, and even a little in the morning. But in June, showers do not count for much. An hour after a storm, it can hardly be seen that the beautiful blonde day has wept. The earth, in summer, is as quickly dried as the cheek of a child. At that period of the solstice, the light of full noonday is, so to speak, poignant. It takes everything. It applies itself to the earth, and superposes itself with a sort of suction. One would say that the sun was thirsty. A shower is but a glass of water; a rainstorm is instantly drunk up. In the morning everything was dripping, in the afternoon everything is powdered over.

Nothing is so worthy of admiration as foliage washed by the rain and wiped by the rays of sunlight; it is warm freshness. The gardens and meadows, having water at their roots, and sun in their flowers, become perfuming-pans of incense, and smoke with all their odors at once. Everything smiles, sings and offers itself. One feels gently intoxicated. The springtime is a provisional paradise, the sun helps man to have patience.

There are beings who demand nothing further; mortals, who, having the azure of heaven, say: "It is enough!" dreamers absorbed in the wonderful, dipping into the idolatry of nature, indifferent to good and evil, contemplators of cosmos and radiantly forgetful of man, who do not understand how people can occupy themselves with the hunger of these, and the thirst of those, with the nudity of the poor in winter, with the lymphatic curvature of the little spinal column, with the pallet, the attic, the dungeon, and the rags of shivering young girls, when they can dream beneath the trees; peaceful and terrible spirits they, and pitilessly satisfied. Strange to say, the infinite suffices them. That great need of man, the finite, which admits of embrace, they ignore. The finite which admits of progress and sublime toil, they do not think about. The indefinite, which is born from the human and divine combination of the infinite and the finite, escapes them. Provided that they are face to face with immensity, they smile. Joy never, ecstasy forever. Their life lies in surrendering their personality in contemplation. The history of humanity is for them only a detailed plan. All is not there; the true All remains without; what is the use of busying oneself over that detail, man? Man suffers, that is quite possible; but look at Aldebaran rising! The mother has no more milk, the new-born babe is dying. I know nothing about that, but just look at this wonderful rosette which a slice of wood-cells of the pine presents under the microscope! Compare the most beautiful Mechlin lace to that if you can! These thinkers forget to love. The zodiac thrives with them to such a point that it prevents their seeing the weeping child. God eclipses their souls. This is a family of minds which are, at once, great and petty. Horace was one of them; so was Goethe. La Fontaine perhaps; magnificent egoists of the infinite, tranquil spectators of sorrow, who do not behold Nero if the weather be fair, for whom the sun conceals the funeral pile, who would look on at an execution by the guillotine in the search for an effect of light, who hear neither the cry nor the sob, nor the death rattle, nor the alarm peal, for whom everything is well, since there is a month of May, who, so long as there are clouds of purple and gold above their heads, declare themselves content, and who are determined to be happy until the radiance of the stars and the songs of the birds are exhausted.

These are dark radiances. They have no suspicion that they are to be pitied. Certainly they are so. He who does not weep does not see. They are to be admired and pitied, as one would both pity and admire a being at once night and day, without eyes beneath his lashes but with a star on his brow.

The indifference of these thinkers, is, according to some, a superior philosophy. That may be; but in this superiority there is some infirmity. One may be immortal and yet limp: witness Vulcan. One may be more than man and less than man. There is incomplete immensity in nature. Who knows whether the sun is not a blind man?

But then, what? In whom can we trust? *Solem quis dicere falsum audeat?* Who shall dare to say that the sun is false? Thus certain geniuses, themselves, certain Very-Lofty mortals, man-stars, may be mistaken?

That which is on high at the summit, at the crest, at the zenith, that which sends down so much light on the earth, sees but little, sees badly, sees not at all? Is not this a desperate state of things? No. But what is there, then, above the sun? The god.

On the 6th of June, 1832, about eleven o'clock in the morning, the Luxembourg, solitary and depopulated, was charming. The quincunxes and flower-beds shed forth balm and dazzling beauty into the sunlight. The branches, wild with the brilliant glow of midday, seemed endeavoring to embrace. In the sycamores there was an uproar of linnets, sparrows triumphed, woodpeckers climbed along the chestnut trees, administering little pecks on the bark. The flower-beds accepted the legitimate royalty of the lilies; the most august of perfumes is that which emanates from whiteness. The peppery odor of the carnations was perceptible. The old crows of Marie de Medici were amorous in the tall trees. The sun gilded, empurpled, set fire to and lighted up the tulips, which are nothing but all the varieties of flame made into flowers. All around the banks of tulips the bees, the sparks of these flame-flowers, hummed. All was grace and gayety, even the impending rain; this relapse, by which the lilies of the valley and the honeysuckles were destined to profit, had nothing disturbing about it; the swallows indulged in the charming threat of flying low. He who was there aspired to happiness; life smelled good; all nature exhaled candor, help, assistance, paternity, caress, dawn. The thoughts which fell from heaven were as sweet as the tiny hand of a baby when one kisses it.

The statues under the trees, white and nude, had robes of shadow pierced with light; these goddesses were all tattered with sunlight; rays hung from them on all sides. Around the great fountain, the earth was already dried up to the point of being burnt. There was sufficient breeze to raise little insurrections of dust here and there. A few yellow leaves, left over from the autumn, chased each other merrily, and seemed to be playing tricks on each other.

This abundance of light had something indescribably reassuring about it. Life, sap, heat, odors overflowed; one was conscious, beneath creation, of the enormous size of the source; in all these breaths permeated with love, in this interchange of reverberations and reflections, in this marvellous expenditure of rays, in this infinite outpouring of liquid gold, one felt the prodigality of the inexhaustible; and, behind this splendor as behind a curtain of flame, one caught a glimpse of God, that millionaire of stars.

Thanks to the sand, there was not a speck of mud; thanks to the rain, there was not a grain of ashes. The clumps of blossoms had just been bathed; every sort of velvet, satin, gold and varnish, which springs from the earth in the form of flowers, was irreproachable. This magnificence was cleanly. The grand silence of happy nature filled the garden. A celestial silence that is compatible with a thousand sorts of music, the cooing of nests, the buzzing of swarms, the flutterings of the breeze. All the harmony of the season was complete in one gracious whole; the entrances and exits of spring took place in proper order; the lilacs ended; the jasmines began; some flowers were tardy, some insects in advance of their time; the van-guard of the red June butterflies fraternized with the rear-guard of the white butterflies of May. The plantain trees were getting their new skins. The breeze hollowed out undulations in the magnificent enormity of the chestnut-trees. It was splendid. A veteran from the neighboring barracks, who was gazing through the fence, said: "Here is the Spring presenting arms and in full uniform."

All nature was breakfasting; creation was at table; this was its hour; the great blue cloth was spread in the sky, and the great green cloth on earth; the sun lighted it all up brilliantly. God was serving the universal repast. Each creature had his pasture or his mess. The ring-dove found his hemp-seed, the chaffinch found his millet, the goldfinch found chickweed, the red-breast found worms, the green finch found flies, the fly found infusoriæ, the bee found flowers. They ate each other somewhat, it is true, which is the misery of evil mixed with good; but not a beast of them all had an empty stomach.

The two little abandoned creatures had arrived in the vicinity of the grand fountain, and, rather bewildered by all this light, they tried to hide themselves, the instinct of the poor and the weak in the presence of even impersonal magnificence; and they kept behind the swans' hutch.

Here and there, at intervals, when the wind blew, shouts, clamor, a sort of tumultuous death rattle, which was the firing, and dull blows, which were discharges of cannon, struck the ear confusedly. Smoke hung over the roofs in the direction of the Halles. A bell, which had the air of an appeal, was ringing in the distance.

These children did not appear to notice these noises. The little one repeated from time to time: "I am hungry."

Almost at the same instant with the children, another couple approached the great basin. They consisted of a goodman, about fifty years of age, who was leading by the hand a little fellow of six. No doubt, a father and his son. The little man of six had a big brioche.

At that epoch, certain houses abutting on the river, in the Rues Madame and d'Enfer, had keys to the Luxembourg garden, of which the lodgers enjoyed the use when the gates were shut, a privilege which was suppressed later on. This father and son came from one of these houses, no doubt.

The two poor little creatures watched "that gentleman" approaching, and hid themselves a little more thoroughly.

He was a bourgeois. The same person, perhaps, whom Marius had one day heard, through his love fever, near the same grand basin, counselling his son "to avoid excesses." He had an affable and haughty air, and a mouth which was always smiling, since it did not shut. This mechanical smile, produced by too much jaw and too little skin, shows the teeth rather than the soul. The child, with his brioche, which he had bitten into but had not finished eating, seemed satiated. The child was dressed as a National Guardsman, owing to the insurrection, and the father had remained clad as a bourgeois out of prudence.

Father and son halted near the fountain where two swans were sporting. This bourgeois appeared to cherish a special admiration for the swans. He resembled them in this sense, that he walked like them.

For the moment, the swans were swimming, which is their principal talent, and they were superb.

If the two poor little beings had listened and if they had been of an age to understand, they might have gathered the words of this grave man. The father was saying to his son:

"The sage lives content with little. Look at me, my son. I do not love pomp. I am never seen in clothes decked with gold lace and stones; I leave that false splendor to badly organized souls."

Here the deep shouts which proceeded from the direction of the Halles burst out with fresh force of bell and uproar.

"What is that?" inquired the child.

The father replied:

"It is the Saturnalia."

All at once, he caught sight of the two little ragged boys behind the green swan-hutch.

"There is the beginning," said he.

And, after a pause, he added:

"Anarchy is entering this garden."

In the meanwhile, his son took a bite of his brioche, spit it out, and, suddenly burst out crying.

"What are you crying about?" demanded his father.

"I am not hungry any more," said the child.

The father's smile became more accentuated.

"One does not need to be hungry in order to eat a cake."

"My cake tires me. It is stale."

"Don't you want any more of it?"

"No."

The father pointed to the swans.

"Throw it to those palmipeds."

The child hesitated. A person may not want any more of his cake; but that is no reason for giving it away.

The father went on:

"Be humane. You must have compassion on animals."

And, taking the cake from his son, he flung it into the basin.

The cake fell very near the edge.

The swans were far away, in the centre of the basin, and busy with some prey. They had seen neither the bourgeois nor the brioche.

The bourgeois, feeling that the cake was in danger of being wasted, and moved by this useless shipwreck, entered upon a telegraphic agitation, which finally attracted the attention of the swans.

They perceived something floating, steered for the edge like ships, as they are, and slowly directed their course toward the brioche, with the stupid majesty which befits white creatures.

"The swans (*cygnes*) understand signs (*signes*)," said the bourgeois, delighted to make a jest.

At that moment, the distant tumult of the city underwent another sudden increase. This time it was sinister. There are some gusts of wind which speak more distinctly than others. The one which was blowing at that moment brought clearly defined drum-beats, clamors, platoon firing, and the dismal replies of the tocsin and the cannon. This coincided with a black cloud which suddenly veiled the sun.

The swans had not yet reached the brioche.

"Let us return home," said the father, "they are attacking the Tuileries."

He grasped his son's hand again. Then he continued:

"From the Tuileries to the Luxembourg, there is but the distance which separates Royalty from the peerage; that is not far. Shots will soon rain down."

VICTOR HUGO

He glanced at the cloud.

"Perhaps it is rain itself that is about to shower down; the sky is joining in; the younger branch is condemned. Let us return home quickly."

"I should like to see the swans eat the brioche," said the child.

The father replied:

"That would be imprudent."

And he led his little bourgeois away.

The son, regretting the swans, turned his head back toward the basin until a corner of the quincunxes concealed it from him.

In the meanwhile, the two little waifs had approached the brioche at the same time as the swans. It was floating on the water. The smaller of them stared at the cake, the elder gazed after the retreating bourgeois.

Father and son entered the labyrinth of walks which leads to the grand flight of steps near the clump of trees on the side of the Rue Madame.

As soon as they had disappeared from view, the elder child hastily flung himself flat on his stomach on the rounding curb of the basin, and clinging to it with his left hand, and leaning over the water, on the verge of falling in, he stretched out his right hand with his stick towards the cake. The swans, perceiving the enemy, made haste, and in so doing, they produced an effect of their breasts which was of service to the little fisher; the water flowed back before the swans, and one of these gentle concentric undulations softly floated the brioche towards the child's wand. Just as the swans came up, the stick touched the cake. The child gave it a brisk rap, drew in the brioche, frightened away the swans, seized the cake, and sprang to his feet. The cake was wet; but they were hungry and thirsty. The elder broke the cake into two portions, a large one and a small one, took the small one for himself, gave the large one to his brother, and said to him:

"Ram that into your muzzle."

# XVII

## Mortuus Pater Filium
## Moriturum Expectat

Marius dashed out of the barricade, Combeferre followed him. But he was too late. Gavroche was dead. Combeferre brought back the basket of cartridges; Marius bore the child.

"Alas!" he thought, "that which the father had done for his father, he was requiting to the son; only, Thénardier had brought back his father alive; he was bringing back the child dead."

When Marius re-entered the redoubt with Gavroche in his arms, his face, like the child, was inundated with blood.

At the moment when he had stooped to lift Gavroche, a bullet had grazed his head; he had not noticed it.

Courfeyrac untied his cravat and with it bandaged Marius' brow.

They laid Gavroche on the same table with Mabeuf, and spread over the two corpses the black shawl. There was enough of it for both the old man and the child.

Combeferre distributed the cartridges from the basket which he had brought in.

This gave each man fifteen rounds to fire.

Jean Valjean was still in the same place, motionless on his stone post. When Combeferre offered him his fifteen cartridges, he shook his head.

"Here's a rare eccentric," said Combeferre in a low voice to Enjolras. "He finds a way of not fighting in this barricade."

"Which does not prevent him from defending it," responded Enjolras.

"Heroism has its originals," resumed Combeferre.

And Courfeyrac, who had overheard, added:

"He is another sort from Father Mabeuf."

One thing which must be noted is, that the fire which was battering the barricade hardly disturbed the interior. Those who have never traversed the whirlwind of this sort of war can form no idea of the singular moments of tranquillity mingled with these convulsions. Men go and come, they talk, they jest, they lounge. Some one whom we know heard a combatant say to him in the midst of the grape-shot: "We are here as at a bachelor breakfast." The redoubt of the Rue de la

Chanvrerie, we repeat, seemed very calm within. All mutations and all phases had been, or were about to be, exhausted. The position, from critical, had become menacing, and, from menacing, was probably about to become desperate. In proportion as the situation grew gloomy, the glow of heroism empurpled the barricade more and more. Enjolras, who was grave, dominated it, in the attitude of a young Spartan sacrificing his naked sword to the sombre genius, Epidotas.

Combeferre, wearing an apron, was dressing the wounds: Bossuet and Feuilly were making cartridges with the powder-flask picked up by Gavroche on the dead corporal, and Bossuet said to Feuilly: "We are soon to take the diligence for another planet"; Courfeyrac was disposing and arranging on some paving-stones which he had reserved for himself near Enjolras, a complete arsenal, his sword-cane, his gun, two holster pistols, and a cudgel, with the care of a young girl setting a small dunkerque in order. Jean Valjean stared silently at the wall opposite him. An artisan was fastening Mother Hucheloup's big straw hat on his head with a string, "for fear of sun-stroke," as he said. The young men from the Cougourde d'Aix were chatting merrily among themselves, as though eager to speak patois for the last time. Joly, who had taken Widow Hucheloup's mirror from the wall, was examining his tongue in it. Some combatants, having discovered a few crusts of rather mouldy bread, in a drawer, were eagerly devouring them. Marius was disturbed with regard to what his father was about to say to him.

# XVIII

## The Vulture Become Prey

We must insist upon one psychological fact peculiar to barricades. Nothing which is characteristic of that surprising war of the streets should be omitted.

Whatever may have been the singular inward tranquillity which we have just mentioned, the barricade, for those who are inside it, remains, nonetheless, a vision.

There is something of the apocalypse in civil war, all the mists of the unknown are commingled with fierce flashes, revolutions are sphinxes, and any one who has passed through a barricade thinks he has traversed a dream.

The feelings to which one is subject in these places we have pointed out in the case of Marius, and we shall see the consequences; they are both more and less than life. On emerging from a barricade, one no longer knows what one has seen there. One has been terrible, but one knows it not. One has been surrounded with conflicting ideas which had human faces; one's head has been in the light of the future. There were corpses lying prone there, and phantoms standing erect. The hours were colossal and seemed hours of eternity. One has lived in death. Shadows have passed by. What were they?

One has beheld hands on which there was blood; there was a deafening horror; there was also a frightful silence; there were open mouths which shouted, and other open mouths which held their peace; one was in the midst of smoke, of night, perhaps. One fancied that one had touched the sinister ooze of unknown depths; one stares at something red on one's finger nails. One no longer remembers anything.

Let us return to the Rue de la Chanvrerie.

All at once, between two discharges, the distant sound of a clock striking the hour became audible.

"It is midday," said Combeferre.

The twelve strokes had not finished striking when Enjolras sprang to his feet, and from the summit of the barricade hurled this thundering shout:

"Carry stones up into the houses; line the windowsills and the roofs with them. Half the men to their guns, the other half to the paving-stones. There is not a minute to be lost."

A squad of sappers and miners, axe on shoulder, had just made their appearance in battle array at the end of the street.

This could only be the head of a column; and of what column? The attacking column, evidently; the sappers charged with the demolition of the barricade must always precede the soldiers who are to scale it.

They were, evidently, on the brink of that moment which M. Clermont-Tonnerre, in 1822, called "the tug of war."

Enjolras' order was executed with the correct haste which is peculiar to ships and barricades, the only two scenes of combat where escape is impossible. In less than a minute, two thirds of the stones which Enjolras had had piled up at the door of Corinthe had been carried up to the first floor and the attic, and before a second minute had elapsed, these stones, artistically set one upon the other, walled up the sash-window on the first floor and the windows in the roof to half their height. A few loop-holes carefully planned by Feuilly, the principal architect, allowed of the passage of the gun-barrels. This armament of the windows could be effected all the more easily since the firing of grape-shot had ceased. The two cannons were now discharging ball against the centre of the barrier in order to make a hole there, and, if possible, a breach for the assault.

When the stones destined to the final defence were in place, Enjolras had the bottles which he had set under the table where Mabeuf lay, carried to the first floor.

"Who is to drink that?" Bossuet asked him.

"They," replied Enjolras.

Then they barricaded the window below, and held in readiness the iron cross-bars which served to secure the door of the wine-shop at night.

The fortress was complete. The barricade was the rampart, the wine-shop was the dungeon. With the stones which remained they stopped up the outlet.

As the defenders of a barricade are always obliged to be sparing of their ammunition, and as the assailants know this, the assailants combine their arrangements with a sort of irritating leisure, expose themselves to fire prematurely, though in appearance more than in reality, and take their ease. The preparations for attack are always made with a certain methodical deliberation; after which, the lightning strikes.

This deliberation permitted Enjolras to take a review of everything and to perfect everything. He felt that, since such men were to die, their death ought to be a masterpiece.

He said to Marius: "We are the two leaders. I will give the last orders inside. Do you remain outside and observe."

Marius posted himself on the lookout upon the crest of the barricade.

Enjolras had the door of the kitchen, which was the ambulance, as the reader will remember, nailed up.

"No splashing of the wounded," he said.

He issued his final orders in the tap-room in a curt, but profoundly tranquil tone; Feuilly listened and replied in the name of all.

"On the first floor, hold your axes in readiness to cut the staircase. Have you them?"

"Yes," said Feuilly.

"How many?"

"Two axes and a pole-axe."

"That is good. There are now twenty-six combatants of us on foot. How many guns are there?"

"Thirty-four."

"Eight too many. Keep those eight guns loaded like the rest and at hand. Swords and pistols in your belts. Twenty men to the barricade. Six ambushed in the attic windows, and at the window on the first floor to fire on the assailants through the loop-holes in the stones. Let not a single worker remain inactive here. Presently, when the drum beats the assault, let the twenty below stairs rush to the barricade. The first to arrive will have the best places."

These arrangements made, he turned to Javert and said:

"I am not forgetting you."

And, laying a pistol on the table, he added:

"The last man to leave this room will smash the skull of this spy."

"Here?" inquired a voice.

"No, let us not mix their corpses with our own. The little barricade of the Mondétour lane can be scaled. It is only four feet high. The man is well pinioned. He shall be taken thither and put to death."

There was some one who was more impassive at that moment than Enjolras, it was Javert. Here Jean Valjean made his appearance.

He had been lost among the group of insurgents. He stepped forth and said to Enjolras:

"You are the commander?"

"Yes."

"You thanked me a while ago."

"In the name of the Republic. The barricade has two saviors, Marius Pontmercy and yourself."

"Do you think that I deserve a recompense?"

"Certainly."

"Well, I request one."

"What is it?"

"That I may blow that man's brains out."

Javert raised his head, saw Jean Valjean, made an almost imperceptible movement, and said:

"That is just."

As for Enjolras, he had begun to re-load his rifle; he cut his eyes about him:

"No objections."

And he turned to Jean Valjean:

"Take the spy."

Jean Valjean did, in fact, take possession of Javert, by seating himself on the end of the table. He seized the pistol, and a faint click announced that he had cocked it.

Almost at the same moment, a blast of trumpets became audible.

"Take care!" shouted Marius from the top of the barricade.

Javert began to laugh with that noiseless laugh which was peculiar to him, and gazing intently at the insurgents, he said to them:

"You are in no better case than I am."

"All out!" shouted Enjolras.

The insurgents poured out tumultuously, and, as they went, received in the back,—may we be permitted the expression,—this sally of Javert's:

"We shall meet again shortly!"

# XIX

## Jean Valjean Takes His Revenge

When Jean Valjean was left alone with Javert, he untied the rope which fastened the prisoner across the middle of the body, and the knot of which was under the table. After this he made him a sign to rise.

Javert obeyed with that indefinable smile in which the supremacy of enchained authority is condensed.

Jean Valjean took Javert by the martingale, as one would take a beast of burden by the breast-band, and, dragging the latter after him, emerged from the wine-shop slowly, because Javert, with his impeded limbs, could take only very short steps.

Jean Valjean had the pistol in his hand.

In this manner they crossed the inner trapezium of the barricade. The insurgents, all intent on the attack, which was imminent, had their backs turned to these two.

Marius alone, stationed on one side, at the extreme left of the barricade, saw them pass. This group of victim and executioner was illuminated by the sepulchral light which he bore in his own soul.

Jean Valjean with some difficulty, but without relaxing his hold for a single instant, made Javert, pinioned as he was, scale the little entrenchment in the Mondétour lane.

When they had crossed this barrier, they found themselves alone in the lane. No one saw them. Among the heap they could distinguish a livid face, streaming hair, a pierced hand and the half nude breast of a woman. It was Éponine. The corner of the houses hid them from the insurgents. The corpses carried away from the barricade formed a terrible pile a few paces distant.

Javert gazed askance at this body, and, profoundly calm, said in a low tone:

"It strikes me that I know that girl."

Then he turned to Jean Valjean.

Jean Valjean thrust the pistol under his arm and fixed on Javert a look which it required no words to interpret: "Javert, it is I."

Javert replied:

"Take your revenge."

Jean Valjean drew from his pocket a knife, and opened it.

"A clasp-knife!" exclaimed Javert, "you are right. That suits you better."

Jean Valjean cut the martingale which Javert had about his neck, then he cut the cords on his wrists, then, stooping down, he cut the cord on his feet; and, straightening himself up, he said to him:

"You are free."

Javert was not easily astonished. Still, master of himself though he was, he could not repress a start. He remained open-mouthed and motionless.

Jean Valjean continued:

"I do not think that I shall escape from this place. But if, by chance, I do, I live, under the name of Fauchelevent, in the Rue de l'Homme Armé, No. 7."

Javert snarled like a tiger, which made him half open one corner of his mouth, and he muttered between his teeth:

"Have a care."

"Go," said Jean Valjean.

Javert began again:

"Thou saidst Fauchelevent, Rue de l'Homme Armé?"

"Number 7."

Javert repeated in a low voice:—"Number 7."

He buttoned up his coat once more, resumed the military stiffness between his shoulders, made a half turn, folded his arms and, supporting his chin on one of his hands, he set out in the direction of the Halles. Jean Valjean followed him with his eyes:

A few minutes later, Javert turned round and shouted to Jean Valjean:

"You annoy me. Kill me, rather."

Javert himself did not notice that he no longer addressed Jean Valjean as "thou."

"Be off with you," said Jean Valjean.

Javert retreated slowly. A moment later he turned the corner of the Rue des Prêcheurs.

When Javert had disappeared, Jean Valjean fired his pistol in the air.

Then he returned to the barricade and said:

"It is done."

In the meanwhile, this is what had taken place.

Marius, more intent on the outside than on the interior, had not, up to that time, taken a good look at the pinioned spy in the dark background of the tap-room.

When he beheld him in broad daylight, striding over the barricade in order to proceed to his death, he recognized him. Something suddenly recurred to his mind. He recalled the inspector of the Rue de Pontoise, and the two pistols which the latter had handed to him and which he, Marius, had used in this very barricade, and not only did he recall his face, but his name as well.

This recollection was misty and troubled, however, like all his ideas.

It was not an affirmation that he made, but a question which he put to himself:

"Is not that the inspector of police who told me that his name was Javert?"

Perhaps there was still time to intervene in behalf of that man. But, in the first place, he must know whether this was Javert.

Marius called to Enjolras, who had just stationed himself at the other extremity of the barricade:

"Enjolras!"

"What?"

"What is the name of yonder man?"

"What man?"

"The police agent. Do you know his name?"

"Of course. He told us."

"What is it?"

"Javert."

Marius sprang to his feet.

At that moment, they heard the report of the pistol.

Jean Valjean reappeared and cried: "It is done."

A gloomy chill traversed Marius' heart.

# XX

## THE DEAD ARE IN THE RIGHT AND THE LIVING ARE NOT IN THE WRONG

The death agony of the barricade was about to begin.

Everything contributed to its tragic majesty at that supreme moment; a thousand mysterious crashes in the air, the breath of armed masses set in movement in the streets which were not visible, the intermittent gallop of cavalry, the heavy shock of artillery on the march, the firing by squads, and the cannonades crossing each other in the labyrinth of Paris, the smokes of battle mounting all gilded above the roofs, indescribable and vaguely terrible cries, lightnings of menace everywhere, the tocsin of Saint-Merry, which now had the accents of a sob, the mildness of the weather, the splendor of the sky filled with sun and clouds, the beauty of the day, and the alarming silence of the houses.

For, since the preceding evening, the two rows of houses in the Rue de la Chanvrerie had become two walls; ferocious walls, doors closed, windows closed, shutters closed.

In those days, so different from those in which we live, when the hour was come, when the people wished to put an end to a situation, which had lasted too long, with a charter granted or with a legal country, when universal wrath was diffused in the atmosphere, when the city consented to the tearing up of the pavements, when insurrection made the bourgeoisie smile by whispering its password in its ear, then the inhabitant, thoroughly penetrated with the revolt, so to speak, was the auxiliary of the combatant, and the house fraternized with the improvised fortress which rested on it. When the situation was not ripe, when the insurrection was not decidedly admitted, when the masses disowned the movement, all was over with the combatants, the city was changed into a desert around the revolt, souls grew chilled, refuges were nailed up, and the street turned into a defile to help the army to take the barricade.

A people cannot be forced, through surprise, to walk more quickly than it chooses. Woe to whomsoever tries to force its hand! A people does not let itself go at random. Then it abandons the insurrection to itself. The insurgents become noxious, infected with the plague. A house is an escarpment, a door is a refusal, a façade is a wall. This wall hears, sees and will not. It might open and save you. No. This wall is a judge. It gazes at you and condemns you. What dismal things are closed houses. They seem dead, they are living. Life which is, as it were, suspended there, persists there. No one has gone out of them for four and twenty hours, but no one is missing from them. In the interior of that rock, people go and come, go to bed and rise again; they are a family party there; there they eat and drink; they are afraid, a terrible thing! Fear excuses this fearful lack of hospitality; terror is mixed with it, an extenuating circumstance. Sometimes, even, and this has been actually seen, fear turns to passion; fright may change into fury, as prudence does into rage; hence this wise saying: "The enraged moderates." There are outbursts of supreme terror, whence springs wrath like a mournful smoke.—"What do these people want? What have they come there to do? Let them get out of the scrape. So much the worse for them. It is their fault. They are only getting what they deserve. It does not concern us. Here is our poor street all riddled with balls. They are a pack of rascals. Above all things, don't open the door."—And the house assumes the air of a tomb. The insurgent is in the death-throes in front of that house; he sees the grape-shot and naked swords drawing near; if he cries, he knows that they are listening to him, and that no one will come; there stand walls which might protect him, there are men who might save him; and these walls have ears of flesh, and these men have bowels of stone.

Whom shall he reproach?

No one and every one.

The incomplete times in which we live.

It is always at its own risk and peril that Utopia is converted into revolution, and from philosophical protest becomes an armed protest, and from Minerva turns to Pallas.

The Utopia which grows impatient and becomes revolt knows what awaits it; it almost always comes too soon. Then it becomes resigned, and stoically accepts catastrophe in lieu of triumph. It serves those who deny it without complaint, even excusing them, and even disculpates them, and its magnanimity consists in consenting to abandonment. It is indomitable in the face of obstacles and gentle towards ingratitude.

Is this ingratitude, however?

Yes, from the point of view of the human race.

VICTOR HUGO

No, from the point of view of the individual.

Progress is man's mode of existence. The general life of the human race is called Progress, the collective stride of the human race is called Progress. Progress advances; it makes the great human and terrestrial journey towards the celestial and the divine; it has its halting places where it rallies the laggard troop, it has its stations where it meditates, in the presence of some splendid Canaan suddenly unveiled on its horizon, it has its nights when it sleeps; and it is one of the poignant anxieties of the thinker that he sees the shadow resting on the human soul, and that he gropes in darkness without being able to awaken that slumbering Progress.

"God is dead, perhaps," said Gerard de Nerval one day to the writer of these lines, confounding progress with God, and taking the interruption of movement for the death of Being.

He who despairs is in the wrong. Progress infallibly awakes, and, in short, we may say that it marches on, even when it is asleep, for it has increased in size. When we behold it erect once more, we find it taller. To be always peaceful does not depend on progress any more than it does on the stream; erect no barriers, cast in no boulders; obstacles make water froth and humanity boil. Hence arise troubles; but after these troubles, we recognize the fact that ground has been gained. Until order, which is nothing else than universal peace, has been established, until harmony and unity reign, progress will have revolutions as its halting-places.

What, then, is progress? We have just enunciated it; the permanent life of the peoples.

Now, it sometimes happens, that the momentary life of individuals offers resistance to the eternal life of the human race.

Let us admit without bitterness, that the individual has his distinct interests, and can, without forfeiture, stipulate for his interest, and defend it; the present has its pardonable dose of egotism; momentary life has its rights, and is not bound to sacrifice itself constantly to the future. The generation which is passing in its turn over the earth, is not forced to abridge it for the sake of the generations, its equal, after all, who will have their turn later on.—"I exist," murmurs that some one whose name is All. "I am young and in love, I am old and I wish to repose, I am the father of a family, I toil, I prosper, I am successful in business, I have houses to lease, I have money in the government funds, I am happy, I have a wife and children, I have all this, I desire to live, leave me in peace."—Hence, at certain hours, a profound cold broods over the magnanimous vanguard of the human race.

Utopia, moreover, we must admit, quits its radiant sphere when it makes war. It, the truth of to-morrow, borrows its mode of procedure, battle, from the lie of yesterday. It, the future, behaves like the past. It, pure idea, becomes a deed of violence. It complicates its heroism with a violence for which it is just that it should be held to answer; a violence of occasion and expedient, contrary to principle, and for which it is fatally punished. The Utopia, insurrection, fights with the old military code in its fist; it shoots spies, it executes traitors; it suppresses living beings and flings them into unknown darkness. It makes use of death, a serious matter. It seems as though Utopia had no longer any faith in radiance, its irresistible and incorruptible force. It strikes with the sword. Now, no sword is simple. Every blade has two edges; he who wounds with the one is wounded with the other.

Having made this reservation, and made it with all severity, it is impossible for us not to admire, whether they succeed or not, those the glorious combatants of the future, the confessors of Utopia. Even when they miscarry, they are worthy of veneration; and it is, perhaps, in failure, that they possess the most majesty. Victory, when it is in accord with progress, merits the applause of the people; but a heroic defeat merits their tender compassion. The one is magnificent, the other sublime. For our own part, we prefer martyrdom to success. John Brown is greater than Washington, and Pisacane is greater than Garibaldi.

It certainly is necessary that some one should take the part of the vanquished.

We are unjust towards these great men who attempt the future, when they fail.

Revolutionists are accused of sowing fear abroad. Every barricade seems a crime. Their theories are incriminated, their aim suspected, their ulterior motive is feared, their conscience denounced. They are reproached with raising, erecting, and heaping up, against the reigning social state, a mass of miseries, of griefs, of iniquities, of wrongs, of despairs, and of tearing from the lowest depths blocks of shadow in order therein to embattle themselves and to combat. People shout to them: "You are tearing up the pavements of hell!" They might reply: "That is because our barricade is made of good intentions."

The best thing, assuredly, is the pacific solution. In short, let us agree that when we behold the pavement, we think of the bear, and it is a good will which renders society uneasy. But it depends on society to save itself, it is to its own good will that we make our appeal. No violent remedy is necessary. To study evil amiably, to prove its existence, then to cure it. It is to this that we invite it.

However that may be, even when fallen, above all when fallen, these men, who at every point of the universe, with their eyes fixed on France, are striving for the grand work with the inflexible logic of the ideal, are august; they give their life a free offering to progress; they accomplish the will of Providence; they perform a religious act. At the appointed hour, with as much disinterestedness as an actor who answers to his cue, in obedience to the divine stage-manager, they enter the tomb. And this hopeless combat, this stoical disappearance they accept in order to bring about the supreme and universal consequences, the magnificent and irresistibly human movement begun on the 14th of July, 1789; these soldiers are priests. The French revolution is an act of God.

Moreover, there are, and it is proper to add this distinction to the distinctions already pointed out in another chapter,—there are accepted revolutions, revolutions which are called revolutions; there are refused revolutions, which are called riots.

An insurrection which breaks out, is an idea which is passing its examination before the people. If the people lets fall a black ball, the idea is dried fruit; the insurrection is a mere skirmish.

Waging war at every summons and every time that Utopia desires it, is not the thing for the peoples. Nations have not always and at every hour the temperament of heroes and martyrs.

They are positive. *A priori*, insurrection is repugnant to them, in the first place, because it often results in a catastrophe, in the second place, because it always has an abstraction as its point of departure.

Because, and this is a noble thing, it is always for the ideal, and for the ideal alone, that those who sacrifice themselves do thus sacrifice themselves. An insurrection is an enthusiasm. Enthusiasm may wax wroth; hence the appeal to arms. But every insurrection, which aims at a government or a régime, aims higher. Thus, for instance, and we insist upon it, what the chiefs of the insurrection of 1832, and, in particular, the young enthusiasts of the Rue de la Chanvrerie were combating, was not precisely Louis Philippe. The majority of them, when talking freely, did justice to this king who stood midway between monarchy and revolution; no one hated him. But they attacked the younger branch of the divine right in Louis Philippe as they had attacked its elder branch in Charles X; and that which they wished to overturn in overturning royalty in France, was, as we have explained, the usurpation of man over man, and of privilege over right in the entire universe. Paris without a king has as result the world without despots. This is the manner in which they reasoned. Their aim was distant no doubt, vague perhaps, and it retreated in the face of their efforts; but it was great.

Thus it is. And we sacrifice ourselves for these visions, which are almost always illusions for the sacrificed, but illusions with which, after all, the whole of human certainty is mingled. We throw ourselves into these tragic affairs and become intoxicated with that which we are about to do. Who knows? We may succeed. We are few in number, we have a whole army arrayed against us; but we are defending right, the natural law, the sovereignty of each one over himself from which no abdication is possible, justice and truth, and in case of need, we die like the three hundred Spartans. We do not think of Don Quixote but of Leonidas. And we march straight before us, and once pledged, we do not draw back, and we rush onwards with head held low, cherishing as our hope an unprecedented victory, revolution completed, progress set free again, the aggrandizement of the human race, universal deliverance; and in the event of the worst, Thermopylæ.

These passages of arms for the sake of progress often suffer shipwreck, and we have just explained why. The crowd is restive in the presence of the impulses of paladins. Heavy masses, the multitudes which are fragile because of their very weight, fear adventures; and there is a touch of adventure in the ideal.

Moreover, and we must not forget this, interests which are not very friendly to the ideal and the sentimental are in the way. Sometimes the stomach paralyzes the heart.

The grandeur and beauty of France lies in this, that she takes less from the stomach than other nations: she more easily knots the rope about her loins. She is the first awake, the last asleep. She marches forwards. She is a seeker.

This arises from the fact that she is an artist.

The ideal is nothing but the culminating point of logic, the same as the beautiful is nothing but the summit of the true. Artistic peoples are also consistent peoples. To love beauty is to see the light. That is why the torch of Europe, that is to say of civilization, was first borne by Greece, who passed it on to Italy, who handed it on to France. Divine, illuminating nations of scouts! *Vitælampada tradunt.*

It is an admirable thing that the poetry of a people is the element of its progress. The amount of civilization is measured by the quantity of imagination. Only, a civilizing people should remain a manly people. Corinth, yes; Sybaris, no. Whoever becomes effeminate makes himself a bastard. He must be neither a dilettante nor a virtuoso: but he must be artistic. In the matter of civilization, he must not refine, but he must sublime. On this condition, one gives to the human race the pattern of the ideal.

The modern ideal has its type in art, and its means is science. It is through science that it will realize that august vision of the poets, the socially beautiful. Eden will be reconstructed by A+B. At the point which civilization has now reached, the exact is a necessary element of the splendid, and the artistic sentiment is not only served, but completed by the scientific organ; dreams must be calculated. Art, which is the conqueror, should have for support science, which is the walker; the solidity of the creature which is ridden is of importance. The modern spirit is the genius of Greece with the genius of India as its vehicle; Alexander on the elephant.

Races which are petrified in dogma or demoralized by lucre are unfit to guide civilization. Genuflection before the idol or before money wastes away the muscles which walk and the will which advances. Hieratic or mercantile absorption lessens a people's power of radiance, lowers its horizon by lowering its level, and deprives it of that intelligence, at once both human and divine of the universal goal, which makes missionaries of nations. Babylon has no ideal; Carthage has no ideal. Athens and Rome have and keep, throughout all the nocturnal darkness of the centuries, halos of civilization.

France is in the same quality of race as Greece and Italy. She is Athenian in the matter of beauty, and Roman in her greatness. Moreover, she is good. She gives herself. Oftener than is the case with other races, is she in the humor for self-devotion and sacrifice. Only, this humor seizes upon her, and again abandons her. And therein lies the great peril for those who run when she desires only to walk, or who walk on when she desires to halt. France has her relapses into materialism, and, at certain instants, the ideas which obstruct that sublime brain have no longer anything which recalls French greatness and are of the dimensions of a Missouri or a South Carolina. What is to be done in such a case? The giantess plays at being a dwarf; immense France has her freaks of pettiness. That is all.

To this there is nothing to say. Peoples, like planets, possess the right to an eclipse. And all is well, provided that the light returns and that the eclipse does not degenerate into night. Dawn and resurrection are synonymous. The reappearance of the light is identical with the persistence of the *I*.

Let us state these facts calmly. Death on the barricade or the tomb in exile, is an acceptable occasion for devotion. The real name of devotion is disinterestedness. Let the abandoned allow themselves to be abandoned, let the exiled allow themselves to be exiled, and let us confine ourselves to entreating great nations not to retreat too far, when they do retreat. One must not push too far in descent under pretext of a return to reason.

Matter exists, the minute exists, interest exists, the stomach exists; but the stomach must not be the sole wisdom. The life of the moment has its rights, we admit, but permanent life has its rights also. Alas! the fact that one is mounted does not preclude a fall. This can be seen in history more frequently than is desirable: A nation is great, it tastes the ideal, then it bites the mire, and finds it good; and if it be asked how it happens that it has abandoned Socrates for Falstaff, it replies: "Because I love statesmen."

One word more before returning to our subject, the conflict.

A battle like the one which we are engaged in describing is nothing else than a convulsion towards the ideal. Progress trammelled is sickly, and is subject to these tragic epilepsies. With that malady of progress, civil war, we have been obliged to come in contact in our passage. This is one of the fatal phases, at once act and entr'acte of that drama whose pivot is a social condemnation, and whose veritable title is *Progress*.

Progress!

The cry to which we frequently give utterance is our whole thought; and, at the point of this drama which we have now reached, the idea which it contains having still more than one trial to undergo, it is, perhaps, permitted to us, if not to lift the veil from it, to at least allow its light to shine through.

The book which the reader has under his eye at this moment is, from one end to the other, as a whole and in detail, whatever may be its intermittences, exceptions and faults, the march from evil to good, from the unjust to the just, from night to day, from appetite to conscience, from rottenness to life, from hell to heaven, from nothingness to God. Point of departure: matter; point of arrival: the soul. The hydra at the beginning, the angel at the end.

# XXI

## The Heroes

All at once, the drum beat the charge.

The attack was a hurricane. On the evening before, in the darkness, the barricade had been approached silently, as by a boa. Now, in broad daylight, in that widening street, surprise was decidedly impossible, rude force had, moreover, been unmasked, the cannon had begun the roar, the army hurled itself on the barricade. Fury now became skill. A powerful detachment of infantry of the line, broken at regular intervals, by the National Guard and the Municipal Guard on foot, and supported by serried masses which could be heard though not seen, debauched into the street at a run, with drums beating, trumpets braying, bayonets levelled, the sappers at their head, and, imperturbable under the projectiles, charged straight for the barricade with the weight of a brazen beam against a wall.

The wall held firm.

The insurgents fired impetuously. The barricade once scaled had a mane of lightning flashes. The assault was so furious, that for one moment, it was inundated with assailants; but it shook off the soldiers as the lion shakes off the dogs, and it was only covered with besiegers as the cliff is covered with foam, to reappear, a moment later, beetling, black and formidable.

The column, forced to retreat, remained massed in the street, unprotected but terrible, and replied to the redoubt with a terrible discharge of musketry. Any one who has seen fireworks will recall the sheaf formed of interlacing lightnings which is called a bouquet. Let the reader picture to himself this bouquet, no longer vertical but horizontal, bearing a bullet, buckshot or a biscaïen at the tip of each one of its jets of flame, and picking off dead men one after another from its clusters of lightning. The barricade was underneath it.

On both sides, the resolution was equal. The bravery exhibited there was almost barbarous and was complicated with a sort of heroic ferocity which began by the sacrifice of self.

This was the epoch when a National Guardsman fought like a Zouave. The troop wished to make an end of it, insurrection was desirous of fighting. The acceptance of the death agony in the flower of youth and in the flush of health turns intrepidity into frenzy. In this fray, each one underwent the broadening growth of the death hour. The street was strewn with corpses.

The barricade had Enjolras at one of its extremities and Marius at the other. Enjolras, who carried the whole barricade in his head, reserved and sheltered himself; three soldiers fell, one after the other, under his embrasure, without having even seen him; Marius fought unprotected. He made himself a target. He stood with more than half his body above the breastworks. There is no more violent prodigal than the avaricious man who takes the bit in his teeth; there is no man more terrible in action than a dreamer. Marius was formidable and pensive. In battle he was as in a dream. One would have pronounced him a phantom engaged in firing a gun.

The insurgents' cartridges were giving out; but not their sarcasms. In this whirlwind of the sepulchre in which they stood, they laughed.

Courfeyrac was bareheaded.

"What have you done with your hat?" Bossuet asked him.

Courfeyrac replied:

"They have finally taken it away from me with cannon-balls."

Or they uttered haughty comments.

"Can any one understand," exclaimed Feuilly bitterly, "those men,— (and he cited names, well-known names, even celebrated names, some belonging to the old army)—who had promised to join us, and taken an oath to aid us, and who had pledged their honor to it, and who are our generals, and who abandon us!"

And Combeferre restricted himself to replying with a grave smile.

"There are people who observe the rules of honor as one observes the stars, from a great distance."

The interior of the barricade was so strewn with torn cartridges that one would have said that there had been a snowstorm.

The assailants had numbers in their favor; the insurgents had position. They were at the top of a wall, and they thundered point-blank upon the soldiers tripping over the dead and wounded and entangled in the escarpment. This barricade, constructed as it was and admirably buttressed, was really one of those situations where a handful of men hold a legion in check. Nevertheless, the attacking column, constantly recruited and enlarged under the shower of bullets, drew inexorably nearer, and now, little by little, step by step, but surely, the army closed in around the barricade as the vice grasps the wine-press.

One assault followed another. The horror of the situation kept increasing.

Then there burst forth on that heap of paving-stones, in that Rue de la Chanvrerie, a battle worthy of a wall of Troy. These haggard, ragged, exhausted men, who had had nothing to eat for four and twenty hours, who had not slept, who had but a few more rounds to fire, who were fumbling in their pockets which had been emptied of cartridges, nearly all of whom were wounded, with head or arm bandaged with black and blood-stained linen, with holes in their clothes from which the blood trickled, and who were hardly armed with poor guns and notched swords, became Titans. The barricade was ten times attacked, approached, assailed, scaled, and never captured.

In order to form an idea of this struggle, it is necessary to imagine fire set to a throng of terrible courages, and then to gaze at the conflagration. It was not a combat, it was the interior of a furnace; there mouths breathed the flame; there countenances were extraordinary. The human form seemed impossible there, the combatants flamed forth there, and it was formidable to behold the going and coming in that red glow of those salamanders of the fray.

The successive and simultaneous scenes of this grand slaughter we renounce all attempts at depicting. The epic alone has the right to fill twelve thousand verses with a battle.

One would have pronounced this that hell of Brahmanism, the most redoubtable of the seventeen abysses, which the Veda calls the Forest of Swords.

They fought hand to hand, foot to foot, with pistol shots, with blows of the sword, with their fists, at a distance, close at hand, from above, from below, from everywhere, from the roofs of the houses, from the windows of the wine-shop, from the cellar windows, whither some had crawled. They were one against sixty.

The façade of Corinthe, half demolished, was hideous. The window, tattooed with grape-shot, had lost glass and frame and was nothing now but a shapeless hole, tumultuously blocked with paving-stones.

Bossuet was killed; Feuilly was killed; Courfeyrac was killed; Combeferre, transfixed by three blows from a bayonet in the breast at the moment when he was lifting up a wounded soldier, had only time to cast a glance to heaven when he expired.

Marius, still fighting, was so riddled with wounds, particularly in the head, that his countenance disappeared beneath the blood, and one would have said that his face was covered with a red kerchief.

Enjolras alone was not struck. When he had no longer any weapon, he reached out his hands to right and left and an insurgent thrust some arm or other into his fist. All he had left was the stumps of four swords; one more than François I. at Marignan. Homer says: "Diomedes cuts the throat of Axylus, son of Teuthranis, who dwelt in happy Arisba; Euryalus, son of Mecistæus, exterminates Dresos and Opheltios, Esepius, and that Pedasus whom the naiad Abarbarea bore to the blameless Bucolion; Ulysses overthrows Pidytes of Percosius; Antilochus, Ablerus; Polypætes, Astyalus; Polydamas, Otos, of Cyllene; and Teucer, Aretaon. Meganthios dies under the blows of Euripylus' pike. Agamemnon, king of the heroes, flings to earth Elatos, born in the rocky city which is laved by the sounding river Satnoïs." In our old poems of exploits, Esplandian attacks the giant marquis Swantibore with a cobbler's shoulder-stick of fire, and the latter defends himself by stoning the hero with towers which he plucks up by the roots. Our ancient mural frescoes show us the two Dukes of Bretagne and Bourbon, armed, emblazoned and crested in war-like guise, on horseback and approaching each other, their battle-axes in hand, masked with iron, gloved with iron, booted with iron, the one caparisoned in ermine, the other draped in azure: Bretagne with his lion between the two horns of his crown, Bourbon helmeted with a monster fleur de lys on his visor. But, in order to be superb, it is not necessary to wear, like Yvon, the ducal morion, to have in the fist, like Esplandian, a living flame, or, like Phyles, father of Polydamas, to have brought back from Ephyra a good suit of mail, a present from the king of men, Euphetes; it suffices to give one's life for a conviction or a loyalty. This ingenuous little soldier, yesterday a peasant of Bauce or Limousin, who prowls with his clasp-knife by his side, around the children's nurses in the Luxembourg garden, this pale young student bent over a piece of anatomy or a book, a blond youth who shaves his beard with scissors,—take both of them, breathe upon them with a breath of duty, place them face to face in the Carrefour Boucherat or in the blind alley Planche-Mibray, and let the one fight for his flag, and the other for his ideal, and let both of them imagine that they are fighting for their country; the struggle will be colossal; and the shadow which this raw recruit and this sawbones in conflict will produce in that grand epic field where humanity is striving, will equal the shadow cast by Megaryon, King of Lycia, tiger-filled, crushing in his embrace the immense body of Ajax, equal to the gods.

# XXII

## FOOT TO FOOT

When there were no longer any of the leaders left alive, except Enjolras and Marius at the two extremities of the barricade, the centre, which had so long sustained Courfeyrac, Joly, Bossuet, Feuilly and Combeferre, gave way. The cannon, though it had not effected a practicable breach, had made a rather large hollow in the middle of the redoubt; there, the summit of the wall had disappeared before the balls, and had crumbled away; and the rubbish which had fallen, now inside, now outside, had, as it accumulated, formed two piles in the nature of slopes on the two sides of the barrier, one on the inside, the other on the outside. The exterior slope presented an inclined plane to the attack.

A final assault was there attempted, and this assault succeeded. The mass bristling with bayonets and hurled forward at a run, came up with irresistible force, and the serried front of battle of the attacking column made its appearance through the smoke on the crest of the battlements. This time, it was decisive. The group of insurgents who were defending the centre retreated in confusion.

Then the gloomy love of life awoke once more in some of them. Many, finding themselves under the muzzles of this forest of guns, did not wish to die. This is a moment when the instinct of self-preservation emits howls, when the beast reappears in men. They were hemmed in by the lofty, six-story house which formed the background of their redoubt. This house might prove their salvation. The building was barricaded, and walled, as it were, from top to bottom. Before the troops of the line had reached the interior of the redoubt, there was time for a door to open and shut, the space of a flash of lightning was sufficient for that, and the door of that house, suddenly opened a crack and closed again instantly, was life for these despairing men. Behind this house, there were streets, possible flight, space. They set to knocking at that door with the butts of their guns, and with kicks, shouting, calling, entreating, wringing their hands. No one opened. From the little window on the third floor, the head of the dead man gazed down upon them.

But Enjolras and Marius, and the seven or eight rallied about them, sprang forward and protected them. Enjolras had shouted to the soldiers: "Don't advance!" and as an officer had not obeyed, Enjolras had killed the officer. He was now in the little inner court of the redoubt, with his back planted against the Corinthe building, a sword in one hand, a rifle in the other, holding open the door of the wine-shop which he barred against assailants. He shouted to the desperate men:—"There is but one door open; this one."—And shielding them with his body, and facing an entire battalion alone, he made them pass in behind him. All precipitated themselves thither. Enjolras, executing with his rifle, which he now used like a cane, what single-stick players call a "covered rose" round his head, levelled the bayonets around and in front of him, and was the last to enter; and then ensued a horrible moment, when the soldiers tried to make their way in, and the insurgents strove to bar them out. The door was slammed with such violence, that, as it fell back into its frame, it showed the five fingers of a soldier who had been clinging to it, cut off and glued to the post.

Marius remained outside. A shot had just broken his collar bone, he felt that he was fainting and falling. At that moment, with eyes already shut, he felt the shock of a vigorous hand seizing him, and the swoon in which his senses vanished, hardly allowed him time for the thought, mingled with a last memory of Cosette:—"I am taken prisoner. I shall be shot."

Enjolras, not seeing Marius among those who had taken refuge in the wine-shop, had the same idea. But they had reached a moment when each man has not the time to meditate on his own death. Enjolras fixed the bar across the door, and bolted it, and double-locked it with key and chain, while those outside were battering furiously at it, the soldiers with the butts of their muskets, the sappers with their axes. The assailants were grouped about that door. The siege of the wine-shop was now beginning.

The soldiers, we will observe, were full of wrath.

The death of the artillery-sergeant had enraged them, and then, a still more melancholy circumstance. During the few hours which had preceded the attack, it had been reported among them that the insurgents were mutilating their prisoners, and that there was the headless body of a soldier in the wine-shop. This sort of fatal rumor is the usual accompaniment of civil wars, and it was a false report of this kind which, later on, produced the catastrophe of the Rue Transnonain.

When the door was barricaded, Enjolras said to the others:

"Let us sell our lives dearly."

Then he approached the table on which lay Mabeuf and Gavroche. Beneath the black cloth two straight and rigid forms were visible, one large, the other small, and the two faces were vaguely outlined beneath the cold folds of the shroud. A hand projected from beneath the winding sheet and hung near the floor. It was that of the old man.

Enjolras bent down and kissed that venerable hand, just as he had kissed his brow on the preceding evening.

These were the only two kisses which he had bestowed in the course of his life.

Let us abridge the tale. The barricade had fought like a gate of Thebes; the wine-shop fought like a house of Saragossa. These resistances are dogged. No quarter. No flag of truce possible. Men are willing to die, provided their opponent will kill them.

When Suchet says:—"Capitulate,"—Palafox replies: "After the war with cannon, the war with knives." Nothing was lacking in the capture by assault of the Hucheloup wine-shop; neither paving-stones raining from the windows and the roof on the besiegers and exasperating the soldiers by crushing them horribly, nor shots fired from the attic-windows and the cellar, nor the fury of attack, nor, finally, when the door yielded, the frenzied madness of extermination. The assailants, rushing into the wine-shop, their feet entangled in the panels of the door which had been beaten in and flung on the ground, found not a single combatant there. The spiral staircase, hewn asunder with the axe, lay in the middle of the tap-room, a few wounded men were just breathing their last, every one who was not killed was on the first floor, and from there, through the hole in the ceiling, which had formed the entrance of the stairs, a terrific fire burst forth. It was the last of their cartridges. When they were exhausted, when these formidable men on the point of death had no longer either powder or ball, each grasped in his hands two of the bottles which Enjolras had reserved, and of which we have spoken, and held the scaling party in check with these frightfully fragile clubs. They were bottles of aquafortis.

We relate these gloomy incidents of carnage as they occurred. The besieged man, alas! converts everything into a weapon. Greek fire did not disgrace Archimedes, boiling pitch did not disgrace Bayard. All war is a thing of terror, and there is no choice in it. The musketry of the besiegers, though confined and embarrassed by being directed from below upwards, was deadly. The rim of the hole in the ceiling was speedily surrounded by heads of the slain, whence dripped long, red and smoking streams, the uproar was indescribable; a close and burning smoke almost produced night over this combat. Words are lacking to express horror when it has reached this pitch. There were no longer men in this conflict, which was now infernal. They were no longer giants matched with colossi. It resembled Milton and Dante rather than Homer. Demons attacked, spectres resisted.

It was heroism become monstrous.

# XXIII

## Orestes Fasting and Pylades Drunk

At length, by dint of mounting on each other's backs, aiding themselves with the skeleton of the staircase, climbing up the walls, clinging to the ceiling, slashing away at the very brink of the trap-door, the last one who offered resistance, a score of assailants, soldiers, National Guardsmen, municipal guardsmen, in utter confusion, the majority disfigured by wounds in the face during that redoubtable ascent, blinded by blood, furious, rendered savage, made an irruption into the apartment on the first floor. There they found only one man still on his feet, Enjolras. Without cartridges, without sword, he had nothing in his hand now but the barrel of his gun whose stock he had broken over the head of those who were entering. He had placed the billiard table between his assailants and himself; he had retreated into the corner of the room, and there, with haughty eye, and head borne high, with this stump of a weapon in his hand, he was still so alarming as to speedily create an empty space around him. A cry arose:

"He is the leader! It was he who slew the artillery-man. It is well that he has placed himself there. Let him remain there. Let us shoot him down on the spot."

"Shoot me," said Enjolras.

And flinging away his bit of gun-barrel, and folding his arms, he offered his breast.

The audacity of a fine death always affects men. As soon as Enjolras folded his arms and accepted his end, the din of strife ceased in the room, and this chaos suddenly stilled into a sort of sepulchral solemnity. The menacing majesty of Enjolras disarmed and motionless, appeared to oppress this tumult, and this young man, haughty, bloody, and charming, who alone had not a wound, who was as indifferent as an invulnerable being, seemed, by the authority of his tranquil glance, to constrain this sinister rabble to kill him respectfully. His beauty, at that moment augmented by his pride, was resplendent, and he was fresh and rosy after the fearful four and twenty hours which had just elapsed, as though he could no more be fatigued than wounded. It was of him, possibly, that a witness spoke afterwards, before the council of war: "There was an insurgent whom I heard called Apollo." A National Guardsman who had taken aim at Enjolras, lowered his gun, saying: "It seems to me that I am about to shoot a flower."

Twelve men formed into a squad in the corner opposite Enjolras, and silently made ready their guns.

Then a sergeant shouted:

"Take aim!"

An officer intervened.

"Wait."

And addressing Enjolras:

"Do you wish to have your eyes bandaged?"

"No."

"Was it you who killed the artillery sergeant?"

"Yes."

Grantaire had waked up a few moments before.

Grantaire, it will be remembered, had been asleep ever since the preceding evening in the upper room of the wine-shop, seated on a chair and leaning on the table.

He realized in its fullest sense the old metaphor of "dead drunk." The hideous potion of absinthe-porter and alcohol had thrown him into a lethargy. His table being small, and not suitable for the barricade, he had been left in possession of it. He was still in the same posture, with his breast bent over the table, his head lying flat on his arms, surrounded by glasses, beer-jugs and bottles. His was the overwhelming slumber of the torpid bear and the satiated leech. Nothing had had any effect upon it, neither the fusillade, nor the cannon-balls, nor the grape-shot which had made its way through the window into the room where he was. Nor the tremendous uproar of the assault. He merely replied to the cannonade, now and then, by a snore. He seemed to be waiting there for a bullet which should spare him the trouble of waking. Many corpses were strewn around him; and, at the first glance, there was nothing to distinguish him from those profound sleepers of death.

Noise does not rouse a drunken man; silence awakens him. The fall of everything around him only augmented Grantaire's prostration; the crumbling of all things was his lullaby. The sort of halt which the tumult underwent in the presence of Enjolras was a shock to this heavy slumber. It had the effect of a carriage going at full speed, which suddenly comes to a dead stop. The persons dozing within it wake up. Grantaire rose to his feet with a start, stretched out his arms, rubbed his eyes, stared, yawned, and understood.

A fit of drunkenness reaching its end resembles a curtain which is torn away. One beholds, at a single glance and as a whole, all that it has concealed. All suddenly presents itself to the memory; and the drunkard who has known nothing of what has been taking place during the last twenty-four hours, has no sooner opened his eyes than he is perfectly informed. Ideas recur to him with abrupt lucidity; the obliteration of intoxication, a sort of steam which has obscured the brain, is dissipated, and makes way for the clear and sharply outlined importunity of realities.

Relegated, as he was, to one corner, and sheltered behind the billiard-table, the soldiers whose eyes were fixed on Enjolras, had not even noticed Grantaire, and the sergeant was preparing to repeat his order: "Take aim!" when all at once, they heard a strong voice shout beside them:

"Long live the Republic! I'm one of them."

Grantaire had risen. The immense gleam of the whole combat which he had missed, and in which he had had no part, appeared in the brilliant glance of the transfigured drunken man.

He repeated: "Long live the Republic!" crossed the room with a firm stride and placed himself in front of the guns beside Enjolras.

"Finish both of us at one blow," said he.

And turning gently to Enjolras, he said to him:

"Do you permit it?"

Enjolras pressed his hand with a smile.

This smile was not ended when the report resounded.

Enjolras, pierced by eight bullets, remained leaning against the wall, as though the balls had nailed him there. Only, his head was bowed.

Grantaire fell at his feet, as though struck by a thunderbolt.

A few moments later, the soldiers dislodged the last remaining insurgents, who had taken refuge at the top of the house. They fired into the attic through a wooden lattice. They fought under the very roof. They flung bodies, some of them still alive, out through the windows. Two light-infantrymen, who tried to lift the shattered omnibus, were slain by two shots fired from the attic. A man in a blouse was flung down from it, with a bayonet wound in the abdomen, and breathed his last on the ground. A soldier and an insurgent slipped together on the sloping slates of the roof, and, as they would not release each other, they fell, clasped in a ferocious embrace. A similar conflict went on in the cellar. Shouts, shots, a fierce trampling. Then silence. The barricade was captured.

The soldiers began to search the houses round about, and to pursue the fugitives.

# XXIV

## Prisoner

Marius was, in fact, a prisoner.

The hand which had seized him from behind and whose grasp he had felt at the moment of his fall and his loss of consciousness was that of Jean Valjean.

Jean Valjean had taken no other part in the combat than to expose himself in it. Had it not been for him, no one, in that supreme phase of agony, would have thought of the wounded. Thanks to him, everywhere present in the carnage, like a providence, those who fell were picked up, transported to the tap-room, and cared for. In the intervals, he reappeared on the barricade. But nothing which could resemble a blow, an attack or even personal defence proceeded from his hands. He held his peace and lent succor. Moreover, he had received only a few scratches. The bullets would have none of him. If suicide formed part of what he had meditated on coming to this sepulchre, to that spot, he had not succeeded. But we doubt whether he had thought of suicide, an irreligious act.

Jean Valjean, in the thick cloud of the combat, did not appear to see Marius; the truth is, that he never took his eyes from the latter. When a shot laid Marius low, Jean Valjean leaped forward with the agility of a tiger, fell upon him as on his prey, and bore him off.

The whirlwind of the attack was, at that moment, so violently concentrated upon Enjolras and upon the door of the wine-shop, that no one saw Jean Valjean sustaining the fainting Marius in his arms, traverse the unpaved field of the barricade and disappear behind the angle of the Corinthe building.

The reader will recall this angle which formed a sort of cape on the street; it afforded shelter from the bullets, the grape-shot, and all eyes, and a few square feet of space. There is sometimes a chamber which does not burn in the midst of a conflagration, and in the midst of raging seas, beyond a promontory or at the extremity of a blind alley of shoals, a tranquil nook. It was in this sort of fold in the interior trapezium of the barricade, that Éponine had breathed her last.

There Jean Valjean halted, let Marius slide to the ground, placed his back against the wall, and cast his eyes about him.

The situation was alarming.

For an instant, for two or three perhaps, this bit of wall was a shelter, but how was he to escape from this massacre? He recalled the anguish which he had suffered in the Rue Polonceau eight years before, and in what manner he had contrived to make his escape; it was difficult then, to-day it was impossible. He had before him that deaf and implacable house, six stories in height, which appeared to be inhabited only by a dead man leaning out of his window; he had on his right the rather low barricade, which shut off the Rue de la Petite Truanderie; to pass this obstacle seemed easy, but beyond the crest of the barrier a line of bayonets was visible. The troops of the line were posted on the watch behind that barricade. It was evident, that to pass the barricade was to go in quest of the fire of the platoon, and that any head which should run the risk of lifting itself above the top of that wall of stones would serve as a target for sixty shots. On his left he had the field of battle. Death lurked round the corner of that wall.

What was to be done?

Only a bird could have extricated itself from this predicament.

And it was necessary to decide on the instant, to devise some expedient, to come to some decision. Fighting was going on a few paces away; fortunately, all were raging around a single point, the door of the wine-shop; but if it should occur to one soldier, to one single soldier, to turn the corner of the house, or to attack him on the flank, all was over.

Jean Valjean gazed at the house facing him, he gazed at the barricade at one side of him, then he looked at the ground, with the violence of the last extremity, bewildered, and as though he would have liked to pierce a hole there with his eyes.

By dint of staring, something vaguely striking in such an agony began to assume form and outline at his feet, as though it had been a power of glance which made the thing desired unfold. A few paces distant he perceived, at the base of the small barrier so pitilessly guarded and watched on the exterior, beneath a disordered mass of paving-stones which partly concealed it, an iron grating, placed flat and on a level with the soil. This grating, made of stout, transverse bars, was about two feet square. The frame of paving-stones which supported it had been torn up, and it was, as it were, unfastened.

Through the bars a view could be had of a dark aperture, something like the flue of a chimney, or the pipe of a cistern. Jean Valjean darted forward. His old art of escape rose to his brain like an illumination. To thrust aside the stones, to raise the grating, to lift Marius, who was as inert as a dead body, upon his shoulders, to descend, with this burden on his loins, and with the aid of his elbows and knees into that sort of well, fortunately not very deep, to let the heavy trap, upon which the loosened stones rolled down afresh, fall into its place behind him, to gain his footing on a flagged surface three metres below the surface,— all this was executed like that which one does in dreams, with the strength of a giant and the rapidity of an eagle; this took only a few minutes.

Jean Valjean found himself with Marius, who was still unconscious, in a sort of long, subterranean corridor.

There reigned profound peace, absolute silence, night.

The impression which he had formerly experienced when falling from the wall into the convent recurred to him. Only, what he was carrying to-day was not Cosette; it was Marius. He could barely hear the formidable tumult in the wine-shop, taken by assault, like a vague murmur overhead.

BOOK SECOND
THE INTESTINE OF THE LEVIATHAN

# I

## The Land Impoverished by the Sea

Paris casts twenty-five millions yearly into the water. And this without metaphor. How, and in what manner? Day and night. With what object? With no object. With what intention? With no intention. Why? For no reason. By means of what organ? By means of its intestine. What is its intestine? The sewer.

Twenty-five millions is the most moderate approximative figure which the valuations of special science have set upon it.

Science, after having long groped about, now knows that the most fecundating and the most efficacious of fertilizers is human manure. The Chinese, let us confess it to our shame, knew it before us. Not a Chinese peasant—it is Eckberg who says this,—goes to town without bringing back with him, at the two extremities of his bamboo pole, two full buckets of what we designate as filth. Thanks to human dung, the earth in China is still as young as in the days of Abraham. Chinese wheat yields a hundred fold of the seed. There is no guano comparable in fertility with the detritus of a capital. A great city is the most mighty of dung-makers. Certain success would attend the experiment of employing the city to manure the plain. If our gold is manure, our manure, on the other hand, is gold.

What is done with this golden manure? It is swept into the abyss.

Fleets of vessels are despatched, at great expense, to collect the dung of petrels and penguins at the South Pole, and the incalculable element of opulence which we have on hand, we send to the sea. All the human and animal manure which the world wastes, restored to the land instead of being cast into the water, would suffice to nourish the world.

Those heaps of filth at the gate-posts, those tumbrils of mud which jolt through the street by night, those terrible casks of the street department, those fetid drippings of subterranean mire, which the pavements hide from you,—do you know what they are? They are the meadow in flower, the green grass, wild thyme, thyme and sage, they are game, they are cattle, they are the satisfied bellows of great oxen in the evening, they are perfumed hay, they are golden wheat, they are the bread on your table, they are the warm blood in your veins, they are health, they are joy, they are life. This is the will of that mysterious creation which is transformation on earth and transfiguration in heaven.

Restore this to the great crucible; your abundance will flow forth from it. The nutrition of the plains furnishes the nourishment of men.

You have it in your power to lose this wealth, and to consider me ridiculous to boot. This will form the master-piece of your ignorance.

Statisticians have calculated that France alone makes a deposit of half a milliard every year, in the Atlantic, through the mouths of her rivers. Note this: with five hundred millions we could pay one quarter of the expenses of our budget. The cleverness of man is such that he prefers to get rid of these five hundred millions in the gutter. It is the very substance of the people that is carried off, here drop by drop, there wave after wave, the wretched outpour of our sewers into the rivers, and the gigantic collection of our rivers into the ocean. Every hiccough of our sewers costs us a thousand francs. From this spring two results, the land impoverished, and the water tainted. Hunger arising from the furrow, and disease from the stream.

It is notorious, for example, that at the present hour, the Thames is poisoning London.

So far as Paris is concerned, it has become indispensable of late, to transport the mouths of the sewers downstream, below the last bridge.

A double tubular apparatus, provided with valves and sluices, sucking up and driving back, a system of elementary drainage, simple as the lungs of a man, and which is already in full working order in many communities in England, would suffice to conduct the pure water of the fields into our cities, and to send back to the fields the rich water of the cities, and this easy exchange, the simplest in the world, would retain among us the five hundred millions now thrown away. People are thinking of other things.

The process actually in use does evil, with the intention of doing good. The intention is good, the result is melancholy. Thinking to purge the city, the population is blanched like plants raised in cellars. A sewer is a mistake. When drainage, everywhere, with its double function, restoring what it takes, shall have replaced the sewer, which is a simple impoverishing washing, then, this being combined with the data of a now social economy, the product of the earth will be increased tenfold, and the problem of misery will be singularly lightened. Add the suppression of parasitism, and it will be solved.

In the meanwhile, the public wealth flows away to the river, and leakage takes place. Leakage is the word. Europe is being ruined in this manner by exhaustion.

As for France, we have just cited its figures. Now, Paris contains one twenty-fifth of the total population of France, and Parisian guano being the richest of all, we understate the truth when we value the loss on the part of Paris at twenty-five millions in the half milliard which France annually rejects. These twenty-five millions, employed in assistance and enjoyment, would double the splendor of Paris. The city spends them in sewers. So that we may say that Paris's great prodigality, its wonderful festival, its Beaujon folly, its orgy, its stream of gold from full hands, its pomp, its luxury, its magnificence, is its sewer system.

It is in this manner that, in the blindness of a poor political economy, we drown and allow to float downstream and to be lost in the gulfs the well-being of all. There should be nets at Saint-Cloud for the public fortune.

Economically considered, the matter can be summed up thus: Paris is a spendthrift. Paris, that model city, that patron of well-arranged capitals, of which every nation strives to possess a copy, that metropolis of the ideal, that august country of the initiative, of impulse and of effort, that centre and that dwelling of minds, that nation-city, that hive of the future, that marvellous combination of Babylon and Corinth, would make a peasant of the Fo-Kian shrug his shoulders, from the point of view which we have just indicated.

Imitate Paris and you will ruin yourselves.

Moreover, and particularly in this immemorial and senseless waste, Paris is itself an imitator.

These surprising exhibitions of stupidity are not novel; this is no young folly. The ancients did like the moderns. "The sewers of Rome," says Liebig, "have absorbed all the well-being of the Roman peasant." When the Campagna of Rome was ruined by the Roman sewer, Rome exhausted Italy, and when she had put Italy in her sewer, she poured in Sicily, then Sardinia, then Africa. The sewer of Rome has engulfed the world. This cesspool offered its engulfment to the city and the universe. *Urbi et orbi.* Eternal city, unfathomable sewer.

Rome sets the example for these things as well as for others.

Paris follows this example with all the stupidity peculiar to intelligent towns.

For the requirements of the operation upon the subject of which we have just explained our views, Paris has beneath it another Paris; a Paris of sewers; which has its streets, its crossroads, its squares, its blind-alleys, its arteries, and its circulation, which is of mire and minus the human form.

For nothing must be flattered, not even a great people; where there is everything there is also ignominy by the side of sublimity; and, if Paris contains Athens, the city of light, Tyre, the city of might, Sparta, the city of virtue, Nineveh, the city of marvels, it also contains Lutetia, the city of mud.

However, the stamp of its power is there also, and the Titanic sink of Paris realizes, among monuments, that strange ideal realized in humanity by some men like Macchiavelli, Bacon and Mirabeau, grandiose vileness.

The sub-soil of Paris, if the eye could penetrate its surface, would present the aspect of a colossal madrepore. A sponge has no more partitions and ducts than the mound of earth for a circuit of six leagues round about, on which rests the great and ancient city. Not to mention its catacombs, which are a separate cellar, not to mention the inextricable trellis-work of gas pipes, without reckoning the vast tubular system for the distribution of fresh water which ends in the pillar fountains, the sewers alone form a tremendous, shadowy network under the two banks; a labyrinth which has its slope for its guiding thread.

There appears, in the humid mist, the rat which seems the product to which Paris has given birth.

# II

## Ancient History of the Sewer

L et the reader imagine Paris lifted off like a cover, the subterranean network of sewers, from a bird's-eye view, will outline on the banks a species of large branch grafted on the river. On the right bank, the belt sewer will form the trunk of this branch, the secondary ducts will form the branches, and those without exit the twigs.

This figure is but a summary one and half exact, the right angle, which is the customary angle of this species of subterranean ramifications, being very rare in vegetation.

A more accurate image of this strange geometrical plan can be formed by supposing that one is viewing some eccentric oriental alphabet, as intricate as a thicket, against a background of shadows, and the misshapen letters should be welded one to another in apparent confusion, and as at haphazard, now by their angles, again by their extremities.

Sinks and sewers played a great part in the Middle Ages, in the Lower Empire and in the Orient of old. The masses regarded these beds of decomposition, these monstrous cradles of death, with a fear that was almost religious. The vermin ditch of Benares is no less conducive to giddiness than the lions' ditch of Babylon. Teglath-Phalasar, according to the rabbinical books, swore by the sink of Nineveh. It was from the sewer of Münster that John of Leyden produced his false moon, and it was from the cesspool of Kekscheb that oriental menalchme, Mokanna, the veiled prophet of Khorassan, caused his false sun to emerge.

The history of men is reflected in the history of sewers. The Germoniæ narrated Rome. The sewer of Paris has been an ancient and formidable thing. It has been a sepulchre, it has served as an asylum. Crime, intelligence, social protest, liberty of conscience, thought, theft, all that human laws persecute or have persecuted, is hidden in that hole; the *maillotins* in the fourteenth century, the *tire-laine* of the fifteenth, the Huguenots in the sixteenth, Morin's *illuminated* in the seventeenth, the *chauffeurs* (brigands) in the eighteenth. A hundred years ago, the nocturnal blow of the dagger emerged thence, the pickpocket in danger slipped thither; the forest had its cave, Paris had its sewer. Vagrancy, that Gallic *picareria*, accepted the sewer as the adjunct of the Cour des Miracles, and at evening, it returned thither, fierce and sly, through the Maubuée outlet, as into a bed-chamber.

It was quite natural, that those who had the blind-alley Vide-Gousset, (Empty-Pocket) or the Rue Coupe-Gorge (Cut-Throat), for the scene of their daily labor, should have for their domicile by night the culvert of the Chemin-Vert, or the catch basin of Hurepoix. Hence a throng of souvenirs. All sorts of phantoms haunt these long, solitary corridors; everywhere is putrescence and miasma; here and there are breathing-holes, where Villon within converses with Rabelais without.

The sewer in ancient Paris is the rendezvous of all exhaustions and of all attempts. Political economy therein spies a detritus, social philosophy there beholds a residuum.

The sewer is the conscience of the city. Everything there converges and confronts everything else. In that livid spot there are shades, but there are no longer any secrets. Each thing bears its true form, or at least, its definitive form. The mass of filth has this in its favor, that it is not a liar. Ingenuousness has taken refuge there. The mask of Basil is to be found there, but one beholds its cardboard and its strings and the inside as well as the outside, and it is accentuated by honest mud. Scapin's false nose is its next-door neighbor. All the uncleannesses of civilization, once past their use, fall into this trench of truth, where the immense social sliding ends. They are there engulfed, but they display themselves there. This mixture is a confession. There, no more false appearances, no plastering over is possible, filth removes its shirt, absolute denudation puts to the rout all illusions and mirages, there is nothing more except what really exists, presenting the sinister form of that which is coming to an end. There, the bottom of a bottle indicates drunkenness, a basket-handle tells a tale of domesticity; there the core of an apple which has entertained literary opinions becomes an apple-core once more; the effigy on the big sou becomes frankly covered with verdigris, Caiphas' spittle meets Falstaff's puking, the louis-d'or which comes from the gaming-house jostles the nail whence hangs the rope's end of the suicide. A livid fœtus rolls along, enveloped in the spangles which danced at the Opera last Shrove-Tuesday, a cap which has pronounced judgment on men wallows beside a mass of rottenness which was formerly Margoton's petticoat; it is more than fraternization, it is equivalent to addressing each other as *thou*. All which was formerly rouged, is washed free. The last veil is torn away. A sewer is a cynic. It tells everything.

The sincerity of foulness pleases us, and rests the soul. When one has passed one's time in enduring upon earth the spectacle of the great airs which reasons of state, the oath, political sagacity, human justice, professional probity, the austerities of situation, incorruptible robes all assume, it solaces one to enter a sewer and to behold the mire which befits it.

This is instructive at the same time. We have just said that history passes through the sewer. The Saint-Barthélemys filter through there, drop by drop, between the paving-stones. Great public assassinations, political and religious butcheries, traverse this underground passage of civilization, and thrust their corpses there. For the eye of the thinker, all historic murderers are to be found there, in that hideous penumbra, on their knees, with a scrap of their winding-sheet for an apron, dismally sponging out their work. Louis XI is there with Tristan, François I. with Duprat, Charles IX is there with his mother, Richelieu is there with Louis XIII, Louvois is there, Letellier is there, Hébert and Maillard are there, scratching the stones, and trying to make the traces of their actions disappear. Beneath these vaults one hears the brooms of spectres. One there breathes the enormous fetidness of social catastrophes. One beholds reddish reflections in the corners. There flows a terrible stream, in which bloody hands have been washed.

The social observer should enter these shadows. They form a part of his laboratory. Philosophy is the microscope of the thought. Everything desires to flee from it, but nothing escapes it. Tergiversation is useless. What side of oneself does one display in evasions? the shameful side. Philosophy pursues with its glance, probes the evil, and does not permit it to escape into nothingness. In the obliteration of things which disappear, in the watching of things which vanish, it recognizes all. It reconstructs the purple from the rag, and the woman from the scrap of her dress. From the cesspool, it reconstitutes the city; from mud, it reconstructs manners; from the potsherd it infers the amphora or the jug. By the imprint of a finger-nail on a piece of parchment, it recognizes the difference which separates the Jewry of the Judengasse from the Jewry of the Ghetto. It re-discovers in what remains that which has been, good, evil, the true, the blood-stain of the palace, the ink-blot of the cavern, the drop of sweat from the brothel, trials undergone, temptations welcomed, orgies cast forth, the turn which characters have taken as they became abased, the trace of prostitution in souls of which their grossness rendered them capable, and on the vesture of the porters of Rome the mark of Messalina's elbowing.

# III

## BRUNESEAU

The sewer of Paris in the Middle Ages was legendary. In the sixteenth century, Henri II attempted a bore, which failed. Not a hundred years ago, the cesspool, Mercier attests the fact, was abandoned to itself, and fared as best it might.

Such was this ancient Paris, delivered over to quarrels, to indecision, and to gropings. It was tolerably stupid for a long time. Later on, '89 showed how understanding comes to cities. But in the good, old times, the capital had not much head. It did not know how to manage its own affairs either morally or materially, and could not sweep out filth any better than it could abuses. Everything presented an obstacle, everything raised a question. The sewer, for example, was refractory to every itinerary. One could no more find one's bearings in the sewer than one could understand one's position in the city; above the unintelligible, below the inextricable; beneath the confusion of tongues there reigned the confusion of caverns; Dædalus backed up Babel.

Sometimes the Paris sewer took a notion to overflow, as though this misunderstood Nile were suddenly seized with a fit of rage. There occurred, infamous to relate, inundations of the sewer. At times, that stomach of civilization digested badly, the cesspool flowed back into the throat of the city, and Paris got an after-taste of her own filth. These resemblances of the sewer to remorse had their good points; they were warnings; very badly accepted, however; the city waxed indignant at the audacity of its mire, and did not admit that the filth should return. Drive it out better.

The inundation of 1802 is one of the actual memories of Parisians of the age of eighty. The mud spread in cross-form over the Place des Victoires, where stands the statue of Louis XIV; it entered the Rue Saint-Honoré by the two mouths to the sewer in the Champs-Élysées, the Rue Saint-Florentin through the Saint-Florentin sewer, the Rue Pierre-à-Poisson through the sewer de la Sonnerie, the Rue Popincourt, through the sewer of the Chemin-Vert, the Rue de la Roquette, through the sewer of the Rue de Lappe; it covered the drain of the Rue des Champs-Élysées to the height of thirty-five centimetres; and, to the

South, through the vent of the Seine, performing its functions in inverse sense, it penetrated the Rue Mazarine, the Rue de l'Échaudé, and the Rue des Marais, where it stopped at a distance of one hundred and nine metres, a few paces distant from the house in which Racine had lived, respecting, in the seventeenth century, the poet more than the King. It attained its maximum depth in the Rue Saint-Pierre, where it rose to the height of three feet above the flag-stones of the water-spout, and its maximum length in the Rue Saint-Sabin, where it spread out over a stretch two hundred and thirty-eight metres in length.

At the beginning of this century, the sewer of Paris was still a mysterious place. Mud can never enjoy a good fame; but in this case its evil renown reached the verge of the terrible. Paris knew, in a confused way, that she had under her a terrible cavern. People talked of it as of that monstrous bed of Thebes in which swarmed centipedes fifteen long feet in length, and which might have served Behemoth for a bathtub. The great boots of the sewermen never ventured further than certain well-known points. We were then very near the epoch when the scavenger's carts, from the summit of which Sainte-Foix fraternized with the Marquis de Créqui, discharged their loads directly into the sewer. As for cleaning out,—that function was entrusted to the pouring rains which encumbered rather than swept away. Rome left some poetry to her sewer, and called it the Gemoniæ; Paris insulted hers, and entitled it the Polypus-Hole. Science and superstition were in accord, in horror. The Polypus hole was no less repugnant to hygiene than to legend. The goblin was developed under the fetid covering of the Mouffetard sewer; the corpses of the Marmousets had been cast into the sewer de la Barillerie; Fagon attributed the redoubtable malignant fever of 1685 to the great hiatus of the sewer of the Marais, which remained yawning until 1833 in the Rue Saint-Louis, almost opposite the sign of the *Gallant Messenger*. The mouth of the sewer of the Rue de la Mortellerie was celebrated for the pestilences which had their source there; with its grating of iron, with points simulating a row of teeth, it was like a dragon's maw in that fatal street, breathing forth hell upon men. The popular imagination seasoned the sombre Parisian sink with some indescribably hideous intermixture of the infinite. The sewer had no bottom. The sewer was the lower world. The idea of exploring these leprous regions did not even occur to the police. To try that unknown thing, to cast the plummet into that shadow, to set out on a voyage of discovery in that abyss—who would have dared? It was alarming. Nevertheless, some one did present himself. The cesspool had its Christopher Columbus.

One day, in 1805, during one of the rare apparitions which the Emperor made in Paris, the Minister of the Interior, some Decrès or Crétet or other, came to the master's intimate levee. In the Carrousel there was audible the clanking of swords of all those extraordinary soldiers of the great Republic, and of the great Empire; then Napoleon's door was blocked with heroes; men from the Rhine, from the Escaut, from the Adige, and from the Nile; companions of Joubert, of Desaix, of Marceau, of Hoche, of Kléber; the aérostiers of Fleurus, the grenadiers of Mayence, the pontoon-builders of Genoa, hussars whom the Pyramids had looked down upon, artillerists whom Junot's cannonball had spattered with mud, cuirassiers who had taken by assault the fleet lying at anchor in the Zuyderzee; some had followed Bonaparte upon the bridge of Lodi, others had accompanied Murat in the trenches of Mantua, others had preceded Lannes in the hollow road of Montebello. The whole army of that day was present there, in the court-yard of the Tuileries, represented by a squadron or a platoon, and guarding Napoleon in repose; and that was the splendid epoch when the grand army had Marengo behind it and Austerlitz before it.—"Sire," said the Minister of the Interior to Napoleon, "yesterday I saw the most intrepid man in your Empire."—"What man is that?" said the Emperor brusquely, "and what has he done?"—"He wants to do something, Sire."—"What is it?"—"To visit the sewers of Paris."

This man existed and his name was Bruneseau.

# IV

The visit took place. It was a formidable campaign; a nocturnal battle against pestilence and suffocation. It was, at the same time, a voyage of discovery. One of the survivors of this expedition, an intelligent workingman, who was very young at the time, related curious details with regard to it, several years ago, which Bruneseau thought himself obliged to omit in his report to the prefect of police, as unworthy of official style. The processes of disinfection were, at that epoch, extremely rudimentary. Hardly had Bruneseau crossed the first articulations of that subterranean network, when eight laborers out of the twenty refused to go any further. The operation was complicated; the visit entailed the necessity of cleaning; hence it was necessary to cleanse and at the same time, to proceed; to note the entrances of water, to count the gratings and the vents, to lay out in detail the branches, to indicate the currents at the point where they parted, to define the respective bounds of the divers basins, to sound the small sewers grafted on the principal sewer, to measure the height under the key-stone of each drain, and the width, at the spring of the vaults as well as at the bottom, in order to determine the arrangements with regard to the level of each water-entrance, either of the bottom of the arch, or on the soil of the street. They advanced with toil. The lanterns pined away in the foul atmosphere. From time to time, a fainting sewerman was carried out. At certain points, there were precipices. The soil had given away, the pavement had crumbled, the sewer had changed into a bottomless well; they found nothing solid; a man disappeared suddenly; they had great difficulty in getting him out again. On the advice of Fourcroy, they lighted large cages filled with tow steeped in resin, from time to time, in spots which had been sufficiently disinfected. In some places, the wall was covered with misshapen fungi,—one would have said tumors; the very stone seemed diseased within this unbreathable atmosphere.

Bruneseau, in his exploration, proceeded down hill. At the point of separation of the two water-conduits of the Grand-Hurleur, he deciphered upon a projecting stone the date of 1550; this stone indicated the limits where Philibert Delorme, charged by Henri II with visiting the subterranean drains of Paris, had halted. This stone was the mark of the sixteenth century on the sewer; Bruneseau found the handiwork of the seventeenth century once more in the Ponceau drain of the old Rue Vieille-du-Temple, vaulted between 1600 and 1650; and the handiwork of the eighteenth in the western section of the collecting canal, walled and vaulted in 1740. These two vaults, especially the less ancient, that of 1740, were more cracked and decrepit than the masonry of the belt sewer, which dated from 1412, an epoch when the brook of fresh water of Ménilmontant was elevated to the dignity of the Grand Sewer of Paris, an advancement analogous to that of a peasant who should become first *valet de chambre* to the King; something like Gros-Jean transformed into Lebel.

Here and there, particularly beneath the Court-House, they thought they recognized the hollows of ancient dungeons, excavated in the very sewer itself. Hideous *in-pace*. An iron neck-collar was hanging in one of these cells. They walled them all up. Some of their finds were singular; among others, the skeleton of an ourang-outan, who had disappeared from the Jardin des Plantes in 1800, a disappearance probably connected with the famous and indisputable apparition of the devil in the Rue des Bernardins, in the last year of the eighteenth century. The poor devil had ended by drowning himself in the sewer.

Beneath this long, arched drain which terminated at the Arche-Marion, a perfectly preserved rag-picker's basket excited the admiration of all connoisseurs. Everywhere, the mire, which the sewermen came to handle with intrepidity, abounded in precious objects, jewels of gold and silver, precious stones, coins. If a giant had filtered this cesspool, he would have had the riches of centuries in his lair. At the point where the two branches of the Rue du Temple and of the Rue Sainte-Avoye separate, they picked up a singular Huguenot medal in copper, bearing on one side the pig hooded with a cardinal's hat, and on the other, a wolf with a tiara on his head.

The most surprising rencounter was at the entrance to the Grand Sewer. This entrance had formerly been closed by a grating of which nothing but the hinges remained. From one of these hinges hung a dirty and shapeless rag which, arrested there in its passage, no doubt, had floated there in the darkness and finished its process of being torn apart. Bruneseau held his lantern close to this rag and examined it. It was of very fine batiste, and in one of the corners, less frayed than the rest, they made out a heraldic coronet and embroidered above these seven letters: LAVBESP. The crown was the coronet of a Marquis, and the seven letters signified *Laubespine*. They recognized the fact, that what they had before their eyes was a morsel of the shroud of Marat.

Marat in his youth had had amorous intrigues. This was when he was a member of the household of the Comte d'Artois, in the capacity of physician to the Stables. From these love affairs, historically proved, with a great lady, he had retained this sheet. As a waif or a souvenir. At his death, as this was the only linen of any fineness which he had in his house, they buried him in it. Some old women had shrouded him for the tomb in that swaddling-band in which the tragic Friend of the people had enjoyed voluptuousness. Bruneseau passed on. They left that rag where it hung; they did not put the finishing touch to it. Did this arise from scorn or from respect? Marat deserved both. And then, destiny was there sufficiently stamped to make them hesitate to touch it. Besides, the things of the sepulchre must be left in the spot which they select. In short, the relic was a strange one. A Marquise had slept in it; Marat had rotted in it; it had traversed the Pantheon to end with the rats of the sewer. This chamber rag, of which Watteau would formerly have joyfully sketched every fold, had ended in becoming worthy of the fixed gaze of Dante.

The whole visit to the subterranean stream of filth of Paris lasted seven years, from 1805 to 1812. As he proceeded, Bruneseau drew, directed, and completed considerable works; in 1808 he lowered the arch of the Ponceau, and, everywhere creating new lines, he pushed the sewer, in 1809, under the Rue Saint-Denis as far as the fountain of the Innocents; in 1810, under the Rue Froidmanteau and under the Salpêtrière; in 1811 under the Rue Neuve-des-Petits-Pères, under the Rue du Mail, under the Rue de l'Écharpe, under the Place Royale; in 1812, under the Rue de la Paix, and under the Chaussée d'Antin. At the same time, he had the whole network disinfected and rendered healthful. In the second year of his work, Bruneseau engaged the assistance of his son-in-law Nargaud.

It was thus that, at the beginning of the century, ancient society cleansed its double bottom, and performed the toilet of its sewer. There was that much clean, at all events.

Tortuous, cracked, unpaved, full of fissures, intersected by gullies, jolted by eccentric elbows, mounting and descending illogically, fetid, wild, fierce, submerged in obscurity, with cicatrices on its pavements and scars on its walls, terrible,—such was, retrospectively viewed, the antique sewer of Paris. Ramifications in every direction, crossings, of trenches, branches, goose-feet, stars, as in military mines, cœcum, blind alleys, vaults lined with saltpetre, pestiferous pools, scabby sweats, on the walls, drops dripping from the ceilings, darkness; nothing could equal the horror of this old, waste crypt, the digestive apparatus of Babylon, a cavern, ditch, gulf pierced with streets, a titanic mole-burrow, where the mind seems to behold that enormous blind mole, the past, prowling through the shadows, in the filth which has been splendor.

This, we repeat, was the sewer of the past.

# V

## PRESENT PROGRESS

To-day the sewer is clean, cold, straight, correct. It almost realizes the ideal of what is understood in England by the word "respectable." It is proper and grayish; laid out by rule and line; one might almost say as though it came out of a bandbox. It resembles a tradesman who has become a councillor of state. One can almost see distinctly there. The mire there comports itself with decency. At first, one might readily mistake it for one of those subterranean corridors, which were so common in former days, and so useful in flights of monarchs and princes, in those good old times, "when the people loved their kings." The present sewer is a beautiful sewer; the pure style reigns there; the classical rectilinear alexandrine which, driven out of poetry, appears to have taken refuge in architecture, seems mingled with all the stones of that long, dark and whitish vault; each outlet is an arcade; the Rue de Rivoli serves as pattern even in the sewer. However, if the geometrical line is in place anywhere, it is certainly in the drainage trench of a great city. There, everything should be subordinated to the shortest road. The sewer has, nowadays, assumed a certain official aspect. The very police reports, of which it sometimes forms the subject, no longer are wanting in respect towards it. The words which characterize it in administrative language are sonorous and dignified. What used to be called a gut is now called a gallery; what used to be called a hole is now called a surveying orifice. Villon would no longer meet with his ancient temporary provisional lodging. This network of cellars has its immemorial population of prowlers, rodents, swarming in greater numbers than ever; from time to time, an aged and veteran rat risks his head at the window of the sewer and surveys the Parisians; but even these vermin grow tame, so satisfied are they with their subterranean palace. The cesspool no longer retains anything of its primitive ferocity. The rain, which in former days soiled the sewer, now washes it. Nevertheless, do not trust yourself too much to it. Miasmas still inhabit it. It is more hypocritical than irreproachable. The prefecture of police and the commission of health have done their best. But, in spite of all the processes of disinfection, it exhales, a vague, suspicious odor like Tartuffe after confession.

Let us confess, that, taking it all in all, this sweeping is a homage which the sewer pays to civilization, and as, from this point of view, Tartuffe's conscience is a progress over the Augean stables, it is certain that the sewers of Paris have been improved.

It is more than progress; it is transmutation. Between the ancient and the present sewer there is a revolution. What has effected this revolution?

The man whom all the world forgets, and whom we have mentioned, Bruneseau.

# VI

## Future Progress

The excavation of the sewer of Paris has been no slight task. The last ten centuries have toiled at it without being able to bring it to a termination, any more than they have been able to finish Paris. The sewer, in fact, receives all the counter-shocks of the growth of Paris. Within the bosom of the earth, it is a sort of mysterious polyp with a thousand antennæ, which expands below as the city expands above. Every time that the city cuts a street, the sewer stretches out an arm. The old monarchy had constructed only twenty-three thousand three hundred metres of sewers; that was where Paris stood in this respect on the first of January, 1806. Beginning with this epoch, of which we shall shortly speak, the work was usefully and energetically resumed and prosecuted; Napoleon built—the figures are curious—four thousand eight hundred and four metres; Louis XVIII, five thousand seven hundred and nine; Charles X, ten thousand eight hundred and thirty-six; Louis-Philippe, eighty-nine thousand and twenty; the Republic of 1848, twenty-three thousand three hundred and eighty-one; the present government, seventy thousand five hundred; in all, at the present time, two hundred and twenty-six thousand six hundred and ten metres; sixty leagues of sewers; the enormous entrails of Paris. An obscure ramification ever at work; a construction which is immense and ignored.

As the reader sees, the subterranean labyrinth of Paris is to-day more than ten times what it was at the beginning of the century. It is difficult to form any idea of all the perseverance and the efforts which have been required to bring this cesspool to the point of relative perfection in which it now is. It was with great difficulty that the ancient monarchical provostship and, during the last ten years of the eighteenth century, the revolutionary mayoralty, had succeeded in perforating the five leagues of sewer which existed previous to 1806. All sorts of obstacles hindered this operation, some peculiar to the soil, others inherent in the very prejudices of the laborious population of Paris. Paris is built upon a soil which is singularly rebellious to the pick, the hoe, the bore, and to human manipulation. There is nothing more difficult to pierce and to penetrate than the geological formation upon which is superposed the marvellous historical formation called Paris; as soon as work in any form whatsoever is begun and adventures upon this stretch of alluvium, subterranean resistances abound. There are liquid clays, springs, hard rocks, and those soft and deep quagmires which special science calls *moutardes*. The pick advances laboriously through the calcareous layers alternating with very slender threads of clay, and schistose beds in plates incrusted with oyster-shells, the contemporaries of the pre-Adamite oceans. Sometimes a rivulet suddenly bursts through a vault that has been begun, and inundates the laborers; or a layer of marl is laid bare, and rolls down with the fury of a cataract, breaking the stoutest supporting beams like glass. Quite recently, at Villette, when it became necessary to pass the collecting sewer under the Saint-Martin canal without interrupting navigation or emptying the canal, a fissure appeared in the basin of the canal, water suddenly became abundant in the subterranean tunnel, which was beyond the power of the pumping engines; it was necessary to send a diver to explore the fissure which had been made in the narrow entrance of the grand basin, and it was not without great difficulty that it was stopped up. Elsewhere near the Seine, and even at a considerable distance from the river, as for instance, at Belleville, Grand-Rue and Lumière Passage, quicksands are encountered in which one sticks fast, and in which a man sinks visibly. Add suffocation by miasmas, burial by slides, and sudden crumbling of the earth. Add the typhus, with which the workmen become slowly impregnated. In our own day, after having excavated the gallery of Clichy, with a banquette to receive the principal water-conduit of Ourcq, a piece of work which was executed in a trench ten metres deep; after having, in the midst of land-slides, and with the aid of excavations often putrid, and of shoring up, vaulted the Bièvre from the Boulevard de l'Hôpital, as far as the Seine; after having, in order to deliver Paris from the floods of Montmartre and in order to provide an outlet for that river-like pool nine hectares in extent, which crouched near the Barrière des Martyrs, after having, let us state, constructed the line of sewers from the Barrière Blanche to the road of Aubervilliers, in four months, working day and night, at a depth of eleven metres; after having—a thing heretofore unseen—made a subterranean sewer in the Rue Barre-du-Bec, without a trench, six metres below the surface, the superintendent, Monnot, died. After having vaulted three thousand metres of sewer in all quarters of the city, from the Rue Traversière-Saint-Antoine to the Rue de l'Ourcine, after having freed the Carrefour

Censier-Mouffetard from inundations of rain by means of the branch of the Arbalète, after having built the Saint-Georges sewer, on rock and concrete in the fluid sands, after having directed the formidable lowering of the flooring of the vault timber in the Notre-Dame-de-Nazareth branch, Duleau the engineer died. There are no bulletins for such acts of bravery as these, which are more useful, nevertheless, than the brutal slaughter of the field of battle.

The sewers of Paris in 1832 were far from being what they are to-day. Bruneseau had given the impulse, but the cholera was required to bring about the vast reconstruction which took place later on. It is surprising to say, for example, that in 1821, a part of the belt sewer, called the Grand Canal, as in Venice, still stood stagnating uncovered to the sky, in the Rue des Gourdes. It was only in 1821 that the city of Paris found in its pocket the two hundred and sixty-thousand eighty francs and six centimes required for covering this mass of filth. The three absorbing wells, of the Combat, the Cunette, and Saint-Mandé, with their discharging mouths, their apparatus, their cesspools, and their depuratory branches, only date from 1836. The intestinal sewer of Paris has been made over anew, and, as we have said, it has been extended more than tenfold within the last quarter of a century.

Thirty years ago, at the epoch of the insurrection of the 5th and 6th of June, it was still, in many localities, nearly the same ancient sewer. A very great number of streets which are now convex were then sunken causeways. At the end of a slope, where the tributaries of a street or crossroads ended, there were often to be seen large, square gratings with heavy bars, whose iron, polished by the footsteps of the throng, gleamed dangerous and slippery for vehicles, and caused horses to fall. The official language of the Roads and Bridges gave to these gratings the expressive name of *Cassis*.

In 1832, in a number of streets, in the Rue de l'Étoile, the Rue Saint-Louis, the Rue du Temple, the Rue Vieille-du-Temple, the Rue Notre-Dame de Nazareth, the Rue Folie-Méricourt, the Quai aux Fleurs, the Rue du Petit-Musc, the Rue du Normandie, the Rue Pont-Aux-Biches, the Rue des Marais, the Faubourg Saint-Martin, the Rue Notre Dame des-Victoires, the Faubourg Montmartre, the Rue Grange-Batelière, in the Champs-Élysées, the Rue Jacob, the Rue de Tournon, the ancient gothic sewer still cynically displayed its maw. It consisted of enormous voids of stone catch-basins sometimes surrounded by stone posts, with monumental effrontery.

Paris in 1806 still had nearly the same sewers numerically as stated in 1663; five thousand three hundred fathoms. After Bruneseau, on the 1st of January, 1832, it had forty thousand three hundred metres. Between 1806 and 1831, there had been built, on an average, seven hundred and fifty metres annually, afterwards eight and even ten thousand metres of galleries were constructed every year, in masonry, of small stones, with hydraulic mortar which hardens under water, on a cement foundation. At two hundred francs the metre, the sixty leagues of Paris' sewers of the present day represent forty-eight millions.

In addition to the economic progress which we have indicated at the beginning, grave problems of public hygiene are connected with that immense question: the sewers of Paris.

Paris is the centre of two sheets, a sheet of water and a sheet of air. The sheet of water, lying at a tolerably great depth underground, but already sounded by two bores, is furnished by the layer of green clay situated between the chalk and the Jurassic lime-stone; this layer may be represented by a disk five and twenty leagues in circumference; a multitude of rivers and brooks ooze there; one drinks the Seine, the Marne, the Yonne, the Oise, the Aisne, the Cher, the Vienne and the Loire in a glass of water from the well of Grenelle. The sheet of water is healthy, it comes from heaven in the first place and next from the earth; the sheet of air is unhealthy, it comes from the sewer. All the miasms of the cesspool are mingled with the breath of the city; hence this bad breath. The air taken from above a dung-heap, as has been scientifically proved, is purer than the air taken from above Paris. In a given time, with the aid of progress, mechanisms become perfected, and as light increases, the sheet of water will be employed to purify the sheet of air; that is to say, to wash the sewer. The reader knows, that by "washing the sewer" we mean: the restitution of the filth to the earth; the return to the soil of dung and of manure to the fields. Through this simple act, the entire social community will experience a diminution of misery and an augmentation of health. At the present hour, the radiation of diseases from Paris extends to fifty leagues around the Louvre, taken as the hub of this pestilential wheel.

We might say that, for ten centuries, the cesspool has been the disease of Paris. The sewer is the blemish which Paris has in her blood. The popular instinct has never been deceived in it. The occupation of sewermen was formerly almost as perilous, and almost as repugnant to the people, as the occupation of knacker, which was so long held in horror and handed over to the executioner. High wages were necessary to induce a mason to disappear in that fetid mine; the ladder of the cesspool cleaner hesitated to plunge into it; it was said, in proverbial form: "to descend into the sewer is to enter the grave;" and all sorts of hideous legends, as we have said, covered this colossal sink with terror; a dread sink-hole which bears the traces of the revolutions of the globe as of the revolutions of man, and where are to be found vestiges of all cataclysms from the shells of the Deluge to the rag of Marat.

BOOK THIRD
MUD BUT THE SOUL

# I

## The Sewer and its Surprises

It was in the sewers of Paris that Jean Valjean found himself.

Still another resemblance between Paris and the sea. As in the ocean, the diver may disappear there.

The transition was an unheard-of one. In the very heart of the city, Jean Valjean had escaped from the city, and, in the twinkling of an eye, in the time required to lift the cover and to replace it, he had passed from broad daylight to complete obscurity, from midday to midnight, from tumult to silence, from the whirlwind of thunders to the stagnation of the tomb, and, by a vicissitude far more tremendous even than that of the Rue Polonceau, from the most extreme peril to the most absolute obscurity.

An abrupt fall into a cavern; a disappearance into the secret trap-door of Paris; to quit that street where death was on every side, for that sort of sepulchre where there was life, was a strange instant. He remained for several seconds as though bewildered; listening, stupefied. The waste-trap of safety had suddenly yawned beneath him. Celestial goodness had, in a manner, captured him by treachery. Adorable ambuscades of providence!

Only, the wounded man did not stir, and Jean Valjean did not know whether that which he was carrying in that grave was a living being or a dead corpse.

His first sensation was one of blindness. All of a sudden, he could see nothing. It seemed to him too, that, in one instant, he had become deaf. He no longer heard anything. The frantic storm of murder which had been let loose a few feet above his head did not reach him, thanks to the thickness of the earth which separated him from it, as we have said, otherwise than faintly and indistinctly, and like a rumbling, in the depths. He felt that the ground was solid under his feet; that was all; but that was enough. He extended one arm and then the other, touched the walls on both sides, and perceived that the passage was narrow; he slipped, and thus perceived that the pavement was wet. He cautiously put forward one foot, fearing a hole, a sink, some gulf; he discovered that the paving continued. A gust of fetidness informed him of the place in which he stood.

After the lapse of a few minutes, he was no longer blind. A little light fell through the man-hole through which he had descended, and his eyes became accustomed to this cavern. He began to distinguish something. The passage in which he had burrowed—no other word can better express the situation—was walled in behind him. It was one of those blind alleys, which the special jargon terms branches. In front of him there was another wall, a wall like night. The light of the air-hole died out ten or twelve paces from the point where Jean Valjean stood, and barely cast a wan pallor on a few metres of the damp walls of the sewer. Beyond, the opaqueness was massive; to penetrate thither seemed horrible, an entrance into it appeared like an engulfment. A man could, however, plunge into that wall of fog and it was necessary so to do. Haste was even requisite. It occurred to Jean Valjean that the grating which he had caught sight of under the flag-stones might also catch the eye of the soldiery, and that everything hung upon this chance. They also might descend into that well and search it. There was not a minute to be lost. He had deposited Marius on the ground, he picked him up again,—that is the real word for it,—placed him on his shoulders once more, and set out. He plunged resolutely into the gloom.

The truth is, that they were less safe than Jean Valjean fancied. Perils of another sort and no less serious were awaiting them, perchance. After the lightning-charged whirlwind of the combat, the cavern of miasmas and traps; after chaos, the sewer. Jean Valjean had fallen from one circle of hell into another.

When he had advanced fifty paces, he was obliged to halt. A problem presented itself. The passage terminated in another gut which he encountered across his path. There two ways presented themselves. Which should he take? Ought he to turn to the left or to the right? How was he to find his bearings in that black labyrinth? This labyrinth, to which we have already called the reader's attention, has a clue, which is its slope. To follow to the slope is to arrive at the river.

This Jean Valjean instantly comprehended.

He said to himself that he was probably in the sewer des Halles; that if he were to choose the path to the left and follow the slope, he would arrive, in less than a quarter of an hour, at some mouth on the Seine between the Pont au Change and the Pont-Neuf, that is to say, he would make his appearance in broad daylight on the most densely peopled spot in Paris. Perhaps he would come out on some man-hole at the intersection of streets. Amazement of the passers-by at beholding two bleeding men emerge from the earth at their feet. Arrival of the police, a call to arms of the neighboring post of guards. Thus they would be seized before they had even got out. It would be better to plunge into that labyrinth, to confide themselves to that black gloom, and to trust to Providence for the outcome.

He ascended the incline, and turned to the right.

When he had turned the angle of the gallery, the distant glimmer of an air-hole disappeared, the curtain of obscurity fell upon him once more, and he became blind again. Nevertheless, he advanced as rapidly as possible. Marius' two arms were passed round his neck, and the former's feet dragged behind him. He held both these arms with one hand, and groped along the wall with the other. Marius' cheek touched his, and clung there, bleeding. He felt a warm stream which came from Marius trickling down upon him and making its way under his clothes. But a humid warmth near his ear, which the mouth of the wounded man touched, indicated respiration, and consequently, life. The passage along which Jean Valjean was now proceeding was not so narrow as the first. Jean Valjean walked through it with considerable difficulty. The rain of the preceding day had not, as yet, entirely run off, and it created a little torrent in the centre of the bottom, and he was forced to hug the wall in order not to have his feet in the water.

Thus he proceeded in the gloom. He resembled the beings of the night groping in the invisible and lost beneath the earth in veins of shadow.

Still, little by little, whether it was that the distant air-holes emitted a little wavering light in this opaque gloom, or whether his eyes had become accustomed to the obscurity, some vague vision returned to him, and he began once more to gain a confused idea, now of the wall which he touched, now of the vault beneath which he was passing. The pupil dilates in the dark, and the soul dilates in misfortune and ends by finding God there.

It was not easy to direct his course.

The line of the sewer re-echoes, so to speak, the line of the streets which lie above it. There were then in Paris two thousand two hundred streets. Let the reader imagine himself beneath that forest of gloomy branches which is called the sewer. The system of sewers existing at that epoch, placed end to end, would have given a length of eleven leagues. We have said above, that the actual network, thanks to the special activity of the last thirty years, was no less than sixty leagues in extent.

Jean Valjean began by committing a blunder. He thought that he was beneath the Rue Saint-Denis, and it was a pity that it was not so. Under the Rue Saint-Denis there is an old stone sewer which dates from Louis XIII and which runs straight to the collecting sewer, called the Grand Sewer, with but a single elbow, on the right, on the elevation of the ancient Cour des Miracles, and a single branch, the Saint-Martin sewer, whose four arms describe a cross. But the gut of the Petite-Truanderie the entrance to which was in the vicinity of the Corinthe wine-shop has never communicated with the sewer of the Rue Saint-Denis; it ended at the Montmartre sewer, and it was in this that Jean Valjean was entangled. There opportunities of losing oneself abound. The Montmartre sewer is one of the most labyrinthine of the ancient network. Fortunately, Jean Valjean had left behind him the sewer of the markets whose geometrical plan presents the appearance of a multitude of parrots' roosts piled on top of each other; but he had before him more than one embarrassing encounter and more than one street corner—for they are streets—presenting itself in the gloom like an interrogation point; first, on his left, the vast sewer of the Plâtrière, a sort of Chinese puzzle, thrusting out and entangling its chaos of Ts and Zs under the Post-Office and under the rotunda of the Wheat Market, as far as the Seine, where it terminates in a Y; secondly, on his right, the curving corridor of the Rue du Cadran with its three teeth, which are also blind courts; thirdly, on his left, the branch of the Mail, complicated, almost at its inception, with a sort of fork, and proceeding from zig-zag to zig-zag until it ends in the grand crypt of the outlet of the Louvre, truncated and ramified in every direction; and lastly, the blind alley of a passage of the Rue des Jeûneurs, without counting little ducts here and there, before reaching the belt sewer, which alone could conduct him to some issue sufficiently distant to be safe.

Had Jean Valjean had any idea of all that we have here pointed out, he would speedily have perceived, merely by feeling the wall, that he was not in the subterranean gallery of the Rue Saint-Denis. Instead of the ancient stone, instead of the antique architecture, haughty and royal even in the sewer, with pavement and string courses of granite and mortar costing eight hundred livres the fathom, he would have felt under his hand contemporary cheapness, economical expedients, porous stone filled with mortar on a concrete foundation, which costs two hundred francs the metre, and the bourgeoise masonry known as *à petits matériaux*—small stuff; but of all this he knew nothing.

He advanced with anxiety, but with calmness, seeing nothing, knowing nothing, buried in chance, that is to say, engulfed in providence.

By degrees, we will admit, a certain horror seized upon him. The gloom which enveloped him penetrated his spirit. He walked in an enigma. This aqueduct of the sewer is formidable; it interlaces in a dizzy fashion. It is a melancholy thing to be caught in this Paris of shadows. Jean Valjean was obliged to find and even to invent his route without seeing it. In this unknown, every step that he risked might be his last. How was he to get out? should he find an issue? should he find it in time? would that colossal subterranean sponge with its stone cavities, allow itself to be penetrated and pierced? should he there encounter some unexpected knot in the darkness? should he arrive at the inextricable and the impassable? would Marius die there of hemorrhage and he of hunger? should they end by both getting lost, and by furnishing two skeletons in a nook of that night? He did not know. He put all these questions to himself without replying to them. The intestines of Paris form a precipice. Like the prophet, he was in the belly of the monster.

All at once, he had a surprise. At the most unforeseen moment, and without having ceased to walk in a straight line, he perceived that he was no longer ascending; the water of the rivulet was beating against his heels, instead of meeting him at his toes. The sewer was now descending. Why? Was he about to arrive suddenly at the Seine? This danger was a great one, but the peril of retreating was still greater. He continued to advance.

It was not towards the Seine that he was proceeding. The ridge which the soil of Paris forms on its right bank empties one of its watersheds into the Seine and the other into the Grand Sewer. The crest of this ridge which determines the division of the waters describes a very capricious line. The culminating point, which is the point of separation of the currents, is in the Sainte-Avoye sewer, beyond the Rue Michel-le-Comte, in the sewer of the Louvre, near the boulevards, and in the Montmartre sewer, near the Halles. It was this culminating point that Jean Valjean had reached. He was directing his course towards the belt sewer; he was on the right path. But he did not know it.

Every time that he encountered a branch, he felt of its angles, and if he found that the opening which presented itself was smaller than the passage in which he was, he did not enter but continued his route, rightly judging that every narrower way must needs terminate in a blind alley, and could only lead him further from his goal, that is to say, the outlet. Thus he avoided the quadruple trap which was set for him in the darkness by the four labyrinths which we have just enumerated.

At a certain moment, he perceived that he was emerging from beneath the Paris which was petrified by the uprising, where the barricades had suppressed circulation, and that he was entering beneath the living and normal Paris. Overhead he suddenly heard a noise as of thunder, distant but continuous. It was the rumbling of vehicles.

He had been walking for about half an hour, at least according to the calculation which he made in his own mind, and he had not yet thought of rest; he had merely changed the hand with which he was holding Marius. The darkness was more profound than ever, but its very depth reassured him.

All at once, he saw his shadow in front of him. It was outlined on a faint, almost indistinct reddish glow, which vaguely empurpled the flooring vault underfoot, and the vault overhead, and gilded to his right and to his left the two viscous walls of the passage. Stupefied, he turned round.

Behind him, in the portion of the passage which he had just passed through, at a distance which appeared to him immense, piercing the dense obscurity, flamed a sort of horrible star which had the air of surveying him.

It was the gloomy star of the police which was rising in the sewer.

In the rear of that star eight or ten forms were moving about in a confused way, black, upright, indistinct, horrible.

# II

## Explanation

On the day of the sixth of June, a battue of the sewers had been ordered. It was feared that the vanquished might have taken to them for refuge, and Prefect Gisquet was to search occult Paris while General Bugeaud swept public Paris; a double and connected operation which exacted a double strategy on the part of the public force, represented above by the army and below by the police. Three squads of agents and sewermen explored the subterranean drain of Paris, the first on the right bank, the second on the left bank, the third in the city. The agents of police were armed with carabines, with bludgeons, swords and poignards.

That which was directed at Jean Valjean at that moment, was the lantern of the patrol of the right bank.

This patrol had just visited the curving gallery and the three blind alleys which lie beneath the Rue du Cadran. While they were passing their lantern through the depths of these blind alleys, Jean Valjean had encountered on his path the entrance to the gallery, had perceived that it was narrower than the principal passage and had not penetrated thither. He had passed on. The police, on emerging from the gallery du Cadran, had fancied that they heard the sound of footsteps in the direction of the belt sewer. They were, in fact, the steps of Jean Valjean. The sergeant in command of the patrol had raised his lantern, and the squad had begun to gaze into the mist in the direction whence the sound proceeded.

This was an indescribable moment for Jean Valjean.

Happily, if he saw the lantern well, the lantern saw him but ill. It was light and he was shadow. He was very far off, and mingled with the darkness of the place. He hugged the wall and halted. Moreover, he did not understand what it was that was moving behind him. The lack of sleep and food, and his emotions had caused him also to pass into the state of a visionary. He beheld a gleam, and around that gleam, forms. What was it? He did not comprehend.

Jean Valjean having paused, the sound ceased.

The men of the patrol listened, and heard nothing, they looked and saw nothing. They held a consultation.

There existed at that epoch at this point of the Montmartre sewer a sort of crossroads called *de service*, which was afterwards suppressed, on account of the little interior lake which formed there, swallowing up the torrent of rain in heavy storms. The patrol could form a cluster in this open space. Jean Valjean saw these spectres form a sort of circle. These bull-dogs' heads approached each other closely and whispered together.

The result of this council held by the watch dogs was, that they had been mistaken, that there had been no noise, that it was useless to get entangled in the belt sewer, that it would only be a waste of time, but that they ought to hasten towards Saint-Merry; that if there was anything to do, and any "bousingot" to track out, it was in that quarter.

From time to time, parties re-sole their old insults. In 1832, the word bousingot formed the interim between the word jacobin, which had become obsolete, and the word demagogue which has since rendered such excellent service.

The sergeant gave orders to turn to the left, towards the watershed of the Seine.

If it had occurred to them to separate into two squads, and to go in both directions, Jean Valjean would have been captured. All hung on that thread. It is probable that the instructions of the prefecture, foreseeing a possibility of combat and insurgents in force, had forbidden the patrol to part company. The patrol resumed its march, leaving Jean Valjean behind it. Of all this movement, Jean Valjean perceived nothing, except the eclipse of the lantern which suddenly wheeled round.

Before taking his departure, the sergeant, in order to acquit his policeman's conscience, discharged his gun in the direction of Jean Valjean. The detonation rolled from echo to echo in the crypt, like the rumbling of that titanic entrail. A bit of plaster which fell into the stream and splashed up the water a few paces away from Jean Valjean, warned him that the ball had struck the arch over his head.

Slow and measured steps resounded for some time on the timber work, gradually dying away as they retreated to a greater distance; the group of black forms vanished, a glimmer of light oscillated and floated, communicating to the vault a reddish glow which grew fainter, then disappeared; the silence became profound once more, the obscurity became complete, blindness and deafness resumed possession of the shadows; and Jean Valjean, not daring to stir as yet, remained for a long time leaning with his back against the wall, with straining ears, and dilated pupils, watching the disappearance of that phantom patrol.

# III

## The "Spun" Man

This justice must be rendered to the police of that period, that even in the most serious public junctures, it imperturbably fulfilled its duties connected with the sewers and surveillance. A revolt was, in its eyes, no pretext for allowing malefactors to take the bit in their own mouths, and for neglecting society for the reason that the government was in peril. The ordinary service was performed correctly in company with the extraordinary service, and was not troubled by the latter. In the midst of an incalculable political event already begun, under the pressure of a possible revolution, a police agent, "spun" a thief without allowing himself to be distracted by insurrection and barricades.

It was something precisely parallel which took place on the afternoon of the 6th of June on the banks of the Seine, on the slope of the right shore, a little beyond the Pont des Invalides.

There is no longer any bank there now. The aspect of the locality has changed.

On that bank, two men, separated by a certain distance, seemed to be watching each other while mutually avoiding each other. The one who was in advance was trying to get away, the one in the rear was trying to overtake the other.

It was like a game of checkers played at a distance and in silence. Neither seemed to be in any hurry, and both walked slowly, as though each of them feared by too much haste to make his partner redouble his pace.

One would have said that it was an appetite following its prey, and purposely without wearing the air of doing so. The prey was crafty and on its guard.

The proper relations between the hunted pole-cat and the hunting dog were observed. The one who was seeking to escape had an insignificant mien and not an impressive appearance; the one who was seeking to seize him was rude of aspect, and must have been rude to encounter.

The first, conscious that he was the more feeble, avoided the second; but he avoided him in a manner which was deeply furious; any one who could have observed him would have discerned in his eyes the sombre hostility of flight, and all the menace that fear contains.

The shore was deserted; there were no passers-by; not even a boatman nor a lighter-man was in the skiffs which were moored here and there.

It was not easy to see these two men, except from the quay opposite, and to any person who had scrutinized them at that distance, the man who was in advance would have appeared like a bristling, tattered, and equivocal being, who was uneasy and trembling beneath a ragged blouse, and the other like a classic and official personage, wearing the frock-coat of authority buttoned to the chin.

Perchance the reader might recognize these two men, if he were to see them closer at hand.

What was the object of the second man?

Probably to succeed in clothing the first more warmly.

When a man clothed by the state pursues a man in rags, it is in order to make of him a man who is also clothed by the state. Only, the whole question lies in the color. To be dressed in blue is glorious; to be dressed in red is disagreeable.

There is a purple from below.

It is probably some unpleasantness and some purple of this sort which the first man is desirous of shirking.

If the other allowed him to walk on, and had not seized him as yet, it was, judging from all appearances, in the hope of seeing him lead up to some significant meeting-place and to some group worth catching. This delicate operation is called "spinning."

What renders this conjecture entirely probable is that the buttoned-up man, on catching sight from the shore of a hackney-coach on the quay as it was passing along empty, made a sign to the driver; the driver understood, evidently recognized the person with whom he had to deal, turned about and began to follow the two men at the top of the quay, at a foot-pace. This was not observed by the slouching and tattered personage who was in advance.

The hackney-coach rolled along the trees of the Champs-Élysées. The bust of the driver, whip in hand, could be seen moving along above the parapet.

One of the secret instructions of the police authorities to their agents contains this article: "Always have on hand a hackney-coach, in case of emergency."

VICTOR HUGO

While these two men were manœuvring, each on his own side, with irreproachable strategy, they approached an inclined plane on the quay which descended to the shore, and which permitted cab-drivers arriving from Passy to come to the river and water their horses. This inclined plane was suppressed later on, for the sake of symmetry; horses may die of thirst, but the eye is gratified.

It is probable that the man in the blouse had intended to ascend this inclined plane, with a view to making his escape into the Champs-Élysées, a place ornamented with trees, but, in return, much infested with policemen, and where the other could easily exercise violence.

This point on the quay is not very far distant from the house brought to Paris from Moret in 1824, by Colonel Brack, and designated as "the house of François I." A guard house is situated close at hand.

To the great surprise of his watcher, the man who was being tracked did not mount by the inclined plane for watering. He continued to advance along the quay on the shore.

His position was visibly becoming critical.

What was he intending to do, if not to throw himself into the Seine?

Henceforth, there existed no means of ascending to the quay; there was no other inclined plane, no staircase; and they were near the spot, marked by the bend in the Seine towards the Pont de Jéna, where the bank, growing constantly narrower, ended in a slender tongue, and was lost in the water. There he would inevitably find himself blocked between the perpendicular wall on his right, the river on his left and in front of him, and the authorities on his heels.

It is true that this termination of the shore was hidden from sight by a heap of rubbish six or seven feet in height, produced by some demolition or other. But did this man hope to conceal himself effectually behind that heap of rubbish, which one need but skirt? The expedient would have been puerile. He certainly was not dreaming of such a thing. The innocence of thieves does not extend to that point.

The pile of rubbish formed a sort of projection at the water's edge, which was prolonged in a promontory as far as the wall of the quay.

The man who was being followed arrived at this little mound and went round it, so that he ceased to be seen by the other.

The latter, as he did not see, could not be seen; he took advantage of this fact to abandon all dissimulation and to walk very rapidly. In a few moments, he had reached the rubbish heap and passed round it. There he halted in sheer amazement. The man whom he had been pursuing was no longer there.

Total eclipse of the man in the blouse.

The shore, beginning with the rubbish heap, was only about thirty paces long, then it plunged into the water which beat against the wall of the quay. The fugitive could not have thrown himself into the Seine without being seen by the man who was following him. What had become of him?

The man in the buttoned-up coat walked to the extremity of the shore, and remained there in thought for a moment, his fists clenched, his eyes searching. All at once he smote his brow. He had just perceived, at the point where the land came to an end and the water began, a large iron grating, low, arched, garnished with a heavy lock and with three massive hinges. This grating, a sort of door pierced at the base of the quay, opened on the river as well as on the shore. A blackish stream passed under it. This stream discharged into the Seine.

Beyond the heavy, rusty iron bars, a sort of dark and vaulted corridor could be descried. The man folded his arms and stared at the grating with an air of reproach.

As this gaze did not suffice, he tried to thrust it aside; he shook it, it resisted solidly. It is probable that it had just been opened, although no sound had been heard, a singular circumstance in so rusty a grating; but it is certain that it had been closed again. This indicated that the man before whom that door had just opened had not a hook but a key.

This evidence suddenly burst upon the mind of the man who was trying to move the grating, and evoked from him this indignant ejaculation:

"That is too much! A government key!"

Then, immediately regaining his composure, he expressed a whole world of interior ideas by this outburst of monosyllables accented almost ironically: "Come! Come! Come! Come!"

That said, and in the hope of something or other, either that he should see the man emerge or other men enter, he posted himself on the watch behind a heap of rubbish, with the patient rage of a pointer.

The hackney-coach, which regulated all its movements on his, had, in its turn, halted on the quay above him, close to the parapet. The coachman, foreseeing a prolonged wait, encased his horses' muzzles in the bag of oats which is damp at the bottom, and which is so familiar to Parisians, to whom, be it said in parenthesis, the Government sometimes applies it. The rare passers-by on the Pont de Jéna turned their heads, before they pursued their way, to take a momentary glance at these two motionless items in the landscape, the man on the shore, the carriage on the quay.

# IV

## He Also Bears His Cross

Jean Valjean had resumed his march and had not again paused.

This march became more and more laborious. The level of these vaults varies; the average height is about five feet, six inches, and has been calculated for the stature of a man; Jean Valjean was forced to bend over, in order not to strike Marius against the vault; at every step he had to bend, then to rise, and to feel incessantly of the wall. The moisture of the stones, and the viscous nature of the timber framework furnished but poor supports to which to cling, either for hand or foot. He stumbled along in the hideous dung-heap of the city. The intermittent gleams from the air-holes only appeared at very long intervals, and were so wan that the full sunlight seemed like the light of the moon; all the rest was mist, miasma, opaqueness, blackness. Jean Valjean was both hungry and thirsty; especially thirsty; and this, like the sea, was a place full of water where a man cannot drink. His strength, which was prodigious, as the reader knows, and which had been but little decreased by age, thanks to his chaste and sober life, began to give way, nevertheless. Fatigue began to gain on him; and as his strength decreased, it made the weight of his burden increase. Marius, who was, perhaps, dead, weighed him down as inert bodies weigh. Jean Valjean held him in such a manner that his chest was not oppressed, and so that respiration could proceed as well as possible. Between his legs he felt the rapid gliding of the rats. One of them was frightened to such a degree that he bit him. From time to time, a breath of fresh air reached him through the vent-holes of the mouths of the sewer, and reanimated him.

It might have been three hours past midday when he reached the belt-sewer.

He was, at first, astonished at this sudden widening. He found himself, all at once, in a gallery where his outstretched hands could not reach the two walls, and beneath a vault which his head did not touch. The Grand Sewer is, in fact, eight feet wide and seven feet high.

At the point where the Montmartre sewer joins the Grand Sewer, two other subterranean galleries, that of the Rue de Provence, and that of the Abattoir, form a square. Between these four ways, a less sagacious man would have remained undecided. Jean Valjean selected the broadest, that is to say, the belt-sewer. But here the question again came up—should he descend or ascend? He thought that the situation required haste, and that he must now gain the Seine at any risk. In other terms, he must descend. He turned to the left.

It was well that he did so, for it is an error to suppose that the belt-sewer has two outlets, the one in the direction of Bercy, the other towards Passy, and that it is, as its name indicates, the subterranean girdle of the Paris on the right bank. The Grand Sewer, which is, it must be remembered, nothing else than the old brook of Ménilmontant, terminates, if one ascends it, in a blind sack, that is to say, at its ancient point of departure which was its source, at the foot of the knoll of Ménilmontant. There is no direct communication with the branch which collects the waters of Paris beginning with the Quartier Popincourt, and which falls into the Seine through the Amelot sewer above the ancient Isle Louviers. This branch, which completes the collecting sewer, is separated from it, under the Rue Ménilmontant itself, by a pile which marks the dividing point of the waters, between upstream and downstream. If Jean Valjean had ascended the gallery he would have arrived, after a thousand efforts, and broken down with fatigue, and in an expiring condition, in the gloom, at a wall. He would have been lost.

In case of necessity, by retracing his steps a little way, and entering the passage of the Filles-du-Calvaire, on condition that he did not hesitate at the subterranean crossing of the Carrefour Boucherat, and by taking the corridor Saint-Louis, then the Saint-Gilles gut on the left, then turning to the right and avoiding the Saint-Sebastian gallery, he might have reached the Amelot sewer, and thence, provided that he did not go astray in the sort of F which lies under the Bastille, he might have attained the outlet on the Seine near the Arsenal. But in order to do this, he must have been thoroughly familiar with the enormous madrepore of the sewer in all its ramifications and in all its openings. Now, we must again insist that he knew nothing of that frightful drain which he was traversing; and had any one asked him in what he was, he would have answered: "In the night."

His instinct served him well. To descend was, in fact, possible safety.

He left on his right the two narrow passages which branch out in the form of a claw under the Rue Laffitte and the Rue Saint-Georges and the long, bifurcated corridor of the Chaussée d'Antin.

A little beyond an affluent, which was, probably, the Madeleine branch, he halted. He was extremely weary. A passably large air-hole, probably the man-hole in the Rue d'Anjou, furnished a light that was almost vivid. Jean Valjean, with the gentleness of movement which a brother would exercise towards his wounded brother, deposited Marius on the banquette of the sewer. Marius' blood-stained face appeared under the wan light of the air-hole like the ashes at the bottom of a tomb. His eyes were closed, his hair was plastered down on his temples like a painter's brushes dried in red wash; his hands hung limp and dead. A clot of blood had collected in the knot of his cravat; his limbs were cold, and blood was clotted at the corners of his mouth; his shirt had thrust itself into his wounds, the cloth of his coat was chafing the yawning gashes in the living flesh. Jean Valjean, pushing aside the garments with the tips of his fingers, laid his hand upon Marius' breast; his heart was still beating. Jean Valjean tore up his shirt, bandaged the young man's wounds as well as he was able and stopped the flowing blood; then bending over Marius, who still lay unconscious and almost without breathing, in that half light, he gazed at him with inexpressible hatred.

On disarranging Marius' garments, he had found two things in his pockets, the roll which had been forgotten there on the preceding evening, and Marius' pocketbook. He ate the roll and opened the pocketbook. On the first page he found the four lines written by Marius. The reader will recall them:

"My name is Marius Pontmercy. Carry my body to my grandfather, M. Gillenormand, Rue des Filles-du-Calvaire, No. 6, in the Marais."

Jean Valjean read these four lines by the light of the air-hole, and remained for a moment as though absorbed in thought, repeating in a low tone: "Rue des Filles-du-Calvaire, number 6, Monsieur Gillenormand." He replaced the pocketbook in Marius' pocket. He had eaten, his strength had returned to him; he took Marius up once more upon his back, placed the latter's head carefully on his right shoulder, and resumed his descent of the sewer.

The Grand Sewer, directed according to the course of the valley of Ménilmontant, is about two leagues long. It is paved throughout a notable portion of its extent.

This torch of the names of the streets of Paris, with which we are illuminating for the reader Jean Valjean's subterranean march, Jean Valjean himself did not possess. Nothing told him what zone of the city he was traversing, nor what way he had made. Only the growing pallor of the pools of light which he encountered from time to time indicated to him that the sun was withdrawing from the pavement, and that the day would soon be over; and the rolling of vehicles overhead, having become intermittent instead of continuous, then having almost ceased, he concluded that he was no longer under central Paris, and that he was approaching some solitary region, in the vicinity of the outer boulevards, or the extreme outer quays. Where there are fewer houses and streets, the sewer has fewer air-holes. The gloom deepened around Jean Valjean. Nevertheless, he continued to advance, groping his way in the dark.

Suddenly this darkness became terrible.

# V

## In the Case of Sand as in that of Woman, There is a Fineness Which is Treacherous

He felt that he was entering the water, and that he no longer had a pavement under his feet, but only mud.

It sometimes happens, that on certain shores of Bretagne or Scotland a man, either a traveller or a fisherman, while walking at low tide on the beach far from shore, suddenly notices that for several minutes past, he has been walking with some difficulty. The beach under foot is like pitch; his soles stick fast to it; it is no longer sand, it is bird-lime. The strand is perfectly dry, but at every step that he takes, as soon as the foot is raised, the print is filled with water. The eye, however, has perceived no change; the immense beach is smooth and tranquil, all the sand has the same aspect, nothing distinguishes the soil that is solid from that which is not solid; the joyous little cloud of sand-lice continues to leap tumultuously under the feet of the passer-by.

The man pursues his way, he walks on, turns towards the land, endeavors to approach the shore. He is not uneasy. Uneasy about what? Only he is conscious that the heaviness of his feet seems to be increasing at every step that he takes. All at once he sinks in. He sinks in two or three inches. Decidedly, he is not on the right road; he halts to get his bearings. Suddenly he glances at his feet; his feet have disappeared. The sand has covered them. He draws his feet out of the sand, he tries to retrace his steps, he turns back, he sinks in more deeply than before. The sand is up to his ankles, he tears himself free from it and flings himself to the left, the sand reaches to mid-leg, he flings himself to the right, the sand comes up to his knees. Then, with indescribable terror, he recognizes the fact that he is caught in a quicksand, and that he has beneath him that frightful medium in which neither man can walk nor fish can swim. He flings away his burden, if he have one, he lightens himself, like a ship in distress; it is too late, the sand is above his knees.

He shouts, he waves his hat, or his handkerchief, the sand continually gains on him; if the beach is deserted, if the land is too far away, if the bank of sand is too ill-famed, there is no hero in the neighborhood, all is over, he is condemned to be engulfed. He is condemned to that terrible interment, long, infallible, implacable, which it is impossible to either retard or hasten, which lasts for hours, which will not come to an end, which seizes you erect, free, in the flush of health, which drags you down by the feet, which, at every effort that you attempt, at every shout that you utter, draws you a little lower, which has the air of punishing you for your resistance by a redoubled grasp, which forces a man to return slowly to earth, while leaving him time to survey the horizon, the trees, the verdant country, the smoke of the villages on the plain, the sails of the ships on the sea, the birds which fly and sing, the sun and the sky. This engulfment is the sepulchre which assumes a tide, and which mounts from the depths of the earth towards a living man. Each minute is an inexorable layer-out of the dead. The wretched man tries to sit down, to lie down, to climb; every movement that he makes buries him deeper; he straightens himself up, he sinks; he feels that he is being swallowed up; he shrieks, implores, cries to the clouds, wrings his hands, grows desperate. Behold him in the sand up to his belly, the sand reaches to his breast, hc is only a bust now. He uplifts his hands, utters furious groans, clenches his nails on the beach, tries to cling fast to that ashes, supports himself on his elbows in order to raise himself from that soft sheath, and sobs frantically; the sand mounts higher. The sand has reached his shoulders, the sand reaches to his throat; only his face is visible now. His mouth cries aloud, the sand fills it; silence. His eyes still gaze forth, the sand closes them, night. Then his brow decreases, a little hair quivers above the sand; a hand projects, pierces the surface of the beach, waves and disappears. Sinister obliteration of a man.

Sometimes a rider is engulfed with his horse; sometimes the carter is swallowed up with his cart; all founders in that strand. It is shipwreck elsewhere than in the water. It is the earth drowning a man. The earth, permeated with the ocean, becomes a pitfall. It presents itself in the guise of a plain, and it yawns like a wave. The abyss is subject to these treacheries.

This melancholy fate, always possible on certain sea beaches, was also possible, thirty years ago, in the sewers of Paris.

Before the important works, undertaken in 1833, the subterranean drain of Paris was subject to these sudden slides.

The water filtered into certain subjacent strata, which were particularly friable; the foot-way, which was of flag-stones, as in the ancient sewers, or of cement on concrete, as in the new galleries, having no longer an underpinning, gave way. A fold in a flooring of this sort means a crack, means crumbling. The framework crumbled away for a certain length. This crevice, the hiatus of a gulf of mire, was called a *fontis*, in the special tongue. What is a *fontis?* It is the quicksands of the seashore suddenly encountered under the surface of the earth; it is the beach of Mont Saint-Michel in a sewer. The soaked soil is in a state of fusion, as it were; all its molecules are in suspension in soft medium; it is not earth and it is not water. The depth is sometimes very great. Nothing can be more formidable than such an encounter. If the water predominates, death is prompt, the man is swallowed up; if earth predominates, death is slow.

Can any one picture to himself such a death? If being swallowed by the earth is terrible on the seashore, what is it in a cesspool? Instead of the open air, the broad daylight, the clear horizon, those vast sounds, those free clouds whence rains life, instead of those barks descried in the distance, of that hope under all sorts of forms, of probable passers-by, of succor possible up to the very last moment,—instead of all this, deafness, blindness, a black vault, the inside of a tomb already prepared, death in the mire beneath a cover! slow suffocation by filth, a stone box where asphyxia opens its claw in the mire and clutches you by the throat; fetidness mingled with the death-rattle; slime instead of the strand, sulfuretted hydrogen in place of the hurricane, dung in place of the ocean! And to shout, to gnash one's teeth, and to writhe, and to struggle, and to agonize, with that enormous city which knows nothing of it all, over one's head!

Inexpressible is the horror of dying thus! Death sometimes redeems his atrocity by a certain terrible dignity. On the funeral pile, in shipwreck, one can be great; in the flames as in the foam, a superb attitude is possible; one there becomes transfigured as one perishes. But not here. Death is filthy. It is humiliating to expire. The supreme floating visions are abject. Mud is synonymous with shame. It is petty, ugly, infamous. To die in a butt of Malvoisie, like Clarence, is permissible; in the ditch of a scavenger, like Escoubleau, is horrible. To struggle therein is hideous; at the same time that one is going through the death agony, one is floundering about. There are shadows enough for hell, and mire enough to render it nothing but a slough, and the dying man knows not whether he is on the point of becoming a spectre or a frog.

Everywhere else the sepulchre is sinister; here it is deformed.

The depth of the *fontis* varied, as well as their length and their density, according to the more or less bad quality of the sub-soil. Sometimes a *fontis* was three or four feet deep, sometimes eight or ten; sometimes the bottom was unfathomable. Here the mire was almost solid, there almost liquid. In the Lunière fontis, it would have taken a man a day to disappear, while he would have been devoured in five minutes by the Philippeaux slough. The mire bears up more or less, according to its density. A child can escape where a man will perish. The first law of safety is to get rid of every sort of load. Every sewerman who felt the ground giving way beneath him began by flinging away his sack of tools, or his back-basket, or his hod.

The fontis were due to different causes: the friability of the soil; some landslip at a depth beyond the reach of man; the violent summer rains; the incessant flooding of winter; long, drizzling showers. Sometimes the weight of the surrounding houses on a marly or sandy soil forced out the vaults of the subterranean galleries and caused them to bend aside, or it chanced that a flooring vault burst and split under this crushing thrust. In this manner, the heaping up of the Parthénon, obliterated, a century ago, a portion of the vaults of Saint-Geneviève hill. When a sewer was broken in under the pressure of the houses, the mischief was sometimes betrayed in the street above by a sort of space, like the teeth of a saw, between the paving-stones; this crevice was developed in an undulating line throughout the entire length of the cracked vault, and then, the evil being visible, the remedy could be promptly applied. It also frequently happened, that the interior ravages were not revealed by any external scar, and in that case, woe to the sewermen. When they entered without precaution into the sewer, they were liable to be lost. Ancient registers make mention of several scavengers who were buried in fontis in this manner. They give many names; among others, that of the sewerman who was swallowed up in a quagmire under the man-hole of the Rue Carême-Prenant, a certain Blaise Poutrain; this Blaise Poutrain was the brother of Nicholas Poutrain, who was the last grave-digger of the cemetery called the Charnier des Innocents, in 1785, the epoch when that cemetery expired.

There was also that young and charming Vicomte d'Escoubleau, of whom we have just spoken, one of the heroes of the siege of Lérida, where they delivered the assault in silk stockings, with violins at their head. D'Escoubleau, surprised one night at his cousin's, the Duchesse de Sourdis', was drowned in a quagmire of the Beautreillis sewer, in which he had taken refuge in order to escape from the Duke. Madame de Sourdis, when informed of his death, demanded her smelling-bottle, and forgot to weep, through sniffling at her salts. In such cases, there is no love which holds fast; the sewer extinguishes it. Hero refuses to wash the body of Leander. Thisbe stops her nose in the presence of Pyramus and says: "Phew!"

# VI

## THE FONTIS

Jean Valjean found himself in the presence of a fontis.

This sort of quagmire was common at that period in the subsoil of the Champs-Élysées, difficult to handle in the hydraulic works and a bad preservative of the subterranean constructions, on account of its excessive fluidity. This fluidity exceeds even the inconsistency of the sands of the Quartier Saint-Georges, which could only be conquered by a stone construction on a concrete foundation, and the clayey strata, infected with gas, of the Quartier des Martyrs, which are so liquid that the only way in which a passage was effected under the gallery des Martyrs was by means of a cast-iron pipe. When, in 1836, the old stone sewer beneath the Faubourg Saint-Honoré, in which we now see Jean Valjean, was demolished for the purpose of reconstructing it, the quicksand, which forms the subsoil of the Champs-Élysées as far as the Seine, presented such an obstacle, that the operation lasted nearly six months, to the great clamor of the dwellers on the riverside, particularly those who had hotels and carriages. The work was more than unhealthy; it was dangerous. It is true that they had four months and a half of rain, and three floods of the Seine.

The fontis which Jean Valjean had encountered was caused by the downpour of the preceding day. The pavement, badly sustained by the subjacent sand, had given way and had produced a stoppage of the water. Infiltration had taken place, a slip had followed. The dislocated bottom had sunk into the ooze. To what extent? Impossible to say. The obscurity was more dense there than elsewhere. It was a pit of mire in a cavern of night.

Jean Valjean felt the pavement vanishing beneath his feet. He entered this slime. There was water on the surface, slime at the bottom. He must pass it. To retrace his steps was impossible. Marius was dying, and Jean Valjean exhausted. Besides, where was he to go? Jean Valjean advanced. Moreover, the pit seemed, for the first few steps, not to be very deep. But in proportion as he advanced, his feet plunged deeper. Soon he had the slime up to his calves and water above his knees. He walked on, raising Marius in his arms, as far above the water as he could. The mire now reached to his knees, and the water to his waist. He could no longer retreat. This mud, dense enough for one man, could not, obviously, uphold two. Marius and Jean Valjean would have stood a chance of extricating themselves singly. Jean Valjean continued to advance, supporting the dying man, who was, perhaps, a corpse.

The water came up to his arm-pits; he felt that he was sinking; it was only with difficulty that he could move in the depth of ooze which he had now reached. The density, which was his support, was also an obstacle. He still held Marius on high, and with an unheard-of expenditure of force, he advanced still; but he was sinking. He had only his head above the water now and his two arms holding up Marius. In the old paintings of the deluge there is a mother holding her child thus.

He sank still deeper, he turned his face to the rear, to escape the water, and in order that he might be able to breathe; anyone who had seen him in that gloom would have thought that what he beheld was a mask floating on the shadows; he caught a faint glimpse above him of the drooping head and livid face of Marius; he made a desperate effort and launched his foot forward; his foot struck something solid; a point of support. It was high time.

He straightened himself up, and rooted himself upon that point of support with a sort of fury. This produced upon him the effect of the first step in a staircase leading back to life.

The point of support, thus encountered in the mire at the supreme moment, was the beginning of the other watershed of the pavement, which had bent but had not given way, and which had curved under the water like a plank and in a single piece. Well built pavements form a vault and possess this sort of firmness. This fragment of the vaulting, partly submerged, but solid, was a veritable inclined plane, and, once on this plane, he was safe. Jean Valjean mounted this inclined plane and reached the other side of the quagmire.

As he emerged from the water, he came in contact with a stone and fell upon his knees. He reflected that this was but just, and he remained there for some time, with his soul absorbed in words addressed to God.

He rose to his feet, shivering, chilled, foul-smelling, bowed beneath the dying man whom he was dragging after him, all dripping with slime, and his soul filled with a strange light.

# VII

## One Sometimes Runs Aground When One Fancies that One is Disembarking

He set out on his way once more.

However, although he had not left his life in the fontis, he seemed to have left his strength behind him there. That supreme effort had exhausted him. His lassitude was now such that he was obliged to pause for breath every three or four steps, and lean against the wall. Once he was forced to seat himself on the banquette in order to alter Marius' position, and he thought that he should have to remain there. But if his vigor was dead, his energy was not. He rose again.

He walked on desperately, almost fast, proceeded thus for a hundred paces, almost without drawing breath, and suddenly came in contact with the wall. He had reached an elbow of the sewer, and, arriving at the turn with head bent down, he had struck the wall. He raised his eyes, and at the extremity of the vault, far, very far away in front of him, he perceived a light. This time it was not that terrible light; it was good, white light. It was daylight. Jean Valjean saw the outlet.

A damned soul, who, in the midst of the furnace, should suddenly perceive the outlet of Gehenna, would experience what Jean Valjean felt. It would fly wildly with the stumps of its burned wings towards that radiant portal. Jean Valjean was no longer conscious of fatigue, he no longer felt Marius' weight, he found his legs once more of steel, he ran rather than walked. As he approached, the outlet became more and more distinctly defined. It was a pointed arch, lower than the vault, which gradually narrowed, and narrower than the gallery, which closed in as the vault grew lower. The tunnel ended like the interior of a funnel; a faulty construction, imitated from the wickets of penitentiaries, logical in a prison, illogical in a sewer, and which has since been corrected.

Jean Valjean reached the outlet.

There he halted.

It certainly was the outlet, but he could not get out.

The arch was closed by a heavy grating, and the grating, which, to all appearance, rarely swung on its rusty hinges, was clamped to its stone jamb by a thick lock, which, red with rust, seemed like an enormous brick. The keyhole could be seen, and the robust latch, deeply sunk in the iron staple. The door was plainly double-locked. It was one of those prison locks which old Paris was so fond of lavishing.

Beyond the grating was the open air, the river, the daylight, the shore, very narrow but sufficient for escape. The distant quays, Paris, that gulf in which one so easily hides oneself, the broad horizon, liberty. On the right, downstream, the bridge of Jéna was discernible, on the left, upstream, the bridge of the Invalides; the place would have been a propitious one in which to await the night and to escape. It was one of the most solitary points in Paris; the shore which faces the Grand-Caillou. Flies were entering and emerging through the bars of the grating.

It might have been half-past eight o'clock in the evening. The day was declining.

Jean Valjean laid Marius down along the wall, on the dry portion of the vaulting, then he went to the grating and clenched both fists round the bars; the shock which he gave it was frenzied, but it did not move. The grating did not stir. Jean Valjean seized the bars one after the other, in the hope that he might be able to tear away the least solid, and to make of it a lever wherewith to raise the door or to break the lock. Not a bar stirred. The teeth of a tiger are not more firmly fixed in their sockets. No lever; no prying possible. The obstacle was invincible. There was no means of opening the gate.

Must he then stop there? What was he to do? What was to become of him? He had not the strength to retrace his steps, to recommence the journey which he had already taken. Besides, how was he to again traverse that quagmire whence he had only extricated himself as by a miracle? And after the quagmire, was there not the police patrol, which assuredly could not be twice avoided? And then, whither was he to go? What direction should he pursue? To follow the incline would not conduct him to his goal. If he were to reach another outlet, he would find it obstructed by a plug or a grating. Every outlet was, undoubtedly, closed in that manner. Chance had unsealed the grating through which he had entered, but it was evident that all the other sewer mouths were barred. He had only succeeded in escaping into a prison.

All was over. Everything that Jean Valjean had done was useless. Exhaustion had ended in failure.

They were both caught in the immense and gloomy web of death, and Jean Valjean felt the terrible spider running along those black strands and quivering in the shadows. He turned his back to the grating, and fell upon the pavement, hurled to earth rather than seated, close to Marius, who still made no movement, and with his head bent between his knees. This was the last drop of anguish.

Of what was he thinking during this profound depression? Neither of himself nor of Marius. He was thinking of Cosette.

# VIII

## The Torn Coat-Tail

In the midst of this prostration, a hand was laid on his shoulder, and a low voice said to him:

"Half shares."

Some person in that gloom? Nothing so closely resembles a dream as despair. Jean Valjean thought that he was dreaming. He had heard no footsteps. Was it possible? He raised his eyes.

A man stood before him.

This man was clad in a blouse; his feet were bare; he held his shoes in his left hand; he had evidently removed them in order to reach Jean Valjean, without allowing his steps to be heard.

Jean Valjean did not hesitate for an instant. Unexpected as was this encounter, this man was known to him. The man was Thénardier.

Although awakened, so to speak, with a start, Jean Valjean, accustomed to alarms, and steeled to unforeseen shocks that must be promptly parried, instantly regained possession of his presence of mind. Moreover, the situation could not be made worse, a certain degree of distress is no longer capable of a crescendo, and Thénardier himself could add nothing to this blackness of this night.

A momentary pause ensued.

Thénardier, raising his right hand to a level with his forehead, formed with it a shade, then he brought his eyelashes together, by screwing up his eyes, a motion which, in connection with a slight contraction of the mouth, characterizes the sagacious attention of a man who is endeavoring to recognize another man. He did not succeed. Jean Valjean, as we have just stated, had his back turned to the light, and he was, moreover, so disfigured, so bemired, so bleeding that he would have been unrecognizable in full noonday. On the contrary, illuminated by the light from the grating, a cellar light, it is true, livid, yet precise in its lividness, Thénardier, as the energetic popular metaphor expresses it, immediately "leaped into" Jean Valjean's eyes. This inequality of conditions sufficed to assure some advantage to Jean Valjean in that mysterious duel which was on the point of beginning between the two situations and the two men. The encounter took place between Jean Valjean veiled and Thénardier unmasked.

Jean Valjean immediately perceived that Thénardier did not recognize him.

They surveyed each other for a moment in that half-gloom, as though taking each other's measure. Thénardier was the first to break the silence.

"How are you going to manage to get out?"

Jean Valjean made no reply. Thénardier continued:

"It's impossible to pick the lock of that gate. But still you must get out of this."

"That is true," said Jean Valjean.

"Well, half shares then."

"What do you mean by that?"

"You have killed that man; that's all right. I have the key."

Thénardier pointed to Marius. He went on:

"I don't know you, but I want to help you. You must be a friend."

Jean Valjean began to comprehend. Thénardier took him for an assassin.

Thénardier resumed:

"Listen, comrade. You didn't kill that man without looking to see what he had in his pockets. Give me my half. I'll open the door for you."

And half drawing from beneath his tattered blouse a huge key, he added:

"Do you want to see how a key to liberty is made? Look here."

Jean Valjean "remained stupid"—the expression belongs to the elder Corneille—to such a degree that he doubted whether what he beheld was real. It was Providence appearing in horrible guise, and his good angel springing from the earth in the form of Thénardier.

Thénardier thrust his fist into a large pocket concealed under his blouse, drew out a rope and offered it to Jean Valjean.

"Hold on," said he, "I'll give you the rope to boot."

"What is the rope for?"

"You will need a stone also, but you can find one outside. There's a heap of rubbish."

"What am I to do with a stone?"

"Idiot, you'll want to sling that stiff into the river, you'll need a stone and a rope, otherwise it would float on the water."

Jean Valjean took the rope. There is no one who does not occasionally accept in this mechanical way.

Thénardier snapped his fingers as though an idea had suddenly occurred to him.

"Ah, see here, comrade, how did you contrive to get out of that slough yonder? I haven't dared to risk myself in it. Phew! you don't smell good."

After a pause he added:

"I'm asking you questions, but you're perfectly right not to answer. It's an apprenticeship against that cursed quarter of an hour before the examining magistrate. And then, when you don't talk at all, you run no risk of talking too loud. That's no matter, as I can't see your face and as I don't know your name, you are wrong in supposing that I don't know who you are and what you want. I twig. You've broken up that gentleman a bit; now you want to tuck him away somewhere. The river, that great hider of folly, is what you want. I'll get you out of your scrape. Helping a good fellow in a pinch is what suits me to a hair."

While expressing his approval of Jean Valjean's silence, he endeavored to force him to talk. He jostled his shoulder in an attempt to catch a sight of his profile, and he exclaimed, without, however, raising his tone:

"Apropos of that quagmire, you're a hearty animal. Why didn't you toss the man in there?"

Jean Valjean preserved silence.

Thénardier resumed, pushing the rag which served him as a cravat to the level of his Adam's apple, a gesture which completes the capable air of a serious man:

"After all, you acted wisely. The workmen, when they come to-morrow to stop up that hole, would certainly have found the stiff abandoned there, and it might have been possible, thread by thread, straw by straw, to pick up the scent and reach you. Some one has passed through the sewer. Who? Where did he get out? Was he seen to come out? The police are full of cleverness. The sewer is treacherous and tells tales of you. Such a find is a rarity, it attracts attention, very few people make use of the sewers for their affairs, while the river belongs to everybody. The river is the true grave. At the end of a month they fish up your man in the nets at Saint-Cloud. Well, what does one care for that? It's carrion! Who killed that man? Paris. And justice makes no inquiries. You have done well."

The more loquacious Thénardier became, the more mute was Jean Valjean.

Again Thénardier shook him by the shoulder.

"Now let's settle this business. Let's go shares. You have seen my key, show me your money."

Thénardier was haggard, fierce, suspicious, rather menacing, yet amicable.

There was one singular circumstance; Thénardier's manners were not simple; he had not the air of being wholly at his ease; while affecting an air of mystery, he spoke low; from time to time he laid his finger on his mouth, and muttered, "hush!" It was difficult to divine why. There was no one there except themselves. Jean Valjean thought that other ruffians might possibly be concealed in some nook, not very far off, and that Thénardier did not care to share with them.

Thénardier resumed:

"Let's settle up. How much did the stiff have in his bags?"

Jean Valjean searched his pockets.

It was his habit, as the reader will remember, to always have some money about him. The mournful life of expedients to which he had been condemned imposed this as a law upon him. On this occasion, however, he had been caught unprepared. When donning his uniform of a National Guardsman on the preceding evening, he had forgotten, dolefully absorbed as he was, to take his pocket-book. He had only some small change in his fob. He turned out his pocket, all soaked with ooze, and spread out on the banquette of the vault one louis d'or, two five-franc pieces, and five or six large sous.

Thénardier thrust out his lower lip with a significant twist of the neck.

"You knocked him over cheap," said he.

He set to feeling the pockets of Jean Valjean and Marius, with the greatest familiarity. Jean Valjean, who was chiefly concerned in keeping his back to the light, let him have his way.

While handling Marius' coat, Thénardier, with the skill of a pickpocket, and without being noticed by Jean Valjean, tore off a strip which he concealed under his blouse, probably thinking that this morsel of stuff might serve, later on, to identify the assassinated man and the assassin. However, he found no more than the thirty francs.

"That's true," said he, "both of you together have no more than that."

And, forgetting his motto: "half shares," he took all.

He hesitated a little over the large sous. After due reflection, he took them also, muttering:

"Never mind! You cut folks' throats too cheap altogether."

That done, he once more drew the big key from under his blouse.

"Now, my friend, you must leave. It's like the fair here, you pay when you go out. You have paid, now clear out."

And he began to laugh.

Had he, in lending to this stranger the aid of his key, and in making some other man than himself emerge from that portal, the pure and disinterested intention of rescuing an assassin? We may be permitted to doubt this.

Thénardier helped Jean Valjean to replace Marius on his shoulders, then he betook himself to the grating on tiptoe, and barefooted, making Jean Valjean a sign to follow him, looked out, laid his finger on his mouth, and remained for several seconds, as though in suspense; his inspection finished, he placed the key in the lock. The bolt slipped back and the gate swung open. It neither grated nor squeaked. It moved very softly.

It was obvious that this gate and those hinges, carefully oiled, were in the habit of opening more frequently than was supposed. This softness was suspicious; it hinted at furtive goings and comings, silent entrances and exits of nocturnal men, and the wolf-like tread of crime.

The sewer was evidently an accomplice of some mysterious band. This taciturn grating was a receiver of stolen goods.

Thénardier opened the gate a little way, allowing just sufficient space for Jean Valjean to pass out, closed the grating again, gave the key a double turn in the lock and plunged back into the darkness, without making any more noise than a breath. He seemed to walk with the velvet paws of a tiger.

A moment later, that hideous providence had retreated into the invisibility.

Jean Valjean found himself in the open air.

# IX

## Marius Produces on Some One Who is a Judge of the Matter, the Effect of Being Dead

He allowed Marius to slide down upon the shore.

They were in the open air!

The miasmas, darkness, horror lay behind him. The pure, healthful, living, joyous air that was easy to breathe inundated him. Everywhere around him reigned silence, but that charming silence when the sun has set in an unclouded azure sky. Twilight had descended; night was drawing on, the great deliverer, the friend of all those who need a mantle of darkness that they may escape from an anguish. The sky presented itself in all directions like an enormous calm. The river flowed to his feet with the sound of a kiss. The aerial dialogue of the nests bidding each other good night in the elms of the Champs-Élysées was audible. A few stars, daintily piercing the pale blue of the zenith, and visible to reverie alone, formed imperceptible little splendors amid the immensity. Evening was unfolding over the head of Jean Valjean all the sweetness of the infinite.

It was that exquisite and undecided hour which says neither yes nor no. Night was already sufficiently advanced to render it possible to lose oneself at a little distance and yet there was sufficient daylight to permit of recognition at close quarters.

For several seconds, Jean Valjean was irresistibly overcome by that august and caressing serenity; such moments of oblivion do come to men; suffering refrains from harassing the unhappy wretch; everything is eclipsed in the thoughts; peace broods over the dreamer like night; and, beneath the twilight which beams and in imitation of the sky which is illuminated, the soul becomes studded with stars. Jean Valjean could not refrain from contemplating that vast, clear shadow which rested over him; thoughtfully he bathed in the sea of ecstasy and prayer in the majestic silence of the eternal heavens. Then he bent down swiftly to Marius, as though the sentiment of duty had returned to him, and, dipping up water in the hollow of his hand, he gently sprinkled a few drops on the latter's face. Marius' eyelids did not open; but his half-open mouth still breathed.

Jean Valjean was on the point of dipping his hand in the river once more, when, all at once, he experienced an indescribable embarrassment, such as a person feels when there is some one behind him whom he does not see.

We have already alluded to this impression, with which everyone is familiar.

He turned round.

Some one was, in fact, behind him, as there had been a short while before.

A man of lofty stature, enveloped in a long coat, with folded arms, and bearing in his right fist a bludgeon of which the leaden head was visible, stood a few paces in the rear of the spot where Jean Valjean was crouching over Marius.

With the aid of the darkness, it seemed a sort of apparition. An ordinary man would have been alarmed because of the twilight, a thoughtful man on account of the bludgeon. Jean Valjean recognized Javert.

The reader has divined, no doubt, that Thénardier's pursuer was no other than Javert. Javert, after his unlooked-for escape from the barricade, had betaken himself to the prefecture of police, had rendered a verbal account to the Prefect in person in a brief audience, had then immediately gone on duty again, which implied—the note, the reader will recollect, which had been captured on his person—a certain surveillance of the shore on the right bank of the Seine near the Champs-Élysées, which had, for some time past, aroused the attention of the police. There he had caught sight of Thénardier and had followed him. The reader knows the rest.

Thus it will be easily understood that that grating, so obligingly opened to Jean Valjean, was a bit of cleverness on Thénardier's part. Thénardier intuitively felt that Javert was still there; the man spied upon has a scent which never deceives him; it was necessary to fling a bone to that sleuth-hound. An assassin, what a godsend! Such an opportunity must never be allowed to slip. Thénardier, by putting Jean Valjean outside in his stead, provided a prey for the police, forced them to relinquish his scent, made them forget him in a bigger adventure, repaid Javert for his waiting, which always flatters a spy, earned thirty francs, and counted with certainty, so far as he himself was concerned, on escaping with the aid of this diversion.

Jean Valjean had fallen from one danger upon another.

These two encounters, this falling one after the other, from Thénardier upon Javert, was a rude shock.

Javert did not recognize Jean Valjean, who, as we have stated, no longer looked like himself. He did not unfold his arms, he made sure of his bludgeon in his fist, by an imperceptible movement, and said in a curt, calm voice:

"Who are you?"

"I."

"Who is 'I'?"

"Jean Valjean."

Javert thrust his bludgeon between his teeth, bent his knees, inclined his body, laid his two powerful hands on the shoulders of Jean Valjean, which were clamped within them as in a couple of vices, scrutinized him, and recognized him. Their faces almost touched. Javert's look was terrible.

Jean Valjean remained inert beneath Javert's grasp, like a lion submitting to the claws of a lynx.

"Inspector Javert," said he, "you have me in your power. Moreover, I have regarded myself as your prisoner ever since this morning. I did not give you my address with any intention of escaping from you. Take me. Only grant me one favor."

Javert did not appear to hear him. He kept his eyes riveted on Jean Valjean. His chin being contracted, thrust his lips upwards towards his nose, a sign of savage reverie. At length he released Jean Valjean, straightened himself stiffly up without bending, grasped his bludgeon again firmly, and, as though in a dream, he murmured rather than uttered this question:

"What are you doing here? And who is this man?"

He still abstained from addressing Jean Valjean as *thou*.

Jean Valjean replied, and the sound of his voice appeared to rouse Javert:

"It is with regard to him that I desire to speak to you. Dispose of me as you see fit; but first help me to carry him home. That is all that I ask of you."

Javert's face contracted as was always the case when any one seemed to think him capable of making a concession. Nevertheless, he did not say "no."

Again he bent over, drew from his pocket a handkerchief which he moistened in the water and with which he then wiped Marius' blood-stained brow.

"This man was at the barricade," said he in a low voice and as though speaking to himself. "He is the one they called Marius."

A spy of the first quality, who had observed everything, listened to everything, and taken in everything, even when he thought that he was to die; who had played the spy even in his agony, and who, with his elbows leaning on the first step of the sepulchre, had taken notes.

He seized Marius' hand and felt his pulse.

"He is wounded," said Jean Valjean.

"He is a dead man," said Javert.

Jean Valjean replied:

"No. Not yet."

"So you have brought him thither from the barricade?" remarked Javert.

His preoccupation must indeed have been very profound for him not to insist on this alarming rescue through the sewer, and for him not to even notice Jean Valjean's silence after his question.

Jean Valjean, on his side, seemed to have but one thought. He resumed:

"He lives in the Marais, Rue des Filles-du-Calvaire, with his grandfather. I do not recollect his name."

Jean Valjean fumbled in Marius' coat, pulled out his pocket-book, opened it at the page which Marius had pencilled, and held it out to Javert.

There was still sufficient light to admit of reading. Besides this, Javert possessed in his eye the feline phosphorescence of night birds. He deciphered the few lines written by Marius, and muttered: "Gillenormand, Rue des Filles-du Calvaire, No. 6."

Then he exclaimed: "Coachman!"

The reader will remember that the hackney-coach was waiting in case of need.

Javert kept Marius' pocket-book.

A moment later, the carriage, which had descended by the inclined plane of the watering-place, was on the shore. Marius was laid upon the back seat, and Javert seated himself on the front seat beside Jean Valjean.

The door slammed, and the carriage drove rapidly away, ascending the quays in the direction of the Bastille.

They quitted the quays and entered the streets. The coachman, a black form on his box, whipped up his thin horses. A glacial silence reigned in the carriage. Marius, motionless, with his body resting in the corner, and his head drooping on his breast, his arms hanging, his legs stiff, seemed to be awaiting only a coffin; Jean Valjean seemed made of shadow, and Javert of stone, and in that vehicle full of night, whose interior, every time that it passed in front of a street lantern, appeared to be turned lividly wan, as by an intermittent flash of lightning, chance had united and seemed to be bringing face to face the three forms of tragic immobility, the corpse, the spectre, and the statue.

# X

## RETURN OF THE SON WHO WAS PRODIGAL OF HIS LIFE

At every jolt over the pavement, a drop of blood trickled from Marius' hair.

Night had fully closed in when the carriage arrived at No. 6, Rue des Filles-du-Calvaire.

Javert was the first to alight; he made sure with one glance of the number on the carriage gate, and, raising the heavy knocker of beaten iron, embellished in the old style, with a male goat and a satyr confronting each other, he gave a violent peal. The gate opened a little way and Javert gave it a push. The porter half made his appearance yawning, vaguely awake, and with a candle in his hand.

Everyone in the house was asleep. People go to bed betimes in the Marais, especially on days when there is a revolt. This good, old quarter, terrified at the Revolution, takes refuge in slumber, as children, when they hear the Bugaboo coming, hide their heads hastily under their coverlet.

In the meantime Jean Valjean and the coachman had taken Marius out of the carriage, Jean Valjean supporting him under the armpits, and the coachman under the knees.

As they thus bore Marius, Jean Valjean slipped his hand under the latter's clothes, which were broadly rent, felt his breast, and assured himself that his heart was still beating. It was even beating a little less feebly, as though the movement of the carriage had brought about a certain fresh access of life.

Javert addressed the porter in a tone befitting the government, and the presence of the porter of a factious person.

"Some person whose name is Gillenormand?"

"Here. What do you want with him?"

"His son is brought back."

"His son?" said the porter stupidly.

"He is dead."

Jean Valjean, who, soiled and tattered, stood behind Javert, and whom the porter was surveying with some horror, made a sign to him with his head that this was not so.

The porter did not appear to understand either Javert's words or Jean Valjean's sign.

Javert continued:

"He went to the barricade, and here he is."

"To the barricade?" ejaculated the porter.

"He has got himself killed. Go waken his father."

The porter did not stir.

"Go along with you!" repeated Javert.

And he added:

"There will be a funeral here to-morrow."

For Javert, the usual incidents of the public highway were categorically classed, which is the beginning of foresight and surveillance, and each contingency had its own compartment; all possible facts were arranged in drawers, as it were, whence they emerged on occasion, in variable quantities; in the street, uproar, revolt, carnival, and funeral.

The porter contented himself with waking Basque. Basque woke Nicolette; Nicolette roused great-aunt Gillenormand.

As for the grandfather, they let him sleep on, thinking that he would hear about the matter early enough in any case.

Marius was carried up to the first floor, without any one in the other parts of the house being aware of the fact, and deposited on an old sofa in M. Gillenormand's antechamber; and while Basque went in search of a physician, and while Nicolette opened the linen-presses, Jean Valjean felt Javert touch him on the shoulder. He understood and descended the stairs, having behind him the step of Javert who was following him.

The porter watched them take their departure as he had watched their arrival, in terrified somnolence.

They entered the carriage once more, and the coachman mounted his box.

"Inspector Javert," said Jean, "grant me yet another favor."

"What is it?" demanded Javert roughly.

"Let me go home for one instant. Then you shall do whatever you like with me."

Javert remained silent for a few moments, with his chin drawn back into the collar of his great-coat, then he lowered the glass and front:

"Driver," said he, "Rue de l'Homme Armé, No. 7."

# XI

## Concussion in the Absolute

They did not open their lips again during the whole space of their ride.

What did Jean Valjean want? To finish what he had begun; to warn Cosette, to tell her where Marius was, to give her, possibly, some other useful information, to take, if he could, certain final measures. As for himself, so far as he was personally concerned, all was over; he had been seized by Javert and had not resisted; any other man than himself in like situation would, perhaps, have had some vague thoughts connected with the rope which Thénardier had given him, and of the bars of the first cell that he should enter; but, let us impress it upon the reader, after the Bishop, there had existed in Jean Valjean a profound hesitation in the presence of any violence, even when directed against himself.

Suicide, that mysterious act of violence against the unknown which may contain, in a measure, the death of the soul, was impossible to Jean Valjean.

At the entrance to the Rue de l'Homme Armé, the carriage halted, the way being too narrow to admit of the entrance of vehicles. Javert and Jean Valjean alighted.

The coachman humbly represented to "monsieur l'Inspecteur," that the Utrecht velvet of his carriage was all spotted with the blood of the assassinated man, and with mire from the assassin. That is the way he understood it. He added that an indemnity was due him. At the same time, drawing his certificate book from his pocket, he begged the inspector to have the goodness to write him "a bit of an attestation."

Javert thrust aside the book which the coachman held out to him, and said:

"How much do you want, including your time of waiting and the drive?"

"It comes to seven hours and a quarter," replied the man, "and my velvet was perfectly new. Eighty francs, Mr. Inspector."

Javert drew four napoleons from his pocket and dismissed the carriage.

Jean Valjean fancied that it was Javert's intention to conduct him on foot to the post of the Blancs-Manteaux or to the post of the Archives, both of which are close at hand.

They entered the street. It was deserted as usual. Javert followed Jean Valjean. They reached No. 7. Jean Valjean knocked. The door opened.

"It is well," said Javert. "Go upstairs."

He added with a strange expression, and as though he were exerting an effort in speaking in this manner:

"I will wait for you here."

Jean Valjean looked at Javert. This mode of procedure was but little in accord with Javert's habits. However, he could not be greatly surprised that Javert should now have a sort of haughty confidence in him, the confidence of the cat which grants the mouse liberty to the length of its claws, seeing that Jean Valjean had made up his mind to surrender himself and to make an end of it. He pushed open the door, entered the house, called to the porter who was in bed and who had pulled the cord from his couch: "It is I!" and ascended the stairs.

On arriving at the first floor, he paused. All sorrowful roads have their stations. The window on the landing-place, which was a sash-window, was open. As in many ancient houses, the staircase got its light from without and had a view on the street. The street-lantern, situated directly opposite, cast some light on the stairs, and thus effected some economy in illumination.

Jean Valjean, either for the sake of getting the air, or mechanically, thrust his head out of this window. He leaned out over the street. It is short, and the lantern lighted it from end to end. Jean Valjean was overwhelmed with amazement; there was no longer any one there.

Javert had taken his departure.

# XII

## The Grandfather

B asque and the porter had carried Marius into the drawing-room, as he still lay stretched out, motionless, on the sofa upon which he had been placed on his arrival. The doctor who had been sent for had hastened thither. Aunt Gillenormand had risen.

Aunt Gillenormand went and came, in affright, wringing her hands and incapable of doing anything but saying: "Heavens! is it possible?" At times she added: "Everything will be covered with blood." When her first horror had passed off, a certain philosophy of the situation penetrated her mind, and took form in the exclamation: "It was bound to end in this way!" She did not go so far as: "I told you so!" which is customary on this sort of occasion. At the physician's orders, a camp bed had been prepared beside the sofa. The doctor examined Marius, and after having found that his pulse was still beating, that the wounded man had no very deep wound on his breast, and that the blood on the corners of his lips proceeded from his nostrils, he had him placed flat on the bed, without a pillow, with his head on the same level as his body, and even a trifle lower, and with his bust bare in order to facilitate respiration. Mademoiselle Gillenormand, on perceiving that they were undressing Marius, withdrew. She set herself to telling her beads in her own chamber.

The trunk had not suffered any internal injury; a bullet, deadened by the pocket-book, had turned aside and made the tour of his ribs with a hideous laceration, which was of no great depth, and consequently, not dangerous. The long, underground journey had completed the dislocation of the broken collar-bone, and the disorder there was serious. The arms had been slashed with sabre cuts. Not a single scar disfigured his face; but his head was fairly covered with cuts; what would be the result of these wounds on the head? Would they stop short at the hairy cuticle, or would they attack the brain? As yet, this could not be decided. A grave symptom was that they had caused a swoon, and that people do not always recover from such swoons. Moreover, the wounded man had been exhausted by hemorrhage. From the waist down, the barricade had protected the lower part of the body from injury.

Basque and Nicolette tore up linen and prepared bandages; Nicolette sewed them, Basque rolled them. As lint was lacking, the doctor, for the time being, arrested the bleeding with layers of wadding. Beside the bed, three candles burned on a table where the case of surgical instruments lay spread out. The doctor bathed Marius' face and hair with cold water. A full pail was reddened in an instant. The porter, candle in hand, lighted them.

The doctor seemed to be pondering sadly. From time to time, he made a negative sign with his head, as though replying to some question which he had inwardly addressed to himself.

A bad sign for the sick man are these mysterious dialogues of the doctor with himself.

At the moment when the doctor was wiping Marius' face, and lightly touching his still closed eyes with his finger, a door opened at the end of the drawing-room, and a long, pallid figure made its appearance.

This was the grandfather.

The revolt had, for the past two days, deeply agitated, enraged and engrossed the mind of M. Gillenormand. He had not been able to sleep on the previous night, and he had been in a fever all day long. In the evening, he had gone to bed very early, recommending that everything in the house should be well barred, and he had fallen into a doze through sheer fatigue.

Old men sleep lightly; M. Gillenormand's chamber adjoined the drawing-room, and in spite of all the precautions that had been taken, the noise had awakened him. Surprised at the rift of light which he saw under his door, he had risen from his bed, and had groped his way thither.

He stood astonished on the threshold, one hand on the handle of the half-open door, with his head bent a little forward and quivering, his body wrapped in a white dressing-gown, which was straight and as destitute of folds as a winding-sheet; and he had the air of a phantom who is gazing into a tomb.

He saw the bed, and on the mattress that young man, bleeding, white with a waxen whiteness, with closed eyes and gaping mouth, and pallid lips, stripped to the waist, slashed all over with crimson wounds, motionless and brilliantly lighted up.

The grandfather trembled from head to foot as powerfully as ossified limbs can tremble, his eyes, whose corneæ were yellow on account of his great age, were veiled in a sort of vitreous glitter, his whole face assumed in an instant the earthy angles of a skull, his arms fell pendent, as though a spring had broken, and his amazement was betrayed by the outspreading of the fingers of his two aged hands, which quivered all over, his knees formed an angle in front, allowing, through the opening in his dressing-gown, a view of his poor bare legs, all bristling with white hairs, and he murmured:

"Marius!"

"Sir," said Basque, "Monsieur has just been brought back. He went to the barricade, and. . ."

"He is dead!" cried the old man in a terrible voice. "Ah! The rascal!"

Then a sort of sepulchral transformation straightened up this centenarian as erect as a young man.

"Sir," said he, "you are the doctor. Begin by telling me one thing. He is dead, is he not?"

The doctor, who was at the highest pitch of anxiety, remained silent.

M. Gillenormand wrung his hands with an outburst of terrible laughter.

"He is dead! He is dead! He is dead! He has got himself killed on the barricades! Out of hatred to me! He did that to spite me! Ah! You blood-drinker! This is the way he returns to me! Misery of my life, he is dead!"

He went to the window, threw it wide open as though he were stifling, and, erect before the darkness, he began to talk into the street, to the night:

"Pierced, sabred, exterminated, slashed, hacked in pieces! Just look at that, the villain! He knew well that I was waiting for him, and that I had had his room arranged, and that I had placed at the head of my bed his portrait taken when he was a little child! He knew well that he had only to come back, and that I had been recalling him for years, and that I remained by my fireside, with my hands on my knees, not knowing what to do, and that I was mad over it! You knew well, that you had but to return and to say: 'It is I,' and you would have been the master of the house, and that I should have obeyed you, and that you could have done whatever you pleased with your old numskull of a grandfather! you knew that well, and you said:

"No, he is a Royalist, I will not go! And you went to the barricades, and you got yourself killed out of malice! To revenge yourself for what I said to you about Monsieur le Duc de Berry. It is infamous! Go to bed then and sleep tranquilly! he is dead, and this is my awakening."

The doctor, who was beginning to be uneasy in both quarters, quitted Marius for a moment, went to M. Gillenormand, and took his arm. The grandfather turned round, gazed at him with eyes which seemed exaggerated in size and bloodshot, and said to him calmly:

"I thank you, sir. I am composed, I am a man, I witnessed the death of Louis XVI, I know how to bear events. One thing is terrible and that is to think that it is your newspapers which do all the mischief. You will have scribblers, chatterers, lawyers, orators, tribunes, discussions, progress, enlightenment, the rights of man, the liberty of the press, and this is the way that your children will be brought home to you. Ah! Marius! It is abominable! Killed! Dead before me! A barricade! Ah, the scamp! Doctor, you live in this quarter, I believe? Oh! I know you well. I see your cabriolet pass my window. I am going to tell you. You are wrong to think that I am angry. One does not fly into a rage against a dead man. That would be stupid. This is a child whom I have reared. I was already old while he was very young. He played in the Tuileries garden with his little shovel and his little chair, and in order that the inspectors might not grumble, I stopped up the holes that he made in the earth with his shovel, with my cane. One day he exclaimed: Down with Louis XVIII! and off he went. It was no fault of mine. He was all rosy and blond. His mother is dead. Have you ever noticed that all little children are blond? Why is it so? He is the son of one of those brigands of the Loire, but children are innocent of their fathers' crimes. I remember when he was no higher than that. He could not manage to pronounce his Ds. He had a way of talking that was so sweet and indistinct that you would have thought it was a bird chirping. I remember that once, in front of the Hercules Farnese, people formed a circle to admire him and marvel at him, he was so handsome, was that child! He had a head such as you see in pictures. I talked in a deep voice, and I frightened him with my cane, but he knew very well that it was only to make him laugh. In the morning, when he entered my room, I grumbled, but he was like the sunlight to me, all the same. One cannot defend oneself against those brats. They take hold of you, they hold you fast, they never let you go again. The truth is, that there never was a cupid like that child. Now, what can you say for your Lafayettes, your Benjamin Constants, and your Tirecuir de Corcelles who have killed him? This cannot be allowed to pass in this fashion."

He approached Marius, who still lay livid and motionless, and to whom the physician had returned, and began once more to wring his hands. The old man's pallid lips moved as though mechanically, and permitted the passage of words that were barely audible, like breaths in the death agony:

"Ah! heartless lad! Ah! clubbist! Ah! wretch! Ah! Septembrist!"

Reproaches in the low voice of an agonizing man, addressed to a corpse.

Little by little, as it is always indispensable that internal eruptions should come to the light, the sequence of words returned, but the grandfather appeared no longer to have the strength to utter them, his voice was so weak, and extinct, that it seemed to come from the other side of an abyss:

"It is all the same to me, I am going to die too, that I am. And to think that there is not a hussy in Paris who would not have been delighted to make this wretch happy! A scamp who, instead of amusing himself and enjoying life, went off to fight and get himself shot down like a brute! And for whom? Why? For the Republic! Instead of going to dance at the Chaumière, as it is the duty of young folks to do! What's the use of being twenty years old? The Republic, a cursed pretty folly! Poor mothers, beget fine boys, do! Come, he is dead. That will make two funerals under the same carriage gate. So you have got yourself arranged like this for the sake of General Lamarque's handsome eyes! What had that General Lamarque done to you? A slasher! A chatter-box! To get oneself killed for a dead man! If that isn't enough to drive any one mad! Just think of it! At twenty! And without so much as turning his head to see whether he was not leaving something behind him! That's the way poor, good old fellows are forced to die alone, nowadays. Perish in your corner, owl! Well, after all, so much the better, that is what I was hoping for, this will kill me on the spot. I am too old, I am a hundred years old, I am a hundred thousand years old, I ought, by rights, to have been dead long ago. This blow puts an end to it. So all is over, what happiness! What is the good of making him inhale ammonia and all that parcel of drugs? You are wasting your trouble, you fool of a doctor! Come, he's dead, completely dead. I know all about it, I am dead myself too. He hasn't done things by half. Yes, this age is infamous, infamous and that's what I think of you, of your ideas, of your systems, of your masters, of your oracles, of your doctors, of your scape-graces of writers, of your rascally philosophers, and of all the revolutions which, for the last sixty years, have been frightening the flocks of crows in the Tuileries! But you were pitiless in getting yourself killed like this, I shall not even grieve over your death, do you understand, you assassin?"

At that moment, Marius slowly opened his eyes, and his glance, still dimmed by lethargic wonder, rested on M. Gillenormand.

"Marius!" cried the old man. "Marius! My little Marius! my child! my well-beloved son! You open your eyes, you gaze upon me, you are alive, thanks!"

And he fell fainting.

BOOK FOURTH
JAVERT DERAILED

# I

Javert passed slowly down the Rue de l'Homme Armé.

He walked with drooping head for the first time in his life, and likewise, for the first time in his life, with his hands behind his back.

Up to that day, Javert had borrowed from Napoleon's attitudes, only that which is expressive of resolution, with arms folded across the chest; that which is expressive of uncertainty—with the hands behind the back—had been unknown to him. Now, a change had taken place; his whole person, slow and sombre, was stamped with anxiety.

He plunged into the silent streets.

Nevertheless, he followed one given direction.

He took the shortest cut to the Seine, reached the Quai des Ormes, skirted the quay, passed the Grève, and halted at some distance from the post of the Place du Châtelet, at the angle of the Pont Notre-Dame. There, between the Notre-Dame and the Pont au Change on the one hand, and the Quai de la Mégisserie and the Quai aux Fleurs on the other, the Seine forms a sort of square lake, traversed by a rapid.

This point of the Seine is dreaded by mariners. Nothing is more dangerous than this rapid, hemmed in, at that epoch, and irritated by the piles of the mill on the bridge, now demolished. The two bridges, situated thus close together, augment the peril; the water hurries in formidable wise through the arches. It rolls in vast and terrible waves; it accumulates and piles up there; the flood attacks the piles of the bridges as though in an effort to pluck them up with great liquid ropes. Men who fall in there never reappear; the best of swimmers are drowned there.

Javert leaned both elbows on the parapet, his chin resting in both hands, and, while his nails were mechanically twined in the abundance of his whiskers, he meditated.

A novelty, a revolution, a catastrophe had just taken place in the depths of his being; and he had something upon which to examine himself.

Javert was undergoing horrible suffering.

For several hours, Javert had ceased to be simple. He was troubled; that brain, so limpid in its blindness, had lost its transparency; that crystal was clouded. Javert felt duty divided within his conscience, and he could not conceal the fact from himself. When he had so unexpectedly encountered Jean Valjean on the banks of the Seine, there had been in him something of the wolf which regains his grip on his prey, and of the dog who finds his master again.

He beheld before him two paths, both equally straight, but he beheld two; and that terrified him; him, who had never in all his life known more than one straight line. And, the poignant anguish lay in this, that the two paths were contrary to each other. One of these straight lines excluded the other. Which of the two was the true one?

His situation was indescribable.

To owe his life to a malefactor, to accept that debt and to repay it; to be, in spite of himself, on a level with a fugitive from justice, and to repay his service with another service; to allow it to be said to him, "Go," and to say to the latter in his turn: "Be free"; to sacrifice to personal motives duty, that general obligation, and to be conscious, in those personal motives, of something that was also general, and, perchance, superior, to betray society in order to remain true to his conscience; that all these absurdities should be realized and should accumulate upon him,—this was what overwhelmed him.

One thing had amazed him,—this was that Jean Valjean should have done him a favor, and one thing petrified him,—that he, Javert, should have done Jean Valjean a favor.

Where did he stand? He sought to comprehend his position, and could no longer find his bearings.

What was he to do now? To deliver up Jean Valjean was bad; to leave Jean Valjean at liberty was bad. In the first case, the man of authority fell lower than the man of the galleys, in the second, a convict rose above the law, and set his foot upon it. In both cases, dishonor for him, Javert. There was disgrace in any resolution at which he might arrive. Destiny has some extremities which rise perpendicularly from the impossible, and beyond which life is no longer anything but a precipice. Javert had reached one of those extremities.

One of his anxieties consisted in being constrained to think. The very violence of all these conflicting emotions forced him to it. Thought was something to which he was unused, and which was peculiarly painful.

In thought there always exists a certain amount of internal rebellion; and it irritated him to have that within him.

Thought on any subject whatever, outside of the restricted circle of his functions, would have been for him in any case useless and a fatigue; thought on the day which had just passed was a torture. Nevertheless, it was indispensable that he should take a look into his conscience, after such shocks, and render to himself an account of himself.

What he had just done made him shudder. He, Javert, had seen fit to decide, contrary to all the regulations of the police, contrary to the whole social and judicial organization, contrary to the entire code, upon a release; this had suited him; he had substituted his own affairs for the affairs of the public; was not this unjustifiable? Every time that he brought himself face to face with this deed without a name which he had committed, he trembled from head to foot. Upon what should he decide? One sole resource remained to him; to return in all haste to the Rue de l'Homme Armé, and commit Jean Valjean to prison. It was clear that that was what he ought to do. He could not.

Something barred his way in that direction.

Something? What? Is there in the world, anything outside of the tribunals, executory sentences, the police and the authorities? Javert was overwhelmed.

A galley-slave sacred! A convict who could not be touched by the law! And that the deed of Javert!

Was it not a fearful thing that Javert and Jean Valjean, the man made to proceed with vigor, the man made to submit,—that these two men who were both the things of the law, should have come to such a pass, that both of them had set themselves above the law? What then! such enormities were to happen and no one was to be punished! Jean Valjean, stronger than the whole social order, was to remain at liberty, and he, Javert, was to go on eating the government's bread!

His reverie gradually became terrible.

He might, athwart this reverie, have also reproached himself on the subject of that insurgent who had been taken to the Rue des Filles-du-Calvaire; but he never even thought of that. The lesser fault was lost in the greater. Besides, that insurgent was, obviously, a dead man, and, legally, death puts an end to pursuit.

Jean Valjean was the load which weighed upon his spirit.

Jean Valjean disconcerted him. All the axioms which had served him as points of support all his life long, had crumbled away in the presence of this man. Jean Valjean's generosity towards him, Javert, crushed him. Other facts which he now recalled, and which he had formerly treated as lies and folly, now recurred to him as realities. M. Madeleine reappeared behind Jean Valjean, and the two figures were superposed in such fashion that they now formed but one, which was venerable.

Javert felt that something terrible was penetrating his soul—admiration for a convict. Respect for a galley-slave—is that a possible thing? He shuddered at it, yet could not escape from it. In vain did he struggle, he was reduced to confess, in his inmost heart, the sublimity of that wretch. This was odious.

A benevolent malefactor, merciful, gentle, helpful, clement, a convict, returning good for evil, giving back pardon for hatred, preferring pity to vengeance, preferring to ruin himself rather than to ruin his enemy, saving him who had smitten him, kneeling on the heights of virtue, more nearly akin to an angel than to a man. Javert was constrained to admit to himself that this monster existed.

Things could not go on in this manner.

Certainly, and we insist upon this point, he had not yielded without resistance to that monster, to that infamous angel, to that hideous hero, who enraged almost as much as he amazed him. Twenty times, as he sat in that carriage face to face with Jean Valjean, the legal tiger had roared within him. A score of times he had been tempted to fling himself upon Jean Valjean, to seize him and devour him, that is to say, to arrest him. What more simple, in fact? To cry out at the first post that they passed:—"Here is a fugitive from justice, who has broken his ban!" to summon the gendarmes and say to them: "This man is yours!" then to go off, leaving that condemned man there, to ignore the rest and not to meddle further in the matter. This man is forever a prisoner of the law; the law may do with him what it will. What could be more just? Javert had said all this to himself; he had wished to pass beyond, to act, to apprehend the man, and then, as at present, he had not been able to do it; and every time that his arm had been raised convulsively towards Jean Valjean's collar, his hand had fallen back again, as beneath an enormous weight, and in the depths of his thought he had heard a voice, a strange voice crying to him:—"It is well. Deliver up your savior. Then have the basin of Pontius Pilate brought and wash your claws."

Then his reflections reverted to himself and beside Jean Valjean glorified he beheld himself, Javert, degraded.

A convict was his benefactor!

But then, why had he permitted that man to leave him alive? He had the right to be killed in that barricade. He should have asserted that right. It would have been better to summon the other insurgents to his succor against Jean Valjean, to get himself shot by force.

His supreme anguish was the loss of certainty. He felt that he had been uprooted. The code was no longer anything more than a stump in his hand. He had to deal with scruples of an unknown species. There had taken place within him a sentimental revelation entirely distinct from legal affirmation, his only standard of measurement hitherto. To remain in his former uprightness did not suffice. A whole order of unexpected facts had cropped up and subjugated him. A whole new world was dawning on his soul: kindness accepted and repaid, devotion, mercy, indulgence, violences committed by pity on austerity, respect for persons, no more definitive condemnation, no more conviction, the possibility of a tear in the eye of the law, no one knows what justice according to God, running in inverse sense to justice according to men. He perceived amid the shadows the terrible rising of an unknown moral sun; it horrified and dazzled him. An owl forced to the gaze of an eagle.

He said to himself that it was true that there were exceptional cases, that authority might be put out of countenance, that the rule might be inadequate in the presence of a fact, that everything could not be framed within the text of the code, that the unforeseen compelled obedience, that the virtue of a convict might set a snare for the virtue of the functionary, that destiny did indulge in such ambushes, and he reflected with despair that he himself had not even been fortified against a surprise.

He was forced to acknowledge that goodness did exist. This convict had been good. And he himself, unprecedented circumstance, had just been good also. So he was becoming depraved.

He found that he was a coward. He conceived a horror of himself.

Javert's ideal, was not to be human, to be grand, to be sublime; it was to be irreproachable.

Now, he had just failed in this.

How had he come to such a pass? How had all this happened? He could not have told himself. He clasped his head in both hands, but in spite of all that he could do, he could not contrive to explain it to himself.

He had certainly always entertained the intention of restoring Jean Valjean to the law of which Jean Valjean was the captive, and of which he, Javert, was the slave. Not for a single instant while he held him in his grasp had he confessed to himself that he entertained the idea of releasing him. It was, in some sort, without his consciousness, that his hand had relaxed and had let him go free.

All sorts of interrogation points flashed before his eyes. He put questions to himself, and made replies to himself, and his replies frightened him. He asked himself: "What has that convict done, that desperate fellow, whom I have pursued even to persecution, and who has had me under his foot, and who could have avenged himself, and who owed it both to his rancor and to his safety, in leaving me my life, in showing mercy upon me? His duty? No. Something more. And I in showing mercy upon him in my turn—what have I done? My duty? No. Something more. So there is something beyond duty?" Here he took fright; his balance became disjointed; one of the scales fell into the abyss, the other rose heavenward, and Javert was no less terrified by the one which was on high than by the one which was below. Without being in the least in the world what is called Voltairian or a philosopher, or incredulous, being, on the contrary, respectful by instinct, towards the established church, he knew it only as an august fragment of the social whole; order was his dogma, and sufficed for him; ever since he had attained to man's estate and the rank of a functionary, he had centred nearly all his religion in the police. Being,—and here we employ words without the least irony and in their most serious acceptation, being, as we have said, a spy as other men are priests. He had a superior, M. Gisquet; up to that day he had never dreamed of that other superior, God.

This new chief, God, he became unexpectedly conscious of, and he felt embarrassed by him. This unforeseen presence threw him off his bearings; he did not know what to do with this superior, he, who was not ignorant of the fact that the subordinate is bound always to bow, that he must not disobey, nor find fault, nor discuss, and that, in the presence of a superior who amazes him too greatly, the inferior has no other resource than that of handing in his resignation.

But how was he to set about handing in his resignation to God?

However things might stand,—and it was to this point that he reverted constantly,—one fact dominated everything else for him, and that was, that he had just committed a terrible infraction of the law. He had just shut his eyes on an escaped convict who had broken his ban. He had just set a galley-slave at large. He had just robbed the laws of a man who belonged to them. That was what he had done. He no longer understood himself. The very reasons for his action escaped him; only their vertigo was left with him. Up to that moment he had lived with that blind faith which gloomy probity engenders. This faith had quitted him, this probity had deserted him. All that he had believed in melted away. Truths which he did not wish to recognize were besieging him, inexorably. Henceforth, he must be a different man. He was suffering from the strange pains of a conscience abruptly operated on for the cataract. He saw that which it was repugnant to him to behold. He felt himself emptied, useless, put out of joint with his past life, turned out, dissolved. Authority was dead within him. He had no longer any reason for existing.

A terrible situation! to be touched.

To be granite and to doubt! to be the statue of Chastisement cast in one piece in the mould of the law, and suddenly to become aware of the fact that one cherishes beneath one's breast of bronze something absurd and disobedient which almost resembles a heart! To come to the pass of returning good for good, although one has said to oneself up to that day that that good is evil! to be the watch-dog, and to lick the intruder's hand! to be ice and melt! to be the pincers and to turn into a hand! to suddenly feel one's fingers opening! to relax one's grip,—what a terrible thing!

The man-projectile no longer acquainted with his route and retreating!

To be obliged to confess this to oneself: infallibility is not infallible, there may exist error in the dogma, all has not been said when a code speaks, society is not perfect, authority is complicated with vacillation, a crack is possible in the immutable, judges are but men, the law may err, tribunals may make a mistake! to behold a rift in the immense blue pane of the firmament!

That which was passing in Javert was the Fampoux of a rectilinear conscience, the derailment of a soul, the crushing of a probity which had been irresistibly launched in a straight line and was breaking against God. It certainly was singular that the stoker of order, that the engineer of authority, mounted on the blind iron horse with its rigid road, could be unseated by a flash of light! that the immovable, the direct, the correct, the geometrical, the passive, the perfect, could bend! that there should exist for the locomotive a road to Damascus!

God, always within man, and refractory, He, the true conscience, to the false; a prohibition to the spark to die out; an order to the ray to remember the sun; an injunction to the soul to recognize the veritable absolute when confronted with the fictitious absolute, humanity which cannot be lost; the human heart indestructible; that splendid phenomenon, the finest, perhaps, of all our interior marvels, did

Javert understand this? Did Javert penetrate it? Did Javert account for it to himself? Evidently he did not. But beneath the pressure of that incontestable incomprehensibility he felt his brain bursting.

He was less the man transfigured than the victim of this prodigy. In all this he perceived only the tremendous difficulty of existence. It seemed to him that, henceforth, his respiration was repressed forever. He was not accustomed to having something unknown hanging over his head.

Up to this point, everything above him had been, to his gaze, merely a smooth, limpid and simple surface; there was nothing incomprehensible, nothing obscure; nothing that was not defined, regularly disposed, linked, precise, circumscribed, exact, limited, closed, fully provided for; authority was a plane surface; there was no fall in it, no dizziness in its presence. Javert had never beheld the unknown except from below. The irregular, the unforeseen, the disordered opening of chaos, the possible slip over a precipice—this was the work of the lower regions, of rebels, of the wicked, of wretches. Now Javert threw himself back, and he was suddenly terrified by this unprecedented apparition: a gulf on high.

What! one was dismantled from top to bottom! one was disconcerted, absolutely! In what could one trust! That which had been agreed upon was giving way! What! the defect in society's armor could be discovered by a magnanimous wretch! What! an honest servitor of the law could suddenly find himself caught between two crimes—the crime of allowing a man to escape and the crime of arresting him! everything was not settled in the orders given by the State to the functionary! There might be blind alleys in duty! What,—all this was real! was it true that an ex-ruffian, weighed down with convictions, could rise erect and end by being in the right? Was this credible? were there cases in which the law should retire before transfigured crime, and stammer its excuses?— Yes, that was the state of the case! and Javert saw it! and Javert had touched it! and not only could he not deny it, but he had taken part in it. These were realities. It was abominable that actual facts could reach such deformity. If facts did their duty, they would confine themselves to being proofs of the law; facts—it is God who sends them. Was anarchy, then, on the point of now descending from on high?

Thus,—and in the exaggeration of anguish, and the optical illusion of consternation, all that might have corrected and restrained this impression was effaced, and society, and the human race, and the universe were, henceforth, summed up in his eyes, in one simple and terrible feature,—thus the penal laws, the thing judged, the force due to legislation, the decrees of the sovereign courts, the magistracy, the government, prevention, repression, official cruelty, wisdom, legal infallibility, the principle of authority, all the dogmas on which rest political and civil security, sovereignty, justice, public truth, all this was rubbish, a shapeless mass, chaos; he himself, Javert, the spy of order, incorruptibility in the service of the police, the bull-dog providence of society, vanquished and hurled to earth; and, erect, at the summit of all that ruin, a man with a green cap on his head and a halo round his brow; this was the astounding confusion to which he had come; this was the fearful vision which he bore within his soul.

Was this to be endured? No.

A violent state, if ever such existed. There were only two ways of escaping from it. One was to go resolutely to Jean Valjean, and restore to his cell the convict from the galleys. The other. . .

Javert quitted the parapet, and, with head erect this time, betook himself, with a firm tread, towards the station-house indicated by a lantern at one of the corners of the Place du Châtelet.

On arriving there, he saw through the window a sergeant of police, and he entered. Policemen recognize each other by the very way in which they open the door of a station-house. Javert mentioned his name, showed his card to the sergeant, and seated himself at the table of the post on which a candle was burning. On a table lay a pen, a leaden inkstand and paper, provided in the event of possible reports and the orders of the night patrols. This table, still completed by its straw-seated chair, is an institution; it exists in all police stations; it is invariably ornamented with a box-wood saucer filled with sawdust and a wafer box of cardboard filled with red wafers, and it forms the lowest stage of official style. It is there that the literature of the State has its beginning.

Javert took a pen and a sheet of paper, and began to write. This is what he wrote:

A Few Observations for the Good of the Service

"In the first place: I beg Monsieur le Préfet to cast his eyes on this.

"Secondly: prisoners, on arriving after examination, take off their shoes and stand barefoot on the flagstones while they are being searched. Many of them cough on their return to prison. This entails hospital expenses.

"Thirdly: the mode of keeping track of a man with relays of police agents from distance to distance, is good, but, on important occasions, it is requisite that at least two agents should never lose sight of each other, so that, in case one agent should, for any cause, grow weak in his service, the other may supervise him and take his place.

"Fourthly: it is inexplicable why the special regulation of the prison of the Madelonettes interdicts the prisoner from having a chair, even by paying for it.

"Fifthly: in the Madelonettes there are only two bars to the canteen, so that the canteen woman can touch the prisoners with her hand.

"Sixthly: the prisoners called barkers, who summon the other prisoners to the parlor, force the prisoner to pay them two sous to call his name distinctly. This is a theft.

"Seventhly: for a broken thread ten sous are withheld in the weaving shop; this is an abuse of the contractor, since the cloth is none the worse for it.

"Eighthly: it is annoying for visitors to La Force to be obliged to traverse the boys' court in order to reach the parlor of Sainte-Marie-l'Égyptienne.

"Ninthly: it is a fact that any day gendarmes can be overheard relating in the court-yard of the prefecture the interrogations put by the magistrates to prisoners. For a gendarme, who should be sworn to secrecy, to repeat what he has heard in the examination room is a grave disorder.

"Tenthly: Mme. Henry is an honest woman; her canteen is very neat; but it is bad to have a woman keep the wicket to the mouse-trap of the secret cells. This is unworthy of the Conciergerie of a great civilization."

Javert wrote these lines in his calmest and most correct chirography, not omitting a single comma, and making the paper screech under his pen. Below the last line he signed:

JAVERT,
Inspector of the 1st class.
The Post of the Place du Châtelet.
June 7th, 1832, about one o'clock in the morning.

Javert dried the fresh ink on the paper, folded it like a letter, sealed it, wrote on the back: *Note for the administration*, left it on the table, and quitted the post. The glazed and grated door fell to behind him.

Again he traversed the Place du Châtelet diagonally, regained the quay, and returned with automatic precision to the very point which he had abandoned a quarter of an hour previously, leaned on his elbows and found himself again in the same attitude on the same paving-stone of the parapet. He did not appear to have stirred.

The darkness was complete. It was the sepulchral moment which follows midnight. A ceiling of clouds concealed the stars. Not a single light burned in the houses of the city; no one was passing; all of the streets and quays which could be seen were deserted; Notre-Dame and the towers of the Court-House seemed features of the night. A street lantern reddened the margin of the quay. The outlines of the bridges lay shapeless in the mist one behind the other. Recent rains had swollen the river.

The spot where Javert was leaning was, it will be remembered, situated precisely over the rapids of the Seine, perpendicularly above that formidable spiral of whirlpools which loose and knot themselves again like an endless screw.

Javert bent his head and gazed. All was black. Nothing was to be distinguished. A sound of foam was audible; but the river could not be seen. At moments, in that dizzy depth, a gleam of light appeared, and undulated vaguely, water possessing the power of taking light, no one knows whence, and converting it into a snake. The light vanished, and all became indistinct once more. Immensity seemed thrown open there. What lay below was not water, it was a gulf. The wall of the quay, abrupt, confused, mingled with the vapors, instantly concealed from sight, produced the effect of an escarpment of the infinite. Nothing was to be seen, but the hostile chill of the water and the stale odor of the wet stones could be felt. A fierce breath rose from this abyss. The flood in the river, divined rather than perceived, the tragic whispering of the waves, the melancholy vastness of the arches of the bridge, the imaginable fall into that gloomy void, into all that shadow was full of horror.

Javert remained motionless for several minutes, gazing at this opening of shadow; he considered the invisible with a fixity that resembled attention. The water roared. All at once he took off his hat and placed it on the edge of the quay. A moment later, a tall black figure, which a belated passer-by in the distance might have taken for a phantom, appeared erect upon the parapet of the quay, bent over towards the Seine, then drew itself up again, and fell straight down into the shadows; a dull splash followed; and the shadow alone was in the secret of the convulsions of that obscure form which had disappeared beneath the water.

BOOK FIFTH
GRANDSON AND GRANDFATHER

# I

## In Which the Tree with the Zinc Plaster Appears Again

Some time after the events which we have just recorded, Sieur Boulatruelle experienced a lively emotion.

Sieur Boulatruelle was that road-mender of Montfermeil whom the reader has already seen in the gloomy parts of this book.

Boulatruelle, as the reader may, perchance, recall, was a man who was occupied with divers and troublesome matters. He broke stones and damaged travellers on the highway.

Road-mender and thief as he was, he cherished one dream; he believed in the treasures buried in the forest of Montfermeil. He hoped some day to find the money in the earth at the foot of a tree; in the meanwhile, he lived to search the pockets of passers-by.

Nevertheless, for an instant, he was prudent. He had just escaped neatly. He had been, as the reader is aware, picked up in Jondrette's garret in company with the other ruffians. Utility of a vice: his drunkenness had been his salvation. The authorities had never been able to make out whether he had been there in the quality of a robber or a man who had been robbed. An order of *nolle prosequi*, founded on his well authenticated state of intoxication on the evening of the ambush, had set him at liberty. He had taken to his heels. He had returned to his road from Gagny to Lagny, to make, under administrative supervision, broken stone for the good of the state, with downcast mien, in a very pensive mood, his ardor for theft somewhat cooled; but he was addicted nonetheless tenderly to the wine which had recently saved him.

As for the lively emotion which he had experienced a short time after his return to his road-mender's turf-thatched cot, here it is:

One morning, Boulatruelle, while on his way as was his wont, to his work, and possibly also to his ambush, a little before daybreak caught sight, through the branches of the trees, of a man, whose back alone he saw, but the shape of whose shoulders, as it seemed to him at that distance and in the early dusk, was not entirely unfamiliar to him. Boulatruelle, although intoxicated, had a correct and lucid memory, a defensive arm that is indispensable to any one who is at all in conflict with legal order.

"Where the deuce have I seen something like that man yonder?" he said to himself. But he could make himself no answer, except that the man resembled some one of whom his memory preserved a confused trace.

However, apart from the identity which he could not manage to catch, Boulatruelle put things together and made calculations. This man did not belong in the country-side. He had just arrived there. On foot, evidently. No public conveyance passes through Montfermeil at that hour. He had walked all night. Whence came he? Not from a very great distance; for he had neither haversack, nor bundle. From Paris, no doubt. Why was he in these woods? why was he there at such an hour? what had he come there for?

Boulatruelle thought of the treasure. By dint of ransacking his memory, he recalled in a vague way that he had already, many years before, had a similar alarm in connection with a man who produced on him the effect that he might well be this very individual.

"By the deuce," said Boulatruelle, "I'll find him again. I'll discover the parish of that parishioner. This prowler of Patron-Minette has a reason, and I'll know it. People can't have secrets in my forest if I don't have a finger in the pie."

He took his pick-axe which was very sharply pointed.

"There now," he grumbled, "is something that will search the earth and a man."

And, as one knots one thread to another thread, he took up the line of march at his best pace in the direction which the man must follow, and set out across the thickets.

When he had compassed a hundred strides, the day, which was already beginning to break, came to his assistance. Footprints stamped in the sand, weeds trodden down here and there, heather crushed, young branches in the brushwood bent and in the act of straightening themselves up again with the graceful deliberation of the arms of a pretty woman who stretches herself when she wakes, pointed out to him a sort of track. He followed it, then lost it. Time was flying. He plunged deeper into the woods and came to a sort of eminence. An early huntsman who was passing in the distance along a path, whistling the air of Guillery, suggested to him the idea of climbing a tree. Old as he was, he was agile. There stood close at hand a beech-tree of great

VICTOR HUGO

size, worthy of Tityrus and of Boulatruelle. Boulatruelle ascended the beech as high as he was able.

The idea was a good one. On scrutinizing the solitary waste on the side where the forest is thoroughly entangled and wild, Boulatruelle suddenly caught sight of his man.

Hardly had he got his eye upon him when he lost sight of him.

The man entered, or rather, glided into, an open glade, at a considerable distance, masked by large trees, but with which Boulatruelle was perfectly familiar, on account of having noticed, near a large pile of porous stones, an ailing chestnut-tree bandaged with a sheet of zinc nailed directly upon the bark. This glade was the one which was formerly called the Blaru-bottom. The heap of stones, destined for no one knows what employment, which was visible there thirty years ago, is doubtless still there. Nothing equals a heap of stones in longevity, unless it is a board fence. They are temporary expedients. What a reason for lasting!

Boulatruelle, with the rapidity of joy, dropped rather than descended from the tree. The lair was unearthed, the question now was to seize the beast. That famous treasure of his dreams was probably there.

It was no small matter to reach that glade. By the beaten paths, which indulge in a thousand teasing zigzags, it required a good quarter of an hour. In a bee-line, through the underbrush, which is peculiarly dense, very thorny, and very aggressive in that locality, a full half hour was necessary. Boulatruelle committed the error of not comprehending this. He believed in the straight line; a respectable optical illusion which ruins many a man. The thicket, bristling as it was, struck him as the best road.

"Let's take to the wolves' Rue de Rivoli," said he.

Boulatruelle, accustomed to taking crooked courses, was on this occasion guilty of the fault of going straight.

He flung himself resolutely into the tangle of undergrowth.

He had to deal with holly bushes, nettles, hawthorns, eglantines, thistles, and very irascible brambles. He was much lacerated.

At the bottom of the ravine he found water which he was obliged to traverse.

At last he reached the Blaru-bottom, after the lapse of forty minutes, sweating, soaked, breathless, scratched, and ferocious.

There was no one in the glade. Boulatruelle rushed to the heap of stones. It was in its place. It had not been carried off.

As for the man, he had vanished in the forest. He had made his escape. Where? in what direction? into what thicket? Impossible to guess.

And, heartrending to say, there, behind the pile of stones, in front of the tree with the sheet of zinc, was freshly turned earth, a pick-axe, abandoned or forgotten, and a hole.

The hole was empty.

"Thief!" shrieked Boulatruelle, shaking his fist at the horizon.

# II

## Marius, Emerging from Civil War, Makes Ready for Domestic War

For a long time, Marius was neither dead nor alive. For many weeks he lay in a fever accompanied by delirium, and by tolerably grave cerebral symptoms, caused more by the shocks of the wounds on the head than by the wounds themselves.

He repeated Cosette's name for whole nights in the melancholy loquacity of fever, and with the sombre obstinacy of agony. The extent of some of the lesions presented a serious danger, the suppuration of large wounds being always liable to become re-absorbed, and consequently, to kill the sick man, under certain atmospheric conditions; at every change of weather, at the slightest storm, the physician was uneasy.

"Above all things," he repeated, "let the wounded man be subjected to no emotion." The dressing of the wounds was complicated and difficult, the fixation of apparatus and bandages by cerecloths not having been invented as yet, at that epoch. Nicolette used up a sheet "as big as the ceiling," as she put it, for lint. It was not without difficulty that the chloruretted lotions and the nitrate of silver overcame the gangrene. As long as there was any danger, M. Gillenormand, seated in despair at his grandson's pillow, was, like Marius, neither alive nor dead.

Every day, sometimes twice a day, a very well dressed gentleman with white hair,—such was the description given by the porter,—came to inquire about the wounded man, and left a large package of lint for the dressings.

Finally, on the 7th of September, four months to a day, after the sorrowful night when he had been brought back to his grandfather in a dying condition, the doctor declared that he would answer for Marius. Convalescence began. But Marius was forced to remain for two months more stretched out on a long chair, on account of the results called up by the fracture of his collar-bone. There always is a last wound like that which will not close, and which prolongs the dressings indefinitely, to the great annoyance of the sick person.

However, this long illness and this long convalescence saved him from all pursuit. In France, there is no wrath, not even of a public character, which six months will not extinguish. Revolts, in the present state of society, are so much the fault of every one, that they are followed by a certain necessity of shutting the eyes.

Let us add, that the inexcusable Gisquet order, which enjoined doctors to lodge information against the wounded, having outraged public opinion, and not opinion alone, but the King first of all, the wounded were covered and protected by this indignation; and, with the exception of those who had been made prisoners in the very act of combat, the councils of war did not dare to trouble any one. So Marius was left in peace.

M. Gillenormand first passed through all manner of anguish, and then through every form of ecstasy. It was found difficult to prevent his passing every night beside the wounded man; he had his big armchair carried to Marius' bedside; he required his daughter to take the finest linen in the house for compresses and bandages. Mademoiselle Gillenormand, like a sage and elderly person, contrived to spare the fine linen, while allowing the grandfather to think that he was obeyed. M. Gillenormand would not permit any one to explain to him, that for the preparation of lint batiste is not nearly so good as coarse linen, nor new linen as old linen. He was present at all the dressings of the wounds from which Mademoiselle Gillenormand modestly absented herself. When the dead flesh was cut away with scissors, he said: "Aïe! aïe!" Nothing was more touching than to see him with his gentle, senile palsy, offer the wounded man a cup of his cooling-draught. He overwhelmed the doctor with questions. He did not observe that he asked the same ones over and over again.

On the day when the doctor announced to him that Marius was out of danger, the good man was in a delirium. He made his porter a present of three louis. That evening, on his return to his own chamber, he danced a gavotte, using his thumb and forefinger as castanets, and he sang the following song:

> *"Jeanne est née à Fougère*
> *Vrai nid d'une bergère;*
> *J'adore son jupon,*
> *Fripon.*

> *"Amour, tu vis en elle;*
> *Car c'est dans sa prunelle*
> *Que tu mets ton carquois.*
> *Narquois!*

> *"Moi, je la chante, et j'aime,*
> *Plus que Diane même,*
> *Jeanne et ses durs tetons*
> *Bretons."*

Then he knelt upon a chair, and Basque, who was watching him through the half-open door, made sure that he was praying.

Up to that time, he had not believed in God.

At each succeeding phase of improvement, which became more and more pronounced, the grandfather raved. He executed a multitude of mechanical actions full of joy; he ascended and descended the stairs, without knowing why. A pretty female neighbor was amazed one morning at receiving a big bouquet; it was M. Gillenormand who had sent it to her. The husband made a jealous scene. M. Gillenormand tried to draw Nicolette upon his knees. He called Marius, "M. le Baron." He shouted: "Long live the Republic!"

Every moment, he kept asking the doctor: "Is he no longer in danger?" He gazed upon Marius with the eyes of a grandmother. He brooded over him while he ate. He no longer knew himself, he no longer rendered himself an account of himself. Marius was the master of the house, there was abdication in his joy, he was the grandson of his grandson.

In the state of joy in which he then was, he was the most venerable of children. In his fear lest he might fatigue or annoy the convalescent, he stepped behind him to smile. He was content, joyous, delighted, charming, young. His white locks added a gentle majesty to the gay radiance of his visage. When grace is mingled with wrinkles, it is adorable. There is an indescribable aurora in beaming old age.

As for Marius, as he allowed them to dress his wounds and care for him, he had but one fixed idea: Cosette.

After the fever and delirium had left him, he did not again pronounce her name, and it might have been supposed that he no longer thought of her. He held his peace, precisely because his soul was there.

He did not know what had become of Cosette; the whole affair of the Rue de la Chanvrerie was like a cloud in his memory; shadows that were almost indistinct, floated through his mind, Éponine, Gavroche, Mabeuf, the Thénardiers, all his friends gloomily intermingled with the smoke of the barricade; the strange passage of M. Fauchelevent through that adventure produced on him the effect of a puzzle in a tempest; he understood nothing connected with his own life, he did not know how nor by whom he had been saved, and no one of those around him knew this; all that they had been able to tell him was, that he had been brought home at night in a hackney-coach, to the Rue des Filles-du-Calvaire; past, present, future were nothing more to him than the mist of a vague idea; but in that fog there was one immovable point, one clear and precise outline, something made of granite, a resolution, a will; to find Cosette once more. For him, the idea of life was not distinct from the idea of Cosette. He had decreed in his heart that he would not accept the one without the other, and he was immovably resolved to exact of any person whatever, who should desire to force him to live,—from his grandfather, from fate, from hell,—the restitution of his vanished Eden.

He did not conceal from himself the fact that obstacles existed.

Let us here emphasize one detail, he was not won over and was but little softened by all the solicitude and tenderness of his grandfather. In the first place, he was not in the secret; then, in his reveries of an invalid, which were still feverish, possibly, he distrusted this tenderness as a strange and novel thing, which had for its object his conquest. He remained cold. The grandfather absolutely wasted his poor old smile. Marius said to himself that it was all right so long as he, Marius, did not speak, and let things take their course; but that when it became a question of Cosette, he would find another face, and that his grandfather's true attitude would be unmasked. Then there would be an unpleasant scene; a recrudescence of family questions, a confrontation of positions, every sort of sarcasm and all manner of objections at one and the same time, Fauchelevent, Coupelevent, fortune, poverty, a stone about his neck, the future. Violent resistance; conclusion: a refusal. Marius stiffened himself in advance.

And then, in proportion as he regained life, the old ulcers of his memory opened once more, he reflected again on the past, Colonel Pontmercy placed himself once more between M. Gillenormand and him, Marius, he told himself that he had no true kindness to expect from a person who had been so unjust and so hard to his father. And with health, there returned to him a sort of harshness towards his grandfather. The old man was gently pained by this. M. Gillenormand, without however allowing it to appear, observed that Marius, ever since the latter had been brought back to him and had regained consciousness, had not once called him father. It is true that he did not say "monsieur" to him; but he contrived not to say either the one or the other, by means of a certain way of turning his phrases. Obviously, a crisis was approaching.

As almost always happens in such cases, Marius skirmished before giving battle, by way of proving himself. This is called "feeling the ground." One morning it came to pass that M. Gillenormand spoke slightingly of the Convention, apropos of a newspaper which had fallen into his hands, and gave vent to a Royalist harangue on Danton, Saint-Juste and Robespierre.—"The men of '93 were giants," said Marius with severity. The old man held his peace, and uttered not a sound during the remainder of that day.

Marius, who had always present to his mind the inflexible grandfather of his early years, interpreted this silence as a profound concentration of wrath, augured from it a hot conflict, and augmented his preparations for the fray in the inmost recesses of his mind.

He decided that, in case of a refusal, he would tear off his bandages, dislocate his collar-bone, that he would lay bare all the wounds which he had left, and would reject all food. His wounds were his munitions of war. He would have Cosette or die.

He awaited the propitious moment with the crafty patience of the sick.

That moment arrived.

# III

## Marius Attacked

One day, M. Gillenormand, while his daughter was putting in order the phials and cups on the marble of the commode, bent over Marius and said to him in his tenderest accents: "Look here, my little Marius, if I were in your place, I would eat meat now in preference to fish. A fried sole is excellent to begin a convalescence with, but a good cutlet is needed to put a sick man on his feet."

Marius, who had almost entirely recovered his strength, collected the whole of it, drew himself up into a sitting posture, laid his two clenched fists on the sheets of his bed, looked his grandfather in the face, assumed a terrible air, and said:

"This leads me to say something to you."

"What is it?"

"That I wish to marry."

"Agreed," said his grandfather.—And he burst out laughing.

"How agreed?"

"Yes, agreed. You shall have your little girl."

Marius, stunned and overwhelmed with the dazzling shock, trembled in every limb.

M. Gillenormand went on:

"Yes, you shall have her, that pretty little girl of yours. She comes every day in the shape of an old gentleman to inquire after you. Ever since you were wounded, she has passed her time in weeping and making lint. I have made inquiries. She lives in the Rue de l'Homme Armé, No. 7. Ah! There we have it! Ah! so you want her! Well, you shall have her. You're caught. You had arranged your little plot, you had said to yourself:—'I'm going to signify this squarely to my grandfather, to that mummy of the Regency and of the Directory, to that ancient beau, to that Dorante turned Géronte; he has indulged in his frivolities also, that he has, and he has had his love affairs, and his grisettes and his Cosettes; he has made his rustle, he has had his wings, he has eaten of the bread of spring; he certainly must remember it.' Ah! you take the cockchafer by the horns. That's good. I offer you a cutlet and you answer me: 'By the way, I want to marry.' There's a transition for you! Ah! you reckoned on a bickering! You do not know that I am an old coward. What do you say to that? You are vexed? You did not expect to find your grandfather still more foolish than yourself, you are wasting the discourse which you meant to bestow upon me, Mr. Lawyer, and that's vexatious. Well, so much the worse, rage away. I'll do whatever you wish, and that cuts you short, imbecile! Listen. I have made my inquiries, I'm cunning too; she is charming, she is discreet, it is not true about the lancer, she has made heaps of lint, she's a jewel, she adores you, if you had died, there would have been three of us, her coffin would have accompanied mine. I have had an idea, ever since you have been better, of simply planting her at your bedside, but it is only in romances that young girls are brought to the bedsides of handsome young wounded men who interest them. It is not done. What would your aunt have said to it? You were nude three quarters of the time, my good fellow. Ask Nicolette, who has not left you for a moment, if there was any possibility of having a woman here. And then, what would the doctor have said? A pretty girl does not cure a man of fever. In short, it's all right, let us say no more about it, all's said, all's done, it's all settled, take her. Such is my ferocity. You see, I perceived that you did not love me. I said to myself: 'Here now, I have my little Cosette right under my hand, I'm going to give her to him, he will be obliged to love me a little then, or he must tell the reason why.' Ah! so you thought that the old man was going to storm, to put on a big voice, to shout no, and to lift his cane at all that aurora. Not a bit of it. Cosette, so be it; love, so be it; I ask nothing better. Pray take the trouble of getting married, sir. Be happy, my well-beloved child."

That said, the old man burst forth into sobs.

And he seized Marius' head, and pressed it with both arms against his breast, and both fell to weeping. This is one of the forms of supreme happiness.

"Father!" cried Marius.

"Ah, so you love me!" said the old man.

An ineffable moment ensued. They were choking and could not speak.

At length the old man stammered:

"Come! his mouth is unstopped at last. He has said: 'Father' to me."

Marius disengaged his head from his grandfather's arms, and said gently:

"But, father, now that I am quite well, it seems to me that I might see her."

"Agreed again, you shall see her to-morrow."

"Father!"

"What?"

"Why not to-day?"

"Well, to-day then. Let it be to-day. You have called me 'father' three times, and it is worth it. I will attend to it. She shall be brought hither. Agreed, I tell you. It has already been put into verse. This is the ending of the elegy of the 'Jeune Malade' by André Chénier, by André Chénier whose throat was cut by the ras. . . by the giants of '93."

M. Gillenormand fancied that he detected a faint frown on the part of Marius, who, in truth, as we must admit, was no longer listening to him, and who was thinking far more of Cosette than of 1793.

The grandfather, trembling at having so inopportunely introduced André Chénier, resumed precipitately:

"Cut his throat is not the word. The fact is that the great revolutionary geniuses, who were not malicious, that is incontestable, who were heroes, pardi! found that André Chénier embarrassed them somewhat, and they had him guillot. . . that is to say, those great men on the 7th of Thermidor, besought André Chénier, in the interests of public safety, to be so good as to go. . ."

M. Gillenormand, clutched by the throat by his own phrase, could not proceed. Being able neither to finish it nor to retract it, while his daughter arranged the pillow behind Marius, who was overwhelmed with so many emotions, the old man rushed headlong, with as much rapidity as his age permitted, from the bed-chamber, shut the door behind him, and, purple, choking and foaming at the mouth, his eyes starting from his head, he found himself nose to nose with honest Basque, who was blacking boots in the anteroom. He seized Basque by the collar, and shouted full in his face in fury:—"By the hundred thousand Javottes of the devil, those ruffians did assassinate him!"

"Who, sir?"

"André Chénier!"

"Yes, sir," said Basque in alarm.

VICTOR HUGO

# IV

## Mademoiselle Gillenormand Ends by No Longer Thinking it a Bad Thing that M. Fauchelevent Should Have Entered With Something Under His Arm

osette and Marius beheld each other once more.

What that interview was like we decline to say. There are things which one must not attempt to depict; the sun is one of them.

The entire family, including Basque and Nicolette, were assembled in Marius' chamber at the moment when Cosette entered it.

Precisely at that moment, the grandfather was on the point of blowing his nose; he stopped short, holding his nose in his handkerchief, and gazing over it at Cosette.

She appeared on the threshold; it seemed to him that she was surrounded by a glory.

"Adorable!" he exclaimed.

Then he blew his nose noisily.

Cosette was intoxicated, delighted, frightened, in heaven. She was as thoroughly alarmed as any one can be by happiness. She stammered all pale, yet flushed, she wanted to fling herself into Marius' arms, and dared not. Ashamed of loving in the presence of all these people. People are pitiless towards happy lovers; they remain when the latter most desire to be left alone. Lovers have no need of any people whatever.

With Cosette, and behind her, there had entered a man with white hair who was grave yet smiling, though with a vague and heartrending smile. It was "Monsieur Fauchelevent"; it was Jean Valjean.

He was very well dressed, as the porter had said, entirely in black, in perfectly new garments, and with a white cravat.

The porter was a thousand leagues from recognizing in this correct bourgeois, in this probable notary, the fear-inspiring bearer of the corpse, who had sprung up at his door on the night of the 7th of June, tattered, muddy, hideous, haggard, his face masked in blood and mire, supporting in his arms the fainting Marius; still, his porter's scent was aroused. When M. Fauchelevent arrived with Cosette, the porter had not been able to refrain from communicating to his wife this aside: "I don't know why it is, but I can't help fancying that I've seen that face before."

M. Fauchelevent in Marius' chamber, remained apart near the door. He had under his arm, a package which bore considerable resemblance to an octavo volume enveloped in paper. The enveloping paper was of a greenish hue, and appeared to be mouldy.

"Does the gentleman always have books like that under his arm?" Mademoiselle Gillenormand, who did not like books, demanded in a low tone of Nicolette.

"Well," retorted M. Gillenormand, who had overheard her, in the same tone, "he's a learned man. What then? Is that his fault? Monsieur Boulard, one of my acquaintances, never walked out without a book under his arm either, and he always had some old volume hugged to his heart like that."

And, with a bow, he said aloud:

"Monsieur Tranchelevent. . ."

Father Gillenormand did not do it intentionally, but inattention to proper names was an aristocratic habit of his.

"Monsieur Tranchelevent, I have the honor of asking you, on behalf of my grandson, Baron Marius Pontmercy, for the hand of Mademoiselle."

Monsieur Tranchelevent bowed.

"That's settled," said the grandfather.

And, turning to Marius and Cosette, with both arms extended in blessing, he cried:

"Permission to adore each other!"

They did not require him to repeat it twice. So much the worse! the chirping began. They talked low. Marius, resting on his elbow on his reclining chair, Cosette standing beside him. "Oh, heavens!" murmured Cosette, "I see you once again! it is thou! it is you! The idea of going and fighting like that! But why? It is horrible. I have been dead for four months. Oh! how wicked it was of you to go to that battle! What had I done to you? I pardon you, but you will never do it again. A little while ago, when they came to tell us to come to you, I still thought that I was about to die, but it was from joy. I was so sad! I have not taken the time to dress myself, I must frighten people with my looks! What will your relatives say to see me in a crumpled collar? Do speak! You let me do all the talking. We are still in the Rue de l'Homme Armé. It seems that your shoulder was terrible. They told me that you could put your fist in it. And then, it seems that they cut your flesh with the scissors. That is frightful. I have cried till I have no eyes left. It is queer that a person can suffer like that. Your grandfather has a very kindly air. Don't disturb yourself, don't rise on your elbow, you will injure yourself. Oh! how happy I am! So our unhappiness is over! I am quite foolish. I had things to say to you, and I no longer know in the least what they were. Do you still love me? We live in the Rue de l'Homme Armé. There is no garden. I made lint all the time; stay, sir, look, it is your fault, I have a callous on my fingers."

"Angel!" said Marius.

*Angel* is the only word in the language which cannot be worn out. No other word could resist the merciless use which lovers make of it.

Then as there were spectators, they paused and said not a word more, contenting themselves with softly touching each other's hands.

M. Gillenormand turned towards those who were in the room and cried:

"Talk loud, the rest of you. Make a noise, you people behind the scenes. Come, a little uproar, the deuce! so that the children can chatter at their ease."

And, approaching Marius and Cosette, he said to them in a very low voice:

"Call each other *thou*. Don't stand on ceremony."

Aunt Gillenormand looked on in amazement at this irruption of light in her elderly household. There was nothing aggressive about this amazement; it was not the least in the world like the scandalized and envious glance of an owl at two turtledoves, it was the stupid eye of a poor innocent seven and fifty years of age; it was a life which had been a failure gazing at that triumph, love.

"Mademoiselle Gillenormand senior," said her father to her, "I told you that this is what would happen to you."

He remained silent for a moment, and then added:

"Look at the happiness of others."

Then he turned to Cosette.

"How pretty she is! how pretty she is! She's a Greuze. So you are going to have that all to yourself, you scamp! Ah! my rogue, you are getting off nicely with me, you are happy; if I were not fifteen years too old, we would fight with swords to see which of us should have her. Come now! I am in love with you, mademoiselle. It's perfectly simple.

It is your right. You are in the right. Ah! what a sweet, charming little wedding this will make! Our parish is Saint-Denis du Saint Sacrament, but I will get a dispensation so that you can be married at Saint-Paul. The church is better. It was built by the Jesuits. It is more coquettish. It is opposite the fountain of Cardinal de Birague. The masterpiece of Jesuit architecture is at Namur. It is called Saint-Loup. You must go there after you are married. It is worth the journey. Mademoiselle, I am quite of your mind, I think girls ought to marry; that is what they are made for. There is a certain Sainte-Catherine whom I should always like to see uncoiffed. It's a fine thing to remain a spinster, but it is chilly. The Bible says: Multiply. In order to save the people, Jeanne d'Arc is needed; but in order to make people, what is needed is Mother Goose. So, marry, my beauties. I really do not see the use in remaining a spinster! I know that they have their chapel apart in the church, and that they fall back on the Society of the Virgin; but, sapristi, a handsome husband, a fine fellow, and at the expiration of a year, a big, blond brat who nurses lustily, and who has fine rolls of fat on his thighs, and who musses up your breast in handfuls with his little rosy paws, laughing the while like the dawn,—that's better than holding a candle at vespers, and chanting *Turris Eburnea!*"

The grandfather executed a pirouette on his eighty-year-old heels, and began to talk again like a spring that has broken loose once more:

"Ainsi, bornant les cours de tes rêvasseries,

Alcippe, il est donc vrai, dans peu tu te maries."

"By the way!"

"What is it, father?"

"Have not you an intimate friend?"

"Yes, Courfeyrac."

"What has become of him?"

"He is dead."

"That is good."

He seated himself near them, made Cosette sit down, and took their four hands in his aged and wrinkled hands:

"She is exquisite, this darling. She's a masterpiece, this Cosette! She is a very little girl and a very great lady. She will only be a Baroness, which is a come down for her; she was born a Marquise. What eyelashes she has! Get it well fixed in your noddles, my children, that you are in the true road. Love each other. Be foolish about it. Love is the folly of men and the wit of God. Adore each other. Only," he added, suddenly becoming gloomy, "what a misfortune! It has just occurred to me! More than half of what I possess is swallowed up in an annuity; so long as I live, it will not matter, but after my death, a score of years hence, ah! my poor children, you will not have a sou! Your beautiful white hands, Madame la Baronne, will do the devil the honor of pulling him by the tail."

At this point they heard a grave and tranquil voice say:

"Mademoiselle Euphrasie Fauchelevent possesses six hundred thousand francs."

It was the voice of Jean Valjean.

So far he had not uttered a single word, no one seemed to be aware that he was there, and he had remained standing erect and motionless, behind all these happy people.

"What has Mademoiselle Euphrasie to do with the question?" inquired the startled grandfather.

"I am she," replied Cosette.

"Six hundred thousand francs?" resumed M. Gillenormand.

"Minus fourteen or fifteen thousand francs, possibly," said Jean Valjean.

And he laid on the table the package which Mademoiselle Gillenormand had mistaken for a book.

Jean Valjean himself opened the package; it was a bundle of bank-notes. They were turned over and counted. There were five hundred notes for a thousand francs each, and one hundred and sixty-eight of five hundred. In all, five hundred and eighty-four thousand francs.

"This is a fine book," said M. Gillenormand.

"Five hundred and eighty-four thousand francs!" murmured the aunt.

"This arranges things well, does it not, Mademoiselle Gillenormand senior?" said the grandfather. "That devil of a Marius has ferreted out the nest of a millionaire grisette in his tree of dreams! Just trust to the love affairs of young folks now, will you! Students find studentesses with six hundred thousand francs. Cherubino works better than Rothschild."

"Five hundred and eighty-four thousand francs!" repeated Mademoiselle Gillenormand, in a low tone. "Five hundred and eighty-four! one might as well say six hundred thousand!"

As for Marius and Cosette, they were gazing at each other while this was going on; they hardly heeded this detail.

# V

## Deposit Your Money in a Forest Rather than with a Notary

The reader has, no doubt, understood, without necessitating a lengthy explanation, that Jean Valjean, after the Champmathieu affair, had been able, thanks to his first escape of a few days' duration, to come to Paris and to withdraw in season, from the hands of Laffitte, the sum earned by him, under the name of Monsieur Madeleine, at Montreuil-sur-Mer; and that fearing that he might be recaptured,—which eventually happened—he had buried and hidden that sum in the forest of Montfermeil, in the locality known as the Blaru-bottom. The sum, six hundred and thirty thousand francs, all in bank-bills, was not very bulky, and was contained in a box; only, in order to preserve the box from dampness, he had placed it in a coffer filled with chestnut shavings. In the same coffer he had placed his other treasures, the Bishop's candlesticks. It will be remembered that he had carried off the candlesticks when he made his escape from Montreuil-sur-Mer. The man seen one evening for the first time by Boulatruelle, was Jean Valjean. Later on, every time that Jean Valjean needed money, he went to get it in the Blaru-bottom. Hence the absences which we have mentioned. He had a pickaxe somewhere in the heather, in a hiding-place known to himself alone. When he beheld Marius convalescent, feeling that the hour was at hand, when that money might prove of service, he had gone to get it; it was he again, whom Boulatruelle had seen in the woods, but on this occasion, in the morning instead of in the evening. Boulatreulle inherited his pickaxe.

The actual sum was five hundred and eighty-four thousand, five hundred francs. Jean Valjean withdrew the five hundred francs for himself.—"We shall see hereafter," he thought.

The difference between that sum and the six hundred and thirty thousand francs withdrawn from Laffitte represented his expenditure in ten years, from 1823 to 1833. The five years of his stay in the convent had cost only five thousand francs.

Jean Valjean set the two candlesticks on the chimney-piece, where they glittered to the great admiration of Toussaint.

Moreover, Jean Valjean knew that he was delivered from Javert. The story had been told in his presence, and he had verified the fact in the *Moniteur*, how a police inspector named Javert had been found drowned under a boat belonging to some laundresses, between the Pont au Change and the Pont-Neuf, and that a writing left by this man, otherwise irreproachable and highly esteemed by his superiors, pointed to a fit of mental aberration and a suicide.—"In fact," thought Jean Valjean, "since he left me at liberty, once having got me in his power, he must have been already mad."

# VI

## The Two Old Men Do Everything, Each One After His Own Fashion, to Render Cosette Happy

Everything was made ready for the wedding. The doctor, on being consulted, declared that it might take place in February. It was then December. A few ravishing weeks of perfect happiness passed.

The grandfather was not the least happy of them all. He remained for a quarter of an hour at a time gazing at Cosette.

"The wonderful, beautiful girl!" he exclaimed. "And she has so sweet and good an air! she is, without exception, the most charming girl that I have ever seen in my life. Later on, she'll have virtues with an odor of violets. How graceful! one cannot live otherwise than nobly with such a creature. Marius, my boy, you are a Baron, you are rich, don't go to pettifogging, I beg of you."

Cosette and Marius had passed abruptly from the sepulchre to paradise. The transition had not been softened, and they would have been stunned, had they not been dazzled by it.

"Do you understand anything about it?" said Marius to Cosette.

"No," replied Cosette, "but it seems to me that the good God is caring for us."

Jean Valjean did everything, smoothed away every difficulty, arranged everything, made everything easy. He hastened towards Cosette's happiness with as much ardor, and, apparently with as much joy, as Cosette herself.

As he had been a mayor, he understood how to solve that delicate problem, with the secret of which he alone was acquainted, Cosette's civil status. If he were to announce her origin bluntly, it might prevent the marriage, who knows? He extricated Cosette from all difficulties. He concocted for her a family of dead people, a sure means of not encountering any objections. Cosette was the only scion of an extinct family; Cosette was not his own daughter, but the daughter of the other Fauchelevent. Two brothers Fauchelevent had been gardeners to the convent of the Petit-Picpus. Inquiry was made at that convent; the very best information and the most respectable references abounded; the good nuns, not very apt and but little inclined to fathom questions of paternity, and not attaching any importance to the matter, had never understood exactly of which of the two Fauchelevents Cosette was the daughter. They said what was wanted and they said it with zeal. An *acte de notoriété* was drawn up. Cosette became in the eyes of the law, Mademoiselle Euphrasie Fauchelevent. She was declared an orphan, both father and mother being dead. Jean Valjean so arranged it that he was appointed, under the name of Fauchelevent, as Cosette's guardian, with M. Gillenormand as supervising guardian over him.

As for the five hundred and eighty thousand francs, they constituted a legacy bequeathed to Cosette by a dead person, who desired to remain unknown. The original legacy had consisted of five hundred and ninety-four thousand francs; but ten thousand francs had been expended on the education of Mademoiselle Euphrasie, five thousand francs of that amount having been paid to the convent. This legacy, deposited in the hands of a third party, was to be turned over to Cosette at her majority, or at the date of her marriage. This, taken as a whole, was very acceptable, as the reader will perceive, especially when the sum due was half a million. There were some peculiarities here and there, it is true, but they were not noticed; one of the interested parties had his eyes blindfolded by love, the others by the six hundred thousand francs.

Cosette learned that she was not the daughter of that old man whom she had so long called father. He was merely a kinsman; another Fauchelevent was her real father. At any other time this would have broken her heart. But at the ineffable moment which she was then passing through, it cast but a slight shadow, a faint cloud, and she was so full of joy that the cloud did not last long. She had Marius. The young man arrived, the old man was effaced; such is life.

And then, Cosette had, for long years, been habituated to seeing enigmas around her; every being who has had a mysterious childhood is always prepared for certain renunciations.

Nevertheless, she continued to call Jean Valjean: Father.

Cosette, happy as the angels, was enthusiastic over Father Gillenormand. It is true that he overwhelmed her with gallant compliments and presents. While Jean Valjean was building up for Cosette a normal situation in society and an unassailable status, M. Gillenormand was superintending the basket of wedding gifts. Nothing so amused him as being magnificent. He had given to Cosette a robe of Binche guipure which had descended to him from his own grandmother.

"These fashions come up again," said he, "ancient things are the rage, and the young women of my old age dress like the old women of my childhood."

He rifled his respectable chests of drawers in Coromandel lacquer, with swelling fronts, which had not been opened for years.—"Let us hear the confession of these dowagers," he said, "let us see what they have in their paunches." He noisily violated the pot-bellied drawers of all his wives, of all his mistresses and of all his grandmothers. Pekins, damasks, lampas, painted moires, robes of shot gros de Tours, India kerchiefs embroidered in gold that could be washed, dauphines without a right or wrong side, in the piece, Genoa and Alençon point lace, parures in antique goldsmith's work, ivory bon-bon boxes ornamented with microscopic battles, gewgaws and ribbons—he lavished everything on Cosette. Cosette, amazed, desperately in love with Marius, and wild with gratitude towards M. Gillenormand, dreamed of a happiness without limit clothed in satin and velvet. Her wedding basket seemed to her to be upheld by seraphim. Her soul flew out into the azure depths, with wings of Mechlin lace.

The intoxication of the lovers was only equalled, as we have already said, by the ecstasy of the grandfather. A sort of flourish of trumpets went on in the Rue des Filles-du-Calvaire.

Every morning, a fresh offering of bric-à-brac from the grandfather to Cosette. All possible knickknacks glittered around her.

One day Marius, who was fond of talking gravely in the midst of his bliss, said, apropos of I know not what incident:

"The men of the revolution are so great, that they have the prestige of the ages, like Cato and like Phocion, and each one of them seems to me an antique memory."

"Moire antique!" exclaimed the old gentleman. "Thanks, Marius. That is precisely the idea of which I was in search."

And on the following day, a magnificent dress of tea-rose colored moire antique was added to Cosette's wedding presents.

From these fripperies, the grandfather extracted a bit of wisdom.

"Love is all very well; but there must be something else to go with it. The useless must be mingled with happiness. Happiness is only the necessary. Season that enormously with the superfluous for me. A palace and her heart. Her heart and the Louvre. Her heart and the grand waterworks of Versailles. Give me my shepherdess and try to make her a duchess. Fetch me Phyllis crowned with corn-flowers, and add a hundred thousand francs income. Open for me a bucolic perspective as far as you can see, beneath a marble colonnade. I consent to the bucolic and also to the fairy spectacle of marble and gold. Dry happiness resembles dry bread. One eats, but one does not dine. I want the superfluous, the useless, the extravagant, excess, that which serves no purpose. I remember to have seen, in the Cathedral of Strasburg, a clock, as tall as a three-story house which marked the hours, which had the kindness to indicate the hour, but which had not the air of being made for that; and which, after having struck midday, or midnight,— midday, the hour of the sun, or midnight, the hour of love,—or any other hour that you like, gave you the moon and the stars, the earth and the sea, birds and fishes, Phœbus and Phœbe, and a host of things which emerged from a niche, and the twelve apostles, and the Emperor Charles the Fifth, and Éponine, and Sabinus, and a throng of little gilded goodmen, who played on the trumpet to boot. Without reckoning delicious chimes which it sprinkled through the air, on every occasion, without any one's knowing why. Is a petty bald clock-face which merely tells the hour equal to that? For my part, I am of the opinion of the big clock of Strasburg, and I prefer it to the cuckoo clock from the Black Forest."

M. Gillenormand talked nonsense in connection with the wedding, and all the fripperies of the eighteenth century passed pell-mell through his dithyrambs.

"You are ignorant of the art of festivals. You do not know how to organize a day of enjoyment in this age," he exclaimed. "Your nineteenth century is weak. It lacks excess. It ignores the rich, it ignores the noble. In everything it is clean-shaven. Your third estate is insipid, colorless, odorless, and shapeless. The dreams of your bourgeois who set up, as they express it: a pretty boudoir freshly decorated, violet, ebony and calico. Make way! Make way! the Sieur Curmudgeon is marrying Mademoiselle Clutch-penny. Sumptuousness and splendor. A louis d'or has been stuck to a candle. There's the epoch for you. My demand is that I may flee from it beyond the Sarmatians. Ah! in 1787, I predict that all was lost, from the day when I beheld the Duc de Rohan, Prince de Léon, Duc de Chabot, Duc de Montbazon, Marquis de Soubise, Vicomte de Thouars, peer of France, go to Longchamps in a tapecu! That has borne its fruits. In this century, men attend to business, they gamble on 'Change, they win money, they are stingy. People take care of their surfaces and varnish them; every one is dressed as though just out of a bandbox, washed, soaped, scraped, shaved, combed, waked, smoothed, rubbed, brushed, cleaned on the outside, irreproachable, polished as a pebble, discreet, neat, and at the same time, death of my life, in the depths of their consciences they have dung-heaps and cesspools that are enough to make a cow-herd who blows his nose in his fingers, recoil. I grant to this age the device: 'Dirty Cleanliness.' Don't be vexed, Marius, give me permission to speak; I say no evil of the people as you see, I am always harping on your people, but do look favorably on my dealing a bit of a slap to the bourgeoisie. I belong to it. He who loves well lashes well. Thereupon, I say plainly, that nowadays people marry, but that they no longer know how to marry. Ah! it is true, I regret the grace of the ancient manners. I regret everything about them, their elegance, their chivalry, those courteous and delicate ways, that joyous luxury which every one possessed, music forming part of the wedding, a symphony above stairs, a beating of drums below stairs, the dances, the joyous faces round the table, the fine-spun gallant compliments, the songs, the fireworks, the frank laughter, the devil's own row, the huge knots of ribbon. I regret the bride's garter. The bride's garter is cousin to the girdle of Venus. On what does the war of Troy turn? On Helen's garter, parbleu! Why did they fight, why did Diomed the divine break over the head of Meriones that great brazen helmet of ten points? why did Achilles and Hector hew each other up with vast blows of their lances? Because Helen allowed Paris to take her garter. With Cosette's garter, Homer would construct the *Iliad*. He would put in his poem, a loquacious old fellow, like me, and he would call him Nestor. My friends, in bygone days, in those amiable days of yore, people married wisely; they had a good contract, and then they had a good carouse. As soon as Cujas had taken his departure, Gamacho entered. But, in sooth! the stomach is an agreeable beast which demands its due, and which wants to have its wedding also. People supped well, and had at table a beautiful neighbor without a guimpe so that her throat was only moderately concealed. Oh! the large laughing mouths, and how gay we were in those days! youth was a bouquet; every young man terminated in a branch of lilacs or a tuft of roses; whether he was a shepherd or a warrior; and if, by chance, one was a captain of dragoons, one found means to call oneself Florian. People thought much of looking well. They embroidered and tinted themselves. A bourgeois had the air of a flower, a Marquis had the air of a precious stone. People had no straps to their boots, they had no boots. They were spruce, shining, waved, lustrous, fluttering, dainty, coquettish, which did not at all prevent their wearing swords by their sides. The humming-bird has beak and claws. That was the day of the *Galland Indies*. One of the sides of that century was delicate, the other was magnificent; and by the green cabbages! people amused themselves. To-day, people are serious. The bourgeois is avaricious, the bourgeoise is a prude; your century is unfortunate. People would drive away the Graces as being too low in the neck. Alas! beauty is concealed as though it were ugliness. Since the revolution, everything, including the ballet-dancers, has had its trousers; a mountebank dancer must be grave; your rigadoons are doctrinarian. It is necessary to be majestic. People would be greatly annoyed if they did not carry their chins in their cravats. The ideal of an urchin of twenty when he marries, is to resemble M. Royer-Collard. And do you know what one arrives at with that majesty? at being petty. Learn this: joy is not only joyous; it is great. But be in love gayly then, what the deuce! marry, when you marry, with fever and giddiness, and tumult, and the uproar of happiness! Be grave in church, well and good. But, as soon as the mass is finished, sarpejou! you must make a dream whirl around the bride. A marriage should be royal and chimerical; it should promenade its ceremony from the cathedral of Rheims to the pagoda of Chanteloup. I have a horror of a paltry wedding. Ventregoulette! be in Olympus for that one day, at least. Be one of the gods. Ah! people might be sylphs. Games and Laughter, argiraspides; they are stupids. My friends, every recently made bridegroom ought to be Prince Aldobrandini. Profit by that unique minute in life to soar away to the empyrean with the swans and the eagles, even if you do have to fall back on the morrow into the bourgeoisie of the frogs. Don't economize on the nuptials, do not prune them of their splendors; don't scrimp on the day when you beam. The wedding is not the housekeeping. Oh! if I were to carry out my fancy, it would be gallant, violins would be heard under the trees. Here is my programme: sky-blue and silver. I would mingle with the festival the rural divinities, I would convoke the Dryads and the Nereids. The nuptials of Amphitrite, a rosy cloud, nymphs with well dressed locks and entirely naked, an Academician offering quatrains to the goddess, a chariot drawn by marine monsters.

> "*Triton trottait devant, et tirait de sa conque*
> *Des sons si ravissants qu'il ravissait quiconque!*"

—there's a festive programme, there's a good one, or else I know nothing of such matters, deuce take it!"

While the grandfather, in full lyrical effusion, was listening to himself, Cosette and Marius grew intoxicated as they gazed freely at each other.

Aunt Gillenormand surveyed all this with her imperturbable placidity. Within the last five or six months she had experienced a certain amount of emotions. Marius returned, Marius brought back bleeding, Marius brought back from a barricade, Marius dead, then living, Marius reconciled, Marius betrothed, Marius wedding a poor girl, Marius wedding a millionairess. The six hundred thousand francs had been her last surprise. Then, her indifference of a girl taking her first communion returned to her. She went regularly to service, told her beads, read her euchology, mumbled *Aves* in one corner of the house, while *I love you* was being whispered in the other, and she beheld Marius and Cosette in a vague way, like two shadows. The shadow was herself.

There is a certain state of inert asceticism in which the soul, neutralized by torpor, a stranger to that which may be designated as the business of living, receives no impressions, either human, or pleasant or painful, with the exception of earthquakes and catastrophes. This devotion, as Father Gillenormand said to his daughter, corresponds to a cold in the head. You smell nothing of life. Neither any bad, nor any good odor.

Moreover, the six hundred thousand francs had settled the elderly spinster's indecision. Her father had acquired the habit of taking her so little into account, that he had not consulted her in the matter of consent to Marius' marriage. He had acted impetuously, according to his wont, having, a despot-turned slave, but a single thought,—to satisfy Marius. As for the aunt,—it had not even occurred to him that the aunt existed, and that she could have an opinion of her own, and, sheep as she was, this had vexed her. Somewhat resentful in her inmost soul, but impassible externally, she had said to herself: "My father has settled the question of the marriage without reference to me; I shall settle the question of the inheritance without consulting him." She was rich, in fact, and her father was not. She had reserved her decision on this point. It is probable that, had the match been a poor one, she would have left him poor. "So much the worse for my nephew! he is wedding a beggar, let him be a beggar himself!" But Cosette's half-million pleased the aunt, and altered her inward situation so far as this pair of lovers were concerned. One owes some consideration to six hundred thousand francs, and it was evident that she could not do otherwise than leave her fortune to these young people, since they did not need it.

It was arranged that the couple should live with the grandfather—M. Gillenormand insisted on resigning to them his chamber, the finest in the house. "That will make me young again," he said. "It's an old plan of mine. I have always entertained the idea of having a wedding in my chamber."

He furnished this chamber with a multitude of elegant trifles. He had the ceiling and walls hung with an extraordinary stuff, which he had by him in the piece, and which he believed to have emanated from Utrecht with a buttercup-colored satin ground, covered with velvet auricula blossoms.—"It was with that stuff," said he, "that the bed of the Duchesse d'Anville at la Roche-Guyon was draped."—On the chimney-piece, he set a little figure in Saxe porcelain, carrying a muff against her nude stomach.

M. Gillenormand's library became the lawyer's study, which Marius needed; a study, it will be remembered, being required by the council of the order.

# VII

## The Effects of Dreams Mingled With Happiness

The lovers saw each other every day. Cosette came with M. Fauchelevent.—"This is reversing things," said Mademoiselle Gillenormand, "to have the bride come to the house to do the courting like this." But Marius' convalescence had caused the habit to become established, and the armchairs of the Rue des Filles-du-Calvaire, better adapted to interviews than the straw chairs of the Rue de l'Homme Armé, had rooted it. Marius and M. Fauchelevent saw each other, but did not address each other. It seemed as though this had been agreed upon. Every girl needs a chaperon. Cosette could not have come without M. Fauchelevent. In Marius' eyes, M. Fauchelevent was the condition attached to Cosette. He accepted it. By dint of discussing political matters, vaguely and without precision, from the point of view of the general amelioration of the fate of all men, they came to say a little more than "yes" and "no." Once, on the subject of education, which Marius wished to have free and obligatory, multiplied under all forms lavished on every one, like the air and the sun in a word, respirable for the entire population, they were in unison, and they almost conversed. M. Fauchelevent talked well, and even with a certain loftiness of language—still he lacked something indescribable. M. Fauchelevent possessed something less and also something more, than a man of the world.

Marius, inwardly, and in the depths of his thought, surrounded with all sorts of mute questions this M. Fauchelevent, who was to him simply benevolent and cold. There were moments when doubts as to his own recollections occurred to him. There was a void in his memory, a black spot, an abyss excavated by four months of agony.—Many things had been lost therein. He had come to the point of asking himself whether it were really a fact that he had seen M. Fauchelevent, so serious and so calm a man, in the barricade.

This was not, however, the only stupor which the apparitions and the disappearances of the past had left in his mind. It must not be supposed that he was delivered from all those obsessions of the memory which force us, even when happy, even when satisfied, to glance sadly behind us. The head which does not turn backwards towards horizons that have vanished contains neither thought nor love. At times, Marius clasped his face between his hands, and the vague and tumultuous past traversed the twilight which reigned in his brain. Again he beheld Mabeuf fall, he heard Gavroche singing amid the grape-shot, he felt beneath his lips the cold brow of Éponine; Enjolras, Courfeyrac, Jean Prouvaire, Combeferre, Bossuet, Grantaire, all his friends rose erect before him, then dispersed into thin air. Were all those dear, sorrowful, valiant, charming or tragic beings merely dreams? had they actually existed? The revolt had enveloped everything in its smoke. These great fevers create great dreams. He questioned himself; he felt himself; all these vanished realities made him dizzy. Where were they all then? was it really true that all were dead? A fall into the shadows had carried off all except himself. It all seemed to him to have disappeared as though behind the curtain of a theatre. There are curtains like this which drop in life. God passes on to the following act.

And he himself—was he actually the same man? He, the poor man, was rich; he, the abandoned, had a family; he, the despairing, was to marry Cosette. It seemed to him that he had traversed a tomb, and that he had entered into it black and had emerged from it white, and in that tomb the others had remained. At certain moments, all these beings of the past, returned and present, formed a circle around him, and overshadowed him; then he thought of Cosette, and recovered his serenity; but nothing less than this felicity could have sufficed to efface that catastrophe.

M. Fauchelevent almost occupied a place among these vanished beings. Marius hesitated to believe that the Fauchelevent of the barricade was the same as this Fauchelevent in flesh and blood, sitting so gravely beside Cosette. The first was, probably, one of those nightmares occasioned and brought back by his hours of delirium. However, the natures of both men were rigid, no question from Marius to M. Fauchelevent was possible. Such an idea had not even occurred to him. We have already indicated this characteristic detail.

Two men who have a secret in common, and who, by a sort of tacit agreement, exchange not a word on the subject, are less rare than is commonly supposed.

Once only, did Marius make the attempt. He introduced into the conversation the Rue de la Chanvrerie, and, turning to M. Fauchelevent, he said to him:

"Of course, you are acquainted with that street?"

"What street?"

"The Rue de la Chanvrerie."

"I have no idea of the name of that street," replied M. Fauchelevent, in the most natural manner in the world.

The response which bore upon the name of the street and not upon the street itself, appeared to Marius to be more conclusive than it really was.

"Decidedly," thought he, "I have been dreaming. I have been subject to a hallucination. It was some one who resembled him. M. Fauchelevent was not there."

# VIII

## Two Men Impossible to Find

Marius' enchantment, great as it was, could not efface from his mind other pre-occupations.

While the wedding was in preparation, and while awaiting the date fixed upon, he caused difficult and scrupulous retrospective researches to be made.

He owed gratitude in various quarters; he owed it on his father's account, he owed it on his own.

There was Thénardier; there was the unknown man who had brought him, Marius, back to M. Gillenormand.

Marius endeavored to find these two men, not intending to marry, to be happy, and to forget them, and fearing that, were these debts of gratitude not discharged, they would leave a shadow on his life, which promised so brightly for the future.

It was impossible for him to leave all these arrears of suffering behind him, and he wished, before entering joyously into the future, to obtain a quittance from the past.

That Thénardier was a villain detracted nothing from the fact that he had saved Colonel Pontmercy. Thénardier was a ruffian in the eyes of all the world except Marius.

And Marius, ignorant of the real scene in the battle field of Waterloo, was not aware of the peculiar detail, that his father, so far as Thénardier was concerned was in the strange position of being indebted to the latter for his life, without being indebted to him for any gratitude.

None of the various agents whom Marius employed succeeded in discovering any trace of Thénardier. Obliteration appeared to be complete in that quarter. Madame Thénardier had died in prison pending the trial. Thénardier and his daughter Azelma, the only two remaining of that lamentable group, had plunged back into the gloom. The gulf of the social unknown had silently closed above those beings. On the surface there was not visible so much as that quiver, that trembling, those obscure concentric circles which announce that something has fallen in, and that the plummet may be dropped.

Madame Thénardier being dead, Boulatruelle being eliminated from the case, Claquesous having disappeared, the principal persons accused having escaped from prison, the trial connected with the ambush in the Gorbeau house had come to nothing.

That affair had remained rather obscure. The bench of Assizes had been obliged to content themselves with two subordinates. Panchaud, alias Printanier, alias Bigrenaille, and Demi-Liard, alias Deux-Milliards, who had been inconsistently condemned, after a hearing of both sides of the case, to ten years in the galleys. Hard labor for life had been the sentence pronounced against the escaped and contumacious accomplices.

Thénardier, the head and leader, had been, through contumacy, likewise condemned to death.

This sentence was the only information remaining about Thénardier, casting upon that buried name its sinister light like a candle beside a bier.

Moreover, by thrusting Thénardier back into the very remotest depths, through a fear of being re-captured, this sentence added to the density of the shadows which enveloped this man.

As for the other person, as for the unknown man who had saved Marius, the researches were at first to some extent successful, then came to an abrupt conclusion. They succeeded in finding the carriage which had brought Marius to the Rue des Filles-du-Calvaire on the evening of the 6th of June.

The coachman declared that, on the 6th of June, in obedience to the commands of a police-agent, he had stood from three o'clock in the afternoon until nightfall on the Quai des Champs-Élysées, above the outlet of the Grand Sewer; that, towards nine o'clock in the evening, the grating of the sewer, which abuts on the bank of the river, had opened; that a man had emerged therefrom, bearing on his shoulders another man, who seemed to be dead; that the agent, who was on the watch at that point, had arrested the living man and had seized the dead man; that, at the order of the police-agent, he, the coachman, had taken "all those folks" into his carriage; that they had first driven to the Rue des Filles-du-Calvaire; that they had there deposited the dead man; that the dead man was Monsieur Marius, and that he, the coachman, recognized him perfectly, although he was alive "this time"; that afterwards, they had entered the vehicle again, that he had whipped up his horses; a few paces from the gate of the Archives, they had called to him to halt; that there, in the street, they had paid him and left him, and that the police-agent had led the other man away; that he knew nothing more; that the night had been very dark.

Marius, as we have said, recalled nothing. He only remembered that he had been seized from behind by an energetic hand at the moment when he was falling backwards into the barricade; then, everything vanished so far as he was concerned.

He had only regained consciousness at M. Gillenormand's.

He was lost in conjectures.

He could not doubt his own identity. Still, how had it come to pass that, having fallen in the Rue de la Chanvrerie, he had been picked up by the police-agent on the banks of the Seine, near the Pont des Invalides?

Some one had carried him from the Quartier des Halles to the Champs-Élysées. And how? Through the sewer. Unheard-of devotion!

Some one? Who?

This was the man for whom Marius was searching.

Of this man, who was his savior, nothing; not a trace; not the faintest indication.

Marius, although forced to preserve great reserve, in that direction, pushed his inquiries as far as the prefecture of police. There, no more than elsewhere, did the information obtained lead to any enlightenment.

The prefecture knew less about the matter than did the hackney-coachman. They had no knowledge of any arrest having been made on the 6th of June at the mouth of the Grand Sewer.

No report of any agent had been received there upon this matter, which was regarded at the prefecture as a fable. The invention of this fable was attributed to the coachman.

A coachman who wants a gratuity is capable of anything, even of imagination. The fact was assured, nevertheless, and Marius could not doubt it, unless he doubted his own identity, as we have just said.

Everything about this singular enigma was inexplicable.

What had become of that man, that mysterious man, whom the coachman had seen emerge from the grating of the Grand Sewer bearing upon his back the unconscious Marius, and whom the police-agent on the watch had arrested in the very act of rescuing an insurgent? What had become of the agent himself?

Why had this agent preserved silence? Had the man succeeded in making his escape? Had he bribed the agent? Why did this man give no sign of life to Marius, who owed everything to him? His disinterestedness was no less tremendous than his devotion. Why had not that man appeared again? Perhaps he was above compensation, but no one is above gratitude. Was he dead? Who was the man? What sort of a face had he? No one could tell him this.

The coachman answered: "The night was very dark." Basque and Nicolette, all in a flutter, had looked only at their young master all covered with blood.

The porter, whose candle had lighted the tragic arrival of Marius, had been the only one to take note of the man in question, and this is the description that he gave:

"That man was terrible."

Marius had the blood-stained clothing which he had worn when he had been brought back to his grandfather preserved, in the hope that it would prove of service in his researches.

On examining the coat, it was found that one skirt had been torn in a singular way. A piece was missing.

One evening, Marius was speaking in the presence of Cosette and Jean Valjean of the whole of that singular adventure, of the innumerable inquiries which he had made, and of the fruitlessness of his efforts. The cold countenance of "Monsieur Fauchelevent" angered him.

He exclaimed, with a vivacity which had something of wrath in it:

"Yes, that man, whoever he may have been, was sublime. Do you know what he did, sir? He intervened like an archangel. He must have flung himself into the midst of the battle, have stolen me away, have opened the sewer, have dragged me into it and have carried me through it! He must have traversed more than a league and a half in those frightful subterranean galleries, bent over, weighed down, in the dark, in the cesspool,—more than a league and a half, sir, with a corpse upon his back! And with what object? With the sole object of saving the corpse. And that corpse I was. He said to himself: 'There may still be a glimpse of life there, perchance; I will risk my own existence for that miserable spark!' And his existence he risked not once but twenty times! And every step was a danger. The proof of it is, that on emerging from the sewer, he was arrested. Do you know, sir, that that man did all this? And he had no recompense to expect. What was I? An insurgent. What was I? One of the conquered. Oh! if Cosette's six hundred thousand francs were mine. . ."

"They are yours," interrupted Jean Valjean.

"Well," resumed Marius, "I would give them all to find that man once more."

Jean Valjean remained silent.

BOOK SIXTH
THE SLEEPLESS NIGHT

# I

## The 16th of February, 1833

The night of the 16th to the 17th of February, 1833, was a blessed night. Above its shadows heaven stood open. It was the wedding night of Marius and Cosette.

The day had been adorable.

It had not been the grand festival dreamed by the grandfather, a fairy spectacle, with a confusion of cherubim and Cupids over the heads of the bridal pair, a marriage worthy to form the subject of a painting to be placed over a door; but it had been sweet and smiling.

The manner of marriage in 1833 was not the same as it is to-day. France had not yet borrowed from England that supreme delicacy of carrying off one's wife, of fleeing, on coming out of church, of hiding oneself with shame from one's happiness, and of combining the ways of a bankrupt with the delights of the Song of Songs. People had not yet grasped to the full the chastity, exquisiteness, and decency of jolting their paradise in a posting-chaise, of breaking up their mystery with clic-clacs, of taking for a nuptial bed the bed of an inn, and of leaving behind them, in a commonplace chamber, at so much a night, the most sacred of the souvenirs of life mingled pell-mell with the tête-à-tête of the conductor of the diligence and the maid-servant of the inn.

In this second half of the nineteenth century in which we are now living, the mayor and his scarf, the priest and his chasuble, the law and God no longer suffice; they must be eked out by the Postilion de Lonjumeau; a blue waistcoat turned up with red, and with bell buttons, a plaque like a vantbrace, knee-breeches of green leather, oaths to the Norman horses with their tails knotted up, false galloons, varnished hat, long powdered locks, an enormous whip and tall boots. France does not yet carry elegance to the length of doing like the English nobility, and raining down on the post-chaise of the bridal pair a hail storm of slippers trodden down at heel and of worn-out shoes, in memory of Churchill, afterwards Marlborough, or Malbrouck, who was assailed on his wedding-day by the wrath of an aunt which brought him good luck. Old shoes and slippers do not, as yet, form a part of our nuptial celebrations; but patience, as good taste continues to spread, we shall come to that.

In 1833, a hundred years ago, marriage was not conducted at a full trot.

Strange to say, at that epoch, people still imagined that a wedding was a private and social festival, that a patriarchal banquet does not spoil a domestic solemnity, that gayety, even in excess, provided it be honest, and decent, does happiness no harm, and that, in short, it is a good and a venerable thing that the fusion of these two destinies whence a family is destined to spring, should begin at home, and that the household should thenceforth have its nuptial chamber as its witness.

And people were so immodest as to marry in their own homes.

The marriage took place, therefore, in accordance with this now superannuated fashion, at M. Gillenormand's house.

Natural and commonplace as this matter of marrying is, the banns to publish, the papers to be drawn up, the mayoralty, and the church produce some complication. They could not get ready before the 16th of February.

Now, we note this detail, for the pure satisfaction of being exact, it chanced that the 16th fell on Shrove Tuesday. Hesitations, scruples, particularly on the part of Aunt Gillenormand.

"Shrove Tuesday!" exclaimed the grandfather, "so much the better. There is a proverb:

> *"Mariage un Mardi gras*
> *N'aura point enfants ingrats.'*

Let us proceed. Here goes for the 16th! Do you want to delay, Marius?"

"No, certainly not!" replied the lover.

"Let us marry, then," cried the grandfather.

Accordingly, the marriage took place on the 16th, notwithstanding the public merrymaking. It rained that day, but there is always in the sky a tiny scrap of blue at the service of happiness, which lovers see, even when the rest of creation is under an umbrella.

On the preceding evening, Jean Valjean handed to Marius, in the presence of M. Gillenormand, the five hundred and eighty-four thousand francs.

As the marriage was taking place under the régime of community of property, the papers had been simple.

Henceforth, Toussaint was of no use to Jean Valjean; Cosette inherited her and promoted her to the rank of lady's maid.

As for Jean Valjean, a beautiful chamber in the Gillenormand house had been furnished expressly for him, and Cosette had said to him in such an irresistible manner: "Father, I entreat you," that she had almost persuaded him to promise that he would come and occupy it.

A few days before that fixed on for the marriage, an accident happened to Jean Valjean; he crushed the thumb of his right hand. This was not a serious matter; and he had not allowed any one to trouble himself about it, nor to dress it, nor even to see his hurt, not even Cosette. Nevertheless, this had forced him to swathe his hand in a linen bandage, and to carry his arm in a sling, and had prevented his signing. M. Gillenormand, in his capacity of Cosette's supervising-guardian, had supplied his place.

We will not conduct the reader either to the mayor's office or to the church. One does not follow a pair of lovers to that extent, and one is accustomed to turn one's back on the drama as soon as it puts a wedding nosegay in its buttonhole. We will confine ourselves to noting an incident which, though unnoticed by the wedding party, marked the transit from the Rue des Filles-du-Calvaire to the church of Saint-Paul.

At that epoch, the northern extremity of the Rue Saint-Louis was in process of repaving. It was barred off, beginning with the Rue du Parc-Royal. It was impossible for the wedding carriages to go directly to Saint-Paul. They were obliged to alter their course, and the simplest way was to turn through the boulevard. One of the invited guests observed that it was Shrove Tuesday, and that there would be a jam of vehicles.— "Why?" asked M. Gillenormand—"Because of the maskers."—"Capital," said the grandfather, "let us go that way. These young folks are on the way to be married; they are about to enter the serious part of life. This will prepare them for seeing a bit of the masquerade."

They went by way of the boulevard. The first wedding coach held Cosette and Aunt Gillenormand, M. Gillenormand and Jean Valjean. Marius, still separated from his betrothed according to usage, did not come until the second. The nuptial train, on emerging from the Rue des Filles-du-Calvaire, became entangled in a long procession of vehicles which formed an endless chain from the Madeleine to the Bastille, and from the Bastille to the Madeleine. Maskers abounded on the boulevard. In spite of the fact that it was raining at intervals, Merry-Andrew, Pantaloon and Clown persisted. In the good humor of that winter of 1833, Paris had disguised itself as Venice. Such Shrove Tuesdays are no longer to be seen nowadays. Everything which exists being a scattered Carnival, there is no longer any Carnival.

The sidewalks were overflowing with pedestrians and the windows with curious spectators. The terraces which crown the peristyles of the theatres were bordered with spectators. Besides the maskers, they stared at that procession—peculiar to Shrove Tuesday as to Longchamps,—of vehicles of every description, citadines, tapissières, carioles, cabriolets marching in order, rigorously riveted to each other by the police regulations, and locked into rails, as it were. Any one in these vehicles is at once a spectator and a spectacle. Police sergeants maintained, on the sides of the boulevard, these two interminable parallel files, moving in contrary directions, and saw to it that nothing interfered with that double current, those two brooks of carriages, flowing, the one downstream, the other upstream, the one towards the Chaussée d'Antin, the other towards the Faubourg Saint-Antoine. The carriages of the peers of France and of the Ambassadors, emblazoned with coats of arms, held the middle of the way, going and coming freely. Certain joyous and magnificent trains, notably that of the Bœuf Gras, had the same privilege. In this gayety of Paris, England cracked her whip; Lord Seymour's post-chaise, harassed by a nickname from the populace, passed with great noise.

In the double file, along which the municipal guards galloped like sheep-dogs, honest family coaches, loaded down with great-aunts and grandmothers, displayed at their doors fresh groups of children in disguise, Clowns of seven years of age, Columbines of six, ravishing little creatures, who felt that they formed an official part of the public mirth, who were imbued with the dignity of their harlequinade, and who possessed the gravity of functionaries.

From time to time, a hitch arose somewhere in the procession of vehicles; one or other of the two lateral files halted until the knot was disentangled; one carriage delayed sufficed to paralyze the whole line. Then they set out again on the march.

The wedding carriages were in the file proceeding towards the Bastille, and skirting the right side of the Boulevard. At the top of the Pont-aux-Choux, there was a stoppage. Nearly at the same moment, the other file, which was proceeding towards the Madeleine, halted also. At that point of the file there was a carriage-load of maskers.

These carriages, or to speak more correctly, these wagon-loads of maskers are very familiar to Parisians. If they were missing on a Shrove Tuesday, or at the Mid-Lent, it would be taken in bad part, and people would say: "There's something behind that. Probably the ministry is about to undergo a change." A pile of Cassandras, Harlequins and Columbines, jolted along high above the passers-by, all possible grotesquenesses, from the Turk to the savage, Hercules supporting Marquises, fishwives who would have made Rabelais stop up his ears just as the Mænads made Aristophanes drop his eyes, tow wigs, pink tights, dandified hats, spectacles of a grimacer, three-cornered hats of Janot tormented with a butterfly, shouts directed at pedestrians, fists on hips, bold attitudes, bare shoulders, immodesty unchained; a chaos of shamelessness driven by a coachman crowned with flowers; this is what that institution was like.

Greece stood in need of the chariot of Thespis, France stands in need of the hackney-coach of Vadé.

Everything can be parodied, even parody. The Saturnalia, that grimace of antique beauty, ends, through exaggeration after exaggeration, in Shrove Tuesday; and the Bacchanal, formerly crowned with sprays of vine leaves and grapes, inundated with sunshine, displaying her marble breast in a divine semi-nudity, having at the present day lost her shape under the soaked rags of the North, has finally come to be called the Jack-pudding.

The tradition of carriage-loads of maskers runs back to the most ancient days of the monarchy. The accounts of Louis XI allot to the bailiff of the palace "twenty sous, Tournois, for three coaches of mascarades in the crossroads." In our day, these noisy heaps of creatures are accustomed to have themselves driven in some ancient cuckoo carriage, whose imperial they load down, or they overwhelm a hired landau, with its top thrown back, with their tumultuous groups. Twenty of them ride in a carriage intended for six. They cling to the seats, to the rumble, on the cheeks of the hood, on the shafts. They even bestride the carriage lamps. They stand, sit, lie, with their knees drawn up in a knot, and their legs hanging. The women sit on the men's laps. Far away, above the throng of heads, their wild pyramid is visible. These carriage-loads form mountains of mirth in the midst of the rout. Collé, Panard and Piron flow from it, enriched with slang. This carriage which has become colossal through its freight, has an air of conquest. Uproar reigns in front, tumult behind. People vociferate, shout, howl, there they break forth and writhe with enjoyment; gayety roars; sarcasm flames forth, joviality is flaunted like a red flag; two jades there drag farce blossomed forth into an apotheosis; it is the triumphal car of laughter.

A laughter that is too cynical to be frank. In truth, this laughter is suspicious. This laughter has a mission. It is charged with proving the Carnival to the Parisians.

These fishwife vehicles, in which one feels one knows not what shadows, set the philosopher to thinking. There is government therein. There one lays one's finger on a mysterious affinity between public men and public women.

It certainly is sad that turpitude heaped up should give a sum total of gayety, that by piling ignominy upon opprobrium the people should be enticed, that the system of spying, and serving as caryatids to prostitution should amuse the rabble when it confronts them, that the crowd loves to behold that monstrous living pile of tinsel rags, half dung, half light, roll by on four wheels howling and laughing, that they should clap their hands at this glory composed of all shames, that there would be no festival for the populace, did not the police promenade in their midst these sorts of twenty-headed hydras of joy. But what can be done about it? These be-ribboned and be-flowered tumbrils of mire are insulted and pardoned by the laughter of the public. The laughter of all is the accomplice of universal degradation. Certain unhealthy festivals disaggregate the people and convert them into the populace. And populaces, like tyrants, require buffoons. The King has Roquelaure, the populace has the Merry-Andrew. Paris is a great, mad city on every occasion that it is a great sublime city. There the Carnival forms part of politics. Paris,—let us confess it—willingly allows infamy to furnish it with comedy. She only demands of her masters—when she has masters—one thing: "Paint me the mud." Rome was of the same mind. She loved Nero. Nero was a titanic lighterman.

Chance ordained, as we have just said, that one of these shapeless clusters of masked men and women, dragged about on a vast calash, should halt on the left of the boulevard, while the wedding train halted on the right. The carriage-load of masks caught sight of the wedding carriage containing the bridal party opposite them on the other side of the boulevard.

"Hullo!" said a masker, "here's a wedding."

"A sham wedding," retorted another. "We are the genuine article."

And, being too far off to accost the wedding party, and fearing also, the rebuke of the police, the two maskers turned their eyes elsewhere.

At the end of another minute, the carriage-load of maskers had their hands full, the multitude set to yelling, which is the crowd's caress to masquerades; and the two maskers who had just spoken had to face the throng with their comrades, and did not find the entire repertory of projectiles of the fishmarkets too extensive to retort to the enormous verbal attacks of the populace. A frightful exchange of metaphors took place between the maskers and the crowd.

In the meanwhile, two other maskers in the same carriage, a Spaniard with an enormous nose, an elderly air, and huge black moustache, and a gaunt fishwife, who was quite a young girl, masked with a *loup*, had also noticed the wedding, and while their companions and the passers-by were exchanging insults, they had held a dialogue in a low voice.

Their aside was covered by the tumult and was lost in it. The gusts of rain had drenched the front of the vehicle, which was wide open; the breezes of February are not warm; as the fishwife, clad in a low-necked gown, replied to the Spaniard, she shivered, laughed and coughed.

Here is their dialogue:

"Say, now."

"What, daddy?"

"Do you see that old cove?"

"What old cove?"

"Yonder, in the first wedding-cart, on our side."

"The one with his arm hung up in a black cravat?"

"Yes."

"Well?"

"I'm sure that I know him."

"Ah!"

"I'm willing that they should cut my throat, and I'm ready to swear that I never said either you, thou, or I, in my life, if I don't know that Parisian." (*pantinois.*)

"Paris in Pantin to-day."

"Can you see the bride if you stoop down?"

"No."

"And the bridegroom?"

"There's no bridegroom in that trap."

"Bah!"

"Unless it's the old fellow."

"Try to get a sight of the bride by stooping very low."

"I can't."

"Never mind, that old cove who has something the matter with his paw I know, and that I'm positive."

"And what good does it do to know him?"

"No one can tell. Sometimes it does!"

"I don't care a hang for old fellows, that I don't!"

"I know him."

"Know him, if you want to."

"How the devil does he come to be one of the wedding party?"

"We are in it, too."

"Where does that wedding come from?"

"How should I know?"

"Listen."

"Well, what?"

"There's one thing you ought to do."

"What's that?"

"Get off of our trap and spin that wedding."

"What for?"

"To find out where it goes, and what it is. Hurry up and jump down, trot, my girl, your legs are young."

"I can't quit the vehicle."

"Why not?"

"I'm hired."

"Ah, the devil!"

"I owe my fishwife day to the prefecture."

"That's true."

"If I leave the cart, the first inspector who gets his eye on me will arrest me. You know that well enough."

"Yes, I do."

"I'm bought by the government for to-day."

"All the same, that old fellow bothers me."

"Do the old fellows bother you? But you're not a young girl."

"He's in the first carriage."

"Well?"

"In the bride's trap."

"What then?"

"So he is the father."

"What concern is that of mine?"

"I tell you that he's the father."

"As if he were the only father."

"Listen."

"What?"

"I can't go out otherwise than masked. Here I'm concealed, no one knows that I'm here. But to-morrow, there will be no more maskers. It's Ash Wednesday. I run the risk of being nabbed. I must sneak back into my hole. But you are free."

"Not particularly."

"More than I am, at any rate."

"Well, what of that?"

"You must try to find out where that wedding party went to."

"Where it went?"

"Yes."

"I know."

"Where is it going then?"

"To the Cadran-Bleu."

"In the first place, it's not in that direction."

"Well! to la Rapée."

"Or elsewhere."

"It's free. Wedding parties are at liberty."

"That's not the point at all. I tell you that you must try to learn for me what that wedding is, who that old cove belongs to, and where that wedding pair lives."

"I like that! that would be queer. It's so easy to find out a wedding party that passed through the street on a Shrove Tuesday, a week afterwards. A pin in a hay-mow! It ain't possible!"

"That don't matter. You must try. You understand me, Azelma."

The two files resumed their movement on both sides of the boulevard, in opposite directions, and the carriage of the maskers lost sight of the "trap" of the bride.

# II

## JEAN VALJEAN STILL WEARS HIS ARM IN A SLING

To realize one's dream. To whom is this accorded? There must be elections for this in heaven; we are all candidates, unknown to ourselves; the angels vote. Cosette and Marius had been elected.

Cosette, both at the mayor's office and at church, was dazzling and touching. Toussaint, assisted by Nicolette, had dressed her.

Cosette wore over a petticoat of white taffeta, her robe of Binche guipure, a veil of English point, a necklace of fine pearls, a wreath of orange flowers; all this was white, and, from the midst of that whiteness she beamed forth. It was an exquisite candor expanding and becoming transfigured in the light. One would have pronounced her a virgin on the point of turning into a goddess.

Marius' handsome hair was lustrous and perfumed; here and there, beneath the thick curls, pale lines—the scars of the barricade—were visible.

The grandfather, haughty, with head held high, amalgamating more than ever in his toilet and his manners all the elegances of the epoch of Barras, escorted Cosette. He took the place of Jean Valjean, who, on account of his arm being still in a sling, could not give his hand to the bride.

Jean Valjean, dressed in black, followed them with a smile.

"Monsieur Fauchelevent," said the grandfather to him, "this is a fine day. I vote for the end of afflictions and sorrows. Henceforth, there must be no sadness anywhere. Pardieu, I decree joy! Evil has no right to exist. That there should be any unhappy men is, in sooth, a disgrace to the azure of the sky. Evil does not come from man, who is good at bottom. All human miseries have for their capital and central government hell, otherwise, known as the Devil's Tuileries. Good, here I am uttering demagogical words! As far as I am concerned, I have no longer any political opinions; let all men be rich, that is to say, mirthful, and I confine myself to that."

When, at the conclusion of all the ceremonies, after having pronounced before the mayor and before the priest all possible "yesses," after having signed the registers at the municipality and at the sacristy, after having exchanged their rings, after having knelt side by side under the pall of white moire in the smoke of the censer, they arrived, hand in hand, admired and envied by all, Marius in black, she in white, preceded by the suisse, with the epaulets of a colonel, tapping the pavement with his halberd, between two rows of astonished spectators, at the portals of the church, both leaves of which were thrown wide open, ready to enter their carriage again, and all being finished, Cosette still could not believe that it was real. She looked at Marius, she looked at the crowd, she looked at the sky: it seemed as though she feared that she should wake up from her dream. Her amazed and uneasy air added something indescribably enchanting to her beauty. They entered the same carriage to return home, Marius beside Cosette; M. Gillenormand and Jean Valjean sat opposite them; Aunt Gillenormand had withdrawn one degree, and was in the second vehicle.

"My children," said the grandfather, "here you are, Monsieur le Baron and Madame la Baronne, with an income of thirty thousand livres."

And Cosette, nestling close to Marius, caressed his ear with an angelic whisper: "So it is true. My name is Marius. I am Madame Thou."

These two creatures were resplendent. They had reached that irrevocable and irrecoverable moment, at the dazzling intersection of all youth and all joy. They realized the verses of Jean Prouvaire; they were forty years old taken together. It was marriage sublimated; these two children were two lilies. They did not see each other, they did not contemplate each other. Cosette perceived Marius in the midst of a glory; Marius perceived Cosette on an altar. And on that altar, and in that glory, the two apotheoses mingling, in the background, one knows not how, behind a cloud for Cosette, in a flash for Marius, there was the ideal thing, the real thing, the meeting of the kiss and the dream, the nuptial pillow. All the torments through which they had passed came back to them in intoxication. It seemed to them that their sorrows, their sleepless nights, their tears, their anguish, their terrors, their despair, converted into caresses and rays of light, rendered still more charming the charming hour which was approaching; and that their griefs were but so many handmaidens who were preparing the toilet of joy. How good it is to have suffered! Their unhappiness formed a halo round their happiness. The long agony of their love was terminating in an ascension.

It was the same enchantment in two souls, tinged with voluptuousness in Marius, and with modesty in Cosette. They said to each other in low tones: "We will go back to take a look at our little garden in the Rue Plumet." The folds of Cosette's gown lay across Marius.

Such a day is an ineffable mixture of dream and of reality. One possesses and one supposes. One still has time before one to divine. The emotion on that day, of being at midday and of dreaming of midnight is indescribable. The delights of these two hearts overflowed upon the crowd, and inspired the passers-by with cheerfulness.

People halted in the Rue Saint-Antoine, in front of Saint-Paul, to gaze through the windows of the carriage at the orange-flowers quivering on Cosette's head.

Then they returned home to the Rue des Filles-du-Calvaire. Marius, triumphant and radiant, mounted side by side with Cosette the staircase up which he had been borne in a dying condition. The poor, who had trooped to the door, and who shared their purses, blessed them. There were flowers everywhere. The house was no less fragrant than the church; after the incense, roses. They thought they heard voices carolling in the infinite; they had God in their hearts; destiny appeared to them like a ceiling of stars; above their heads they beheld the light of a rising sun. All at once, the clock struck. Marius glanced at Cosette's charming bare arm, and at the rosy things which were vaguely visible through the lace of her bodice, and Cosette, intercepting Marius' glance, blushed to her very hair.

Quite a number of old family friends of the Gillenormand family had been invited; they pressed about Cosette. Each one vied with the rest in saluting her as Madame la Baronne.

The officer, Théodule Gillenormand, now a captain, had come from Chartres, where he was stationed in garrison, to be present at the wedding of his cousin Pontmercy. Cosette did not recognize him.

He, on his side, habituated as he was to have women consider him handsome, retained no more recollection of Cosette than of any other woman.

"How right I was not to believe in that story about the lancer!" said Father Gillenormand, to himself.

Cosette had never been more tender with Jean Valjean. She was in unison with Father Gillenormand; while he erected joy into aphorisms and maxims, she exhaled goodness like a perfume. Happiness desires that all the world should be happy.

She regained, for the purpose of addressing Jean Valjean, inflections of voice belonging to the time when she was a little girl. She caressed him with her smile.

A banquet had been spread in the dining-room.

Illumination as brilliant as the daylight is the necessary seasoning of a great joy. Mist and obscurity are not accepted by the happy. They do not consent to be black. The night, yes; the shadows, no. If there is no sun, one must be made.

The dining-room was full of gay things. In the centre, above the white and glittering table, was a Venetian lustre with flat plates, with all sorts of colored birds, blue, violet, red, and green, perched amid the candles; around the chandelier, girandoles, on the walls, sconces with triple and quintuple branches; mirrors, silverware, glassware, plate, porcelain, faïence, pottery, gold and silversmith's work, all was sparkling and gay. The empty spaces between the candelabra were filled in with bouquets, so that where there was not a light, there was a flower.

In the antechamber, three violins and a flute softly played quartettes by Haydn.

Jean Valjean had seated himself on a chair in the drawing-room, behind the door, the leaf of which folded back upon him in such a manner as to nearly conceal him. A few moments before they sat down to table, Cosette came, as though inspired by a sudden whim, and made him a deep courtesy, spreading out her bridal toilet with both hands, and with a tenderly roguish glance, she asked him:

"Father, are you satisfied?"

"Yes," said Jean Valjean, "I am content!"

"Well, then, laugh."

Jean Valjean began to laugh.

A few moments later, Basque announced that dinner was served.

The guests, preceded by M. Gillenormand with Cosette on his arm, entered the dining-room, and arranged themselves in the proper order around the table.

Two large armchairs figured on the right and left of the bride, the first for M. Gillenormand, the other for Jean Valjean. M. Gillenormand took his seat. The other armchair remained empty.

They looked about for M. Fauchelevent.

He was no longer there.

M. Gillenormand questioned Basque.

"Do you know where M. Fauchelevent is?"

"Sir," replied Basque, "I do, precisely. M. Fauchelevent told me to say to you, sir, that he was suffering, his injured hand was paining him somewhat, and that he could not dine with Monsieur le Baron and

Madame la Baronne. That he begged to be excused, that he would come to-morrow. He has just taken his departure."

That empty armchair chilled the effusion of the wedding feast for a moment. But, if M. Fauchelevent was absent, M. Gillenormand was present, and the grandfather beamed for two. He affirmed that M. Fauchelevent had done well to retire early, if he were suffering, but that it was only a slight ailment. This declaration sufficed. Moreover, what is an obscure corner in such a submersion of joy? Cosette and Marius were passing through one of those egotistical and blessed moments when no other faculty is left to a person than that of receiving happiness. And then, an idea occurred to M. Gillenormand.—"Pardieu, this armchair is empty. Come hither, Marius. Your aunt will permit it, although she has a right to you. This armchair is for you. That is legal and delightful. Fortunatus beside Fortunata."—Applause from the whole table. Marius took Jean Valjean's place beside Cosette, and things fell out so that Cosette, who had, at first, been saddened by Jean Valjean's absence, ended by being satisfied with it. From the moment when Marius took his place, and was the substitute, Cosette would not have regretted God himself. She set her sweet little foot, shod in white satin, on Marius' foot.

The armchair being occupied, M. Fauchelevent was obliterated; and nothing was lacking.

And, five minutes afterward, the whole table from one end to the other, was laughing with all the animation of forgetfulness.

At dessert, M. Gillenormand, rising to his feet, with a glass of champagne in his hand—only half full so that the palsy of his eighty years might not cause an overflow,—proposed the health of the married pair.

"You shall not escape two sermons," he exclaimed. "This morning you had one from the curé, this evening you shall have one from your grandfather. Listen to me; I will give you a bit of advice: Adore each other. I do not make a pack of gyrations, I go straight to the mark, be happy. In all creation, only the turtledoves are wise. Philosophers say: 'Moderate your joys.' I say: 'Give rein to your joys.' Be as much smitten with each other as fiends. Be in a rage about it. The philosophers talk stuff and nonsense. I should like to stuff their philosophy down their gullets again. Can there be too many perfumes, too many open rose-buds, too many nightingales singing, too many green leaves, too much aurora in life? can people love each other too much? can people please each other too much? Take care, Estelle, thou art too pretty! Have a care, Nemorin, thou art too handsome! Fine stupidity, in sooth! Can people enchant each other too much, cajole each other too much, charm each other too much? Can one be too much alive, too happy? Moderate your joys. Ah, indeed! Down with the philosophers! Wisdom consists in jubilation. Make merry, let us make merry. Are we happy because we are good, or are we good because we are happy? Is the Sancy diamond called the Sancy because it belonged to Harley de Sancy, or because it weighs six hundred carats? I know nothing about it, life is full of such problems; the important point is to possess the Sancy and happiness. Let us be happy without quibbling and quirking. Let us obey the sun blindly. What is the sun? It is love. He who says love, says woman. Ah! ah! behold omnipotence—women. Ask that demagogue of a Marius if he is not the slave of that little tyrant of a Cosette. And of his own free will, too, the coward! Woman! There is no Robespierre who keeps his place but woman reigns. I am no longer Royalist except towards that royalty. What is Adam? The kingdom of Eve. No '89 for Eve. There has been the royal sceptre surmounted by a fleur-de-lys, there has been the imperial sceptre surmounted by a globe, there has been the sceptre of Charlemagne, which was of iron, there has been the sceptre of Louis the Great, which was of gold,—the revolution twisted them between its thumb and forefinger, ha'penny straws; it is done with, it is broken, it lies on the earth, there is no longer any sceptre, but make me a revolution against that little embroidered handkerchief, which smells of patchouli! I should like to see you do it. Try. Why is it so solid? Because it is a gewgaw. Ah! you are the nineteenth century? Well, what then? And we have been as foolish as you. Do not imagine that you have effected much change in the universe, because your trip-gallant is called the cholera-morbus, and because your *pourrée* is called the cachuca. In fact, the women must always be loved. I defy you to escape from that. These friends are our angels. Yes, love, woman, the kiss forms a circle from which I defy you to escape; and, for my own part, I should be only too happy to re-enter it. Which of you has seen the planet Venus, the coquette of the abyss, the Célimène of the ocean, rise in the infinite, calming all here below? The ocean is a rough Alcestis. Well, grumble as he will, when Venus appears he is forced to smile. That brute beast submits. We are all made so. Wrath, tempest, claps of thunder, foam to the very ceiling. A woman enters on the scene, a planet rises; flat on your face! Marius was fighting six months ago; to-day he is married. That is well. Yes, Marius, yes, Cosette, you are in the right. Exist boldly for each other, make us burst with rage that we cannot do the same, idealize each other, catch in your beaks all the tiny blades of felicity that exist on earth, and arrange yourselves a nest for life. Pardi, to love, to be loved, what a fine miracle when one is young! Don't imagine that you have invented that. I, too, have had my dream, I, too, have meditated, I, too, have sighed; I, too, have had a moonlight soul. Love is a child six thousand years old. Love has the right to a long white beard. Methusalem is a street arab beside Cupid. For sixty centuries men and women have got out of their scrape by loving. The devil, who is cunning, took to hating man; man, who is still more cunning, took to loving woman. In this way he does more good than the devil does him harm. This craft was discovered in the days of the terrestrial paradise. The invention is old, my friends, but it is perfectly new. Profit by it. Be Daphnis and Chloe, while waiting to become Philemon and Baucis. Manage so that, when you are with each other, nothing shall be lacking to you, and that Cosette may be the sun for Marius, and that Marius may be the universe to Cosette. Cosette, let your fine weather be the smile of your husband; Marius, let your rain be your wife's tears. And let it never rain in your household. You have filched the winning number in the lottery; you have gained the great prize, guard it well, keep it under lock and key, do not squander it, adore each other and snap your fingers at all the rest. Believe what I say to you. It is good sense. And good sense cannot lie. Be a religion to each other. Each man has his own fashion of adoring God. Saperlotte! the best way to adore God is to love one's wife. *I love thee!* that's my catechism. He who loves is orthodox. The oath of Henri IV places sanctity somewhere between feasting and drunkenness. Ventre-saint-gris! I don't belong to the religion of that oath. Woman is forgotten in it. This astonishes me on the part of Henri IV. My friends, long live women! I am old, they say; it's astonishing how much I feel in the mood to be young. I should like to go and listen to the bagpipes in the woods. Children who contrive to be beautiful and contented,—that intoxicates me. I would like greatly to get married, if any one would have me. It is impossible to imagine that God could have made us for anything but this: to idolize, to coo, to preen ourselves, to be dove-like, to be dainty, to bill and coo our loves from morn to night, to gaze at one's image in one's little wife, to be proud, to be triumphant, to plume oneself; that is the aim of life. There, let not that displease you which we used to think in our day, when we were young folks. Ah! vertu-bamboche! what charming women there were in those days, and what pretty little faces and what lovely lasses! I committed my ravages among them. Then love each other. If people did not love each other, I really do not see what use there would be in having any springtime; and for my own part, I should pray the good God to shut up all the beautiful things that he shows us, and to take away from us and put back in his box, the flowers, the birds, and the pretty maidens. My children, receive an old man's blessing."

The evening was gay, lively and agreeable. The grandfather's sovereign good humor gave the key-note to the whole feast, and each person regulated his conduct on that almost centenarian cordiality. They danced a little, they laughed a great deal; it was an amiable wedding. Goodman Days of Yore might have been invited to it. However, he was present in the person of Father Gillenormand.

There was a tumult, then silence.

The married pair disappeared.

A little after midnight, the Gillenormand house became a temple.

Here we pause. On the threshold of wedding nights stands a smiling angel with his finger on his lips.

The soul enters into contemplation before that sanctuary where the celebration of love takes place.

There should be flashes of light athwart such houses. The joy which they contain ought to make its escape through the stones of the walls in brilliancy, and vaguely illuminate the gloom. It is impossible that this sacred and fatal festival should not give off a celestial radiance to the infinite. Love is the sublime crucible wherein the fusion of the man and the woman takes place; the being one, the being triple, the being final, the human trinity proceeds from it. This birth of two souls into one, ought to be an emotion for the gloom. The lover is the priest; the ravished virgin is terrified. Something of that joy ascends to God. Where true marriage is, that is to say, where there is love, the ideal enters in. A nuptial bed makes a nook of dawn amid the shadows. If it were given to the eye of the flesh to scan the formidable and charming visions of the upper life, it is probable that we should behold the forms of night, the winged unknowns, the blue passers of the invisible, bend down, a throng of sombre heads, around the luminous house, satisfied, showering benedictions, pointing out to each other the virgin wife gently alarmed, sweetly terrified, and bearing the reflection of human bliss upon their divine countenances. If at that supreme hour, the wedded pair, dazzled with voluptuousness and believing themselves alone, were to listen, they would hear in their chamber a confused rustling of wings. Perfect happiness implies a mutual understanding with the angels. That dark little chamber has all heaven for its ceiling. When two mouths, rendered sacred by love, approach to create, it is impossible that there should not be, above that ineffable kiss, a quivering throughout the immense mystery of stars.

These felicities are the true ones. There is no joy outside of these joys. Love is the only ecstasy. All the rest weeps.

To love, or to have loved,—this suffices. Demand nothing more. There is no other pearl to be found in the shadowy folds of life. To love is a fulfilment.

# III

## THE INSEPARABLE

What had become of Jean Valjean?

Immediately after having laughed, at Cosette's graceful command, when no one was paying any heed to him, Jean Valjean had risen and had gained the antechamber unperceived. This was the very room which, eight months before, he had entered black with mud, with blood and powder, bringing back the grandson to the grandfather. The old wainscoting was garlanded with foliage and flowers; the musicians were seated on the sofa on which they had laid Marius down. Basque, in a black coat, knee-breeches, white stockings and white gloves, was arranging roses round all of the dishes that were to be served. Jean Valjean pointed to his arm in its sling, charged Basque to explain his absence, and went away.

The long windows of the dining-room opened on the street. Jean Valjean stood for several minutes, erect and motionless in the darkness, beneath those radiant windows. He listened. The confused sounds of the banquet reached his ear. He heard the loud, commanding tones of the grandfather, the violins, the clatter of the plates, the bursts of laughter, and through all that merry uproar, he distinguished Cosette's sweet and joyous voice.

He quitted the Rue des Filles-du-Calvaire, and returned to the Rue de l'Homme Armé.

In order to return thither, he took the Rue Saint-Louis, the Rue Culture-Sainte-Catherine, and the Blancs-Manteaux; it was a little longer, but it was the road through which, for the last three months, he had become accustomed to pass every day on his way from the Rue de l'Homme Armé to the Rue des Filles-du-Calvaire, in order to avoid the obstructions and the mud in the Rue Vieille-du-Temple.

This road, through which Cosette had passed, excluded for him all possibility of any other itinerary.

Jean Valjean entered his lodgings. He lighted his candle and mounted the stairs. The apartment was empty. Even Toussaint was no longer there. Jean Valjean's step made more noise than usual in the chambers. All the cupboards stood open. He penetrated to Cosette's bedroom. There were no sheets on the bed. The pillow, covered with ticking, and without a case or lace, was laid on the blankets folded up on the foot of the mattress, whose covering was visible, and on which no one was ever to sleep again. All the little feminine objects which Cosette was attached to had been carried away; nothing remained except the heavy furniture and the four walls. Toussaint's bed was despoiled in like manner. One bed only was made up, and seemed to be waiting some one, and this was Jean Valjean's bed.

Jean Valjean looked at the walls, closed some of the cupboard doors, and went and came from one room to another.

Then he sought his own chamber once more, and set his candle on a table.

He had disengaged his arm from the sling, and he used his right hand as though it did not hurt him.

He approached his bed, and his eyes rested, was it by chance? was it intentionally? on the *inseparable* of which Cosette had been jealous, on the little portmanteau which never left him. On his arrival in the Rue de l'Homme Armé, on the 4th of June, he had deposited it on a round table near the head of his bed. He went to this table with a sort of vivacity, took a key from his pocket, and opened the valise.

From it he slowly drew forth the garments in which, ten years before, Cosette had quitted Montfermeil; first the little gown, then the black fichu, then the stout, coarse child's shoes which Cosette might almost have worn still, so tiny were her feet, then the fustian bodice, which was very thick, then the knitted petticoat, next the apron with pockets, then the woollen stockings. These stockings, which still preserved the graceful form of a tiny leg, were no longer than Jean Valjean's hand. All this was black of hue. It was he who had brought those garments to Montfermeil for her. As he removed them from the valise, he laid them on the bed. He fell to thinking. He called up memories. It was in winter, in a very cold month of December, she was shivering, half-naked, in rags, her poor little feet were all red in their wooden shoes. He, Jean Valjean, had made her abandon those rags to clothe herself in these mourning habiliments. The mother must have felt pleased in her grave, to see her daughter wearing mourning for her, and, above all, to see that she was properly clothed, and that she was warm. He thought of that forest of Montfermeil; they had traversed it together, Cosette and he; he thought of what the weather had been, of the leafless trees, of the wood destitute of birds, of the sunless sky; it mattered not, it was charming. He arranged the tiny garments on the bed, the fichu next to the petticoat, the stockings beside the shoes, and he looked at them, one after the other. She was no taller than that, she had her big doll in her arms, she had put her louis d'or in the pocket of that apron, she had laughed, they walked hand in hand, she had no one in the world but him.

Then his venerable, white head fell forward on the bed, that stoical old heart broke, his face was engulfed, so to speak, in Cosette's garments, and if any one had passed up the stairs at that moment, he would have heard frightful sobs.

# IV

## The Immortal Liver

The old and formidable struggle, of which we have already witnessed so many phases, began once more.

Jacob struggled with the angel but one night. Alas! how many times have we beheld Jean Valjean seized bodily by his conscience, in the darkness, and struggling desperately against it!

Unheard-of conflict! At certain moments the foot slips; at other moments the ground crumbles away underfoot. How many times had that conscience, mad for the good, clasped and overthrown him! How many times had the truth set her knee inexorably upon his breast! How many times, hurled to earth by the light, had he begged for mercy! How many times had that implacable spark, lighted within him, and upon him by the Bishop, dazzled him by force when he had wished to be blind! How many times had he risen to his feet in the combat, held fast to the rock, leaning against sophism, dragged in the dust, now getting the upper hand of his conscience, again overthrown by it! How many times, after an equivoque, after the specious and treacherous reasoning of egotism, had he heard his irritated conscience cry in his ear: "A trip! you wretch!" How many times had his refractory thoughts rattled convulsively in his throat, under the evidence of duty! Resistance to God. Funereal sweats. What secret wounds which he alone felt bleed! What excoriations in his lamentable existence! How many times he had risen bleeding, bruised, broken, enlightened, despair in his heart, serenity in his soul! and, vanquished, he had felt himself the conqueror. And, after having dislocated, broken, and rent his conscience with red-hot pincers, it had said to him, as it stood over him, formidable, luminous, and tranquil: "Now, go in peace!"

But on emerging from so melancholy a conflict, what a lugubrious peace, alas!

Nevertheless, that night Jean Valjean felt that he was passing through his final combat.

A heart-rending question presented itself.

Predestinations are not all direct; they do not open out in a straight avenue before the predestined man; they have blind courts, impassable alleys, obscure turns, disturbing crossroads offering the choice of many ways. Jean Valjean had halted at that moment at the most perilous of these crossroads.

He had come to the supreme crossing of good and evil. He had that gloomy intersection beneath his eyes. On this occasion once more, as had happened to him already in other sad vicissitudes, two roads opened out before him, the one tempting, the other alarming.

Which was he to take?

He was counselled to the one which alarmed him by that mysterious index finger which we all perceive whenever we fix our eyes on the darkness.

Once more, Jean Valjean had the choice between the terrible port and the smiling ambush.

Is it then true? the soul may recover; but not fate. Frightful thing! an incurable destiny!

This is the problem which presented itself to him:

In what manner was Jean Valjean to behave in relation to the happiness of Cosette and Marius? It was he who had willed that happiness, it was he who had brought it about; he had, himself, buried it in his entrails, and at that moment, when he reflected on it, he was able to enjoy the sort of satisfaction which an armorer would experience on recognizing his factory mark on a knife, on withdrawing it, all smoking, from his own breast.

Cosette had Marius, Marius possessed Cosette. They had everything, even riches. And this was his doing.

But what was he, Jean Valjean, to do with this happiness, now that it existed, now that it was there? Should he force himself on this happiness? Should he treat it as belonging to him? No doubt, Cosette did belong to another; but should he, Jean Valjean, retain of Cosette all that he could retain? Should he remain the sort of father, half seen but respected, which he had hitherto been? Should he, without saying a word, bring his past to that future? Should he present himself there, as though he had a right, and should he seat himself, veiled, at that luminous fireside? Should he take those innocent hands into his tragic hands, with a smile? Should he place upon the peaceful fender of the Gillenormand drawing-room those feet of his, which dragged behind them the disgraceful shadow of the law? Should he enter into participation in the fair fortunes of Cosette and Marius? Should he render the obscurity on his brow and the cloud upon theirs still more dense? Should he place his catastrophe as a third associate in their felicity? Should he continue to hold his peace? In a word, should he be the sinister mute of destiny beside these two happy beings?

We must have become habituated to fatality and to encounters with it, in order to have the daring to raise our eyes when certain questions appear to us in all their horrible nakedness. Good or evil stands behind this severe interrogation point. What are you going to do? demands the sphinx.

This habit of trial Jean Valjean possessed. He gazed intently at the sphinx.

He examined the pitiless problem under all its aspects.

Cosette, that charming existence, was the raft of this shipwreck. What was he to do? To cling fast to it, or to let go his hold?

If he clung to it, he should emerge from disaster, he should ascend again into the sunlight, he should let the bitter water drip from his garments and his hair, he was saved, he should live.

And if he let go his hold?

Then the abyss.

Thus he took sad council with his thoughts. Or, to speak more correctly, he fought; he kicked furiously internally, now against his will, now against his conviction.

Happily for Jean Valjean that he had been able to weep. That relieved him, possibly. But the beginning was savage. A tempest, more furious than the one which had formerly driven him to Arras, broke loose within him. The past surged up before him facing the present; he compared them and sobbed. The silence of tears once opened, the despairing man writhed.

He felt that he had been stopped short.

Alas! in this fight to the death between our egotism and our duty, when we thus retreat step by step before our immutable ideal, bewildered, furious, exasperated at having to yield, disputing the ground, hoping for a possible flight, seeking an escape, what an abrupt and sinister resistance does the foot of the wall offer in our rear!

To feel the sacred shadow which forms an obstacle!

The invisible inexorable, what an obsession!

Then, one is never done with conscience. Make your choice, Brutus; make your choice, Cato. It is fathomless, since it is God. One flings into that well the labor of one's whole life, one flings in one's fortune, one flings in one's riches, one flings in one's success, one flings in one's liberty or fatherland, one flings in one's well-being, one flings in one's repose, one flings in one's joy! More! more! more! Empty the vase! tip the urn! One must finish by flinging in one's heart.

Somewhere in the fog of the ancient hells, there is a tun like that.

Is not one pardonable, if one at last refuses! Can the inexhaustible have any right? Are not chains which are endless above human strength? Who would blame Sisyphus and Jean Valjean for saying: "It is enough!"

The obedience of matter is limited by friction; is there no limit to the obedience of the soul? If perpetual motion is impossible, can perpetual self-sacrifice be exacted?

The first step is nothing, it is the last which is difficult. What was the Champmathieu affair in comparison with Cosette's marriage and of that which it entailed? What is a re-entrance into the galleys, compared to entrance into the void?

Oh, first step that must be descended, how sombre art thou! Oh, second step, how black art thou!

How could he refrain from turning aside his head this time?

Martyrdom is sublimation, corrosive sublimation. It is a torture which consecrates. One can consent to it for the first hour; one seats oneself on the throne of glowing iron, one places on one's head the crown of hot iron, one accepts the globe of red hot iron, one takes the sceptre of red hot iron, but the mantle of flame still remains to be donned, and comes there not a moment when the miserable flesh revolts and when one abdicates from suffering?

At length, Jean Valjean entered into the peace of exhaustion.

He weighed, he reflected, he considered the alternatives, the mysterious balance of light and darkness.

Should he impose his galleys on those two dazzling children, or should he consummate his irremediable engulfment by himself? On one side lay the sacrifice of Cosette, on the other that of himself.

At what solution should he arrive? What decision did he come to?

What resolution did he take? What was his own inward definitive response to the unbribable interrogatory of fatality? What door did he decide to open? Which side of his life did he resolve upon closing and condemning? Among all the unfathomable precipices which surrounded him, which was his choice? What extremity did he accept? To which of the gulfs did he nod his head?

His dizzy reverie lasted all night long.

He remained there until daylight, in the same attitude, bent double over that bed, prostrate beneath the enormity of fate, crushed, perchance, alas! with clenched fists, with arms outspread at right angles, like a man crucified who has been un-nailed, and flung face down on the earth. There he remained for twelve hours, the twelve long hours of a long winter's night, ice-cold, without once raising his head, and without uttering a word. He was as motionless as a corpse, while his thoughts wallowed on the earth and soared, now like the hydra, now like the eagle. Any one to behold him thus motionless would have pronounced him dead; all at once he shuddered convulsively, and his mouth, glued to Cosette's garments, kissed them; then it could be seen that he was alive.

Who could see? Since Jean Valjean was alone, and there was no one there.

The One who is in the shadows.

BOOK SEVENTH
THE LAST DRAUGHT FROM THE CUP

# I

## The Seventh Circle and the Eighth Heaven

The days that follow weddings are solitary. People respect the meditations of the happy pair. And also, their tardy slumbers, to some degree. The tumult of visits and congratulations only begins later on. On the morning of the 17th of February, it was a little past midday when Basque, with napkin and feather-duster under his arm, busy in setting his antechamber to rights, heard a light tap at the door. There had been no ring, which was discreet on such a day. Basque opened the door, and beheld M. Fauchelevent. He introduced him into the drawing-room, still encumbered and topsy-turvy, and which bore the air of a field of battle after the joys of the preceding evening.

"*Dame*, sir," remarked Basque, "we all woke up late."

"Is your master up?" asked Jean Valjean.

"How is Monsieur's arm?" replied Basque.

"Better. Is your master up?"

"Which one? the old one or the new one?"

"Monsieur Pontmercy."

"Monsieur le Baron," said Basque, drawing himself up.

A man is a Baron most of all to his servants. He counts for something with them; they are what a philosopher would call, bespattered with the title, and that flatters them. Marius, be it said in passing, a militant republican as he had proved, was now a Baron in spite of himself. A small revolution had taken place in the family in connection with this title. It was now M. Gillenormand who clung to it, and Marius who detached himself from it. But Colonel Pontmercy had written: "My son will bear my title." Marius obeyed. And then, Cosette, in whom the woman was beginning to dawn, was delighted to be a Baroness.

"Monsieur le Baron?" repeated Basque. "I will go and see. I will tell him that M. Fauchelevent is here."

"No. Do not tell him that it is I. Tell him that some one wishes to speak to him in private, and mention no name."

"Ah!" ejaculated Basque.

"I wish to surprise him."

"Ah!" ejaculated Basque once more, emitting his second "ah!" as an explanation of the first.

And he left the room.

Jean Valjean remained alone.

The drawing-room, as we have just said, was in great disorder. It seemed as though, by lending an ear, one might still hear the vague noise of the wedding. On the polished floor lay all sorts of flowers which had fallen from garlands and head-dresses. The wax candles, burned to stumps, added stalactites of wax to the crystal drops of the chandeliers. Not a single piece of furniture was in its place. In the corners, three or four armchairs, drawn close together in a circle, had the appearance of continuing a conversation. The whole effect was cheerful. A certain grace still lingers round a dead feast. It has been a happy thing. On the chairs in disarray, among those fading flowers, beneath those extinct lights, people have thought of joy. The sun had succeeded to the chandelier, and made its way gayly into the drawing-room.

Several minutes elapsed. Jean Valjean stood motionless on the spot where Basque had left him. He was very pale. His eyes were hollow, and so sunken in his head by sleeplessness that they nearly disappeared in their orbits. His black coat bore the weary folds of a garment that has been up all night. The elbows were whitened with the down which the friction of cloth against linen leaves behind it.

Jean Valjean stared at the window outlined on the polished floor at his feet by the sun.

There came a sound at the door, and he raised his eyes.

Marius entered, his head well up, his mouth smiling, an indescribable light on his countenance, his brow expanded, his eyes triumphant. He had not slept either.

"It is you, father!" he exclaimed, on catching sight of Jean Valjean; "that idiot of a Basque had such a mysterious air! But you have come too early. It is only half past twelve. Cosette is asleep."

That word: "Father," said to M. Fauchelevent by Marius, signified: supreme felicity. There had always existed, as the reader knows, a lofty wall, a coldness and a constraint between them; ice which must be broken or melted. Marius had reached that point of intoxication when the wall was lowered, when the ice dissolved, and when M. Fauchelevent was to him, as to Cosette, a father.

He continued: his words poured forth, as is the peculiarity of divine paroxysms of joy.

"How glad I am to see you! If you only knew how we missed you yesterday! Good morning, father. How is your hand? Better, is it not?"

And, satisfied with the favorable reply which he had made to himself, he pursued:

"We have both been talking about you. Cosette loves you so dearly! You must not forget that you have a chamber here, We want nothing more to do with the Rue de l'Homme Armé. We will have no more of it at all. How could you go to live in a street like that, which is sickly, which is disagreeable, which is ugly, which has a barrier at one end, where one is cold, and into which one cannot enter? You are to come and install yourself here. And this very day. Or you will have to deal with Cosette. She means to lead us all by the nose, I warn you. You have your own chamber here, it is close to ours, it opens on the garden; the trouble with the clock has been attended to, the bed is made, it is all ready, you have only to take possession of it. Near your bed Cosette has placed a huge, old, easy-chair covered with Utrecht velvet and she has said to it: 'Stretch out your arms to him.' A nightingale comes to the clump of acacias opposite your windows, every spring. In two months more you will have it. You will have its nest on your left and ours on your right. By night it will sing, and by day Cosette will prattle. Your chamber faces due South. Cosette will arrange your books for you, your Voyages of Captain Cook and the other,—Vancouver's and all your affairs. I believe that there is a little valise to which you are attached, I have fixed upon a corner of honor for that. You have conquered my grandfather, you suit him. We will live together. Do you play whist? you will overwhelm my grandfather with delight if you play whist. It is you who shall take Cosette to walk on the days when I am at the courts, you shall give her your arm, you know, as you used to, in the Luxembourg. We are absolutely resolved to be happy. And you shall be included in it, in our happiness, do you hear, father? Come, will you breakfast with us to-day?"

"Sir," said Jean Valjean, "I have something to say to you. I am an ex-convict."

The limit of shrill sounds perceptible can be overleaped, as well in the case of the mind as in that of the ear. These words: "I am an ex-convict," proceeding from the mouth of M. Fauchelevent and entering the ear of Marius overshot the possible. It seemed to him that something had just been said to him; but he did not know what. He stood with his mouth wide open.

Then he perceived that the man who was addressing him was frightful. Wholly absorbed in his own dazzled state, he had not, up to that moment, observed the other man's terrible pallor.

Jean Valjean untied the black cravat which supported his right arm, unrolled the linen from around his hand, bared his thumb and showed it to Marius.

"There is nothing the matter with my hand," said he.

Marius looked at the thumb.

"There has not been anything the matter with it," went on Jean Valjean.

There was, in fact, no trace of any injury.

Jean Valjean continued:

"It was fitting that I should be absent from your marriage. I absented myself as much as was in my power. So I invented this injury in order that I might not commit a forgery, that I might not introduce a flaw into the marriage documents, in order that I might escape from signing."

Marius stammered.

"What is the meaning of this?"

"The meaning of it is," replied Jean Valjean, "that I have been in the galleys."

"You are driving me mad!" exclaimed Marius in terror.

"Monsieur Pontmercy," said Jean Valjean, "I was nineteen years in the galleys. For theft. Then, I was condemned for life for theft, for a second offence. At the present moment, I have broken my ban."

In vain did Marius recoil before the reality, refuse the fact, resist the evidence, he was forced to give way. He began to understand, and, as always happens in such cases, he understood too much. An inward shudder of hideous enlightenment flashed through him; an idea which made him quiver traversed his mind. He caught a glimpse of a wretched destiny for himself in the future.

"Say all, say all!" he cried. "You are Cosette's father!"

And he retreated a couple of paces with a movement of indescribable horror.

Jean Valjean elevated his head with so much majesty of attitude that he seemed to grow even to the ceiling.

"It is necessary that you should believe me here, sir; although our oath to others may not be received in law. . ."

Here he paused, then, with a sort of sovereign and sepulchral authority, he added, articulating slowly, and emphasizing the syllables:

". . . You will believe me. I the father of Cosette! before God, no. Monsieur le Baron Pontmercy, I am a peasant of Faverolles. I earned my living by pruning trees. My name is not Fauchelevent, but Jean Valjean. I am not related to Cosette. Reassure yourself."

Marius stammered:

"Who will prove that to me?"

"I. Since I tell you so."

Marius looked at the man. He was melancholy yet tranquil. No lie could proceed from such a calm. That which is icy is sincere. The truth could be felt in that chill of the tomb.

"I believe you," said Marius.

Jean Valjean bent his head, as though taking note of this, and continued:

"What am I to Cosette? A passer-by. Ten years ago, I did not know that she was in existence. I love her, it is true. One loves a child whom one has seen when very young, being old oneself. When one is old, one feels oneself a grandfather towards all little children. You may, it seems to me, suppose that I have something which resembles a heart. She was an orphan. Without either father or mother. She needed me. That is why I began to love her. Children are so weak that the first comer, even a man like me, can become their protector. I have fulfilled this duty towards Cosette. I do not think that so slight a thing can be called a good action; but if it be a good action, well, say that I have done it. Register this attenuating circumstance. To-day, Cosette passes out of my life; our two roads part. Henceforth, I can do nothing for her. She is Madame Pontmercy. Her providence has changed. And Cosette gains by the change. All is well. As for the six hundred thousand francs, you do not mention them to me, but I forestall your thought, they are a deposit. How did that deposit come into my hands? What does that matter? I restore the deposit. Nothing more can be demanded of me. I complete the restitution by announcing my true name. That concerns me. I have a reason for desiring that you should know who I am."

And Jean Valjean looked Marius full in the face.

All that Marius experienced was tumultuous and incoherent. Certain gusts of destiny produce these billows in our souls.

We have all undergone moments of trouble in which everything within us is dispersed; we say the first things that occur to us, which are not always precisely those which should be said. There are sudden revelations which one cannot bear, and which intoxicate like baleful wine. Marius was stupefied by the novel situation which presented itself to him, to the point of addressing that man almost like a person who was angry with him for this avowal.

"But why," he exclaimed, "do you tell me all this? Who forces you to do so? You could have kept your secret to yourself. You are neither denounced, nor tracked nor pursued. You have a reason for wantonly making such a revelation. Conclude. There is something more. In what connection do you make this confession? What is your motive?"

"My motive?" replied Jean Valjean in a voice so low and dull that one would have said that he was talking to himself rather than to Marius. "From what motive, in fact, has this convict just said 'I am a convict'? Well, yes! the motive is strange. It is out of honesty. Stay, the unfortunate point is that I have a thread in my heart, which keeps me fast. It is when one is old that that sort of thread is particularly solid. All life falls in ruin around one; one resists. Had I been able to tear out that thread, to break it, to undo the knot or to cut it, to go far away, I should have been safe. I had only to go away; there are diligences in the Rue Bouloy; you are happy; I am going. I have tried to break that thread, I have jerked at it, it would not break, I tore my heart with it. Then I said: 'I cannot live anywhere else than here.' I must stay. Well, yes, you are right, I am a fool, why not simply remain here? You offer me a chamber in this house, Madame Pontmercy is sincerely attached to me, she said to the armchair: 'Stretch out your arms to him,' your grandfather demands nothing better than to have me, I suit him, we shall live together, and take our meals in common, I shall give Cosette my arm. . . Madame Pontmercy, excuse me, it is a habit, we shall have but one roof, one table, one fire, the same chimney-corner in winter, the same promenade in summer, that is joy, that is happiness, that is everything. We shall live as one family. One family!"

At that word, Jean Valjean became wild. He folded his arms, glared at the floor beneath his feet as though he would have excavated an abyss therein, and his voice suddenly rose in thundering tones:

"As one family! No. I belong to no family. I do not belong to yours. I do not belong to any family of men. In houses where people are among themselves, I am superfluous. There are families, but there is nothing of the sort for me. I am an unlucky wretch; I am left outside. Did I have a father and mother? I almost doubt it. On the day when I gave that child in marriage, all came to an end. I have seen her happy, and that she is with a man whom she loves, and that there exists here a kind old man, a household of two angels, and all joys in that house, and that it was well, I said to myself: 'Enter thou not.' I could have lied, it is true, have deceived you all, and remained Monsieur Fauchelevent. So long as it was for her, I could lie; but now it would be for myself, and I must not. It was sufficient for me to hold my peace, it is true, and all would go on. You ask me what has forced me to speak? a very odd thing; my conscience. To hold my peace was very easy, however. I passed the night in trying to persuade myself to it; you questioned me, and what I have just said to you is so extraordinary that you have the right to do it; well, yes, I have passed the night in alleging reasons to myself, and I gave myself very good reasons, I have done what I could. But there are two things in which I have not succeeded; in breaking the thread that holds me fixed, riveted and sealed here by the heart, or in silencing some one who speaks softly to me when I am alone. That is why I have come hither to tell you everything this morning. Everything or nearly everything. It is useless to tell you that which concerns only myself; I keep that to myself. You know the essential points. So I have taken my mystery and have brought it to you. And I have disembowelled my secret before your eyes. It was not a resolution that was easy to take. I struggled all night long. Ah! you think that I did not tell myself that this was no Champmathieu affair, that by concealing my name I was doing no one any injury, that the name of Fauchelevent had been given to me by Fauchelevent himself, out of gratitude for a service rendered to him, and that I might assuredly keep it, and that I should be happy in that chamber which you offer me, that I should not be in any one's way, that I should be in my own little corner, and that, while you would have Cosette, I should have the idea that I was in the same house with her. Each one of us would have had his share of happiness. If I continued to be Monsieur Fauchelevent, that would arrange everything. Yes, with the exception of my soul. There was joy everywhere upon my surface, but the bottom of my soul remained black. It is not enough to be happy, one must be content. Thus I should have remained Monsieur Fauchelevent, thus I should have concealed my true visage, thus, in the presence of your expansion, I should have had an enigma, thus, in the midst of your full noonday, I should have had shadows, thus, without crying ''ware,' I should have simply introduced the galleys to your fireside, I should have taken my seat at your table with the thought that if you knew who I was, you would drive me from it, I should have allowed myself to be served by domestics who, had they known, would have said: 'How horrible!' I should have touched you with my elbow, which you have a right to dislike, I should have filched your clasps of the hand! There would have existed in your house a division of respect between venerable white locks and tainted white locks; at your most intimate hours, when all hearts thought themselves open to the very bottom to all the rest, when we four were together, your grandfather, you two and myself, a stranger would have been present! I should have been side by side with you in your existence, having for my only care not to disarrange the cover of my dreadful pit. Thus, I, a dead man, should have thrust myself upon you who are living beings. I should have condemned her to myself forever. You and Cosette and I would have had all three of our heads in the green cap! Does it not make you shudder? I am only the most crushed of men; I should have been the most monstrous of men. And I should have committed that crime every day! And I should have had that face of night upon my visage every day! every day! And I should have communicated to you a share in my taint every day! every day! to you, my dearly beloved, my children, to you, my innocent creatures! Is it nothing to hold one's peace? is it a simple matter to keep silence? No, it is not simple. There is a silence which lies. And my lie, and my fraud and my indignity, and my cowardice and my treason and my crime, I should have drained drop by drop, I should have spit it out, then swallowed it again, I should have finished at midnight and have begun again at midday, and my 'good morning' would have lied, and my 'good night' would have lied, and I should have slept on it, I should have eaten it, with my bread, and I should have looked Cosette in the face, and I should have responded to the smile of the angel by the smile of the damned soul, and I should have been an abominable villain! Why should I do it? in order to be happy. In order to be happy. Have I the right to be happy? I stand outside of life, sir."

Jean Valjean paused. Marius listened. Such chains of ideas and of anguishes cannot be interrupted. Jean Valjean lowered his voice once more, but it was no longer a dull voice—it was a sinister voice.

"You ask why I speak? I am neither denounced, nor pursued, nor tracked, you say. Yes! I am denounced! yes! I am tracked! By whom? By myself. It is I who bar the passage to myself, and I drag myself, and I push myself, and I arrest myself, and I execute myself, and when one holds oneself, one is firmly held."

And, seizing a handful of his own coat by the nape of the neck and extending it towards Marius:

"Do you see that fist?" he continued. "Don't you think that it holds that collar in such a wise as not to release it? Well! conscience is another grasp! If one desires to be happy, sir, one must never understand duty; for, as soon as one has comprehended it, it is implacable. One would say that it punished you for comprehending it; but no, it rewards you; for it places you in a hell, where you feel God beside you. One has no sooner lacerated his own entrails than he is at peace with himself."

And, with a poignant accent, he added:

"Monsieur Pontmercy, this is not common sense, I am an honest man. It is by degrading myself in your eyes that I elevate myself in my own. This has happened to me once before, but it was less painful then; it was a mere nothing. Yes, an honest man. I should not be so if, through my fault, you had continued to esteem me; now that you despise me, I am so. I have that fatality hanging over me that, not being able to ever have anything but stolen consideration, that consideration humiliates me, and crushes me inwardly, and, in order that I may respect myself, it is necessary that I should be despised. Then I straighten up again. I am a galley-slave who obeys his conscience. I know well that that is most improbable. But what would you have me do about it? it is the fact. I have entered into engagements with myself; I keep them. There are encounters which bind us, there are chances which involve us in duties. You see, Monsieur Pontmercy, various things have happened to me in the course of my life."

Again Jean Valjean paused, swallowing his saliva with an effort, as though his words had a bitter after-taste, and then he went on:

"When one has such a horror hanging over one, one has not the right to make others share it without their knowledge, one has not the right to make them slip over one's own precipice without their perceiving it, one has not the right to let one's red blouse drag upon them, one has no right to slyly encumber with one's misery the happiness of others. It is hideous to approach those who are healthy, and to touch them in the dark with one's ulcer. In spite of the fact that Fauchelevent lent me his name, I have no right to use it; he could give it to me, but I could not take it. A name is an *I*. You see, sir, that I have thought somewhat, I have read a little, although I am a peasant; and you see that I express myself properly. I understand things. I have procured myself an education. Well, yes, to abstract a name and to place oneself under it is dishonest. Letters of the alphabet can be filched, like a purse or a watch. To be a false signature in flesh and blood, to be a living false key, to enter the house of honest people by picking their lock, never more to look straightforward, to forever eye askance, to be infamous within the *I*, no! no! no! no! no! It is better to suffer, to bleed, to weep, to tear one's skin from the flesh with one's nails, to pass nights writhing in anguish, to devour oneself body and soul. That is why I have just told you all this. Wantonly, as you say."

He drew a painful breath, and hurled this final word:

"In days gone by, I stole a loaf of bread in order to live; to-day, in order to live, I will not steal a name."

"To live!" interrupted Marius. "You do not need that name in order to live?"

"Ah! I understand the matter," said Jean Valjean, raising and lowering his head several times in succession.

A silence ensued. Both held their peace, each plunged in a gulf of thoughts. Marius was sitting near a table and resting the corner of his mouth on one of his fingers, which was folded back. Jean Valjean was pacing to and fro. He paused before a mirror, and remained motionless. Then, as though replying to some inward course of reasoning, he said, as he gazed at the mirror, which he did not see:

"While, at present, I am relieved."

He took up his march again, and walked to the other end of the drawing-room. At the moment when he turned round, he perceived that Marius was watching his walk. Then he said, with an inexpressible intonation:

"I drag my leg a little. Now you understand why!"

Then he turned fully round towards Marius:

"And now, sir, imagine this: I have said nothing, I have remained Monsieur Fauchelevent, I have taken my place in your house, I am one of you, I am in my chamber, I come to breakfast in the morning in slippers, in the evening all three of us go to the play, I accompany Madame Pontmercy to the Tuileries, and to the Place Royale, we are together, you think me your equal; one fine day you are there, and I am there, we are conversing, we are laughing; all at once, you hear a voice shouting this name: 'Jean Valjean!' and behold, that terrible hand, the police, darts from the darkness, and abruptly tears off my mask!"

Again he paused; Marius had sprung to his feet with a shudder. Jean Valjean resumed:

"What do you say to that?"

Marius' silence answered for him.

Jean Valjean continued:

"You see that I am right in not holding my peace. Be happy, be in heaven, be the angel of an angel, exist in the sun, be content therewith, and do not trouble yourself about the means which a poor damned wretch takes to open his breast and force his duty to come forth; you have before you, sir, a wretched man."

Marius slowly crossed the room, and, when he was quite close to Jean Valjean, he offered the latter his hand.

But Marius was obliged to step up and take that hand which was not offered, Jean Valjean let him have his own way, and it seemed to Marius that he pressed a hand of marble.

"My grandfather has friends," said Marius; "I will procure your pardon."

"It is useless," replied Jean Valjean. "I am believed to be dead, and that suffices. The dead are not subjected to surveillance. They are supposed to rot in peace. Death is the same thing as pardon."

And, disengaging the hand which Marius held, he added, with a sort of inexorable dignity:

"Moreover, the friend to whom I have recourse is the doing of my duty; and I need but one pardon, that of my conscience."

At that moment, a door at the other end of the drawing-room opened gently half way, and in the opening Cosette's head appeared. They saw only her sweet face, her hair was in charming disorder, her eyelids were still swollen with sleep. She made the movement of a bird, which thrusts its head out of its nest, glanced first at her husband, then at Jean Valjean, and cried to them with a smile, so that they seemed to behold a smile at the heart of a rose:

"I will wager that you are talking politics. How stupid that is, instead of being with me!"

Jean Valjean shuddered.

"Cosette! . . ." stammered Marius.

And he paused. One would have said that they were two criminals.

Cosette, who was radiant, continued to gaze at both of them. There was something in her eyes like gleams of paradise.

"I have caught you in the very act," said Cosette. "Just now, I heard my father Fauchelevent through the door saying: 'Conscience. . . doing my duty. . .' That is politics, indeed it is. I will not have it. People should not talk politics the very next day. It is not right."

"You are mistaken. Cosette," said Marius, "we are talking business. We are discussing the best investment of your six hundred thousand francs. . ."

"That is not it at all," interrupted Cosette. "I am coming. Does anybody want me here?"

And, passing resolutely through the door, she entered the drawing-room. She was dressed in a voluminous white dressing-gown, with a thousand folds and large sleeves which, starting from the neck, fell to her feet. In the golden heavens of some ancient gothic pictures, there are these charming sacks fit to clothe the angels.

She contemplated herself from head to foot in a long mirror, then exclaimed, in an outburst of ineffable ecstasy:

"There was once a King and a Queen. Oh! how happy I am!"

That said, she made a curtsey to Marius and to Jean Valjean.

"There," said she, "I am going to install myself near you in an easy-chair, we breakfast in half an hour, you shall say anything you like, I know well that men must talk, and I will be very good."

Marius took her by the arm and said lovingly to her:

"We are talking business."

"By the way," said Cosette, "I have opened my window, a flock of pierrots has arrived in the garden,—Birds, not maskers. To-day is Ash-Wednesday; but not for the birds."

"I tell you that we are talking business, go, my little Cosette, leave us alone for a moment. We are talking figures. That will bore you."

"You have a charming cravat on this morning, Marius. You are very dandified, monseigneur. No, it will not bore me."

"I assure you that it will bore you."

"No. Since it is you. I shall not understand you, but I shall listen to you. When one hears the voices of those whom one loves, one does not need to understand the words that they utter. That we should be here together—that is all that I desire. I shall remain with you, bah!"

"You are my beloved Cosette! Impossible."

"Impossible!"

"Yes."

"Very good," said Cosette. "I was going to tell you some news. I could have told you that your grandfather is still asleep, that your aunt is at mass, that the chimney in my father Fauchelevent's room smokes, that Nicolette has sent for the chimney-sweep, that Toussaint and Nicolette have already quarrelled, that Nicolette makes sport of Toussaint's stammer. Well, you shall know nothing. Ah! it is impossible? you shall see, gentlemen, that I, in my turn, can say: It is impossible. Then who will be caught? I beseech you, my little Marius, let me stay here with you two."

"I swear to you, that it is indispensable that we should be alone."

"Well, am I anybody?"

Jean Valjean had not uttered a single word. Cosette turned to him:

"In the first place, father, I want you to come and embrace me. What do you mean by not saying anything instead of taking my part? who gave me such a father as that? You must perceive that my family life is very unhappy. My husband beats me. Come, embrace me instantly."

Jean Valjean approached.

Cosette turned toward Marius.

"As for you, I shall make a face at you."

Then she presented her brow to Jean Valjean.

Jean Valjean advanced a step toward her.

Cosette recoiled.

"Father, you are pale. Does your arm hurt you?"

"It is well," said Jean Valjean.

"Did you sleep badly?"

"No."

"Are you sad?"

"No."

"Embrace me if you are well, if you sleep well, if you are content, I will not scold you."

And again she offered him her brow.

Jean Valjean dropped a kiss upon that brow whereon rested a celestial gleam.

"Smile."

Jean Valjean obeyed. It was the smile of a spectre.

"Now, defend me against my husband."

"Cosette! . . ." ejaculated Marius.

"Get angry, father. Say that I must stay. You can certainly talk before me. So you think me very silly. What you say is astonishing! business, placing money in a bank a great matter truly. Men make mysteries out of nothing. I am very pretty this morning. Look at me, Marius."

And with an adorable shrug of the shoulders, and an indescribably exquisite pout, she glanced at Marius.

"I love you!" said Marius.

"I adore you!" said Cosette.

And they fell irresistibly into each other's arms.

"Now," said Cosette, adjusting a fold of her dressing-gown, with a triumphant little grimace, "I shall stay."

"No, not that," said Marius, in a supplicating tone. "We have to finish something."

"Still no?"

Marius assumed a grave tone:

"I assure you, Cosette, that it is impossible."

"Ah! you put on your man's voice, sir. That is well, I go. You, father, have not upheld me. Monsieur my father, monsieur my husband, you are tyrants. I shall go and tell grandpapa. If you think that I am going to return and talk platitudes to you, you are mistaken. I am proud. I shall wait for you now. You shall see, that it is you who are going to be bored without me. I am going, it is well."

And she left the room.

Two seconds later, the door opened once more, her fresh and rosy head was again thrust between the two leaves, and she cried to them:

"I am very angry indeed."

The door closed again, and the shadows descended once more.

It was as though a ray of sunlight should have suddenly traversed the night, without itself being conscious of it.

Marius made sure that the door was securely closed.

"Poor Cosette!" he murmured, "when she finds out. . ."

At that word Jean Valjean trembled in every limb. He fixed on Marius a bewildered eye.

"Cosette! oh yes, it is true, you are going to tell Cosette about this. That is right. Stay, I had not thought of that. One has the strength for one thing, but not for another. Sir, I conjure you, I entreat now, sir, give me your most sacred word of honor, that you will not tell her. Is it not enough that you should know it? I have been able to say it myself without being forced to it, I could have told it to the universe, to the whole world,—it was all one to me. But she, she does not know what it is, it would terrify her. What, a convict! we should be obliged to explain matters to her, to say to her: 'He is a man who has been in the galleys.' She saw the chain-gang pass by one day. Oh! My God!" . . . He dropped into an armchair and hid his face in his hands.

His grief was not audible, but from the quivering of his shoulders it was evident that he was weeping. Silent tears, terrible tears.

There is something of suffocation in the sob. He was seized with a sort of convulsion, he threw himself against the back of the chair as though to gain breath, letting his arms fall, and allowing Marius to see his face inundated with tears, and Marius heard him murmur, so low that his voice seemed to issue from fathomless depths:

"Oh! would that I could die!"

"Be at your ease," said Marius, "I will keep your secret for myself alone."

And, less touched, perhaps, than he ought to have been, but forced, for the last hour, to familiarize himself with something as unexpected as it was dreadful, gradually beholding the convict superposed before his very eyes, upon M. Fauchelevent, overcome, little by little, by that lugubrious reality, and led, by the natural inclination of the situation, to recognize the space which had just been placed between that man and himself, Marius added:

"It is impossible that I should not speak a word to you with regard to the deposit which you have so faithfully and honestly remitted. That is an act of probity. It is just that some recompense should be bestowed on you. Fix the sum yourself, it shall be counted out to you. Do not fear to set it very high."

"I thank you, sir," replied Jean Valjean, gently.

He remained in thought for a moment, mechanically passing the tip of his fore-finger across his thumb-nail, then he lifted up his voice:

"All is nearly over. But one last thing remains for me. . ."

"What is it?"

Jean Valjean struggled with what seemed a last hesitation, and, without voice, without breath, he stammered rather than said:

"Now that you know, do you think, sir, you, who are the master, that I ought not to see Cosette any more?"

"I think that would be better," replied Marius coldly.

"I shall never see her more," murmured Jean Valjean. And he directed his steps towards the door.

He laid his hand on the knob, the latch yielded, the door opened. Jean Valjean pushed it open far enough to pass through, stood motionless for a second, then closed the door again and turned to Marius.

He was no longer pale, he was livid. There were no longer any tears in his eyes, but only a sort of tragic flame. His voice had regained a strange composure.

"Stay, sir," he said. "If you will allow it, I will come to see her. I assure you that I desire it greatly. If I had not cared to see Cosette, I should not have made to you the confession that I have made, I should have gone away; but, as I desired to remain in the place where Cosette is, and to continue to see her, I had to tell you about it honestly. You follow my reasoning, do you not? it is a matter easily understood. You see, I have had her with me for more than nine years. We lived first in that hut on the boulevard, then in the convent, then near the Luxembourg. That was where you saw her for the first time. You remember her blue plush hat. Then we went to the Quartier des Invalides, where there was a railing on a garden, the Rue Plumet. I lived in a little back court-yard, whence I could hear her piano. That was my life. We never left each other. That lasted for nine years and some months. I was like her own father, and she was my child. I do not know whether you understand, Monsieur Pontmercy, but to go away now, never to see her again, never to speak to her again, to no longer have anything, would be hard. If you do not disapprove of it, I will come to see Cosette from time to time. I will not come often. I will not remain long. You shall give orders that I am to be received in the little waiting-room. On the ground floor. I could enter perfectly well by the back door, but that might create surprise perhaps, and it would be better, I think, for me to enter by the usual door. Truly, sir, I should like to see a little more of Cosette. As rarely as you please. Put yourself in my place, I have nothing left but that. And then, we must be cautious. If I no longer come at all, it would produce a bad effect, it would be considered singular. What I can do, by the way, is to come in the afternoon, when night is beginning to fall."

"You shall come every evening," said Marius, "and Cosette will be waiting for you."

"You are kind, sir," said Jean Valjean.

Marius saluted Jean Valjean, happiness escorted despair to the door, and these two men parted.

# II

## The Obscurities Which a Revelation Can Contain

Marius was quite upset.

The sort of estrangement which he had always felt towards the man beside whom he had seen Cosette, was now explained to him. There was something enigmatic about that person, of which his instinct had warned him.

This enigma was the most hideous of disgraces, the galleys. This M. Fauchelevent was the convict Jean Valjean.

To abruptly find such a secret in the midst of one's happiness resembles the discovery of a scorpion in a nest of turtledoves.

Was the happiness of Marius and Cosette thenceforth condemned to such a neighborhood? Was this an accomplished fact? Did the acceptance of that man form a part of the marriage now consummated? Was there nothing to be done?

Had Marius wedded the convict as well?

In vain may one be crowned with light and joy, in vain may one taste the grand purple hour of life, happy love, such shocks would force even the archangel in his ecstasy, even the demigod in his glory, to shudder.

As is always the case in changes of view of this nature, Marius asked himself whether he had nothing with which to reproach himself. Had he been wanting in divination? Had he been wanting in prudence? Had he involuntarily dulled his wits? A little, perhaps. Had he entered upon this love affair, which had ended in his marriage to Cosette, without taking sufficient precautions to throw light upon the surroundings? He admitted,—it is thus, by a series of successive admissions of ourselves in regard to ourselves, that life amends us, little by little,—he admitted the chimerical and visionary side of his nature, a sort of internal cloud peculiar to many organizations, and which, in paroxysms of passion and sorrow, dilates as the temperature of the soul changes, and invades the entire man, to such a degree as to render him nothing more than a conscience bathed in a mist. We have more than once indicated this characteristic element of Marius' individuality.

He recalled that, in the intoxication of his love, in the Rue Plumet, during those six or seven ecstatic weeks, he had not even spoken to Cosette of that drama in the Gorbeau hovel, where the victim had taken up such a singular line of silence during the struggle and the ensuing flight. How had it happened that he had not mentioned this to Cosette? Yet it was so near and so terrible! How had it come to pass that he had not even named the Thénardiers, and, particularly, on the day when he had encountered Éponine? He now found it almost difficult to explain his silence of that time. Nevertheless, he could account for it. He recalled his benumbed state, his intoxication with Cosette, love absorbing everything, that catching away of each other into the ideal, and perhaps also, like the imperceptible quantity of reason mingled with this violent and charming state of the soul, a vague, dull instinct impelling him to conceal and abolish in his memory that redoubtable adventure, contact with which he dreaded, in which he did not wish to play any part, his agency in which he had kept secret, and in which he could be neither narrator nor witness without being an accuser.

Moreover, these few weeks had been a flash of lightning; there had been no time for anything except love.

In short, having weighed everything, turned everything over in his mind, examined everything, whatever might have been the consequences if he had told Cosette about the Gorbeau ambush, even if he had discovered that Jean Valjean was a convict, would that have changed him, Marius? Would that have changed her, Cosette? Would he have drawn back? Would he have adored her any the less? Would he have refrained from marrying her? No. Then there was nothing to regret, nothing with which he need reproach himself. All was well. There is a deity for those drunken men who are called lovers. Marius blind, had followed the path which he would have chosen had he been in full possession of his sight. Love had bandaged his eyes, in order to lead him whither? To paradise.

But this paradise was henceforth complicated with an infernal accompaniment.

Marius' ancient estrangement towards this man, towards this Fauchelevent who had turned into Jean Valjean, was at present mingled with horror.

In this horror, let us state, there was some pity, and even a certain surprise.

This thief, this thief guilty of a second offence, had restored that deposit. And what a deposit! Six hundred thousand francs.

He alone was in the secret of that deposit. He might have kept it all, he had restored it all.

Moreover, he had himself revealed his situation. Nothing forced him to this. If any one learned who he was, it was through himself. In this avowal there was something more than acceptance of humiliation, there was acceptance of peril. For a condemned man, a mask is not a mask, it is a shelter. A false name is security, and he had rejected that false name. He, the galley-slave, might have hidden himself forever in an honest family; he had withstood this temptation. And with what motive? Through a conscientious scruple. He himself explained this with the irresistible accents of truth. In short, whatever this Jean Valjean might be, he was, undoubtedly, a conscience which was awakening. There existed some mysterious re-habilitation which had begun; and, to all appearances, scruples had for a long time already controlled this man. Such fits of justice and goodness are not characteristic of vulgar natures. An awakening of conscience is grandeur of soul.

Jean Valjean was sincere. This sincerity, visible, palpable, irrefragable, evident from the very grief that it caused him, rendered inquiries useless, and conferred authority on all that that man had said.

Here, for Marius, there was a strange reversal of situations. What breathed from M. Fauchelevent? distrust. What did Jean Valjean inspire? confidence.

In the mysterious balance of this Jean Valjean which the pensive Marius struck, he admitted the active principle, he admitted the passive principle, and he tried to reach a balance.

But all this went on as in a storm. Marius, while endeavoring to form a clear idea of this man, and while pursuing Jean Valjean, so to speak, in the depths of his thought, lost him and found him again in a fatal mist.

The deposit honestly restored, the probity of the confession—these were good. This produced a lightening of the cloud, then the cloud became black once more.

Troubled as were Marius' memories, a shadow of them returned to him.

After all, what was that adventure in the Jondrette attic? Why had that man taken to flight on the arrival of the police, instead of entering a complaint?

Here Marius found the answer. Because that man was a fugitive from justice, who had broken his ban.

Another question: Why had that man come to the barricade?

For Marius now once more distinctly beheld that recollection which had reappeared in his emotions like sympathetic ink at the application of heat. This man had been in the barricade. He had not fought there. What had he come there for? In the presence of this question a spectre sprang up and replied: "Javert."

Marius recalled perfectly now that funereal sight of Jean Valjean dragging the pinioned Javert out of the barricade, and he still heard behind the corner of the little Rue Mondétour that frightful pistol shot. Obviously, there was hatred between that police spy and the galley-slave. The one was in the other's way. Jean Valjean had gone to the barricade for the purpose of revenging himself. He had arrived late. He probably knew that Javert was a prisoner there. The Corsican vendetta has penetrated to certain lower strata and has become the law there; it is so simple that it does not astonish souls which are but half turned towards good; and those hearts are so constituted that a criminal, who is in the path of repentance, may be scrupulous in the matter of theft and unscrupulous in the matter of vengeance. Jean Valjean had killed Javert. At least, that seemed to be evident.

This was the final question, to be sure; but to this there was no reply. This question Marius felt like pincers. How had it come to pass that Jean Valjean's existence had elbowed that of Cosette for so long a period?

What melancholy sport of Providence was that which had placed that child in contact with that man? Are there then chains for two which are forged on high? and does God take pleasure in coupling the angel with the demon? So a crime and an innocence can be room-mates in the mysterious galleys of wretchedness? In that defiling of condemned persons which is called human destiny, can two brows pass side by side, the one ingenuous, the other formidable, the one all bathed in the divine whiteness of dawn, the other forever blemished by the flash of an eternal lightning? Who could have arranged that inexplicable pairing off? In what manner, in consequence of what prodigy, had any community of life been established between this celestial little creature and that old criminal?

Who could have bound the lamb to the wolf, and, what was still more incomprehensible, have attached the wolf to the lamb? For the wolf loved the lamb, for the fierce creature adored the feeble one, for, during the space of nine years, the angel had had the monster as her point of support. Cosette's childhood and girlhood, her advent in the daylight, her virginal growth towards life and light, had been sheltered by that hideous devotion. Here questions exfoliated, so to speak, into innumerable enigmas, abysses yawned at the bottoms of abysses, and Marius could no longer bend over Jean Valjean without becoming dizzy. What was this man-precipice?

The old symbols of Genesis are eternal; in human society, such as it now exists, and until a broader day shall effect a change in it, there will always be two men, the one superior, the other subterranean; the one which is according to good is Abel; the other which is according to evil is Cain. What was this tender Cain? What was this ruffian religiously absorbed in the adoration of a virgin, watching over her, rearing her, guarding her, dignifying her, and enveloping her, impure as he was himself, with purity?

What was that cesspool which had venerated that innocence to such a point as not to leave upon it a single spot? What was this Jean Valjean educating Cosette? What was this figure of the shadows which had for its only object the preservation of the rising of a star from every shadow and from every cloud?

That was Jean Valjean's secret; that was also God's secret.

In the presence of this double secret, Marius recoiled. The one, in some sort, reassured him as to the other. God was as visible in this affair as was Jean Valjean. God has his instruments. He makes use of the tool which he wills. He is not responsible to men. Do we know how God sets about the work? Jean Valjean had labored over Cosette. He had, to some extent, made that soul. That was incontestable. Well, what then? The workman was horrible; but the work was admirable. God produces his miracles as seems good to him. He had constructed that charming Cosette, and he had employed Jean Valjean. It had pleased him to choose this strange collaborator for himself. What account have we to demand of him? Is this the first time that the dung-heap has aided the spring to create the rose?

Marius made himself these replies, and declared to himself that they were good. He had not dared to press Jean Valjean on all the points which we have just indicated, but he did not confess to himself that he did not dare to do it. He adored Cosette, he possessed Cosette, Cosette was splendidly pure. That was sufficient for him. What enlightenment did he need? Cosette was a light. Does light require enlightenment? He had everything; what more could he desire? All,—is not that enough? Jean Valjean's personal affairs did not concern him.

And bending over the fatal shadow of that man, he clung fast, convulsively, to the solemn declaration of that unhappy wretch: "I am nothing to Cosette. Ten years ago I did not know that she was in existence."

Jean Valjean was a passer-by. He had said so himself. Well, he had passed. Whatever he was, his part was finished.

Henceforth, there remained Marius to fulfil the part of Providence to Cosette. Cosette had sought the azure in a person like herself, in her lover, her husband, her celestial male. Cosette, as she took her flight, winged and transfigured, left behind her on the earth her hideous and empty chrysalis, Jean Valjean.

In whatever circle of ideas Marius revolved, he always returned to a certain horror for Jean Valjean. A sacred horror, perhaps, for, as we have just pointed out, he felt a *quid divinum* in that man. But do what he would, and seek what extenuation he would, he was certainly forced to fall back upon this: the man was a convict; that is to say, a being who has not even a place in the social ladder, since he is lower than the very lowest rung. After the very last of men comes the convict. The convict is no longer, so to speak, in the semblance of the living. The law has deprived him of the entire quantity of humanity of which it can deprive a man.

Marius, on penal questions, still held to the inexorable system, though he was a democrat and he entertained all the ideas of the law on the subject of those whom the law strikes. He had not yet accomplished all progress, we admit. He had not yet come to distinguish between that which is written by man and that which is written by God, between law and right. He had not examined and weighed the right which man takes to dispose of the irrevocable and the irreparable. He was not shocked by the word *vindicte*. He found it quite simple that certain breaches of the written law should be followed by eternal suffering, and he accepted, as the process of civilization, social damnation. He still stood at this point, though safe to advance infallibly later on, since his nature was good, and, at bottom, wholly formed of latent progress.

In this stage of his ideas, Jean Valjean appeared to him hideous and repulsive. He was a man reproved, he was the convict. That word was for him like the sound of the trump on the Day of Judgment; and, after having reflected upon Jean Valjean for a long time, his final gesture had been to turn away his head. *Vade retro.*

Marius, if we must recognize and even insist upon the fact, while interrogating Jean Valjean to such a point that Jean Valjean had said:

"You are confessing me," had not, nevertheless, put to him two or three decisive questions.

It was not that they had not presented themselves to his mind, but that he had been afraid of them. The Jondrette attic? The barricade? Javert? Who knows where these revelations would have stopped? Jean Valjean did not seem like a man who would draw back, and who knows whether Marius, after having urged him on, would not have himself desired to hold him back?

Has it not happened to all of us, in certain supreme conjunctures, to stop our ears in order that we may not hear the reply, after we have asked a question? It is especially when one loves that one gives way to these exhibitions of cowardice. It is not wise to question sinister situations to the last point, particularly when the indissoluble side of our life is fatally intermingled with them. What a terrible light might have proceeded from the despairing explanations of Jean Valjean, and who knows whether that hideous glare would not have darted forth as far as Cosette? Who knows whether a sort of infernal glow would not have lingered behind it on the brow of that angel? The spattering of a lightning-flash is of the thunder also. Fatality has points of juncture where innocence itself is stamped with crime by the gloomy law of the reflections which give color. The purest figures may forever preserve the reflection of a horrible association. Rightly or wrongly, Marius had been afraid. He already knew too much. He sought to dull his senses rather than to gain further light.

In dismay he bore off Cosette in his arms and shut his eyes to Jean Valjean.

That man was the night, the living and horrible night. How should he dare to seek the bottom of it? It is a terrible thing to interrogate the shadow. Who knows what its reply will be? The dawn may be blackened forever by it.

In this state of mind the thought that that man would, henceforth, come into any contact whatever with Cosette was a heartrending perplexity to Marius.

He now almost reproached himself for not having put those formidable questions, before which he had recoiled, and from which an implacable and definitive decision might have sprung. He felt that he was too good, too gentle, too weak, if we must say the word. This weakness had led him to an imprudent concession. He had allowed himself to be touched. He had been in the wrong. He ought to have simply and purely rejected Jean Valjean. Jean Valjean played the part of fire, and that is what he should have done, and have freed his house from that man.

He was vexed with himself, he was angry with that whirlwind of emotions which had deafened, blinded, and carried him away. He was displeased with himself.

What was he to do now? Jean Valjean's visits were profoundly repugnant to him. What was the use in having that man in his house? What did the man want? Here, he became dismayed, he did not wish to dig down, he did not wish to penetrate deeply; he did not wish to sound himself. He had promised, he had allowed himself to be drawn into a promise; Jean Valjean held his promise; one must keep one's word even to a convict, above all to a convict. Still, his first duty was to Cosette. In short, he was carried away by the repugnance which dominated him.

Marius turned over all this confusion of ideas in his mind, passing from one to the other, and moved by all of them. Hence arose a profound trouble.

It was not easy for him to hide this trouble from Cosette, but love is a talent, and Marius succeeded in doing it.

However, without any apparent object, he questioned Cosette, who was as candid as a dove is white and who suspected nothing; he talked of her childhood and her youth, and he became more and more convinced that that convict had been everything good, paternal and respectable that a man can be towards Cosette. All that Marius had caught a glimpse of and had surmised was real. That sinister nettle had loved and protected that lily.

BOOK EIGHTH
FADING AWAY OF THE TWILIGHT

# I

## The Lower Chamber

On the following day, at nightfall, Jean Valjean knocked at the carriage gate of the Gillenormand house. It was Basque who received him. Basque was in the courtyard at the appointed hour, as though he had received his orders. It sometimes happens that one says to a servant: "You will watch for Mr. So and So, when he arrives."

Basque addressed Jean Valjean without waiting for the latter to approach him:

"Monsieur le Baron has charged me to inquire whether monsieur desires to go upstairs or to remain below?"

"I will remain below," replied Jean Valjean.

Basque, who was perfectly respectful, opened the door of the waiting-room and said:

"I will go and inform Madame."

The room which Jean Valjean entered was a damp, vaulted room on the ground floor, which served as a cellar on occasion, which opened on the street, was paved with red squares and was badly lighted by a grated window.

This chamber was not one of those which are harassed by the feather-duster, the pope's head brush, and the broom. The dust rested tranquilly there. Persecution of the spiders was not organized there. A fine web, which spread far and wide, and was very black and ornamented with dead flies, formed a wheel on one of the window-panes. The room, which was small and low-ceiled, was furnished with a heap of empty bottles piled up in one corner.

The wall, which was daubed with an ochre yellow wash, was scaling off in large flakes. At one end there was a chimney-piece painted in black with a narrow shelf. A fire was burning there; which indicated that Jean Valjean's reply: "I will remain below," had been foreseen.

Two armchairs were placed at the two corners of the fireplace. Between the chairs an old bedside rug, which displayed more foundation thread than wool, had been spread by way of a carpet.

The chamber was lighted by the fire on the hearth and the twilight falling through the window.

Jean Valjean was fatigued. For days he had neither eaten nor slept. He threw himself into one of the armchairs.

Basque returned, set a lighted candle on the chimney-piece and retired. Jean Valjean, his head drooping and his chin resting on his breast, perceived neither Basque nor the candle.

All at once, he drew himself up with a start. Cosette was standing beside him.

He had not seen her enter, but he had felt that she was there.

He turned round. He gazed at her. She was adorably lovely. But what he was contemplating with that profound gaze was not her beauty but her soul.

"Well," exclaimed Cosette, "father, I knew that you were peculiar, but I never should have expected this. What an idea! Marius told me that you wish me to receive you here."

"Yes, it is my wish."

"I expected that reply. Good. I warn you that I am going to make a scene for you. Let us begin at the beginning. Embrace me, father."

And she offered him her cheek.

Jean Valjean remained motionless.

"You do not stir. I take note of it. Attitude of guilt. But never mind, I pardon you. Jesus Christ said: Offer the other cheek. Here it is."

And she presented her other cheek.

Jean Valjean did not move. It seemed as though his feet were nailed to the pavement.

"This is becoming serious," said Cosette. "What have I done to you? I declare that I am perplexed. You owe me reparation. You will dine with us."

"I have dined."

"That is not true. I will get M. Gillenormand to scold you. Grandfathers are made to reprimand fathers. Come. Go upstairs with me to the drawing-room. Immediately."

"Impossible."

Here Cosette lost ground a little. She ceased to command and passed to questioning.

"But why? and you choose the ugliest chamber in the house in which to see me. It's horrible here."

"Thou knowest. . ."

Jean Valjean caught himself up.

"You know, madame, that I am peculiar, I have my freaks."

Cosette struck her tiny hands together.

"Madame! . . . You know! . . . more novelties! What is the meaning of this?"

Jean Valjean directed upon her that heartrending smile to which he occasionally had recourse:

"You wished to be Madame. You are so."

"Not for you, father."

"Do not call me father."

"What?"

"Call me 'Monsieur Jean.' 'Jean,' if you like."

"You are no longer my father? I am no longer Cosette? 'Monsieur Jean'? What does this mean? why, these are revolutions, aren't they? what has taken place? come, look me in the face. And you won't live with us! And you won't have my chamber! What have I done to you? Has anything happened?"

"Nothing."

"Well then?"

"Everything is as usual."

"Why do you change your name?"

"You have changed yours, surely."

He smiled again with the same smile as before and added:

"Since you are Madame Pontmercy, I certainly can be Monsieur Jean."

"I don't understand anything about it. All this is idiotic. I shall ask permission of my husband for you to be 'Monsieur Jean.' I hope that he will not consent to it. You cause me a great deal of pain. One does have freaks, but one does not cause one's little Cosette grief. That is wrong. You have no right to be wicked, you who are so good."

He made no reply.

She seized his hands with vivacity, and raising them to her face with an irresistible movement, she pressed them against her neck beneath her chin, which is a gesture of profound tenderness.

"Oh!" she said to him, "be good!"

And she went on:

"This is what I call being good: being nice and coming and living here,—there are birds here as there are in the Rue Plumet,—living with us, quitting that hole of a Rue de l'Homme Armé, not giving us riddles to guess, being like all the rest of the world, dining with us, breakfasting with us, being my father."

He loosed her hands.

"You no longer need a father, you have a husband."

Cosette became angry.

"I no longer need a father! One really does not know what to say to things like that, which are not common sense!"

"If Toussaint were here," resumed Jean Valjean, like a person who is driven to seek authorities, and who clutches at every branch, "she would be the first to agree that it is true that I have always had ways of my own. There is nothing new in this. I always have loved my black corner."

"But it is cold here. One cannot see distinctly. It is abominable, that it is, to wish to be Monsieur Jean! I will not have you say 'you' to me.

"Just now, as I was coming hither," replied Jean Valjean, "I saw a piece of furniture in the Rue Saint Louis. It was at a cabinet-maker's. If I were a pretty woman, I would treat myself to that bit of furniture. A very neat toilet table in the reigning style. What you call rosewood, I think. It is inlaid. The mirror is quite large. There are drawers. It is pretty."

"Hou! the villainous bear!" replied Cosette.

And with supreme grace, setting her teeth and drawing back her lips, she blew at Jean Valjean. She was a Grace copying a cat.

"I am furious," she resumed. "Ever since yesterday, you have made me rage, all of you. I am greatly vexed. I don't understand. You do not defend me against Marius. Marius will not uphold me against you. I am all alone. I arrange a chamber prettily. If I could have put the good God there I would have done it. My chamber is left on my hands. My lodger sends me into bankruptcy. I order a nice little dinner of Nicolette. We will have nothing to do with your dinner, Madame. And my father Fauchelevent wants me to call him 'Monsieur Jean,' and to receive him in a frightful, old, ugly cellar, where the walls have beards, and where the crystal consists of empty bottles, and the curtains are of spiders' webs! You are singular, I admit, that is your style, but people who get married are granted a truce. You ought not to have begun being singular again instantly. So you are going to be perfectly contented in your abominable Rue de l'Homme Armé. I was very desperate indeed there, that I was. What have you against me? You cause me a great deal of grief. Fi!"

And, becoming suddenly serious, she gazed intently at Jean Valjean and added:

"Are you angry with me because I am happy?"

Ingenuousness sometimes unconsciously penetrates deep. This question, which was simple for Cosette, was profound for Jean Valjean. Cosette had meant to scratch, and she lacerated.

VICTOR HUGO

Jean Valjean turned pale.

He remained for a moment without replying, then, with an inexpressible intonation, and speaking to himself, he murmured:

"Her happiness was the object of my life. Now God may sign my dismissal. Cosette, thou art happy; my day is over."

"Ah, you have said *thou* to me!" exclaimed Cosette.

And she sprang to his neck.

Jean Valjean, in bewilderment, strained her wildly to his breast. It almost seemed to him as though he were taking her back.

"Thanks, father!" said Cosette.

This enthusiastic impulse was on the point of becoming poignant for Jean Valjean. He gently removed Cosette's arms, and took his hat.

"Well?" said Cosette.

"I leave you, Madame, they are waiting for you."

And, from the threshold, he added:

"I have said *thou* to you. Tell your husband that this shall not happen again. Pardon me."

Jean Valjean quitted the room, leaving Cosette stupefied at this enigmatical farewell.

# II

## Another Step Backwards

On the following day, at the same hour, Jean Valjean came.

Cosette asked him no questions, was no longer astonished, no longer exclaimed that she was cold, no longer spoke of the drawing-room, she avoided saying either "father" or "Monsieur Jean." She allowed herself to be addressed as *you*. She allowed herself to be called Madame. Only, her joy had undergone a certain diminution. She would have been sad, if sadness had been possible to her.

It is probable that she had had with Marius one of those conversations in which the beloved man says what he pleases, explains nothing, and satisfies the beloved woman. The curiosity of lovers does not extend very far beyond their own love.

The lower room had made a little toilet. Basque had suppressed the bottles, and Nicolette the spiders.

All the days which followed brought Jean Valjean at the same hour. He came every day, because he had not the strength to take Marius' words otherwise than literally. Marius arranged matters so as to be absent at the hours when Jean Valjean came. The house grew accustomed to the novel ways of M. Fauchelevent. Toussaint helped in this direction: "Monsieur has always been like that," she repeated. The grandfather issued this decree:—"He's an original." And all was said. Moreover, at the age of ninety-six, no bond is any longer possible, all is merely juxtaposition; a newcomer is in the way. There is no longer any room; all habits are acquired. M. Fauchelevent, M. Tranchelevent, Father Gillenormand asked nothing better than to be relieved from "that gentleman." He added:—"Nothing is more common than those originals. They do all sorts of queer things. They have no reason. The Marquis de Canaples was still worse. He bought a palace that he might lodge in the garret. These are fantastic appearances that people affect."

No one caught a glimpse of the sinister foundation. And moreover, who could have guessed such a thing? There are marshes of this description in India. The water seems extraordinary, inexplicable, rippling though there is no wind, and agitated where it should be calm.

One gazes at the surface of these causeless ebullitions; one does not perceive the hydra which crawls on the bottom.

Many men have a secret monster in this same manner, a dragon which gnaws them, a despair which inhabits their night. Such a man resembles other men, he goes and comes. No one knows that he bears within him a frightful parasitic pain with a thousand teeth, which lives within the unhappy man, and of which he is dying. No one knows that this man is a gulf. He is stagnant but deep. From time to time, a trouble of which the onlooker understands nothing appears on his surface. A mysterious wrinkle is formed, then vanishes, then reappears; an air-bubble rises and bursts. It is the breathing of the unknown beast.

Certain strange habits: arriving at the hour when other people are taking their leave, keeping in the background when other people are displaying themselves, preserving on all occasions what may be designated as the wall-colored mantle, seeking the solitary walk, preferring the deserted street, avoiding any share in conversation, avoiding crowds and festivals, seeming at one's ease and living poorly, having one's key in one's pocket, and one's candle at the porter's lodge, however rich one may be, entering by the side door, ascending the private staircase,—all these insignificant singularities, fugitive folds on the surface, often proceed from a formidable foundation.

Many weeks passed in this manner. A new life gradually took possession of Cosette: the relations which marriage creates, visits, the care of the house, pleasures, great matters. Cosette's pleasures were not costly, they consisted in one thing: being with Marius. The great occupation of her life was to go out with him, to remain with him. It was for them a joy that was always fresh, to go out arm in arm, in the face of the sun, in the open street, without hiding themselves, before the whole world, both of them completely alone.

Cosette had one vexation. Toussaint could not get on with Nicolette, the soldering of two elderly maids being impossible, and she went away. The grandfather was well; Marius argued a case here and there; Aunt Gillenormand peacefully led that life aside which sufficed for her, beside the new household. Jean Valjean came every day.

The address as *thou* disappeared, the *you*, the "Madame," the "Monsieur Jean," rendered him another person to Cosette. The care which he had himself taken to detach her from him was succeeding. She became more and more gay and less and less tender. Yet she still loved him sincerely, and he felt it.

One day she said to him suddenly: "You used to be my father, you are no longer my father, you were my uncle, you are no longer my uncle, you were Monsieur Fauchelevent, you are Jean. Who are you then? I don't like all this. If I did not know how good you are, I should be afraid of you."

He still lived in the Rue de l'Homme Armé, because he could not make up his mind to remove to a distance from the quarter where Cosette dwelt.

At first, he only remained a few minutes with Cosette, and then went away.

Little by little he acquired the habit of making his visits less brief. One would have said that he was taking advantage of the authorization of the days which were lengthening, he arrived earlier and departed later.

One day Cosette chanced to say "father" to him. A flash of joy illuminated Jean Valjean's melancholy old countenance. He caught her up: "Say Jean."—"Ah! truly," she replied with a burst of laughter, "Monsieur Jean."—"That is right," said he. And he turned aside so that she might not see him wipe his eyes.

# III

## They Recall the Garden
## of the Rue Plumet

This was the last time. After that last flash of light, complete extinction ensued. No more familiarity, no more good-morning with a kiss, never more that word so profoundly sweet: "My father!" He was at his own request and through his own complicity driven out of all his happinesses one after the other; and he had this sorrow, that after having lost Cosette wholly in one day, he was afterwards obliged to lose her again in detail.

The eye eventually becomes accustomed to the light of a cellar. In short, it sufficed for him to have an apparition of Cosette every day. His whole life was concentrated in that one hour.

He seated himself close to her, he gazed at her in silence, or he talked to her of years gone by, of her childhood, of the convent, of her little friends of those bygone days.

One afternoon,—it was on one of those early days in April, already warm and fresh, the moment of the sun's great gayety, the gardens which surrounded the windows of Marius and Cosette felt the emotion of waking, the hawthorn was on the point of budding, a jewelled garniture of gillyflowers spread over the ancient walls, snapdragons yawned through the crevices of the stones, amid the grass there was a charming beginning of daisies, and buttercups, the white butterflies of the year were making their first appearance, the wind, that minstrel of the eternal wedding, was trying in the trees the first notes of that grand, auroral symphony which the old poets called the springtide,—Marius said to Cosette:—"We said that we would go back to take a look at our garden in the Rue Plumet. Let us go thither. We must not be ungrateful."— And away they flitted, like two swallows towards the spring. This garden of the Rue Plumet produced on them the effect of the dawn. They already had behind them in life something which was like the springtime of their love. The house in the Rue Plumet being held on a lease, still belonged to Cosette. They went to that garden and that house. There they found themselves again, there they forgot themselves. That evening, at the usual hour, Jean Valjean came to the Rue des Filles-du-

Calvaire.—"Madame went out with Monsieur and has not yet returned," Basque said to him. He seated himself in silence, and waited an hour. Cosette did not return. He departed with drooping head.

Cosette was so intoxicated with her walk to "their garden," and so joyous at having "lived a whole day in her past," that she talked of nothing else on the morrow. She did not notice that she had not seen Jean Valjean.

"In what way did you go thither?" Jean Valjean asked her."

"On foot."

"And how did you return?"

"In a hackney carriage."

For some time, Jean Valjean had noticed the economical life led by the young people. He was troubled by it. Marius' economy was severe, and that word had its absolute meaning for Jean Valjean. He hazarded a query:

"Why do you not have a carriage of your own? A pretty coupé would only cost you five hundred francs a month. You are rich."

"I don't know," replied Cosette.

"It is like Toussaint," resumed Jean Valjean. "She is gone. You have not replaced her. Why?"

"Nicolette suffices."

"But you ought to have a maid."

"Have I not Marius?"

"You ought to have a house of your own, your own servants, a carriage, a box at the theatre. There is nothing too fine for you. Why not profit by your riches? Wealth adds to happiness."

Cosette made no reply.

Jean Valjean's visits were not abridged. Far from it. When it is the heart which is slipping, one does not halt on the downward slope.

When Jean Valjean wished to prolong his visit and to induce forgetfulness of the hour, he sang the praises of Marius; he pronounced him handsome, noble, courageous, witty, eloquent, good. Cosette outdid him. Jean Valjean began again. They were never weary. Marius—that word was inexhaustible; those six letters contained volumes. In this manner, Jean Valjean contrived to remain a long time.

It was so sweet to see Cosette, to forget by her side! It alleviated his wounds. It frequently happened that Basque came twice to announce: "M. Gillenormand sends me to remind Madame la Baronne that dinner is served."

On those days, Jean Valjean was very thoughtful on his return home.

Was there, then, any truth in that comparison of the chrysalis which had presented itself to the mind of Marius? Was Jean Valjean really a chrysalis who would persist, and who would come to visit his butterfly?

One day he remained still longer than usual. On the following day he observed that there was no fire on the hearth.—"Hello!" he thought. "No fire."—And he furnished the explanation for himself.—"It is perfectly simple. It is April. The cold weather has ceased."

"Heavens! how cold it is here!" exclaimed Cosette when she entered.

"Why, no," said Jean Valjean.

"Was it you who told Basque not to make a fire then?"

"Yes, since we are now in the month of May."

"But we have a fire until June. One is needed all the year in this cellar."

"I thought that a fire was unnecessary."

"That is exactly like one of your ideas!" retorted Cosette.

On the following day there was a fire. But the two armchairs were arranged at the other end of the room near the door. "—What is the meaning of this?" thought Jean Valjean.

He went for the armchairs and restored them to their ordinary place near the hearth.

This fire lighted once more encouraged him, however. He prolonged the conversation even beyond its customary limits. As he rose to take his leave, Cosette said to him:

"My husband said a queer thing to me yesterday."

"What was it?"

"He said to me: 'Cosette, we have an income of thirty thousand livres. Twenty-seven that you own, and three that my grandfather gives me.' I replied: 'That makes thirty.' He went on: 'Would you have the courage to live on the three thousand?' I answered: 'Yes, on nothing. Provided that it was with you.' And then I asked: 'Why do you say that to me?' He replied: 'I wanted to know.'"

Jean Valjean found not a word to answer. Cosette probably expected some explanation from him; he listened in gloomy silence. He went back to the Rue de l'Homme Armé; he was so deeply absorbed that he mistook the door and instead of entering his own house, he entered the adjoining dwelling. It was only after having ascended nearly two stories that he perceived his error and went down again.

His mind was swarming with conjectures. It was evident that Marius had his doubts as to the origin of the six hundred thousand francs, that he feared some source that was not pure, who knows? that he had even, perhaps, discovered that the money came from him, Jean Valjean, that he hesitated before this suspicious fortune, and was disinclined to take it as his own,—preferring that both he and Cosette should remain poor, rather than that they should be rich with wealth that was not clean.

Moreover, Jean Valjean began vaguely to surmise that he was being shown the door.

On the following day, he underwent something like a shock on entering the ground-floor room. The armchairs had disappeared. There was not a single chair of any sort.

"Ah, what's this!" exclaimed Cosette as she entered, "no chairs! Where are the armchairs?"

"They are no longer here," replied Jean Valjean.

"This is too much!"

Jean Valjean stammered:

"It was I who told Basque to remove them."

"And your reason?"

"I have only a few minutes to stay to-day."

"A brief stay is no reason for remaining standing."

"I think that Basque needed the chairs for the drawing-room."

"Why?"

"You have company this evening, no doubt."

"We expect no one."

Jean Valjean had not another word to say.

Cosette shrugged her shoulders.

"To have the chairs carried off! The other day you had the fire put out. How odd you are!"

"Adieu!" murmured Jean Valjean.

He did not say: "Adieu, Cosette." But he had not the strength to say: "Adieu, Madame."

He went away utterly overwhelmed.

This time he had understood.

On the following day he did not come. Cosette only observed the fact in the evening.

"Why," said she, "Monsieur Jean has not been here today."

And she felt a slight twinge at her heart, but she hardly perceived it, being immediately diverted by a kiss from Marius.

On the following day he did not come.

Cosette paid no heed to this, passed her evening and slept well that night, as usual, and thought of it only when she woke. She was so happy! She speedily despatched Nicolette to M. Jean's house to inquire whether he were ill, and why he had not come on the previous evening. Nicolette brought back the reply of M. Jean that he was not ill. He was busy. He would come soon. As soon as he was able. Moreover, he was on the point of taking a little journey. Madame must remember that it was his custom to take trips from time to time. They were not to worry about him. They were not to think of him.

Nicolette on entering M. Jean's had repeated to him her mistress' very words. That Madame had sent her to inquire why M. Jean had not come on the preceding evening. "—It is two days since I have been there," said Jean Valjean gently.

But the remark passed unnoticed by Nicolette, who did not report it to Cosette.

# IV

## ATTRACTION AND EXTINCTION

During the last months of spring and the first months of summer in 1833, the rare passers-by in the Marais, the petty shopkeepers, the loungers on thresholds, noticed an old man neatly clad in black, who emerged every day at the same hour, towards nightfall, from the Rue de l'Homme Armé, on the side of the Rue Sainte-Croix-de-la-Bretonnerie, passed in front of the Blancs Manteaux, gained the Rue Culture-Sainte-Catherine, and, on arriving at the Rue de l'Écharpe, turned to the left, and entered the Rue Saint-Louis.

There he walked at a slow pace, with his head strained forward, seeing nothing, hearing nothing, his eye immovably fixed on a point which seemed to be a star to him, which never varied, and which was no other than the corner of the Rue des Filles-du-Calvaire. The nearer he approached the corner of the street the more his eye lighted up; a sort of joy illuminated his pupils like an inward aurora, he had a fascinated and much affected air, his lips indulged in obscure movements, as though he were talking to some one whom he did not see, he smiled vaguely and advanced as slowly as possible. One would have said that, while desirous of reaching his destination, he feared the moment when he should be close at hand. When only a few houses remained between him and that street which appeared to attract him his pace slackened, to such a degree that, at times, one might have thought that he was no longer advancing at all. The vacillation of his head and the fixity of his eyeballs suggested the thought of the magnetic needle seeking the pole. Whatever time he spent on arriving, he was obliged to arrive at last; he reached the Rue des Filles-du-Calvaire; then he halted, he trembled, he thrust his head with a sort of melancholy timidity round the corner of the last house, and gazed into that street, and there was in that tragic look something which resembled the dazzling light of the impossible, and the reflection from a paradise that was closed to him. Then a tear, which had slowly gathered in the corner of his lids, and had become large enough to fall, trickled down his cheek, and sometimes stopped at his mouth. The old man tasted its bitter flavor. Thus he remained for several minutes as though made of stone, then he returned by the same road and with the same step, and, in proportion as he retreated, his glance died out.

Little by little, this old man ceased to go as far as the corner of the Rue des Filles-du-Calvaire; he halted half way in the Rue Saint-Louis; sometimes a little further off, sometimes a little nearer.

One day he stopped at the corner of the Rue Culture-Sainte-Catherine and looked at the Rue des Filles-du-Calvaire from a distance. Then he shook his head slowly from right to left, as though refusing himself something, and retraced his steps.

Soon he no longer came as far as the Rue Saint-Louis. He got as far as the Rue Pavée, shook his head and turned back; then he went no further than the Rue des Trois-Pavillons; then he did not overstep the Blancs-Manteaux. One would have said that he was a pendulum which was no longer wound up, and whose oscillations were growing shorter before ceasing altogether.

Every day he emerged from his house at the same hour, he undertook the same trip, but he no longer completed it, and, perhaps without himself being aware of the fact, he constantly shortened it. His whole countenance expressed this single idea: What is the use?—His eye was dim; no more radiance. His tears were also exhausted; they no longer collected in the corner of his eye-lid; that thoughtful eye was dry. The old man's head was still craned forward; his chin moved at times; the folds in his gaunt neck were painful to behold. Sometimes, when the weather was bad, he had an umbrella under his arm, but he never opened it.

The good women of the quarter said: "He is an innocent." The children followed him and laughed.

BOOK NINTH
SUPREME SHADOW, SUPREME DAWN

# I

## PITY FOR THE UNHAPPY, BUT INDULGENCE FOR THE HAPPY

It is a terrible thing to be happy! How content one is! How all-sufficient one finds it! How, being in possession of the false object of life, happiness, one forgets the true object, duty!

Let us say, however, that the reader would do wrong were he to blame Marius.

Marius, as we have explained, before his marriage, had put no questions to M. Fauchelevent, and, since that time, he had feared to put any to Jean Valjean. He had regretted the promise into which he had allowed himself to be drawn. He had often said to himself that he had done wrong in making that concession to despair. He had confined himself to gradually estranging Jean Valjean from his house and to effacing him, as much as possible, from Cosette's mind. He had, in a manner, always placed himself between Cosette and Jean Valjean, sure that, in this way, she would not perceive nor think of the latter. It was more than effacement, it was an eclipse.

Marius did what he considered necessary and just. He thought that he had serious reasons which the reader has already seen, and others which will be seen later on, for getting rid of Jean Valjean without harshness, but without weakness.

Chance having ordained that he should encounter, in a case which he had argued, a former employee of the Laffitte establishment, he had acquired mysterious information, without seeking it, which he had not been able, it is true, to probe, out of respect for the secret which he had promised to guard, and out of consideration for Jean Valjean's perilous position. He believed at that moment that he had a grave duty to perform: the restitution of the six hundred thousand francs to some one whom he sought with all possible discretion. In the meanwhile, he abstained from touching that money.

As for Cosette, she had not been initiated into any of these secrets; but it would be harsh to condemn her also.

There existed between Marius and her an all-powerful magnetism, which caused her to do, instinctively and almost mechanically, what

Marius wished. She was conscious of Marius' will in the direction of "Monsieur Jean," she conformed to it. Her husband had not been obliged to say anything to her; she yielded to the vague but clear pressure of his tacit intentions, and obeyed blindly. Her obedience in this instance consisted in not remembering what Marius forgot. She was not obliged to make any effort to accomplish this. Without her knowing why herself, and without his having any cause to accuse her of it, her soul had become so wholly her husband's that that which was shrouded in gloom in Marius' mind became overcast in hers.

Let us not go too far, however; in what concerns Jean Valjean, this forgetfulness and obliteration were merely superficial. She was rather heedless than forgetful. At bottom, she was sincerely attached to the man whom she had so long called her father; but she loved her husband still more dearly. This was what had somewhat disturbed the balance of her heart, which leaned to one side only.

It sometimes happened that Cosette spoke of Jean Valjean and expressed her surprise. Then Marius calmed her: "He is absent, I think. Did not he say that he was setting out on a journey?"—"That is true," thought Cosette. "He had a habit of disappearing in this fashion. But not for so long." Two or three times she despatched Nicolette to inquire in the Rue de l'Homme Armé whether M. Jean had returned from his journey. Jean Valjean caused the answer "no" to be given.

Cosette asked nothing more, since she had but one need on earth, Marius.

Let us also say that, on their side, Cosette and Marius had also been absent. They had been to Vernon. Marius had taken Cosette to his father's grave.

Marius gradually won Cosette away from Jean Valjean. Cosette allowed it.

Moreover that which is called, far too harshly in certain cases, the ingratitude of children, is not always a thing so deserving of reproach as it is supposed. It is the ingratitude of nature. Nature, as we have elsewhere said, "looks before her." Nature divides living beings into those who are arriving and those who are departing. Those who are departing are turned towards the shadows, those who are arriving towards the light. Hence a gulf which is fatal on the part of the old, and involuntary on the part of the young. This breach, at first insensible, increases slowly, like all separations of branches. The boughs, without becoming detached from the trunk, grow away from it. It is no fault of theirs. Youth goes where there is joy, festivals, vivid lights, love. Old age goes towards the end. They do not lose sight of each other, but there is no longer a close connection. Young people feel the cooling off of life; old people, that of the tomb. Let us not blame these poor children.

# II

## Last Flickerings of a Lamp Without Oil

One day, Jean Valjean descended his staircase, took three steps in the street, seated himself on a post, on that same stone post where Gavroche had found him meditating on the night between the 5th and the 6th of June; he remained there a few moments, then went upstairs again. This was the last oscillation of the pendulum. On the following day he did not leave his apartment. On the day after that, he did not leave his bed.

His portress, who prepared his scanty repasts, a few cabbages or potatoes with bacon, glanced at the brown earthenware plate and exclaimed:

"But you ate nothing yesterday, poor, dear man!"

"Certainly I did," replied Jean Valjean.

"The plate is quite full."

"Look at the water jug. It is empty."

"That proves that you have drunk; it does not prove that you have eaten."

"Well," said Jean Valjean, "what if I felt hungry only for water?"

"That is called thirst, and, when one does not eat at the same time, it is called fever."

"I will eat to-morrow."

"Or at Trinity day. Why not to-day? Is it the thing to say: 'I will eat to-morrow'? The idea of leaving my platter without even touching it! My lady-finger potatoes were so good!"

Jean Valjean took the old woman's hand:

"I promise you that I will eat them," he said, in his benevolent voice.

"I am not pleased with you," replied the portress.

Jean Valjean saw no other human creature than this good woman. There are streets in Paris through which no one ever passes, and houses to which no one ever comes. He was in one of those streets and one of those houses.

While he still went out, he had purchased of a coppersmith, for a few sous, a little copper crucifix which he had hung up on a nail opposite his bed. That gibbet is always good to look at.

A week passed, and Jean Valjean had not taken a step in his room. He still remained in bed. The portress said to her husband:—"The good man upstairs yonder does not get up, he no longer eats, he will not last long. That man has his sorrows, that he has. You won't get it out of my head that his daughter has made a bad marriage."

The porter replied, with the tone of marital sovereignty:

"If he's rich, let him have a doctor. If he is not rich, let him go without. If he has no doctor he will die."

"And if he has one?"

"He will die," said the porter.

The portress set to scraping away the grass from what she called her pavement, with an old knife, and, as she tore out the blades, she grumbled:

"It's a shame. Such a neat old man! He's as white as a chicken."

She caught sight of the doctor of the quarter as he passed the end of the street; she took it upon herself to request him to come upstairs.

"It's on the second floor," said she. "You have only to enter. As the good man no longer stirs from his bed, the door is always unlocked."

The doctor saw Jean Valjean and spoke with him.

When he came down again the portress interrogated him:

"Well, doctor?"

"Your sick man is very ill indeed."

"What is the matter with him?"

"Everything and nothing. He is a man who, to all appearances, has lost some person who is dear to him. People die of that."

"What did he say to you?"

"He told me that he was in good health."

"Shall you come again, doctor?"

"Yes," replied the doctor. "But some one else besides must come."

# III

## A Pen is Heavy to the Man Who Lifted the Fauchelevent's Cart

One evening Jean Valjean found difficulty in raising himself on his elbow; he felt of his wrist and could not find his pulse; his breath was short and halted at times; he recognized the fact that he was weaker than he had ever been before. Then, no doubt under the pressure of some supreme preoccupation, he made an effort, drew himself up into a sitting posture and dressed himself. He put on his old workingman's clothes. As he no longer went out, he had returned to them and preferred them. He was obliged to pause many times while dressing himself; merely putting his arms through his waistcoat made the perspiration trickle from his forehead.

Since he had been alone, he had placed his bed in the antechamber, in order to inhabit that deserted apartment as little as possible.

He opened the valise and drew from it Cosette's outfit.

He spread it out on his bed.

The Bishop's candlesticks were in their place on the chimney-piece. He took from a drawer two wax candles and put them in the candlesticks. Then, although it was still broad daylight,—it was summer,—he lighted them. In the same way candles are to be seen lighted in broad daylight in chambers where there is a corpse.

Every step that he took in going from one piece of furniture to another exhausted him, and he was obliged to sit down. It was not ordinary fatigue which expends the strength only to renew it; it was the remnant of all movement possible to him, it was life drained which flows away drop by drop in overwhelming efforts and which will never be renewed.

The chair into which he allowed himself to fall was placed in front of that mirror, so fatal for him, so providential for Marius, in which he had read Cosette's reversed writing on the blotting book. He caught sight of himself in this mirror, and did not recognize himself. He was eighty years old; before Marius' marriage, he would have hardly been taken for fifty; that year had counted for thirty. What he bore on his brow was no longer the wrinkles of age, it was the mysterious mark of death. The hollowing of that pitiless nail could be felt there. His cheeks were pendulous; the skin of his face had the color which would lead one to think that it already had earth upon it; the corners of his mouth drooped as in the mask which the ancients sculptured on tombs. He gazed into space with an air of reproach; one would have said that he was one of those grand tragic beings who have cause to complain of some one.

He was in that condition, the last phase of dejection, in which sorrow no longer flows; it is coagulated, so to speak; there is something on the soul like a clot of despair.

Night had come. He laboriously dragged a table and the old armchair to the fireside, and placed upon the table a pen, some ink and some paper.

That done, he had a fainting fit. When he recovered consciousness, he was thirsty. As he could not lift the jug, he tipped it over painfully towards his mouth, and swallowed a draught.

As neither the pen nor the ink had been used for a long time, the point of the pen had curled up, the ink had dried away, he was forced to rise and put a few drops of water in the ink, which he did not accomplish without pausing and sitting down two or three times, and he was compelled to write with the back of the pen. He wiped his brow from time to time.

Then he turned towards the bed, and, still seated, for he could not stand, he gazed at the little black gown and all those beloved objects.

These contemplations lasted for hours which seemed minutes.

All at once he shivered, he felt that a child was taking possession of him; he rested his elbows on the table, which was illuminated by the Bishop's candles and took up the pen. His hand trembled. He wrote slowly the few following lines:

"Cosette, I bless thee. I am going to explain to thee. Thy husband was right in giving me to understand that I ought to go away; but there is a little error in what he believed, though he was in the right. He is excellent. Love him well even after I am dead. Monsieur Pontmercy, love my darling child well. Cosette, this paper will be found; this is what I wish to say to thee, thou wilt see the figures, if I have the strength to recall them, listen well, this money is really thine. Here is the whole matter: White jet comes from Norway, black jet comes from England, black glass jewellery comes from Germany. Jet is the lightest, the most precious, the most costly. Imitations can be made in France as well as in Germany. What is needed is a little anvil two inches square, and a lamp burning spirits of wine to soften the wax. The wax was formerly made with resin and lampblack, and cost four livres the pound. I invented a way of making it with gum shellac and turpentine. It does not cost more than thirty sous, and is much better. Buckles are made with a violet glass which is stuck fast, by means of this wax, to a little framework of black iron. The glass must be violet for iron jewellery, and black for gold jewellery. Spain buys a great deal of it. It is the country of jet. . ."

Here he paused, the pen fell from his fingers, he was seized by one of those sobs which at times welled up from the very depths of his being; the poor man clasped his head in both hands, and meditated.

"Oh!" he exclaimed within himself (lamentable cries, heard by God alone), "all is over. I shall never see her more. She is a smile which passed over me. I am about to plunge into the night without even seeing her again. Oh! one minute, one instant, to hear her voice, to touch her dress, to gaze upon her, upon her, the angel! and then to die! It is nothing to die, what is frightful is to die without seeing her. She would smile on me, she would say a word to me, would that do any harm to any one? No, all is over, and forever. Here I am all alone. My God! My God! I shall never see her again!" At that moment there came a knock at the door.

# IV

## A Bottle of Ink Which Only Succeeded in Whitening

That same day, or to speak more accurately, that same evening, as Marius left the table, and was on the point of withdrawing to his study, having a case to look over, Basque handed him a letter saying: "The person who wrote the letter is in the antechamber."

Cosette had taken the grandfather's arm and was strolling in the garden.

A letter, like a man, may have an unprepossessing exterior. Coarse paper, coarsely folded—the very sight of certain missives is displeasing.

The letter which Basque had brought was of this sort.

Marius took it. It smelled of tobacco. Nothing evokes a memory like an odor. Marius recognized that tobacco. He looked at the superscription: "To Monsieur, Monsieur le Baron Pommerci. At his hotel." The recognition of the tobacco caused him to recognize the writing as well. It may be said that amazement has its lightning flashes.

Marius was, as it were, illuminated by one of these flashes.

The sense of smell, that mysterious aid to memory, had just revived a whole world within him. This was certainly the paper, the fashion of folding, the dull tint of ink; it was certainly the well-known handwriting, especially was it the same tobacco.

The Jondrette garret rose before his mind.

Thus, strange freak of chance! one of the two scents which he had so diligently sought, the one in connection with which he had lately again exerted so many efforts and which he supposed to be forever lost, had come and presented itself to him of its own accord.

He eagerly broke the seal, and read:

Monsieur le Baron
    If the Supreme Being had given me the talents, I
might have been baron Thénard, member of the Institute
(acadenmy of ciences), but I am not. I only bear the same
as him, happy if this memory recommends me to the
eccellence of your kindnesses. The benefit with which you

will honor me will be reciprocle. I am in possession of a secret concerning an individual. This individual concerns you. I hold the secret at your disposal desiring to have the honor to be huseful to you. I will furnish you with the simple means of driving from your honorabel family that individual who has no right there, madame la baronne being of lofty birth. The sanctuary of virtue cannot cohabit longer with crime without abdicating.

"I awate in the entichamber the orders of monsieur le baron.

"With respect."

The letter was signed "Thénard."

This signature was not false. It was merely a trifle abridged.

Moreover, the rigmarole and the orthography completed the revelation. The certificate of origin was complete.

Marius' emotion was profound. After a start of surprise, he underwent a feeling of happiness. If he could now but find that other man of whom he was in search, the man who had saved him, Marius, there would be nothing left for him to desire.

He opened the drawer of his secretary, took out several bank-notes, put them in his pocket, closed the secretary again, and rang the bell. Basque half opened the door.

"Show the man in," said Marius.

Basque announced:

"Monsieur Thénard."

A man entered.

A fresh surprise for Marius. The man who entered was an utter stranger to him.

This man, who was old, moreover, had a thick nose, his chin swathed in a cravat, green spectacles with a double screen of green taffeta over his eyes, and his hair was plastered and flattened down on his brow on a level with his eyebrows like the wigs of English coachmen in "high life." His hair was gray. He was dressed in black from head to foot, in garments that were very threadbare but clean; a bunch of seals depending from his fob suggested the idea of a watch. He held in his hand an old hat! He walked in a bent attitude, and the curve in his spine augmented the profundity of his bow.

The first thing that struck the observer was, that this personage's coat, which was too ample although carefully buttoned, had not been made for him.

Here a short digression becomes necessary.

There was in Paris at that epoch, in a low-lived old lodging in the Rue Beautreillis, near the Arsenal, an ingenious Jew whose profession was to change villains into honest men. Not for too long, which might have proved embarrassing for the villain. The change was on sight, for a day or two, at the rate of thirty sous a day, by means of a costume which resembled the honesty of the world in general as nearly as possible. This costumer was called "the Changer"; the pickpockets of Paris had given him this name and knew him by no other. He had a tolerably complete wardrobe. The rags with which he tricked out people were almost probable. He had specialties and categories; on each nail of his shop hung a social status, threadbare and worn; here the suit of a magistrate, there the outfit of a Curé, beyond the outfit of a banker, in one corner the costume of a retired military man, elsewhere the habiliments of a man of letters, and further on the dress of a statesman.

This creature was the costumer of the immense drama which knavery plays in Paris. His lair was the green-room whence theft emerged, and into which roguery retreated. A tattered knave arrived at this dressing-room, deposited his thirty sous and selected, according to the part which he wished to play, the costume which suited him, and on descending the stairs once more, the knave was a somebody. On the following day, the clothes were faithfully returned, and the Changer, who trusted the thieves with everything, was never robbed. There was one inconvenience about these clothes, they "did not fit"; not having been made for those who wore them, they were too tight for one, too loose for another and did not adjust themselves to any one. Every pickpocket who exceeded or fell short of the human average was ill at his ease in the Changer's costumes. It was necessary that one should not be either too fat or too lean. The Changer had foreseen only ordinary men. He had taken the measure of the species from the first rascal who came to hand, who is neither stout nor thin, neither tall nor short. Hence adaptations which were sometimes difficult and from which the Changer's clients extricated themselves as best they might. So much the worse for the exceptions! The suit of the statesman, for instance, black from head to foot, and consequently proper, would have been too large for Pitt and too small for Castelcicala. The costume of a statesman was designated as follows in the Changer's catalogue; we copy:

"A coat of black cloth, trowsers of black wool, a silk waistcoat, boots and linen." On the margin there stood: *ex-ambassador*, and a note which we also copy: "In a separate box, a neatly frizzed peruke, green glasses, seals, and two small quills an inch long, wrapped in cotton." All this belonged to the statesman, the ex-ambassador. This whole costume was, if we may so express ourselves, debilitated; the seams were white, a vague button-hole yawned at one of the elbows; moreover, one of the coat buttons was missing on the breast; but this was only detail; as the hand of the statesman should always be thrust into his coat and laid upon his heart, its function was to conceal the absent button.

If Marius had been familiar with the occult institutions of Paris, he would instantly have recognized upon the back of the visitor whom Basque had just shown in, the statesman's suit borrowed from the pick-me-down-that shop of the Changer.

Marius' disappointment on beholding another man than the one whom he expected to see turned to the newcomer's disadvantage.

He surveyed him from head to foot, while that personage made exaggerated bows, and demanded in a curt tone:

"What do you want?"

The man replied with an amiable grin of which the caressing smile of a crocodile will furnish some idea:

"It seems to me impossible that I should not have already had the honor of seeing Monsieur le Baron in society. I think I actually did meet monsieur personally, several years ago, at the house of Madame la Princesse Bagration and in the drawing-rooms of his Lordship the Vicomte Dambray, peer of France."

It is always a good bit of tactics in knavery to pretend to recognize some one whom one does not know.

Marius paid attention to the manner of this man's speech. He spied on his accent and gesture, but his disappointment increased; the pronunciation was nasal and absolutely unlike the dry, shrill tone which he had expected.

He was utterly routed.

"I know neither Madame Bagration nor M. Dambray," said he. "I have never set foot in the house of either of them in my life."

The reply was ungracious. The personage, determined to be gracious at any cost, insisted.

"Then it must have been at Chateaubriand's that I have seen Monsieur! I know Chateaubriand very well. He is very affable. He sometimes says to me: 'Thénard, my friend. . . won't you drink a glass of wine with me?'"

Marius' brow grew more and more severe:

"I have never had the honor of being received by M. de Chateaubriand. Let us cut it short. What do you want?"

The man bowed lower at that harsh voice.

"Monsieur le Baron, deign to listen to me. There is in America, in a district near Panama, a village called la Joya. That village is composed of a single house, a large, square house of three stories, built of bricks dried in the sun, each side of the square five hundred feet in length, each story retreating twelve feet back of the story below, in such a manner as to leave in front a terrace which makes the circuit of the edifice, in the centre an inner court where the provisions and munitions are kept; no windows, loopholes, no doors, ladders, ladders to mount from the ground to the first terrace, and from the first to the second, and from the second to the third, ladders to descend into the inner court, no doors to the chambers, trap-doors, no staircases to the chambers, ladders; in the evening the traps are closed, the ladders are withdrawn, carbines and blunderbusses trained from the loopholes; no means of entering, a house by day, a citadel by night, eight hundred inhabitants,—that is the village. Why so many precautions? because the country is dangerous; it is full of cannibals. Then why do people go there? because the country is marvellous; gold is found there."

"What are you driving at?" interrupted Marius, who had passed from disappointment to impatience.

"At this, Monsieur le Baron. I am an old and weary diplomat. Ancient civilization has thrown me on my own devices. I want to try savages."

"Well?"

"Monsieur le Baron, egotism is the law of the world. The proletarian peasant woman, who toils by the day, turns round when the diligence passes by, the peasant proprietress, who toils in her field, does not turn round. The dog of the poor man barks at the rich man, the dog of the rich man barks at the poor man. Each one for himself. Self-interest—that's the object of men. Gold, that's the loadstone."

"What then? Finish."

"I should like to go and establish myself at la Joya. There are three of us. I have my spouse and my young lady; a very beautiful girl. The journey is long and costly. I need a little money."

"What concern is that of mine?" demanded Marius.

The stranger stretched his neck out of his cravat, a gesture characteristic of the vulture, and replied with an augmented smile.

"Has not Monsieur le Baron perused my letter?"

There was some truth in this. The fact is, that the contents of the epistle had slipped Marius' mind. He had seen the writing rather than read the letter. He could hardly recall it. But a moment ago a fresh start had been given him. He had noted that detail: "my spouse and my young lady."

He fixed a penetrating glance on the stranger. An examining judge could not have done the look better. He almost lay in wait for him.

He confined himself to replying:

"State the case precisely."

The stranger inserted his two hands in both his fobs, drew himself up without straightening his dorsal column, but scrutinizing Marius in his turn, with the green gaze of his spectacles.

"So be it, Monsieur le Baron. I will be precise. I have a secret to sell to you."

"A secret?"

"A secret."

"Which concerns me?"

"Somewhat."

"What is the secret?"

Marius scrutinized the man more and more as he listened to him.

"I commence gratis," said the stranger. "You will see that I am interesting."

"Speak."

"Monsieur le Baron, you have in your house a thief and an assassin."

Marius shuddered.

"In my house? no," said he.

The imperturbable stranger brushed his hat with his elbow and went on:

"An assassin and a thief. Remark, Monsieur le Baron, that I do not here speak of ancient deeds, deeds of the past which have lapsed, which can be effaced by limitation before the law and by repentance before God. I speak of recent deeds, of actual facts as still unknown to justice at this hour. I continue. This man has insinuated himself into your confidence, and almost into your family under a false name. I am about to tell you his real name. And to tell it to you for nothing."

VICTOR HUGO

"I am listening."

"His name is Jean Valjean."

"I know it."

"I am going to tell you, equally for nothing, who he is."

"Say on."

"He is an ex-convict."

"I know it."

"You know it since I have had the honor of telling you."

"No. I knew it before."

Marius' cold tone, that double reply of "I know it," his laconicism, which was not favorable to dialogue, stirred up some smouldering wrath in the stranger. He launched a furious glance on the sly at Marius, which was instantly extinguished. Rapid as it was, this glance was of the kind which a man recognizes when he has once beheld it; it did not escape Marius. Certain flashes can only proceed from certain souls; the eye, that vent-hole of the thought, glows with it; spectacles hide nothing; try putting a pane of glass over hell!

The stranger resumed with a smile:

"I will not permit myself to contradict Monsieur le Baron. In any case, you ought to perceive that I am well informed. Now what I have to tell you is known to myself alone. This concerns the fortune of Madame la Baronne. It is an extraordinary secret. It is for sale—I make you the first offer of it. Cheap. Twenty thousand francs."

"I know that secret as well as the others," said Marius.

The personage felt the necessity of lowering his price a trifle.

"Monsieur le Baron, say ten thousand francs and I will speak."

"I repeat to you that there is nothing which you can tell me. I know what you wish to say to me."

A fresh flash gleamed in the man's eye. He exclaimed:

"But I must dine to-day, nevertheless. It is an extraordinary secret, I tell you. Monsieur le Baron, I will speak. I speak. Give me twenty francs."

Marius gazed intently at him:

"I know your extraordinary secret, just as I knew Jean Valjean's name, just as I know your name."

"My name?"

"Yes."

"That is not difficult, Monsieur le Baron. I had the honor to write to you and to tell it to you. Thénard."

"—Dier."

"Hey?"

"Thénardier."

"Who's that?"

In danger the porcupine bristles up, the beetle feigns death, the old guard forms in a square; this man burst into laughter.

Then he flicked a grain of dust from the sleeve of his coat with a fillip.

Marius continued:

"You are also Jondrette the workman, Fabantou the comedian, Genflot the poet, Don Alvarès the Spaniard, and Mistress Balizard."

"Mistress what?"

"And you kept a pot-house at Montfermeil."

"A pot-house! Never."

"And I tell you that your name is Thénardier."

"I deny it."

"And that you are a rascal. Here."

And Marius drew a bank-note from his pocket and flung it in his face.

"Thanks! Pardon me! five hundred francs! Monsieur le Baron!"

And the man, overcome, bowed, seized the note and examined it.

"Five hundred francs!" he began again, taken aback. And he stammered in a low voice: "An honest rustler."

Then brusquely:

"Well, so be it!" he exclaimed. "Let us put ourselves at our ease."

And with the agility of a monkey, flinging back his hair, tearing off his spectacles, and withdrawing from his nose by sleight of hand the two quills of which mention was recently made, and which the reader has also met with on another page of this book, he took off his face as the man takes off his hat.

His eye lighted up; his uneven brow, with hollows in some places and bumps in others, hideously wrinkled at the top, was laid bare, his nose had become as sharp as a beak; the fierce and sagacious profile of the man of prey reappeared.

"Monsieur le Baron is infallible," he said in a clear voice whence all nasal twang had disappeared, "I am Thénardier."

And he straightened up his crooked back.

Thénardier, for it was really he, was strangely surprised; he would have been troubled, had he been capable of such a thing. He had come to bring astonishment, and it was he who had received it. This humiliation had been worth five hundred francs to him, and, taking it all in all, he accepted it; but he was nonetheless bewildered.

He beheld this Baron Pontmercy for the first time, and, in spite of his disguise, this Baron Pontmercy recognized him, and recognized him thoroughly. And not only was this Baron perfectly informed as to Thénardier, but he seemed well posted as to Jean Valjean. Who was this almost beardless young man, who was so glacial and so generous, who knew people's names, who knew all their names, and who opened his purse to them, who bullied rascals like a judge, and who paid them like a dupe?

Thénardier, the reader will remember, although he had been Marius' neighbor, had never seen him, which is not unusual in Paris; he had formerly, in a vague way, heard his daughters talk of a very poor young man named Marius who lived in the house. He had written to him, without knowing him, the letter with which the reader is acquainted.

No connection between that Marius and M. le Baron Pontmercy was possible in his mind.

As for the name Pontmercy, it will be recalled that, on the battlefield of Waterloo, he had only heard the last two syllables, for which he always entertained the legitimate scorn which one owes to what is merely an expression of thanks.

However, through his daughter Azelma, who had started on the scent of the married pair on the 16th of February, and through his own personal researches, he had succeeded in learning many things, and, from the depths of his own gloom, he had contrived to grasp more than one mysterious clew. He had discovered, by dint of industry, or, at least, by dint of induction, he had guessed who the man was whom he had encountered on a certain day in the Grand Sewer. From the man he had easily reached the name. He knew that Madame la Baronne Pontmercy was Cosette. But he meant to be discreet in that quarter.

Who was Cosette? He did not know exactly himself. He did, indeed, catch an inkling of illegitimacy, the history of Fantine had always seemed to him equivocal; but what was the use of talking about that? in order to cause himself to be paid for his silence? He had, or thought he had, better wares than that for sale. And, according to all appearances, if he were to come and make to the Baron Pontmercy this revelation— and without proof: "Your wife is a bastard," the only result would be to attract the boot of the husband towards the loins of the revealer.

From Thénardier's point of view, the conversation with Marius had not yet begun. He ought to have drawn back, to have modified his strategy, to have abandoned his position, to have changed his front; but nothing essential had been compromised as yet, and he had five hundred francs in his pocket. Moreover, he had something decisive to say, and, even against this very well-informed and well-armed Baron Pontmercy, he felt himself strong. For men of Thénardier's nature, every dialogue is a combat. In the one in which he was about to engage, what was his situation? He did not know to whom he was speaking, but he did know of what he was speaking, he made this rapid review of his inner forces, and after having said: "I am Thénardier," he waited.

Marius had become thoughtful. So he had hold of Thénardier at last. That man whom he had so greatly desired to find was before him. He could honor Colonel Pontmercy's recommendation.

He felt humiliated that that hero should have owned anything to this villain, and that the letter of change drawn from the depths of the tomb by his father upon him, Marius, had been protested up to that day. It also seemed to him, in the complex state of his mind towards Thénardier, that there was occasion to avenge the Colonel for the misfortune of having been saved by such a rascal. In any case, he was content. He was about to deliver the Colonel's shade from this unworthy creditor at last, and it seemed to him that he was on the point of rescuing his father's memory from the debtors' prison. By the side of this duty there was another—to elucidate, if possible, the source of Cosette's fortune. The opportunity appeared to present itself. Perhaps Thénardier knew something. It might prove useful to see the bottom of this man.

He commenced with this.

Thénardier had caused the "honest rustler" to disappear in his fob, and was gazing at Marius with a gentleness that was almost tender.

Marius broke the silence.

"Thénardier, I have told you your name. Now, would you like to have me tell you your secret—the one that you came here to reveal to me? I have information of my own, also. You shall see that I know more about it than you do. Jean Valjean, as you have said, is an assassin and a thief. A thief, because he robbed a wealthy manufacturer, whose ruin he brought about. An assassin, because he assassinated police-agent Javert."

"I don't understand, sir," ejaculated Thénardier.

"I will make myself intelligible. In a certain arrondissement of the Pas de Calais, there was, in 1822, a man who had fallen out with justice, and who, under the name of M. Madeleine, had regained his status and rehabilitated himself. This man had become a just man in the full force of the term. In a trade, the manufacture of black glass goods, he made the fortune of an entire city. As far as his personal fortune was concerned he made that also, but as a secondary matter, and in some sort, by accident. He was the foster-father of the poor. He founded hospitals, opened schools, visited the sick, dowered young girls, supported widows, and adopted orphans; he was like the guardian angel of the country. He refused the cross, he was appointed Mayor. A liberated convict knew the secret of a penalty incurred by this man in former days; he denounced him, and had him arrested, and profited by the arrest to come to Paris and cause the banker Laffitte,—I have the fact from the cashier himself,—by means of a false signature, to hand over to him the sum of over half a million which belonged to M. Madeleine. This convict who robbed M. Madeleine was Jean Valjean. As for the other fact, you have nothing to tell me about it either. Jean Valjean killed the agent Javert; he shot him with a pistol. I, the person who is speaking to you, was present."

Thénardier cast upon Marius the sovereign glance of a conquered man who lays his hand once more upon the victory, and who has just regained, in one instant, all the ground which he has lost. But the smile returned instantly. The inferior's triumph in the presence of his superior must be wheedling.

Thénardier contented himself with saying to Marius:

"Monsieur le Baron, we are on the wrong track."

And he emphasized this phrase by making his bunch of seals execute an expressive whirl.

"What!" broke forth Marius, "do you dispute that? These are facts."

"They are chimæras. The confidence with which Monsieur le Baron honors me renders it my duty to tell him so. Truth and justice before all things. I do not like to see folks accused unjustly. Monsieur le Baron, Jean Valjean did not rob M. Madeleine and Jean Valjean did not kill Javert."

"This is too much! How is this?"

"For two reasons."

"What are they? Speak."

"This is the first: he did not rob M. Madeleine, because it is Jean Valjean himself who was M. Madeleine."

"What tale are you telling me?"

"And this is the second: he did not assassinate Javert, because the person who killed Javert was Javert."

"What do you mean to say?"

"That Javert committed suicide."

"Prove it! prove it!" cried Marius beside himself.

Thénardier resumed, scanning his phrase after the manner of the ancient Alexandrine measure:

"Police-agent-Ja-vert-was-found-drowned-un-der-a-boat-of-the-Pont-au-Change."

"But prove it!"

Thénardier drew from his pocket a large envelope of gray paper, which seemed to contain sheets folded in different sizes.

"I have my papers," he said calmly.

And he added:

"Monsieur le Baron, in your interests I desired to know Jean Valjean thoroughly. I say that Jean Valjean and M. Madeleine are one and the same man, and I say that Javert had no other assassin than Javert. If I speak, it is because I have proofs. Not manuscript proofs—writing is suspicious, handwriting is complaisant,—but printed proofs."

As he spoke, Thénardier extracted from the envelope two copies of newspapers, yellow, faded, and strongly saturated with tobacco. One of these two newspapers, broken at every fold and falling into rags, seemed much older than the other.

"Two facts, two proofs," remarked Thénardier. And he offered the two newspapers, unfolded, to Marius.

The reader is acquainted with these two papers. One, the most ancient, a number of the *Drapeau Blanc* of the 25th of July, 1823, the text of which can be seen in the first volume, established the identity of M. Madeleine and Jean Valjean.

The other, a *Moniteur* of the 15th of June, 1832, announced the suicide of Javert, adding that it appeared from a verbal report of Javert to the prefect that, having been taken prisoner in the barricade of the Rue de la Chanvrerie, he had owed his life to the magnanimity of an insurgent who, holding him under his pistol, had fired into the air, instead of blowing out his brains.

Marius read. He had evidence, a certain date, irrefragable proof, these two newspapers had not been printed expressly for the purpose of backing up Thénardier's statements; the note printed in the *Moniteur* had been an administrative communication from the Prefecture of Police. Marius could not doubt.

The information of the cashier-clerk had been false, and he himself had been deceived.

Jean Valjean, who had suddenly grown grand, emerged from his cloud. Marius could not repress a cry of joy.

"Well, then this unhappy wretch is an admirable man! the whole of that fortune really belonged to him! he is Madeleine, the providence of a whole countryside! he is Jean Valjean, Javert's savior! he is a hero! he is a saint!"

"He's not a saint, and he's not a hero!" said Thénardier. "He's an assassin and a robber."

And he added, in the tone of a man who begins to feel that he possesses some authority:

"Let us be calm."

Robber, assassin—those words which Marius thought had disappeared and which returned, fell upon him like an ice-cold shower-bath.

"Again!" said he.

"Always," ejaculated Thénardier. "Jean Valjean did not rob Madeleine, but he is a thief. He did not kill Javert, but he is a murderer."

"Will you speak," retorted Marius, "of that miserable theft, committed forty years ago, and expiated, as your own newspapers prove, by a whole life of repentance, of self-abnegation and of virtue?"

"I say assassination and theft, Monsieur le Baron, and I repeat that I am speaking of actual facts. What I have to reveal to you is absolutely unknown. It belongs to unpublished matter. And perhaps you will find in it the source of the fortune so skilfully presented to Madame la Baronne by Jean Valjean. I say skilfully, because, by a gift of that nature it would not be so very unskilful to slip into an honorable house whose comforts one would then share, and, at the same stroke, to conceal one's crime, and to enjoy one's theft, to bury one's name and to create for oneself a family."

"I might interrupt you at this point," said Marius, "but go on."

"Monsieur le Baron, I will tell you all, leaving the recompense to your generosity. This secret is worth massive gold. You will say to me: 'Why do not you apply to Jean Valjean?' For a very simple reason; I know that he has stripped himself, and stripped himself in your favor, and I consider the combination ingenious; but he has no longer a son, he would show me his empty hands, and, since I am in need of some money for my trip to la Joya, I prefer you, you who have it all, to him who has nothing. I am a little fatigued, permit me to take a chair."

Marius seated himself and motioned to him to do the same.

Thénardier installed himself on a tufted chair, picked up his two newspapers, thrust them back into their envelope, and murmured as he pecked at the *Drapeau Blanc* with his nail: "It cost me a good deal of trouble to get this one."

That done he crossed his legs and stretched himself out on the back of the chair, an attitude characteristic of people who are sure of what they are saying, then he entered upon his subject gravely, emphasizing his words:

"Monsieur le Baron, on the 6th of June, 1832, about a year ago, on the day of the insurrection, a man was in the Grand Sewer of Paris, at the point where the sewer enters the Seine, between the Pont des Invalides and the Pont de Jéna."

Marius abruptly drew his chair closer to that of Thénardier. Thénardier noticed this movement and continued with the deliberation of an orator who holds his interlocutor and who feels his adversary palpitating under his words:

"This man, forced to conceal himself, and for reasons, moreover, which are foreign to politics, had adopted the sewer as his domicile and had a key to it. It was, I repeat, on the 6th of June; it might have been eight o'clock in the evening. The man hears a noise in the sewer. Greatly surprised, he hides himself and lies in wait. It was the sound of footsteps, some one was walking in the dark, and coming in his direction. Strange to say, there was another man in the sewer besides himself. The grating of the outlet from the sewer was not far off. A little light which fell through it permitted him to recognize the newcomer, and to see that the man was carrying something on his back. He was walking in a bent attitude. The man who was walking in a bent attitude was an ex-convict, and what he was dragging on his shoulders was a corpse. Assassination caught in the very act, if ever there was such a thing. As for the theft, that is understood; one does not kill a man gratis. This convict was on his way to fling the body into the river. One fact is to be noticed, that before reaching the exit grating, this convict, who had come a long distance in the sewer, must, necessarily, have encountered a frightful quagmire where it seems as though he might have left the body, but the sewermen would have found the assassinated man the very next day, while at work on the quagmire, and that did not suit the assassin's plans. He had preferred to traverse that quagmire with his burden, and his exertions must have been terrible, for it is impossible to risk one's life more completely; I don't understand how he could have come out of that alive."

Marius' chair approached still nearer. Thénardier took advantage of this to draw a long breath. He went on:

"Monsieur le Baron, a sewer is not the Champ de Mars. One lacks everything there, even room. When two men are there, they must meet. That is what happened. The man domiciled there and the passer-by were forced to bid each other good-day, greatly to the regret of both. The passer-by said to the inhabitant:—"You see what I have on my back, I must get out, you have the key, give it to me." That convict was a man of terrible strength. There was no way of refusing. Nevertheless, the man who had the key parleyed, simply to gain time. He examined the dead man, but he could see nothing, except that the latter was young, well dressed, with the air of being rich, and all disfigured with blood. While talking, the man contrived to tear and pull off behind, without the assassin perceiving it, a bit of the assassinated man's coat. A document for conviction, you understand; a means of recovering the trace of things and of bringing home the crime to the criminal. He put this document for conviction in his pocket. After which he opened the grating, made the man go out with his embarrassment on his back, closed the grating again, and ran off, not caring to be mixed up with the remainder of the adventure and above all, not wishing to be present when the assassin threw the assassinated man into the river. Now you comprehend. The man who was carrying the corpse was Jean Valjean; the one who had the key is speaking to you at this moment; and the piece of the coat. . ."

Thénardier completed his phrase by drawing from his pocket, and holding, on a level with his eyes, nipped between his two thumbs and his two forefingers, a strip of torn black cloth, all covered with dark spots.

Marius had sprung to his feet, pale, hardly able to draw his breath, with his eyes riveted on the fragment of black cloth, and, without uttering a word, without taking his eyes from that fragment, he retreated to the wall and fumbled with his right hand along the wall for a key which was in the lock of a cupboard near the chimney.

He found the key, opened the cupboard, plunged his arm into it without looking, and without his frightened gaze quitting the rag which Thénardier still held outspread.

But Thénardier continued:

"Monsieur le Baron, I have the strongest of reasons for believing that the assassinated young man was an opulent stranger lured into a trap by Jean Valjean, and the bearer of an enormous sum of money."

"The young man was myself, and here is the coat!" cried Marius, and he flung upon the floor an old black coat all covered with blood.

Then, snatching the fragment from the hands of Thénardier, he crouched down over the coat, and laid the torn morsel against the tattered skirt. The rent fitted exactly, and the strip completed the coat.

Thénardier was petrified.

This is what he thought: "I'm struck all of a heap."

Marius rose to his feet trembling, despairing, radiant.

He fumbled in his pocket and stalked furiously to Thénardier, presenting to him and almost thrusting in his face his fist filled with bank-notes for five hundred and a thousand francs.

"You are an infamous wretch! you are a liar, a calumniator, a villain. You came to accuse that man, you have only justified him; you wanted to ruin him, you have only succeeded in glorifying him. And it is you who are the thief! And it is you who are the assassin! I saw you, Thénardier Jondrette, in that lair on the Rue de l'Hôpital. I know enough about you to send you to the galleys and even further if I choose. Here are a thousand francs, bully that you are!"

And he flung a thousand franc note at Thénardier.

"Ah! Jondrette Thénardier, vile rascal! Let this serve you as a lesson, you dealer in second-hand secrets, merchant of mysteries, rummager of the shadows, wretch! Take these five hundred francs and get out of here! Waterloo protects you."

"Waterloo!" growled Thénardier, pocketing the five hundred francs along with the thousand.

"Yes, assassin! You there saved the life of a Colonel. . ."

"Of a General," said Thénardier, elevating his head.

"Of a Colonel!" repeated Marius in a rage. "I wouldn't give a ha'penny for a general. And you come here to commit infamies! I tell you that you have committed all crimes. Go! disappear! Only be happy, that is all that I desire. Ah! monster! here are three thousand francs more. Take them. You will depart to-morrow, for America, with your daughter; for your wife is dead, you abominable liar. I shall watch over your departure, you ruffian, and at that moment I will count out to you twenty thousand francs. Go get yourself hung elsewhere!"

"Monsieur le Baron!" replied Thénardier, bowing to the very earth, "eternal gratitude." And Thénardier left the room, understanding nothing, stupefied and delighted with this sweet crushing beneath sacks of gold, and with that thunder which had burst forth over his head in bank-bills.

Struck by lightning he was, but he was also content; and he would have been greatly angered had he had a lightning rod to ward off such lightning as that.

Let us finish with this man at once.

Two days after the events which we are at this moment narrating, he set out, thanks to Marius' care, for America under a false name, with his daughter Azelma, furnished with a draft on New York for twenty thousand francs.

The moral wretchedness of Thénardier, the bourgeois who had missed his vocation, was irremediable. He was in America what he had been in Europe. Contact with an evil man sometimes suffices to corrupt a good action and to cause evil things to spring from it. With Marius' money, Thénardier set up as a slave-dealer.

As soon as Thénardier had left the house, Marius rushed to the garden, where Cosette was still walking.

"Cosette! Cosette!" he cried. "Come! come quick! Let us go. Basque, a carriage! Cosette, come. Ah! My God! It was he who saved my life! Let us not lose a minute! Put on your shawl."

Cosette thought him mad and obeyed.

He could not breathe, he laid his hand on his heart to restrain its throbbing. He paced back and forth with huge strides, he embraced Cosette:

"Ah! Cosette! I am an unhappy wretch!" said he.

Marius was bewildered. He began to catch a glimpse in Jean Valjean of some indescribably lofty and melancholy figure. An unheard-of virtue, supreme and sweet, humble in its immensity, appeared to him. The convict was transfigured into Christ.

Marius was dazzled by this prodigy. He did not know precisely what he beheld, but it was grand.

In an instant, a hackney-carriage stood in front of the door.

Marius helped Cosette in and darted in himself.

"Driver," said he, "Rue de l'Homme Armé, Number 7."

The carriage drove off.

"Ah! what happiness!" ejaculated Cosette. "Rue de l'Homme Armé, I did not dare to speak to you of that. We are going to see M. Jean."

"Thy father! Cosette, thy father more than ever. Cosette, I guess it. You told me that you had never received the letter that I sent you by Gavroche. It must have fallen into his hands. Cosette, he went to the barricade to save me. As it is a necessity with him to be an angel, he saved others also; he saved Javert. He rescued me from that gulf to give me to you. He carried me on his back through that frightful sewer. Ah! I am a monster of ingratitude. Cosette, after having been your providence, he became mine. Just imagine, there was a terrible quagmire enough to drown one a hundred times over, to drown one in mire. Cosette! he made me traverse it. I was unconscious; I saw nothing, I heard nothing, I could know nothing of my own adventure. We are going to bring him back, to take him with us, whether he is willing or not, he shall never leave us again. If only he is at home! Provided only that we can find him, I will pass the rest of my life in venerating him. Yes, that is how it should be, do you see, Cosette? Gavroche must have delivered my letter to him. All is explained. You understand."

Cosette did not understand a word.

"You are right," she said to him.

Meanwhile the carriage rolled on.

# V

## A Night Behind Which There is Day

Jean Valjean turned round at the knock which he heard on his door.
"Come in," he said feebly.

The door opened.

Cosette and Marius made their appearance.

Cosette rushed into the room.

Marius remained on the threshold, leaning against the jamb of the door.

"Cosette!" said Jean Valjean.

And he sat erect in his chair, his arms outstretched and trembling, haggard, livid, gloomy, an immense joy in his eyes.

Cosette, stifling with emotion, fell upon Jean Valjean's breast.

"Father!" said she.

Jean Valjean, overcome, stammered:

"Cosette! she! you! Madame! it is thou! Ah! my God!"

And, pressed close in Cosette's arms, he exclaimed:

"It is thou! thou art here! Thou dost pardon me then!"

Marius, lowering his eyelids, in order to keep his tears from flowing, took a step forward and murmured between lips convulsively contracted to repress his sobs:

"My father!"

"And you also, you pardon me!" Jean Valjean said to him.

Marius could find no words, and Jean Valjean added:

"Thanks."

Cosette tore off her shawl and tossed her hat on the bed.

"It embarrasses me," said she.

And, seating herself on the old man's knees, she put aside his white locks with an adorable movement, and kissed his brow.

Jean Valjean, bewildered, let her have her own way.

Cosette, who only understood in a very confused manner, redoubled her caresses, as though she desired to pay Marius' debt.

Jean Valjean stammered:

"How stupid people are! I thought that I should never see her again. Imagine, Monsieur Pontmercy, at the very moment when you entered,

I was saying to myself: 'All is over. Here is her little gown, I am a miserable man, I shall never see Cosette again,' and I was saying that at the very moment when you were mounting the stairs. Was not I an idiot? Just see how idiotic one can be! One reckons without the good God. The good God says:

"'You fancy that you are about to be abandoned, stupid! No. No, things will not go so. Come, there is a good man yonder who is in need of an angel.' And the angel comes, and one sees one's Cosette again! and one sees one's little Cosette once more! Ah! I was very unhappy."

For a moment he could not speak, then he went on:

"I really needed to see Cosette a little bit now and then. A heart needs a bone to gnaw. But I was perfectly conscious that I was in the way. I gave myself reasons: 'They do not want you, keep in your own course, one has not the right to cling eternally.' Ah! God be praised, I see her once more! Dost thou know, Cosette, thy husband is very handsome? Ah! what a pretty embroidered collar thou hast on, luckily. I am fond of that pattern. It was thy husband who chose it, was it not? And then, thou shouldst have some cashmere shawls. Let me call her thou, Monsieur Pontmercy. It will not be for long."

And Cosette began again:

"How wicked of you to have left us like that! Where did you go? Why have you stayed away so long? Formerly your journeys only lasted three or four days. I sent Nicolette, the answer always was: 'He is absent.' How long have you been back? Why did you not let us know? Do you know that you are very much changed? Ah! what a naughty father! he has been ill, and we have not known it! Stay, Marius, feel how cold his hand is!"

"So you are here! Monsieur Pontmercy, you pardon me!" repeated Jean Valjean.

At that word which Jean Valjean had just uttered once more, all that was swelling Marius' heart found vent.

He burst forth:

"Cosette, do you hear? he has come to that! he asks my forgiveness! And do you know what he has done for me, Cosette? He has saved my life. He has done more—he has given you to me. And after having saved me, and after having given you to me, Cosette, what has he done with himself? He has sacrificed himself. Behold the man. And he says to me the ingrate, to me the forgetful, to me the pitiless, to me the guilty one: Thanks! Cosette, my whole life passed at the feet of this man would be too little. That barricade, that sewer, that furnace, that cesspool,—all that he traversed for me, for thee, Cosette! He carried me away through all the deaths which he put aside before me, and accepted for himself. Every courage, every virtue, every heroism, every sanctity he possesses! Cosette, that man is an angel!"

"Hush! hush!" said Jean Valjean in a low voice. "Why tell all that?"

"But you!" cried Marius with a wrath in which there was veneration, "why did you not tell it to me? It is your own fault, too. You save people's lives, and you conceal it from them! You do more, under the pretext of unmasking yourself, you calumniate yourself. It is frightful."

"I told the truth," replied Jean Valjean.

"No," retorted Marius, "the truth is the whole truth; and that you did not tell. You were Monsieur Madeleine, why not have said so? You saved Javert, why not have said so? I owed my life to you, why not have said so?"

"Because I thought as you do. I thought that you were in the right. It was necessary that I should go away. If you had known about that affair, of the sewer, you would have made me remain near you. I was therefore forced to hold my peace. If I had spoken, it would have caused embarrassment in every way."

"It would have embarrassed what? embarrassed whom?" retorted Marius. "Do you think that you are going to stay here? We shall carry you off. Ah! good heavens! when I reflect that it was by an accident that I have learned all this. You form a part of ourselves. You are her father, and mine. You shall not pass another day in this dreadful house. Do not imagine that you will be here to-morrow."

"To-morrow," said Jean Valjean, "I shall not be here, but I shall not be with you."

"What do you mean?" replied Marius. "Ah! come now, we are not going to permit any more journeys. You shall never leave us again. You belong to us. We shall not loose our hold of you."

"This time it is for good," added Cosette. "We have a carriage at the door. I shall run away with you. If necessary, I shall employ force."

And she laughingly made a movement to lift the old man in her arms.

"Your chamber still stands ready in our house," she went on. "If you only knew how pretty the garden is now! The azaleas are doing very well there. The walks are sanded with river sand; there are tiny violet shells. You shall eat my strawberries. I water them myself. And no more 'madame,' no more 'Monsieur Jean,' we are living under a Republic, everybody says *thou*, don't they, Marius? The programme is changed. If you only knew, father, I have had a sorrow, there was a robin redbreast which had made her nest in a hole in the wall, and a horrible cat ate her. My poor, pretty, little robin red-breast which used to put her head out of her window and look at me! I cried over it. I should have liked to kill the cat. But now nobody cries any more. Everybody laughs, everybody is happy. You are going to come with us. How delighted grandfather will be! You shall have your plot in the garden, you shall cultivate it, and we shall see whether your strawberries are as fine as mine. And, then, I shall do everything that you wish, and then, you will obey me prettily."

Jean Valjean listened to her without hearing her. He heard the music of her voice rather than the sense of her words; one of those large tears which are the sombre pearls of the soul welled up slowly in his eyes.

He murmured:

"The proof that God is good is that she is here."

"Father!" said Cosette.

Jean Valjean continued:

"It is quite true that it would be charming for us to live together. Their trees are full of birds. I would walk with Cosette. It is sweet to be among living people who bid each other 'good-day,' who call to each other in the garden. People see each other from early morning. We should each cultivate our own little corner. She would make me eat her strawberries. I would make her gather my roses. That would be charming. Only. . ."

He paused and said gently:

"It is a pity."

The tear did not fall, it retreated, and Jean Valjean replaced it with a smile.

Cosette took both the old man's hands in hers.

"My God!" said she, "your hands are still colder than before. Are you ill? Do you suffer?"

"I? No," replied Jean Valjean. "I am very well. Only. . ."

He paused.

"Only what?"

"I am going to die presently."

Cosette and Marius shuddered.

"To die!" exclaimed Marius.

"Yes, but that is nothing," said Jean Valjean.

He took breath, smiled and resumed:

"Cosette, thou wert talking to me, go on, so thy little robin red-breast is dead? Speak, so that I may hear thy voice."

Marius gazed at the old man in amazement.

Cosette uttered a heartrending cry.

"Father! my father! you will live. You are going to live. I insist upon your living, do you hear?"

Jean Valjean raised his head towards her with adoration.

"Oh! yes, forbid me to die. Who knows? Perhaps I shall obey. I was on the verge of dying when you came. That stopped me, it seemed to me that I was born again."

"You are full of strength and life," cried Marius. "Do you imagine that a person can die like this? You have had sorrow, you shall have no more. It is I who ask your forgiveness, and on my knees! You are going to live, and to live with us, and to live a long time. We take possession of you once more. There are two of us here who will henceforth have no other thought than your happiness."

"You see," resumed Cosette, all bathed in tears, "that Marius says that you shall not die."

Jean Valjean continued to smile.

"Even if you were to take possession of me, Monsieur Pontmercy, would that make me other than I am? No, God has thought like you and myself, and he does not change his mind; it is useful for me to go. Death is a good arrangement. God knows better than we what we need. May you be happy, may Monsieur Pontmercy have Cosette, may youth wed the morning, may there be around you, my children, lilacs and nightingales; may your life be a beautiful, sunny lawn, may all the enchantments of heaven fill your souls, and now let me, who am good for nothing, die; it is certain that all this is right. Come, be reasonable, nothing is possible now, I am fully conscious that all is over. And then, last night, I drank that whole jug of water. How good thy husband is, Cosette! Thou art much better off with him than with me."

A noise became audible at the door.

It was the doctor entering.

"Good-day, and farewell, doctor," said Jean Valjean. "Here are my poor children."

Marius stepped up to the doctor. He addressed to him only this single word: "Monsieur? . . ." But his manner of pronouncing it contained a complete question.

The doctor replied to the question by an expressive glance.

"Because things are not agreeable," said Jean Valjean, "that is no reason for being unjust towards God."

A silence ensued.

All breasts were oppressed.

Jean Valjean turned to Cosette. He began to gaze at her as though he wished to retain her features for eternity.

In the depths of the shadow into which he had already descended, ecstasy was still possible to him when gazing at Cosette. The reflection of that sweet face lighted up his pale visage.

The doctor felt of his pulse.

"Ah! it was you that he wanted!" he murmured, looking at Cosette and Marius.

And bending down to Marius' ear, he added in a very low voice: "Too late."

Jean Valjean surveyed the doctor and Marius serenely, almost without ceasing to gaze at Cosette.

These barely articulate words were heard to issue from his mouth:

"It is nothing to die; it is dreadful not to live."

All at once he rose to his feet. These accesses of strength are sometimes the sign of the death agony. He walked with a firm step to the wall, thrusting aside Marius and the doctor who tried to help him, detached from the wall a little copper crucifix which was suspended there, and returned to his seat with all the freedom of movement of perfect health, and said in a loud voice, as he laid the crucifix on the table:

"Behold the great martyr."

Then his chest sank in, his head wavered, as though the intoxication of the tomb were seizing hold upon him.

His hands, which rested on his knees, began to press their nails into the stuff of his trousers.

Cosette supported his shoulders, and sobbed, and tried to speak to him, but could not.

Among the words mingled with that mournful saliva which accompanies tears, they distinguished words like the following:

"Father, do not leave us. Is it possible that we have found you only to lose you again?"

It might be said that agony writhes. It goes, comes, advances towards the sepulchre, and returns towards life. There is groping in the action of dying.

Jean Valjean rallied after this semi-swoon, shook his brow as though to make the shadows fall away from it and became almost perfectly lucid once more.

He took a fold of Cosette's sleeve and kissed it.

"He is coming back! doctor, he is coming back," cried Marius.

"You are good, both of you," said Jean Valjean. "I am going to tell you what has caused me pain. What has pained me, Monsieur Pontmercy, is that you have not been willing to touch that money. That money really belongs to your wife. I will explain to you, my children, and for that reason, also, I am glad to see you. Black jet comes from England, white jet comes from Norway. All this is in this paper, which you will read. For bracelets, I invented a way of substituting for slides of soldered sheet iron, slides of iron laid together. It is prettier, better and less costly. You will understand how much money can be made in that way. So Cosette's fortune is really hers. I give you these details, in order that your mind may be set at rest."

The portress had come upstairs and was gazing in at the half-open door. The doctor dismissed her.

But he could not prevent this zealous woman from exclaiming to the dying man before she disappeared: "Would you like a priest?"

"I have had one," replied Jean Valjean.

And with his finger he seemed to indicate a point above his head where one would have said that he saw some one.

It is probable, in fact, that the Bishop was present at this death agony.

Cosette gently slipped a pillow under his loins.

Jean Valjean resumed:

"Have no fear, Monsieur Pontmercy, I adjure you. The six hundred thousand francs really belong to Cosette. My life will have been wasted if you do not enjoy them! We managed to do very well with those glass goods. We rivalled what is called Berlin jewellery. However, we could not equal the black glass of England. A gross, which contains twelve hundred very well cut grains, only costs three francs."

When a being who is dear to us is on the point of death, we gaze upon him with a look which clings convulsively to him and which would fain hold him back.

Cosette gave her hand to Marius, and both, mute with anguish, not knowing what to say to the dying man, stood trembling and despairing before him.

Jean Valjean sank moment by moment. He was failing; he was drawing near to the gloomy horizon.

His breath had become intermittent; a little rattling interrupted it. He found some difficulty in moving his forearm, his feet had lost all movement, and in proportion as the wretchedness of limb and feebleness of body increased, all the majesty of his soul was displayed and spread over his brow. The light of the unknown world was already visible in his eyes.

His face paled and smiled. Life was no longer there, it was something else.

His breath sank, his glance grew grander. He was a corpse on which the wings could be felt.

He made a sign to Cosette to draw near, then to Marius; the last minute of the last hour had, evidently, arrived.

He began to speak to them in a voice so feeble that it seemed to come from a distance, and one would have said that a wall now rose between them and him.

"Draw near, draw near, both of you. I love you dearly. Oh! how good it is to die like this! And thou lovest me also, my Cosette. I knew well that thou still felt friendly towards thy poor old man. How kind it was of thee to place that pillow under my loins! Thou wilt weep for me a little, wilt thou not? Not too much. I do not wish thee to have any real griefs. You must enjoy yourselves a great deal, my children. I forgot to tell you that the profit was greater still on the buckles without tongues than on all the rest. A gross of a dozen dozens cost ten francs and sold for sixty. It really was a good business. So there is no occasion for surprise at the six hundred thousand francs, Monsieur Pontmercy. It is honest money. You may be rich with a tranquil mind. Thou must have a carriage, a box at the theatres now and then, and handsome ball dresses, my Cosette, and then, thou must give good dinners to thy friends, and be very happy. I was writing to Cosette a while ago. She will find my letter. I bequeath to her the two candlesticks which stand on the chimney-piece. They are of silver, but to me they are gold, they are diamonds; they change candles which are placed in them into wax-tapers. I do not know whether the person who gave them to me is pleased with me yonder on high. I have done what I could. My children, you will not forget that I am a poor man, you will have me buried in the first plot of earth that you find, under a stone to mark the spot. This is my wish. No name on the stone. If Cosette cares to come for a little while now and then, it will give me pleasure. And you too, Monsieur Pontmercy. I must admit that I have not always loved you. I ask your pardon for that. Now she and you form but one for me. I feel very grateful to you. I am sure that you make Cosette happy. If you only knew, Monsieur Pontmercy, her pretty rosy cheeks were my delight; when I saw her in the least pale, I was sad. In the chest of drawers, there is a bank-bill for five hundred francs. I have not touched it. It is for the poor. Cosette, dost thou see thy little gown yonder on the bed? dost thou recognize it? That was ten years ago, however. How time flies! We have been very happy. All is over. Do not weep, my children, I am not going very far, I shall see you from there, you will only have to look at night, and you will see me smile. Cosette, dost thou remember Montfermeil? Thou wert in the forest, thou wert greatly terrified; dost thou remember how I took hold of the handle of the water-bucket? That was the first time that I touched thy poor, little hand. It was so cold! Ah! your hands were red then, mademoiselle, they are very white now. And the big doll! dost thou remember? Thou didst call her Catherine. Thou regrettedest not having taken her to the convent! How thou didst make me laugh sometimes, my sweet angel! When it had been raining, thou didst float bits of straw on the gutters, and watch them pass away. One day I gave thee a willow battledore and a shuttlecock with yellow, blue and green feathers. Thou hast forgotten it. Thou wert roguish so young! Thou didst play. Thou didst put cherries in thy ears. Those are things of the past. The forests through which one has passed with one's child, the trees under which one has strolled, the convents where one has concealed oneself, the games, the hearty laughs of childhood, are shadows. I imagined that all that belonged to me. In that lay my stupidity. Those Thénardiers were wicked. Thou must forgive them. Cosette, the moment has come to tell thee the name of thy mother. She was called Fantine. Remember that name—Fantine. Kneel whenever thou utterest it. She suffered much. She loved thee dearly. She had as much unhappiness as thou hast had happiness. That is the way God apportions things. He is there on high, he sees us all, and he knows what he does in the midst of his great stars. I am on the verge of departure, my children. Love each other well and always. There is nothing else but that in the world: love for each other. You will think sometimes of the poor old man who died here. Oh my Cosette, it is not my fault, indeed, that I have not seen thee all this time, it cut me to the heart; I went as far as the corner of the street, I must have produced a queer effect on the people who saw me pass, I was like a madman, I once went out without my hat. I no longer see clearly, my children, I had still other things to say, but never mind. Think a little of me. Come still nearer. I die happy. Give me your dear and well-beloved heads, so that I may lay my hands upon them."

Cosette and Marius fell on their knees, in despair, suffocating with tears, each beneath one of Jean Valjean's hands. Those august hands no longer moved.

He had fallen backwards, the light of the candles illuminated him.

His white face looked up to heaven, he allowed Cosette and Marius to cover his hands with kisses.

He was dead.

The night was starless and extremely dark. No doubt, in the gloom, some immense angel stood erect with wings outspread, awaiting that soul.

# VI

## The Grass Covers and the Rain Effaces

In the cemetery of Père-Lachaise, in the vicinity of the common grave, far from the elegant quarter of that city of sepulchres, far from all the tombs of fancy which display in the presence of eternity all the hideous fashions of death, in a deserted corner, beside an old wall, beneath a great yew tree over which climbs the wild convolvulus, amid dandelions and mosses, there lies a stone. That stone is no more exempt than others from the leprosy of time, of dampness, of the lichens and from the defilement of the birds. The water turns it green, the air blackens it. It is not near any path, and people are not fond of walking in that direction, because the grass is high and their feet are immediately wet. When there is a little sunshine, the lizards come thither. All around there is a quivering of weeds. In the spring, linnets warble in the trees.

This stone is perfectly plain. In cutting it the only thought was the requirements of the tomb, and no other care was taken than to make the stone long enough and narrow enough to cover a man.

No name is to be read there.

Only, many years ago, a hand wrote upon it in pencil these four lines, which have become gradually illegible beneath the rain and the dust, and which are, to-day, probably effaced:

> *Il dort. Quoique le sort fût pour lui bien étrange,*
> *Il vivait. Il mourut quand il n'eut plus son ange.*
> *La chose simplement d'elle-même arriva,*
> *Comme la nuit se fait lorsque le jour s'en va*

# A Note About the Author

Victor Hugo (1802–1885) was a French writer and prominent figure during Europe's Romantic movement. As a child, he traveled across the continent due to his father's position in the Napoleonic army. As a young man, he studied law although his passion was always literature. In 1819, Hugo created *Conservateur Littéraire*, a periodical that featured works from up-and-coming writers. A few years later he published a collection of poems *Odes et Poésies Diverses* followed by the novel *Han d'Islande* in 1825. Hugo has an extensive catalog, yet he's best known for the classics *The Hunchback of Notre-Dame* (1831) and *Les Misérables* (1862).

# A Note from the Publisher

Spanning many genres, from non-fiction essays to literature classics to children's books and lyric poetry, Mint Edition books showcase the master works of our time in a modern new package. The text is freshly typeset, is clean and easy to read, and features a new note about the author in each volume. Many books also include exclusive new introductory material. Every book boasts a striking new cover, which makes it as appropriate for collecting as it is for gift giving. Mint Edition books are only printed when a reader orders them, so natural resources are not wasted. We're proud that our books are never manufactured in excess and exist only in the exact quantity they need to be read and enjoyed.

# bookfinity™

## Discover more of your favorite classics with Bookfinity™.

- Track your reading with custom book lists.
- Get great book recommendations for your personalized Reader Type.
- Add reviews for your favorite books.
- AND MUCH MORE!

Visit **bookfinity.com** and take the fun Reader Type quiz to get started.

Enjoy our classic and modern companion pairings!

## Classic & Modern